TARGET OF OPPORTUNITY

The missiles came like a wall of spears aimed at his head, disgorging smoke as they streaked across the space toward him. He juked his *Warhammer* hard to the right at the last moment, causing some of the shots to miss and fly past him. There was a roar in his ears as the rest of the warheads found their mark.

His secondary display flickered as it tried to track the loss of armor. Flames from one or more warheads lapped up the torso of Harbinger and blackened the lower portion of his cockpit ferroglass. His 'Mech careened under the rumbling impact of the missiles, staggering drunkenly to one side. Smoke, black and gray, wrapped around the Spirit Cat 'Mech, hugging it like a deadly snake attempting to crush the life from him.

Cox fired back with two of his large lasers, both shots hitting the *Vulture* in the legs. The emerald beams stabbed into the knee area, and he saw one plate of her ferrofibrous armor actually pop off from the sudden heat searing a joint. His sensors painted the picture he expected to see; she was reloading her missile racks, planning to finish him off. Caitlin Bauer was probably still puzzled about why he was not rushing forward and taking away her advantage, but she also probably didn't care.

So he turned and ran.

MechWarrior
DARK AGE

TARGET OF
OPPORTUNITY

A BATTLETECH™ NOVEL

Blaine Lee Pardoe

A ROC BOOK

ROC
Published by New American Library, a division of
Penguin Group (USA) Inc., 375 Hudson Street,
New York, New York 10014, USA
Penguin Group (Canada), 10 Alcorn Avenue, Toronto,
Ontario M4V 3B2, Canada (a division of Pearson Penguin Canada Inc.)
Penguin Books Ltd., 80 Strand, London WC2R 0RL, England
Penguin Ireland, 25 St. Stephen's Green, Dublin 2,
Ireland (a division of Penguin Books Ltd.)
Penguin Group (Australia), 250 Camberwell Road, Camberwell, Victoria 3124,
Australia (a division of Pearson Australia Group Pty. Ltd.)
Penguin Books India Pvt. Ltd., 11 Community Centre, Panchsheel Park,
New Delhi - 110 017, India
Penguin Group (NZ), cnr Airborne and Rosedale Roads, Albany,
Auckland 1310, New Zealand (a division of Pearson New Zealand Ltd.)
Penguin Books (South Africa) (Pty.) Ltd., 24 Sturdee Avenue,
Rosebank, Johannesburg 2196, South Africa

Penguin Books Ltd., Registered Offices:
80 Strand, London WC2R 0RL, England

First published by Roc, an imprint of New American Library,
a division of Penguin Group (USA) Inc.

First Printing, February 2005
10 9 8 7 6 5 4 3 2 1

PUBLISHER'S NOTE
This is a work of fiction. Names, characters, places, and incidents either are the product of the author's imagination or are used fictitiously, and any resemblance to actual persons, living or dead, business establishments, events, or locales is entirely coincidental.

If you purchased this book without a cover you should be aware that this book is stolen property. It was reported as "unsold and destroyed" to the publisher and neither the author nor the publisher has received any payment for this "stripped book."

The scanning, uploading, and distribution of this book via the Internet or via any other means without the permission of the publisher is illegal and punishable by law. Please purchase only authorized electronic editions, and do not participate in or encourage electronic piracy of copyrighted materials. Your support of the author's rights is appreciated.

*To my alma mater, Central Michigan University,
and to my family. Peace of Focht be with you all. . . .*

Prologue

ComStar Research and Development Division
Stuttgart, Terra
Prefecture X, The Republic
26 January 3135

Tucker Harwell took a deep breath, tried to force a smile to his face, and stepped into the office. *Be calm,* he told himself. *This is a great opportunity. Don't talk too fast. Don't act too eager.* He was concentrating so hard on what to say and how to say it that he stood like a tall, gawking statue in the doorway. His skinny build belied his appetite, and his medium-length black hair appeared to have been styled with a blender, the combined result of a cowlick on the crown of his head and a lack of interest in the way his hair looked.

The man behind the burnished cherrywood desk, Precentor Malcolm Buhl, looked up and waved him forward. "Mr. Harwell, come in." Buhl was an older man, balding, slightly overweight. Tucker stammered a reply, saying no complete word, then closed the door behind him. The precentor rose and shook Harwell's sweaty hand.

"Have a seat," Precentor Buhl invited, gesturing to one of the black leather chairs facing the desk. Tucker dropped into the deep seat, nervously squirming to find a comfortable spot. As he shifted, the leather groaned; now he was nervous and embarrassed. Tucker pushed up on the bridge of his eyeglasses several times, trying to get them positioned just right. A fingerprint smudged his right lens; he regretted not taking the time to clean them before coming to the meeting. He avoided wearing his glasses when he could, but the correction his eyes needed couldn't be made with surgery, so he wore glasses sometimes. He wore them for this meeting because he wanted to see straight. For a moment he considered cleaning the lens right there, but restrained himself. He didn't want to blow this interview.

"Tucker," Precentor Buhl said soothingly, "you seem nervous. Relax."

"Yes, sir," he replied, then wished he hadn't said the words out loud. *Too formal, Tuck. You don't sound relaxed.* He took another deep breath and looked around the office. It was much nicer than the other middle manager offices he had seen during his career at ComStar. This one had very expensive furniture—a big contrast to the sea of cubicles or the controlled-environment labs where he worked. Behind the precentor, a large window framed a spectacular view of the ages-old pines of Germany's Black Forest, which grew right up to the edges of the ComStar research and development facility. The forest was slowly recovering after being devastated by fire during the Jihad.

"I've been looking over your file. Very impressive, I must say. You just completed the new program at the DeBurke Institute, correct?" Precentor Buhl looked up from the file on his desk and deliberately closed the cover on the material so that Tucker couldn't see it.

"Yes, sir. Just this afternoon—of course, you already know that. Graduated at the top of my class," he replied. The room felt warm; Tucker knew it was his nerves making him hot, but knowing that didn't help cool him down. And despite the pep talk he'd given himself, he knew he was still talking too fast.

"In fact," the precentor recited calmly, staring at the

younger man, "you graduated high school three years early, got your bachelor's degree in two years, your master's in one, your doctorate in three more. If I go by your record, you're something of a prodigy, aren't you, my boy?"

Tucker swallowed, but his throat remained bone dry. "I don't think so, sir. I'm just focused on my work—that's all."

Buhl cast him a wry sideways glance. "The DeBurke Institute is our newest training program, teaching our most advanced research in hyperpulse technology," he replied. "Your instructors all concur. There's nothing more that ComStar can teach you about interstellar communications systems."

"Thank you, sir."

Precentor Buhl paused for a moment, as if considering his next words. "Tucker, do you know what I do here at ComStar?"

Tucker nodded quickly. "Yes, sir. You're in charge of special projects for Primus Mori. Everyone in the class talks about trying to get in to meet you. Anything that is on the cutting edge for research and development, you're in charge of."

Buhl gave him a thin smile. "An overstatement. In a corporate environment like ComStar, people's importance is often exaggerated, my boy. I do, however, handle a number of unique projects. When someone like you comes along, I make a point of finding the right niche for them in the organization." There was a smoothness to this explanation that Tucker guessed meant the precentor was concealing the true nature of his role in the organization. He had no problem with that.

"They say that the best assignments are the ones you arrange," he offered anxiously.

"Another exaggeration, I assure you. Though I have had my share of work cut out for me the last few years. All of us have," he said with a sigh. The reference was not lost on Tucker, or anyone else associated with ComStar. Three years ago the organization had suffered one of its worse setbacks. ComStar was the only Inner Sphere source for interstellar communication, and it had found its entire network under siege by unknown forces.

Hyperpulse generators, or HPGs, formed a vast communications network that linked the worlds of The Republic and the rest of the Inner Sphere. At least that was how it was until 1 August 3132, when the network was taken out. An invasive virus had penetrated the programming of a significant number of HPGs, and when the generators were activated the virus had the effect of altering the frequency on which they broadcast—something that shouldn't have been possible. The result was thousands of fried HPG cores. The more modern HPGs were not impacted by the virus, but they were physically attacked by terrorist actions. The assault was so subtle and so widespread that it took the Inner Sphere—and ComStar—by surprise. When the dust had settled on what became known within ComStar as Gray Monday, more than 80 percent of the interstellar communications network was down. The primary operations screens for ComStar turned gray with static on that day, and most stayed that way.

What followed was chaos.

Worlds were cut off from one another. Almost immediately, petty warlords and would-be rulers rose up all across the Inner Sphere and began trying to carve up Devlin Stone's once-pastoral empire—and one another. Even the old Houses of the Inner Sphere once again took up arms and began to poke at the edges of The Republic. Raids and incursions suddenly were commonplace. The demilitarized Inner Sphere beat its plowshares back into swords.

And everyone blamed ComStar.

ComStar ran the HPG network. ComStar, independent of The Republic, was in charge of maintaining interstellar communications. Most thought that the network would be down for a few days, then a few weeks, but the problems were far deeper than anyone in ComStar suspected. In the early days, rumors had circulated about a few HPGs on far-flung worlds that had been reinitialized and activated, but those stories were mostly lies or wishful thinking. In those dark months that followed Gray Monday, the public stopped looking at ComStar with hope. Many blamed the technicians and leaders of the massive corporate entity for the disruption. Some even went so far as to declare that ComStar had sabotaged its network deliberately, though that made no sense.

The public had a valid reason for doubting ComStar. That reason had a name. It was the Jihad.

"Where were you on Gray Monday, Tucker?"

For members of ComStar, the event was as significant as the fall of the Star League was to the ruling Houses of the Inner Sphere. Gray Monday had forged together the individuals of ComStar as only a crisis could. The question was a bond of honor between the members of the organization.

"I was at the university, delivering a lecture. I remember one of the graduate assistants bursting into the room and telling the class that the entire system was down. I thought it was a joke, kept my class until the end of the session. I remember giving the grad assistant hell for interrupting my lecture. I was reassigned in five hours. They had me helping smooth out message-flow rates down at headquarters in Sydney. I was there for three months, and don't think I saw the light of day all that time."

"Tucker, I will be frank with you. ComStar has been hemorrhaging profits and talented people for some time. I don't want to lose you."

"Sir, I am loyal to ComStar."

"I know that. But I want to make sure we keep you happy, keep you challenged. I don't want you to end up like some of those fanatics I hear about—praying to their hardware to ensure that it works. ComStar needs to move to the future, not get caught in its past."

Praying to the hardware? That was a relic from ComStar's days as a technoreligious order. He hadn't heard any rumors of that behavior reemerging, but apparently it was. "Sir, I'm not like that, not at all."

Buhl straightened in his chair. "Of course you're not, Tucker. So let me see what I can do to keep you challenged. I have an opening that I'm considering you for. Your record shows that your knowledge and understanding of the system makes you more than qualified for this position, but I have one reservation, and I want to be honest with you about it. This is fieldwork. Not some university lab or R & D project. This is serious hands-on work on an HPG on another planet. You'd have a chance to put some of that theory you've learned to the test."

Tucker adjusted his glasses again. His hands broke out in a new sheen of sweat.

"Is this operational work, sir?" He didn't want a job sitting at a workstation watching communications traffic.

Precentor Buhl allowed himself a low chuckle. "No, Tucker. This assignment is not piloting a cubicle. Have you heard of the planet Wyatt?"

Tucker shook his head.

"I'm not surprised. Strangely enough, the virus that took down the network had a subroutine that deleted Wyatt from most online atlases and star charts. Wyatt is in Prefecture VIII. Like most of the Inner Sphere, its HPG was rendered inoperative on Gray Monday. The core of their transmitter was burned out, so we sent a replacement. When it was installed, the HPG could transmit again, but it began to send the same message over and over, millions of times, overloading the receiving network for a few seconds—then the core fried."

Tucker's eyes widened. "Just like what happened on Gray Monday."

"We tried to shut it down, but we were too late. We could find no reason that the core should have failed—no reason at all."

Tucker's face tightened as he thought. Assuming that the HPG crash was intentional, then the new core should have solved Wyatt's problem. The message cascade was an anomaly. Immediately, curiosity overwhelmed his intention to maintain a reserved attitude in the interview.

"I'd start by going over the transmission log, including all subbinary feeds."

Precentor Buhl leaned back in his seat and steepled

his hands in front of him. "I can have that arranged. May I assume that you are interested in the position, even though I haven't told you about the job?"

Tucker nodded once and let a small, excited grin light his face. His mind was saying, "Are you kidding?" but out loud he said only, "Sounds like a real interesting opportunity."

"It is," Buhl replied. "It surely is. Welcome to the project."

Tucker rose, shaking his new boss's hand. "Then the position's mine?"

"Yes."

"I can't wait to tell my father," Tucker replied.

"The replacement HPG core for Wyatt has already been loaded aboard the DropShip *Divine Breeze*. It departs in two days. I've taken the liberty of sending the background data covering the HPG issues on Wyatt to a secured directory in the ship's computer, encoded to your access. In the meantime, I suggest you pack and get your personal affairs in order—see your family and friends." He slid a small noteputer across the desktop. The younger man glanced at it. The tiny screen displayed his transfer orders and the itinerary for the *Divine Breeze*—all filled out and processed.

Tucker was stunned for a full thirty seconds. He knew his mouth was hanging open, but he struggled to find words. "How did you know I'd want the position, sir?"

The precentor smiled. "You don't reach my level in a complex organization like ComStar without knowing something about people, Mr. Harwell." He gestured to the door. "Good luck."

The precentor sat quietly at his desk for a full two minutes, waiting for the knock at the door. When it came, Malcolm Buhl said only, "Enter," and a lithe, stunning woman in her early forties, dressed in a tight-fitting black suit and tie, walked into the office and took a seat across from her manager. She held a noteputer. *Am I her manager or her keeper?* Buhl wondered.

"I assume," she began, leaning back in the chair and

brushing lint off of her lapel, "that you were able to secure Harwell for the task?"

"Of course," Buhl replied. "I trust that you're not surprised?"

"By you, never," Precentor Svetlana Kerr replied, looking straight at Buhl. "Does he know what he's up against?"

The older man shook his balding head. "No. Some of it is in the briefing, and I'll also speak with him while he's in transit to the JumpShip. I intend to downplay the political issues at first, because I want his focus to be on fixing that HPG."

Kerr's face seemed to sour. "Blasted Republic. At least with Exarch Redburn in power we knew what we were dealing with."

Buhl waved his hand in the space between them dismissively. "This isn't just about the Exarch. The Paladin that he assigned to this, Kelson Sorenson, likes to champion causes others would give up as lost—not that our situation falls into that category, of course. He considers himself a man of the people, so I suppose the theory is that he tries harder. I've met with him twice and so has the primus. He's bound and determined to get the HPG network back up, and up now." His eyes widened slightly with his words, as if he were mimicking the expression of the Paladin.

"Has anyone explained to them that willing it to happen isn't the same as making it happen? If we could get the system up, we would. ComStar's a corporation; we make our money transmitting data. It's in our own best interest to get the network back up as soon as possible. But whoever sabotaged it did a damn good job."

"Almost as if it were an inside job, eh?" Buhl said coyly.

"You'd better watch your words," Svetlana replied coldly.

"I'm as tired of the empty accusations as you. It's almost hard to believe that a few generations ago, ComStar all but controlled the Inner Sphere from behind the scenes."

"Don't tell me you're pining for the old days?" she asked sarcastically. "You have to reread your history. We may have controlled thousands of worlds and dictated policies, but we also prayed every time we threw a switch or pressed a button. Dressing like monks—"

"Yes, there was a price to pay for the power we controlled," Buhl cut in. "But back then we were respected. My grandfather used to tell me that being part of ComStar was a high honor. In the last few years, we've been treated like outcasts. People think we downed our own network. They think we sabotaged The Republic."

Svetlana shifted. "With good reason, in some respects. Remember, the Word of Blake was ComStar at one time. Now when most people outside of the organization look at us, they remember the horror of the Jihad."

The mere mention of the Jihad seemed to layer silence over the office. It was the Word of Blake, the religious zealots of the old ComStar, who had savaged the Inner Sphere, plunged it into chaos, war, death, and suffering.

"I know my history," Buhl said testily. "I'm sixth-generation ComStar. Tucker Harwell, he's seventh gen. That was one of the reasons I chose him. His family has seen the light and dark of ComStar. Eventually, he'll come over to our way of thinking." Buhl nodded decisively.

"Are you sure?" Precentor Kerr asked.

Buhl grinned, perhaps for the first time that day. "I'm positive. I set up the DeBurke Institute to overcome this network issue. We've spent the last three years trying to repair technology that we've barely improved on in centuries, rumors of some kind of super HPG aside. Most of the HPG network hardware is more than two hundred years old. Tucker Harwell knows more about HPG and interstellar communications theory than anyone working in the organization in the last century. He represents the future."

"Still," Kerr returned, laying her noteputer on the desktop, "the odds are against him. That HPG on Wyatt already burned out one billion-C-bill core. And Paladin Sorenson, he's sending a Knight Errant to baby-sit us when we install the new one. That's a lot of pressure on an untested kid."

"I agree, but, Svetlana, you are making me feel bad. I had hoped that you'd have more faith in me. I've already sent some insurance to Wyatt to make sure matters are well in hand: you know that, since that asset reports to you. And that 'kid,' as you refer to him, he's tougher than he looks. Yes, he's a prodigy of sorts. But when he was ten, he was hit by a hovercar. They put him in one of our sponsored hospitals. The best medical minds we had said he'd never walk again. It took him two years, but he not only overcame his injuries—he graduated ahead of his peers."

Kerr frowned. "I didn't see that in his record."

"And you won't. You see, Svetlana, I don't always put all of my cards on the table. You don't rise far in this organization without knowing how to hold back some information."

"I've read the reports. The indigs on Wyatt aren't too pleased with our lack of progress. He's not going to get a warm reception. Not to mention what happens if he's successful. You turn on an HPG and that planet becomes a target for anyone who wants to carve out a base of power."

Malcolm Buhl leaned back in his chair and turned to look out at the stark blue sky. "It's all about people, my friend. Weak-minded pundits think that ComStar's strength is our technology, our network, but they are wrong. They see us as a corporation that is too large and cumbersome to act. Wrong again. It is our *people* who make us a force to be reckoned with. There are times I think *we've* forgotten that. Those times are going to change."

Precentor Buhl's face seemed to harden, as if he were angry. "I am going to *make* them change."

Book One

Penance

"There are several defining moments that helped shape the ComStar we all know today. Most people focus on the Word of Blake and the Jihad as the events that define ComStar, but there were much earlier, pivotal events that forged the contemporary organization. Understanding these events helps readers to understand the impact of ComStar on the lives of everyone in the Inner Sphere.

"The first of these events was the formation of ComStar by Jerome Blake. By declaring the interstellar communications network neutral in 2787, at the beginning of the Succession Wars, and seizing control of Terra in 2788, Jerome Blake saved the cradle of mankind from three centuries of devastation.

"The next critical moment was when Conrad Toyama ascended to lead ComStar after Blake's death, and transformed the communications empire into a quasireligious cult. His pretext was simple: preserve knowledge and technology using the same methods employed by the monks during the Dark Ages of Terra. ComStar personnel intoned prayers as they worked, and treated their HPG generators as mystical shrines. Toyama could have no way of knowing the repercussions that would result from the seeds he had sown.

"The third critical moment occurred when ComStar's Explorer Corps discovered the remains of Kerensky's Exodus fleet in the guise of the Clans, and with that discovery triggered the Clan invasion of the Inner Sphere. ComStar accepted the Clan's goals at face value and essentially sold out mankind, providing the Clans with intelligence and logistical support to accomplish their goals—until they learned that the true objective of the Clans was to seize Terra, along with ComStar's base of operations.

"Then, in the spring of 3052, history arrived at a point that literally altered the destiny of mankind.

"The might of the Clans was challenged by Precentor Martial Anastasius Focht leading the Com Guards, ComStar's military arm. The result was the battle of Tukayyid. On that planet, beginning on 1 May 3052, the Clans and the Com Guards faced off in a horrific series of battles, with the fate of the Inner Sphere on the line. The Com Guards fought the Clans to defeat, which ended their drive to Terra for fifteen years. But Primus Myndo Waterly launched a backup plan: a complete shutdown of the HPG network, known as an interdiction, across the Inner Sphere. She hoped that with the battle raging on Tukayyid distracting all the leaders of the Great Houses, ComStar would be able to rise up and seize control of the Inner Sphere.

"Her interdiction, named Operation Scorpion, was doomed from the start. Forewarned, the House governments preemptively seized HPGs on the worlds in their realms, and ComStar began to crumble from within. Within a month the Primus was dead, ComStar had shed its religious trappings and one faction split away from the larger organization: the Word of Blake rejected the reforms of Sharilar Mori and chose to cleave to the technoreligious tenets of ComStar.

"The spring of 3052 would change forever the face of the Inner Sphere."

—*Forward by Historian Harold McCoy*
from his bestselling book,
The Spring of 3052:
Three Months that Changed the Universe,
Commonwealth Press, February 3133.

1

The DropShip *Cambrai* vented excess steam from the environmental system with a deep hissing sound, blasting a manmade fog across the tarmac. The condensed moisture didn't last long in the first light of morning, but it did signal the end of the landing procedures. Alexi Holt stood on the gangway and looked back to watch the massive port-side doors of the *Leopard*-class DropShip crack open.

The *Cambrai* had come all the way from Terra attached to its star-hopping JumpShip, *Star Eagle*, carrying a precious cargo. DropShips ferried materials to and from worlds, while JumpShips carried the DropShips from star to star. First of the cargo was the hardware it carried, including Holt's BattleMech, which filled one of its massive bays. Second, the military hardware and expendables she had brought with her. Finally, the information that its captain would provide upon his own departure from the ship.

With the sabotage and collapse of the HPG network, DropShip and JumpShip captains doubled as couriers of information and the equivalent of stellar pony express riders. Some captains transmitted their data and information as soon as they entered a system. Others, like the *Cambrai*'s captain, waited until they arrived on the planet. Local government officials and businesses often treated DropShip captains like visiting royalty because they anxiously awaited the information and news from The Republic that they carried. Naturally, some captains milked this treatment for all it was worth.

Alexi reached the bottom of the gangway and stepped foot on Wyatt, drawing in a deep breath of air. It was a slightly thinner atmosphere than she was used to, and the air was cold and wet with the morning dew. She inhaled a mixture of smells: the oxidized air near the DropShip's fusion engines, fumes from conventional fuels, the faint aroma of strange plants and pollen. It was sweet, an almost pinelike aroma. She had been on dozens of worlds, and they each had their own smell. Wyatt was no different.

A young officer stepped forward and saluted, and she returned the honor. His uniform was gray and green, and from his rank and estimated age, she could see he was a junior lieutenant—very junior. "Lady Holt, I bring you greetings to Wyatt from Legate Singh. I am Lieutenant Johannson, First Company, Wyatt Militia."

She glanced past the young officer, then looked straight into his eyes. "While I am entitled to be called 'Lady,' I prefer to be called Knight Holt," she stated flatly, but not unkindly. There were many titles for Knights; some of those coined in the past few years were less than complimentary. In general, she scorned the formality. "Where is the legate?"

"He asked me to inform you that he is on maneuvers. While he wishes he could be here to greet you personally, he indicated that he would join you as soon as he returns."

Alexi had read the profile of Legate Edward Singh, and found his resume wanting. Yes, he had a good education and he showed administrative talents, but that information told her nothing about the man. Military academy training did not ensure leadership skills or competency on the field of battle, and she had her doubts. In her experience as a Knight, she had found that several of the legates who had risen to command planet militias were in over their heads. Hopefully, Singh wasn't one of them. He was in the field; that was a good sign. Training troops was important.

Hopefully not too important on this planet, but she knew combat here was a good possibility. She had come to Wyatt with a two-part mission from her Paladin. The first was to "work with ComStar to expedite restoration of the hyperpulse generator." Which meant, bluntly, kick them in the butt. That had been clarified for her by Paladin Sorenson. In three years, ComStar had barely scratched the surface of restoring the HPG network. Sorenson had sent her to light the proverbial fire under the ass of ComStar.

The Republic of the Sphere had been peaceful and thriving until the HPG network had been sabotaged. The new Exarch had tasked Paladin Sorenson with fixing the network. The logic was inescapable: since the crash of the network had led to war; restoring it should restore the stability that existed before. At least, that was the formal line that the Knights took, to support the public opinion. Most, like Knight Errant Alexi Holt, understood that the genie was out of the bottle. Now that the old factions and rivalries had surfaced and production was starting again on weapons of war, it was going to take more than just restoration of interstellar communications to end the conflicts and turmoil.

It was that realization that comprised the second element of her mission. If the HPG could be made operational on Wyatt, the world would become one of the few that had contact with other planets other than by JumpShips and their DropShip shuttles. Wyatt, which had disappeared from most star charts, would suddenly become a world of tempting value. Her secondary protocol for coming to Wyatt was to defend the planet should anyone decide to seize it and its HPG.

Alexi was sent to Wyatt to replace another Knight, Arthur Faust. He had kept the peace on Wyatt for years, and had, in a particular waste of a valuable asset, died in a house fire. She was new to this world, and wanted to walk with a diplomatic light step until she knew the people and their capabilities. She gave the far-too-young lieutenant a solid lock of her gaze. "I have brought a cargo hold full of hardware and munitions with me, Lieutenant. I need that gear secured, transported and stored in a safe facility."

"Yes, ma'am," he replied. "I am here to make the necessary arrangements."

"You'll need some vehicle drivers," she replied. "I've brought some large gifts, compliments of Paladin Sorenson."

"Very good," the man said, taking out a noteputer and stabbing at it furiously with the stylus. "I have arranged quarters for you," he said. "Our standard arrangements for someone of your standing are to berth you in the Royale Hotel in the city. Per the information we received from Paladin Sorenson when he sent word of your coming, I have arranged for a room in the BOQ."

She nodded and favored the lieutenant with a small smile. Good. Alexi had spent enough time in her missions as a Knight Errant in cushy hotels or posh resorts. She had been a Knight for a year before the crash of the HPG network, and had been a guest of state on various assignments. Alexi had not become a Knight for the luxury some felt compelled to provide her. The field of battle was what she liked. State dinners had little appeal for her; she preferred field kit meal packs on an open campfire. To hell with formality and a plush hotel. The BOQ, Bachelor Officers Quarters, would be just fine. Sorenson knew her well.

"Very well," she replied, glancing around the almost-empty tarmac, watching a few workers moving a coolant replacement line to her DropShip. "My BattleMech is

aboard as well. I will take care of it personally. I'll need
a map to the barracks or a guide." The streets sometimes
were not rated to hold the weight of a 50- to 100-ton
BattleMech.

"I will guide you myself," he replied enthusiastically.
She understood the excitement in his voice. Before the
Jihad and Devlin Stone's Reformation, BattleMechs had
been relatively common. Now they were far more rare.
In times of peace, a company of vehicles and a handful
of 'Mechs were often more than enough to defend an
entire world against pirates or other predators. Any
world likely to face an invasion from a House or Clan
needed a much larger force. Most locals were excited by
the prospect of seeing just one 'Mech up close.

She surveyed the tarmac again. More workers appeared, all wearing the dull gray coveralls common at a
spaceport. There was no sign of security; in fact, she
realized the lieutenant had not asked for her identification. The bay of the DropShip carried enough military
hardware to outfit a good-sized militia unit, and she was
chagrined that she had let down her own guard. If someone unscrupulous was here, they might be able to seize
the entire cargo.

Best to be sure. "Before we begin, Lieutenant, I have
to validate a few things."

"Sir?"

"Starting with your identification, and proof that you
have authority to be here," Knight Holt grinned at the
sudden look of fear that washed over the younger officer's face.

It had taken nearly half an hour to confirm that Lieutenant Johannson was who he said he was and that he
indeed was with the Wyatt Militia. Near panic by the
time Knight Holt declared herself satisfied with his bona
fides, the young officer ordered in a platoon of infantry
to guard the DropShip and secure the tarmac. That took
another half hour, but in her mind the result was worth
the wait. The infantry secured the DropShip, but the
spaceport itself was still wide open. She was already

seeing areas where she could "assist" with the training of the personnel under Legate Singh.

She noticed a man leaning against a pallet of crates on the tarmac, apparently gazing at her DropShip. He looked like a biker, a drifter. The beard-stubble on his face was at least two days' growth. He wore sunglasses, and his black hair looked as if it had gone unwashed for the same number of days he had avoided a razor. The knee of his left pants leg was worn through.

She tried to ignore him as she prepared to debark her BattleMech, but something about him nagged at her. The face was familiar. Her mind played over where she could have seen him before. Not on Wyatt, since this was her first time here. She looked back at him, then stared intently across the fifty meters separating them as she focused on trying to remember something about the man watching her DropShip.

Then it came to her. The name. The story. *What is he doing here, now? It can't be a coincidence.*

Reo Jones. His name hit her like a cold blast of winter wind.

His was one of thousands of profiles that she and her peer Knights had reviewed, sent up the chain of command through local operatives and police. His story stood out in her mind. She couldn't quite remember the details, but the fragments that floated to the top were not pleasant. She knew Reo was to be watched; he had close ties to known rogue elements; and that he was considered dangerous but not a direct threat to The Republic.

My day just keeps getting better. . . .

He had been a Knight Errant candidate. On his home world of Mizar, just after the communications blackout, mercenaries working for one faction or another—she couldn't remember—attempted to seize the small armaments factory there. Jones was to defend the pass they would have to use to reach the factory. He failed. The factory was looted then burned by the retreating mercs.

The resulting explosion sent fire raging through the nearby town, killing hundreds. Reo Jones was found after

the mercenaries left, his 'Mech undamaged. He was con-
victed of dereliction of duty, and his name was removed
from consideration for Knighthood—a polite way of saying The Republic didn't want him. His own parents had
died in the attack. He was not like the Black Paladin,
the betrayer Ezekiel Crow, who had sold out Liao and
Northwind. Reo wasn't a traitor; he was a failure. In her
eyes, that made him more pathetic.

More memories surfaced from the briefing she had
seen. Alexi knew that he had served in several low-life
mercenary units, and if word was correct, Jacob Bannson,
the dangerous business tycoon, had taken him onto his
payroll. Then Reo had basically disappeared . . . until
now.

She decided it was best to determine if this was indeed
Reo Jones and confront him now with his presence on
Wyatt, rather than wait until he made his move. She
walked toward him with a military-business stride, but
he appeared to ignore her until she closed the last few
meters. Alexi stopped in front of him and balled her fists
on her hips before she spoke.

"Can I help you?" she demanded.

He turned to face her, removing his sunglasses to reveal deep-set blue eyes. "Why, no, ma'am. It's just that
it's not every day a new Knight Errant arrives on
Wyatt—especially one bringing a lot of hardware along
with her. I'm just a little curious, that's all."

"Why would you care what the Knights Errant are
doing, Mr. Jones?" She used his name deliberately.

"Well, Knight Holt," he drawled, proving he knew her
name as well, "you could say that I'm just an interested
local, wondering why The Republic would suddenly start
paying attention to this little backwater world."

"I'd say that it is none of your business," she retorted.

Reo Jones smiled confidently, totally relaxed. "Maybe.
Maybe not. I like to determine for myself what is my
business."

She gritted her teeth and stepped closer to him so that
her voice wouldn't carry. "I know all about you, Mr.
Jones. If you're here playing lackey for Jacob Bannson,

then you would do well to turn your attention elsewhere."

He shook his head. "There's a lot of stories about me floating around out there. Don't believe everything you hear or read. I thought that Knights Errant were supposed to be smarter than that." It was a minor verbal jab, but she knew her face betrayed his hit.

Alexi abruptly changed the subject, hoping to catch him off guard and perhaps learn something that might be of use.

"How did you end up on Wyatt?"

"I've been here for over a year now," he replied, looking away and studying the DropShip as workers unloaded the massive crates she had brought with her. "I came to Wyatt for a little peace and quiet. It seemed like the perfect place to get away from it all. Heck, it doesn't even show up on the star charts; what could be more isolated than that?"

"So you want me to believe it's a coincidence that you're here?" Doubt hung in the air between them.

Reo shook his head. "Sir Knight, I don't care what you believe." He began to walk away from her, then paused, turning back. "I'm just a simple citizen of The Republic, out for a stroll." He looked at her consideringly and added, "Say hello to Demi-Precentor Faulk for me." He gave her a final broad grin, and walked away.

Alexi watched him go, but made no move to stop him. As a Knight Errant, she had authority to deal with reasonable risks to the security of The Republic, but he had done nothing that she could claim served as probable cause. Reo was just an irritating risk. *No, he's not a risk. What's the word I'm looking for? Wild card.*

She was frustrated by her inability to contain Reo Jones' actions; she was more frustrated by the fact that he knew she was going to meet with the demi-precentor. That meant Reo Jones was either connected, smart, or both. Either way, he deserved close observation.

The ComStar compound on Wyatt looked positively pastoral as Alexi Holt approached. The massive hyperpulse generator and its large dish antenna were pointed upward at the blue sky; it seemed to be both aimed at the sky and awaiting messages that simply were not coming. The size of the massive array forced Alexi to remember that the HPG was essentially a combination of cannon and JumpShip engine. It opened a hole in hyperspace and shot data through that hole to a receiving HPG. The power required for such a near instantaneous connection was staggering, and the size of the structure towering over her conveyed that quite effectively.

She realized that what made the complex seem so peaceful was that this HPG was not throbbing with power. The constant, faint hum she should be hearing was conspicuously missing. And this particular installment looked more like a garden than a communications center. The perimeter of the building consisted of a low stone wall covered with vines. A few security personnel guarded the entrance and patrolled the grounds. Though she had no doubt they were heavily armed and trained to protect the facility, with the HPG not working, there was no real threat.

She paused for a moment and considered the open gates leading to the inner courtyard surrounding the HPG. A century or so ago, this would have been unheard of. In those days, ComStar protected its precious interstellar technology so obsessively that few people even reached the gate of an HPG. Those who did penetrate the aggressive security measures would have been greeted by adepts wearing robes and chanting technological phrases as if they were prayers. But that was a long time ago. The horror of the Jihad had purged the religious elements from ComStar once and for all. No one called on "the Holy Blake." ComStar had returned to its origins as a corporate entity.

Her ID was verified at two checkpoints, then she had to wait in a small reception area for what seemed like an eternity. Finally, a smartly dressed man came and escorted her to the office of the demi-precentor in charge of the Wyatt HPG.

Faulk was a sleek-looking man in his thirties wearing

a precisely pressed suit. His smile revealed perfect white teeth, and his manner reminded her more of a marketing executive than someone struggling to get a complex HPG back on line. His blonde, carefully styled hair stayed in place as he rose and shook her hand, gesturing to a seat in front of his desk.

"I'm David Faulk, Demi-Precentor of Wyatt. Welcome to Wyatt, Sir Knight," he said, taking his own seat.

"Thank you," Alexi replied, surveying the room. The moderately sized office held no personal touches. No photographs of family, no awards—no evidence, in fact, that this actually was Faulk's office.

"I received word of your imminent arrival here a few weeks ago from one of the JumpShips passing through our system. My superiors sent me a message telling me something about your assignment." His words were careful, not revealing too much. But that in itself revealed something about him to Alexi. *A political beast. He's trying to ferret out of me what I think my orders mean.*

"I assume your superiors told you that Exarch Levin has made it a priority for ComStar to get the HPG network operational as soon as possible. Paladin Kelson Sorenson sent me here because he believes you have the potential to restore the HPG here on Wyatt sooner than elsewhere."

He flashed her a quick smirk. "Yes, I'd gathered as much from the media. I trust that Paladin Sorenson understands the complexity of the task we are facing here."

She tipped her head to one side and returned the smirk. "I can assure you, Demi-Precentor, that he doesn't care."

The glint of cockiness faded instantly with her words. "Well, you and the Paladin should care. We've been working very hard to get this generator back online. But we've been plagued with a wide range of problems."

Alexi looked pointedly at Faulk's pristine desk. "Yes, I can see you're working quite hard on the problems. Paladin Sorenson has sent me here to assist you in solving them. Humor me—explain the problems you're facing and what you're doing to fix them."

"Very well," he said, his forehead furrowing slightly as he leaned back in his seat. "On Gray Monday the network went down. It was taken down a few different ways. In our case, the virus appeared to retune the factory settings of our HPG's core, but we're not sure how it did that—it should be impossible."

"Isn't each core preset to work on the destination world?"

"Yes, and the factory settings were worked out hundreds of years ago. In every HPG failure, before the core burned out the system began to send out duplicate messages, millions of them. That's a common symptom of a malfunction for any core, but this cascade happened so quickly that the technicians were unable to shut down the system before the problem destroyed the core."

She had been briefed on this by ComStar HQ on Terra, though the phrase Gray Monday was new to her. "Some of your stations were physically sabotaged by terrorists," she prompted.

Demi-Precentor Faulk nodded. "Our newer facilities weren't as susceptible to the virus. These were taken out by terrorist actions, explosives, sabotage—whatever was needed. Whoever did this knew a great deal about our network." His words revealed his true feelings. Not *the* network. *Our* network.

"I'm with you so far, Demi-Precentor," she replied.

"We had special problems here on Wyatt," he continued. "The damage corrupted our HPG core. The core's the heart of the generator, and ours was not only depolarized, it also suffered an imbalance. As you have pointed out, each HPG core is uniquely constructed and tuned for the generator for which it's intended. This has to be done in the factory, because the tuning requires equipment and skills you can't duplicate in the field. It took months to get one built for us, then shipped from Terra. Remember, Knight Holt, that we lost more than eighty percent of the network. Wyatt wasn't the only station that had this problem, so there were a lot of cores being built."

"I am aware of the scope of the problem," she replied.

"We got our core, installed it, and spent weeks on troubleshooting and simulations. Everything checked out fine. We turned it on, and initial start-up was perfect. When we sent our test message, it started replicating. A few thousand at first, then a few million. We started overloading the receiving station that was online with us."

"You knew it was going to burn out," she replied.

He nodded. "I finally ordered our technicians to physically cut the power to the core."

"Then what happened?"

"Pulling the plug damaged the new core. The imbalance in the core fried the firmware and resonator assembly. What happened here was a new problem, one we hadn't encountered before."

Alexi sat silent for a long moment. "Well, Demi-Precentor, what is ComStar doing to fix it?"

He glared at her. "I told you, this is a problem we have never encountered before. Plus, we fried the replacement core. That part alone costs billions of C-bills to manufacture and months to custom-build."

"I understand," she returned. "But you still haven't answered my question."

"A replacement core is being shipped here as we speak. Also, my superiors have told me to inform you that they have sent one of their most gifted technicians, some sort of savant on HPG mechanics, to accompany the new core. ComStar wishes to assure you and your Paladin that we are fully committed to the repair of the Wyatt HPG as soon as possible and are providing the resources to make that happen."

"I appreciate the official position of ComStar," Alexi said back, choosing her words carefully. "When does this replacement core arrive?"

"The hardware and installation technicians are due in-system in a week," he replied curtly. "In the meantime, I will arrange for you to inspect our generator and facilities and review our records, per your Paladin's request."

She nodded, standing. "I appreciate your cooperation, Demi-Precentor," she said again. "One more question;

this genius technician who is coming, what can you tell me about him?"

"Nothing more than his name," Faulk replied. "Harwell. Tucker Harwell. Also, that his sister, an INN researcher for ComStar, was reassigned here to help him adjust more quickly to working in the field."

Alexi nodded. "When you get a chance, please send me what personnel data you can on him. I'm staying in the militia barracks."

2

Customs, Adriana Spaceport
Kinross, Wyatt
The Republic, Prefecture VIII
17 April 3135

The customs agent eyed him suspiciously. At least, Tucker felt he was giving him the eye. The line for customs was short, only Tucker and five other ComStar techs who had arrived on the same ship, but it seemed like the process was taking forever. The customs area was hot and humid, making him feel sticky. The overweight, Asian-looking man used a small metallic wand to stab at his clothing and shaving kit, obviously looking for something that just as obviously wasn't there. Adding to Tucker's misery, he had picked up a sinus infection two days ago, making his head stuffy and his eyes itchy.

The customs office didn't make him feel any better. It was a plain, white-walled brick building floored in lifeless gray carpeting and illuminated with flat-panel white lights. It smacked of a government facility: no pictures on the walls other than posters warning visitors about the risks of bringing unauthorized foods to Wyatt. From the look of the facility, it was in need of maintenance, probably the least of which was the paint chipped off the walls and the plentiful scuff marks. Tucker also noticed that it was not set up to handle a lot of people. Wyatt didn't get a lot of visitors.

The man stared at his identification again, scrutinizing the holoimage and then Tucker. "You're ComStar, eh?"

"Yes," he said, wiping his raw, red nose.

"Here to fix our HPG, I suppose," the customs agent sniffed, handing back Tucker's identification.

"That's the hope," Tucker said, stuffing the ID into his inner jacket pocket. "Our security detail and parts are still aboard the ship, waiting for your people's clearance. With any luck we'll have you up and running in a few weeks." His voice rang with confidence.

"Luck?" the agent said with contempt. "Bloody ComStar."

Tucker cocked his head to the side. He had not heard that exact phrase before, and never heard ComStar spoken about with such disdain. "Excuse me?"

"You heard me," the customs agent said, snapping shut Tucker's suitcase. "What? You think because you're ComStar that you're special? Let me tell you, boy-o, most thinking people think ComStar was the ones that took down the network. And here you come with the parts, three years later, to fix something that you damaged."

Tucker was speechless for a moment, stunned by the vehemence from this total stranger. A new voice shattered the strained silence. "I take it, officer, that you are done here?" Tucker turned and saw a friendly face, one that made him smile.

"Maybe I am, maybe I'm not," the customs agent groused.

The woman, older than Tucker and just slightly shorter, barely lowered the tone of her voice. "If you have charges you wish to file, do so. If you have evidence or probable cause to detain this man, declare your case and act on it. Otherwise, he leaves now," she said, pointing at Tucker.

The customs agent glared at her. "Bloody ComStar," he repeated. "Get him out of here," he said, turning his back and walking away. Tucker walked a few steps before turning to the woman and embracing her. "Patricia, what are you doing here?"

She smiled warmly. Her hair was worn straight and unadorned and she tossed her head slightly to get it back in place after his hug. "Can't I show up to welcome my little brother?"

"But how did you know I was here?"

"I met with Precentor Buhl several months ago. He told me that he was considering you for an assignment, and arranged for me to be sent to Wyatt."

Tucker was astonished. That was impossible. "Patricia, I was still in school then. I hadn't even talked to Buhl about an assignment."

She smiled more broadly and shrugged her shoulders. "From what I hear, he's a very astute man. He must have had you in mind for months before meeting you. He must have wanted you to have a friendly face here."

He stood with his mouth half-open, stunned. He had heard that Buhl was a visionary, that he was one of the true leaders of ComStar. Now Tucker had witnessed that quality. The interview he had gone through was just a formality. Precentor Buhl had planned on sending him to Wyatt long before they had actually met. His respect for the man went up a notch.

"Incredible," was all he managed to stammer. "What have they got you doing here?"

She patted him on the back as they walked out of the customs area. "Archives research for INN. Wyatt was the site of an aerotech production facility before the Jihad. Bowie Industries was destroyed in the first few weeks of fighting, and the defending Com Guards were wiped out to the last man. ComStar has me documenting what happened to the facility. They fund quite a bit of historical research." She spoke casually about her work, as if it were boring. "But what about you? Congratulations are obviously in order for passing your training."

"Thanks. I graduated at the top of my class—I guess

that's why they picked me for this," he replied as they stepped outside. The air was warm and humid, but not as oppressive as in the customs office, and the sun felt good on his skin after the artificial light inside. From what he could see of the city it was old; the brickwork and roof lines spoke of a different age, a different century.

Old cities, at least big ones, were a rarity now on Earth, because the Word of Blake Jihad had destroyed so many of them. For someone like Tucker, who had spent his whole life on Terra but never traveled, the weight of the construction was awe-inspiring. "It's pretty," he commented. "But do all of the locals feel the same as that customs agent?"

"What do you mean?" Patricia's tone was carefully neutral.

"Hating ComStar. Do they all hate us?"

"No," she said reassuringly. "Not everyone. But you have to remember, Tucker, with the network down on most worlds, we're not treated with the respect that we deserve. Most people are suspicious of us at best— memories of the Jihad die hard. And if they've lost money as a result of Gray Monday, they are also more than a little angry at us. I guess that's just part of the burden we carry until the network is back up." He wished he could dismiss her words. As a brand-new graduate of the premier HPG education in the Inner Sphere, it was hard to accept that, as a member of ComStar, he was seen as tainted. He hoped that attitude wouldn't factor into the job he came to do.

"I suppose I should get to the compound and report to the demi. How is this Demi-Precentor Faulk to work with?"

Patricia grimaced. "Well, let's just say he isn't a fan of outside interference."

No problem. "No sweat, Patricia. I'm here to help him."

She reached up and ran her fingers through his disheveled hair, messing it up even more. "That's one of your more endearing characteristics, Tucker . . . your innocence. You think you're coming to Wyatt to help him out, and on paper that's the way it is. But don't let your naivete cloud your thinking. Put yourself in the demi-precentor's shoes. Everyone has an ego, and he's been working on this problem for three years. . . ."

Tucker cocked his head and smiled back, not completely sure what she was warning him about. Within an hour he understood.

From the shadow of a gantry, she watched Legate Edward Singh as he stood in front of his *Panther* BattleMech, watching the technicians swing the gantry into place so that they could gain access to the torso of the massive war machine. Standing three stories tall, the *Panther* was the epitome of warfare technology. The 'Mech's stats scrolled across her brain. Capable of moving at 43 kilometers per hour, in the hands of a good MechWarrior it could blast a city block into slag in a matter of minutes. At thirty-five tons, *Panther*s were classified as light 'Mechs. The Lords Light 2 Extended Range Particle Projector Cannon (ER PPC) that dominated its right arm was ominous even with the 'Mech powered down and secured. Even idled in the Militia's repair bay, the *Panther* was menacing, its humanoid shape seeming to lean forward, as if ready to rush out into battle.

Knight Alexi Holt surveyed Singh as he micromanaged the technicians. He occasionally ran his hand over the top of his head, pulling what few long strands of hair he had remaining over the encroaching bald spot that crowned his brow. She watched him carefully, soaking up details. His position on the planet made him someone to be reckoned with. He had been on maneuvers since she arrived on Wyatt, and had offered her only a short holocommunication greeting in that time. Not even an invitation to join him in the field.

Deciding she had seen enough, she walked toward the legate, exuding the confidence of years earned through disciplined military training and experience. The legate made eye contact with her just as she extended her hand to him. "Legate Singh. I am—"

"Knight Holt," he said, cutting her off. "Pleased to meet you. I'm only sorry that you had to come under such circumstances. Arthur Faust was an honored Knight and colleague."

"He will be missed."

"Yes, he will." Singh paused for a moment. "Regardless of the circumstances, however, welcome to Wyatt. I trust your accommodations meet with your approval?"

She returned his handshake and surveyed him up close. His dirt brown hair was combed over his bald spot. Shaved circles on the side of his head interrupted the remaining hairline, indicating where his neurohelmet, the device that connected the BattleMech to the pilot and allowed him or her to keep the war machine upright and balanced, made contact with his scalp. That he shaved for the contact points supported the impression made by the comb-over, the pressed uniform, the hint of expensive cologne in the air near him, and the fact that he returned from field maneuvers without any sign of sweat. As a 'Mech pilot herself, she knew that there was no measurable improvement in neurohelmet contact by removing hair from the contact points. The legate appeared to be in good shape, but there was something *soft* about him that she couldn't quite identify. She wondered how that softness affected the performance of the Militia.

"My quarters are fine, thank you. I took the liberty of loading the hardware I brought into the south garage."

He smiled absently, glancing back at a technician who was removing one of the armor plates on his 'Mech's torso. "Whatever you need is yours to take, Knight Holt."

"I had hoped," she said neutrally, "that you would invite me to join you in the field. I would have liked to observe the Militia's performance."

The legate's head swiveled back toward hers in surprise. "Really? I apologize for not inviting you. The message the governor and I received stated that you were here to work with ComStar."

"That's true," she replied. "But like Knight Faust, I am also charged with the defense of Wyatt. If ComStar succeeds in reactivating the HPG, Wyatt becomes a tempting target."

The legate chuckled, then stopped when he saw that she was not joking. "No offense, Knight Holt, but I doubt that. Since the Jihad and the destruction of that Bowie Aerospace plant, Wyatt has ceased to be of interest to anyone . . . working HPG or not. From what I've been told, we disappeared off most of the star charts when the network went down, making attacking us even more difficult."

She allowed herself a courtesy smile, one she had practiced often for just such situations. "I understand your viewpoint. But I made it here, as do merchant ships on a regular basis. Wyatt is not hidden. And a functioning HPG would make you a prized world—a member of a very select community of planets."

Legate Singh shrugged off her words. "I suppose I should trust what you say, since you *are* an expert in such matters. Rest assured, Knight Holt, the Wyatt Militia is ready and able to defend our world against any incursion."

"Just to be sure," she returned, "I brought with me some additional hardware and vehicles. It's not much, but it may be enough to trip up anyone foolish enough to come here."

"That's good news," Singh replied. "We can never have too much defense. Perhaps we can meet later and look over your inventory. I can assemble my key officers and they can brief you on our readiness and unit efficiencies. For now, I need to oversee the work on my *Panther*."

"I look forward to our meeting." Alexi stepped away, a little nervous with what she had learned about the man responsible for defending Wyatt. He was a micromanager, yet he didn't know his unit's readiness—he relied on his subordinates for that information. Looks were important to him, not actions—otherwise she would have been invited to the field to watch the maneuvers. There was more than his cologne that bothered her.

*   *   *

The older man tossed Tucker's paperwork to the control panel as if it were garbage. "So I'm supposed to give *you* full run of *my* HPG. It is *not* my fault that the last HPG core failed. I ought to send you packing back to Terra to tell those cube-heads that they aren't going to pin these problems on my personnel record." Demi-Precentor Faulk's face turned deep crimson as he spoke. Anger ran with each word. The other technicians in the HPG control room looked up, and the fear on their faces told Tucker they were used to these outbursts.

Tucker was flustered. "With all due respect, sir, I'm here to help you with the installation."

"You? Some snot-nosed college puke fresh out of a classroom is going to walk into this HPG and help me? My family has been with ComStar for fifty years. My father was the demi here and I was practically raised in this control room. When our HPG was up, I could tell by the *sound* of it if it was working at peak efficiency. You walk in here and say you can help? Pah!" He turned away, and Tucker wondered just how close the demi-precentor was to throwing a punch at him. The three technicians in the control room rose in unison and left the room as quietly as mice. He was alone with the precentor.

Patricia had been right. That stung, too. His older sister had always seemed to be one step ahead of him when it came to matters of common sense. He tried again.

"Sir, I assure you that no one on Terra mentioned you in relation to the problems with the last HPG core. I was told only that they wanted to make sure you had all of the assets necessary to pull off this installation." Tucker paused for a moment, and tried following the path Patricia had suggested. "Personally, I was hoping this opportunity would allow me to learn some fieldwork techniques from you, since you've been working this hardware for so many years."

Demi-Precentor Faulk smoothed the lapels of his suit. "I want you to understand your position here, Adept Harwell," he said in a more normal tone. "This is my world, my HPG. You take your orders from me. You do what I tell you to—nothing more, nothing less. You don't take a dump around here without clearing it with me first. It's bad enough I have to nursemaid that damn Knight Errant poking through my operations; I'll be damned if I'm going to put up with some kid telling me what to do."

Tucker recoiled slightly at his words. The reference to the Knight Errant just confused him; he'd have to figure that out later. "Sir, I'll do what I was sent here to do. Precentor Buhl's orders were to oversee the installation of the core, coordinating my work with you. I'm not sure that those orders are open to interpretation."

"Buhl? Malcolm Buhl?"

"Yes, sir," Tucker said, retrieving his paperwork from the control console. "It's here in the transfer orders."

This time Demi-Precentor Faulk stared at the orders intently, actually reading them through. It took a painfully uncomfortable minute, while Tucker stared silently at him. The HVAC in the control room kicked in, humming enough fan-borne white noise to make the room seem even quieter.

Faulk set the paperwork back on the console. "So Precentor Buhl sent you personally, and your orders are clear. Fine. I'll work with you, Harwell. But there are two things you should know. First, if anything goes wrong with this HPG core, I'll make sure you're the one to blame. Second, you should know that the man you're working for is a real political beast. You hitch your career to his coattails, and you may just find yourself sweeping reception lounges."

Tucker nodded. He was not leveraging Precentor Buhl for anything, so the words were empty for him.

"Very well, sir. I guess the first thing we need to do is get the new core moved here from the DropShip." Faulk turned away, grumbling some sort of agreement. Tucker wondered what he meant by his comment regarding Precentor Buhl, and made a mental note to ask Patricia about it. If anyone would have insights to Buhl and Faulk, it would be her.

The Mill Tails of McPherson
Marcus
The Republic, Prefecture VIII

Galaxy Commander Kev Rosse of the Spirit Cats sat cross-legged by the bonfire and embraced its warmth. Around him, stretching for kilometers in every direction, were enormous piles of mining debris. Most of these were dotted with clumps of scrub brush and trees, brittle and bone-dry. Marcus had long been a mining world, and the mill tailings, the debris left from the mining operations, had dotted this continent for centuries. A cool breeze shifted the heavy air, stirring up tiny tornadoes of black dust. Each gust whipped ashes and embers into the air from the fire.

Star Captain Cox felt that the mountains of waste rock were a perfect place for the Galaxy commander to hold an enclave of the Spirit Cats. Prying eyes from the local population would not come to such a wasteland. Any military force trying to spy on their gathering, including Marcus' planetary militia, would find their scans hampered if not completely blocked by all of the mineral and radioactive element traces in the mill-tailings. Here, in these badlands, the Spirit Cats could meet in private to discuss what was important to their Clan.

Their future.

Kev Rosse was a tall, gaunt, imposing figure. Even in the light of the bonfire, his eyes seemed deep and brooding. Dressed in a warrior's jumpsuit, his body seemed so skinny that you could count his ribs. As Star Captain Cox approached the fire, he studied his commanding officer with appreciation. Much had come to pass since the collapse of the HPG network in The Republic, and Galaxy Commander Rosse had led the Spirit Cats far in that time. Star Captain Cox gave him a silent nod as they made eye contact, a greeting of respect. He took off his half-cloak and dropped down in front of the fire. Two other Star captains emerged from the shadows and did the same.

The Spirit Cats had fought with Devlin Stone to free the Inner Sphere from the Jihad. Warriors of Clan Nova Cat, those naming themselves the Spirit Cats followed Kev Rosse on his quest to find a sanctuary for the Clan—a goal that might seem a contradiction for a society bred for war. Rosse saw the collapse of the HPG network as the beginning of a great storm that would surely consume The Republic of the Sphere, if not all of the Inner Sphere and, led by a vision, sought a new home for his Clan. The men and women who followed him believed his vision would lead the Nova Cats to great glory, but until that day respected Khan Jacali Nostra by pursuing their quest apart from the main body of the Clan.

As the last of his Star captains arrived and sat down near the fire, Rosse gazed solemnly at each leader. When he spoke, his voice was deeper than his physical frame would seem to allow. "I bid you, as Spirit Cats, seekers of the true vision, welcome to our meeting. May our forebears grant us the vision and wisdom to do what is best for our people."

"Seyla," they responded in unison.

"I have called this Clave of my command to convey important news to you," Rosse said deliberately, as if he were preaching. "The providence of the Great Kerenskys came to me five months ago. I experienced a vision . . . one that I wish to share with you."

Cox glanced at the other Star captains gathered around the bonfire and saw each of them transfixed on their leader. He understood their loyalties and feelings. The Spirit Cats were true to their past and heritage. Kev Rosse saw to that, and they respected his insight. That he was planning to speak to them of his vision stirred all their imaginations: the Spirit Cats placed great weight on the visions of their leader.

Rosse closed his eyes as he spoke, as if he could still see the scene of his dream. "I awoke and saw the stars above me, spread throughout the heavens in their ordained places. As I watched, one star disappeared from the night, its light extinguished as if it had never shined. That star called to me. I heard it call my soul. When I awoke, I considered this vision, meditating on its meaning. I believe my vision means this: we must investigate this star and determine it is the sanctuary for our Clan. This star is the planet Wyatt in this Prefecture."

One of the Star captains, a slender woman named Caitlin Bauer, spoke first. "Galaxy Commander, how are you so sure that Wyatt is the world that called to you?"

Rosse smiled before answering. "When the HPG network collapsed, the virus responsible for its collapse did something unexpected. It deleted Wyatt from the stellar cartography atlases in hundreds of thousands of databases—including ComStar's own maps. Thus, the star disappeared.

"I further learned that, the week I experienced my vision, ComStar had attempted to restore the HPG on that world, but it had failed. This star has disappeared two times, and the second time it called out to me. Also in my vision, I saw a man holding the light from this star in his hands, and I knew he was a Lightbringer. My vision bids our Clan to investigate this planet. We must learn if Wyatt is the world where our Clan can survive the coming firestorm of war."

His words stirred Cox's heart and courage, for he had had such a vision himself. He considered if he should support his leader's vision with his own, but held his tongue.

"That planet is only a jump away," said Star Captain Falstaff Taylor. "We should have convened there rather than here. We could have learned the truth together, *quiaff?*"

"Neg," Rosse replied. "We must conserve our strength for the day we fight to earn our sanctuary. One may go to Wyatt, along with his command. The rest must continue searching other worlds."

Star Captain Taylor smiled. "Then we shall settle this according to Clan traditions. Galaxy Commander, I am prepared to fight for the right to take my command to this world. Honor me by accepting my opening bid of two Stars to prove I am most worthy." Kev Rosse nodded.

Star Captain Caitlin Bauer spoke up next. "Such a bid for the right to fulfill the geas of our people insults the honor of the Spirit Cats. I bid one Star of my warriors to prove that I am most fit to fulfill this quest."

Star Captain Franks, a tall black-skinned warrior, spoke next. "Surely my fellow Star captains are not serious. The Purifiers Black Stallion Trinary is of tougher mettle. I bid three Points for the right to go to Wyatt in our Clan's name." Spirit Cat units followed the standard Clan organizational structure, plus each had a name that was earned on a vision quest. The naming of each Trinary and Star in the command structure required a ritual of fasting, battle, tests of endurance, and the vision of the commanding officers.

Star Captain Bauer's face reddened. "The prowess of the Black Stallions of the Purifiers is acknowledged by my Omicron Stealth Cats Trinary, but we cannot accept the implication that we are not the most worthy. I bid two Points for the right to travel to this Wyatt."

Cox let the last bid hang in the air. He would be pleased to win the right to challenge Star Captain Bauer for the right to investigate Wyatt. Several Star captains did not bid, their units most likely undergoing refit and repair from other engagements. Now was the time for him to make his bid, to give honor to the Spirit Cats.

"Galaxy Commander," he said slowly. "This disappearing star also has spoken to me. My visions also have shown me a man holding the light of a vanished star. While I wish I could grant the honor of battle to my Purifier Pouncers Trinary, I must instead honor them with a victory in their name. I bid myself, augmented, against any who would challenge for the right to confirm your vision." He turned to face Star Captain Bauer.

She gritted her teeth as she moved restlessly on the opposite side of the bonfire. The choice was hers. She could let him go, or contest him. Her eyes seemed to flare as she returned his gaze. "Such bravery cannot be proven by words alone. With your permission, Galaxy Commander, I shall face Star Captain Cox in a Trial of Equals, a test of our skills. The winner between us shall fulfill your vision."

Kev Rosse smiled, only for a second. "Such is the way of our people. Bargained well and done. Prepare your 'Mechs for battle."

3

"**S**o your first day was quite busy, from what I heard," Patricia said as she stirred her soup. The bustle of the restaurant distracted Tucker, but he felt safe talking there. It was unlikely anyone could hear him over the sounds of conversation, the clanking of dishes, and the throbbing music bouncing off the cheap decor.

"Word travels fast," he replied, taking a spoonful of his chili and blowing on it to cool it before eating it.

"It's a small city, and an even smaller compound. You're new, and I've been here long enough to build up some contacts in our organization. From what I gathered, you and the demi-precentor spent most of your time locking horns."

"Faulk is a . . ." he hesitated. If he had been sitting with anyone but his sister, he would have cursed the man. Instead, Tucker drew a long breath and blew it out, focusing on his control and composure, then stirred his chili and finished with, ". . . complex person."

"You're the master of understatement," she chuckled.

"He hates me."

"He doesn't know you well enough to hate you, Tucker."

He shook his head. "You didn't hear him chew me out when that core arrived. All I was doing was scanning it for magnetic residue. Standard-freaking procedure and he yells at me for a good ten minutes."

She shook her head in a mirror of his own motion a moment before. "Tucker, you've just got to accept that he considers you a threat. He's faced a few lately, not the least of which is a Knight Errant being sent here to oversee this installation and reactivation."

Tucker cocked his head. "Yeah, he mentioned that when I arrived this morning. Why has a Paladin dispatched a Knight here?"

Patricia daintily drank her soup, taking a moment to wipe her lips. She glanced around to make sure that no one was close enough to listen. "Bear in mind, no one's really saying anything solid. But it sounds to me like the new Exarch is putting pressure on ComStar to get the HPG network back up and running . . . right now. A Paladin named Sorenson has sent out a few Knights Errant to worlds like this one, where we are close to finishing repairs and restoration. Their mission is to 'encourage' us to get the repairs done faster."

Tucker allowed himself a chuckle. "What does a Knight Errant know about HPG operations?"

"She seems to be a quick learner," Patricia countered. "I haven't met her yet, since no one has offered to introduce me. But I have talked to some of the other station personnel. This Knight Errant seems really to be wrapping her head around the problem that you're going to be dealing with."

"What's your take on all of this?"

"I think it's a political hot potato. The Republic is under pressure to get the HPG back up, so they're putting pressure on ComStar, which in turn is going to put pressure on you. None of this helps us get the HPG network repaired; in fact, the unnecessary pressure is a distraction. I understand their logic, though. Until the network went down, The Republic was safe and doing fine. Since it went down, we've faced invasions, incursions, betrayal, you name it." She took another sip of her soup and paused for a moment. "Which brings up the question, how is it going with the new HPG core?"

Tucker made a face and was immediately embarrassed by letting his feelings show. Patricia was the member of his family he felt closest to, and he always wanted to impress her. She was the one person whose opinion of him mattered. *Maybe she'll just think the chili is too hot.* "After Demi-Precentor Faulk made sure I knew that if anything went wrong, it was my butt in a sling—not his," he said brightly. "I oversaw the delivery of the new core from the DropShip. We've begun the preliminary testing that needs to be done before we install it. So far, it looks like it arrived intact."

"So it appears this core will work?"

Tucker shook his head. "The last core tested perfectly, too. It wasn't until they fired up the HPG that it began to send out duplicate messages, overloading the network. It's too early to say. I'm not one-hundred-percent convinced that the problem is the core to begin with."

"Meaning?"

He gave her a grin. It was the same expression he used for any layman when it came to explaining technical matters. Stellar communications was a complicated process, and Tucker had discovered that his so-called peers and family members found the technical details too overwhelming. It only took a few sentences of explanation for their eyes to glaze over. "Everyone is focused on the core as the root of the problem. I'm just saying that I'm going to take a look at everything."

Patricia lowered her spoon. "I know that you'll do what is necessary, Tucker. It's just that ComStar seems to have a lot riding on this. If you can fix this HPG, well, you'll be doing a lot to improve the organization's image, and not just on Wyatt."

Tucker understood. There was more on the table than just Wyatt. The presence of the Knight Errant told him that this was not an ordinary repair job that he had been sent on. "I'm going to do whatever it takes to make this startup and re-initialization a success, Patricia. When we power up that core, it *has* to work."

"I'm glad to hear you say that."

There was a short silence as they both applied themselves to finishing their food.

"You haven't asked about Mom and Dad," he said in a neutral voice. He looked at her as he spoke, and he saw that for the first time since she had picked him up at the spaceport, she refused to make eye contact.

"I got a message to Mom right before I was assigned here. I assume that they're okay or you would have said something." Her tone changed as well. Patricia and her father had done more fighting than talking in the last few years.

"He's getting old, Patricia. Maybe the two of you could patch things up." He allowed a little hope to creep into his voice.

She shook her head. "Tucker, you know better than anyone what he's like. You went into the technical side of the organization. You were always his favorite because of that. Me, I opted to work on nontechnical things. Dad's just set in his ways; he's old-school ComStar. He's not going to be civil to me until I become a tech like you. You know I'm right."

Tucker frowned. "I know that he's getting older and is someday going to die, and if you don't work things out with him, you'll have missed your chance forever."

Patricia paused for a moment. "You're probably right. Maybe after this assignment I'll rotate to Terra for a few days—drop in and see them. Will that make you happy?"

"It's a start," he replied.

She glanced at her wrist and winced. "It's getting late, and I assure you that our demi is going to want you up and at 'em first thing in the morning. You'd better get settled in."

Tucker nodded, pulled his napkin off his lap and tossed it on the table. "You're right. Walk you back to the compound?"

Patricia shook her head. "No, I've got an errand to run. I'll pop in tomorrow and see how you're doing— deal?"

"Deal."

Sitting at a small booth on the other side of Schuler's Restaurant, he stared down at his noteputer as it hummed with activity. Her image came up. Patricia Harwell. INN researcher. He cocked his eyebrow. It had taken a while for the data he had requested to arrive, and her file was pretty thin for a career adept.

He studied her image on the small viewscreen and glanced over as she and her brother Tucker rose from their table. The data had cost a lot of money to obtain; ComStar personnel files were pricey, but his benefactor was willing—eager—to spend the cash. Wyatt was an isolated world, the last place anyone would suspect that Jacob Bannson would have any people or hardware.

Tucker Harwell's data was more intriguing. *A child genius.* It appeared on the surface that, by sending Harwell to Wyatt, ComStar was serious about repairing the HPG. But his trained eyes cut through the data quickly, reading between the lines. He's young, smart, but never had a hands-on assignment in his career.

Reo Jones leaned back in the booth and shut off the noteputer. *Damn peculiar.* ComStar sends in a researcher with a scanty resume, then sends in her brother along with a new HPG core. Add in a new Knight Errant, and the backwater planet that he had come to suddenly seemed like the center of the universe. There was more going on here than what he saw.

Reo wasn't sure what it all meant, but he knew that he needed to get to the bottom of it. His inquiries about Knight Alexi Holt's presence had offered few results. He already knew her background. From the gossip he had picked up from the ComStar adepts who frequented the local bars and restaurants, he had learned that she was in an ongoing battle with Demi-Precentor Faulk . . . who was irritated with her unwanted inspecting and questioning.

Reo allowed himself a silent chuckle. *I wonder if she's learned just how much of a wimp our dear legate really is?* Reo knew that Legate Singh had his own secrets. His connections were the kind that could get someone killed. Wyatt suddenly had all of the makings for going from a boring little world to a world of potential excitement.

The Mill Tails of McPherson
Marcus
The Republic, Prefecture VIII

The scrap ore and debris piles rock rose up like small gray-and-tan mountains. Atop of each of the perimeter mounds, as much as a kilometer apart, small fires burned and warriors of the Spirit Cats stood and sat. They formed a great Circle of Equals, marking the boundaries of the combat trial. The early-morning sunrise over Marcus was slow in coming. The thick storm clouds made it seem more like twilight than morning. Gusts of wind whipped into the valleys of flat rock that filled the spaces between the mill tailings, sending small clouds of grinding dust into the air.

Star Captain Cox moved his *Warhammer IIC,* the "Harbinger," slowly around the base of one of the mounds, watching both his secondary tactical display and his cockpit view of the combat area. The fight had started off quickly. Star Captain Caitlin Bauer was piloting a *Vulture,* painted in the gray-and-white-striped pattern of her Trinary. His 'Mech wore two shades of gray and a long diagonal stripe of red across the torso, like a sash of honor. Bauer's *Vulture* mounted four Type XX "Great Bow" long-range missile racks, each holding twenty warheads. The *Vulture* was a deadly missile boat and at long range could eat him up.

Tactical doctrine in fighting such a BattleMech either on the battlefield or in trial combat was simple. Rush in, move fast, get close, and rip it up. Harbinger carried twenty more tons of armor and weapons. What any warrior should do in this kind of fight was clear.

Cox smiled. He knew he was not any warrior.

He hadn't rushed in. He held back, whittling away at her with his General Systems large lasers. The emerald green beams of light from his lasers had found their mark several times, scoring blackened scars across her legs and torso, searing off armor plating in the process. She had given back what she could; several deadly salvos of missiles had savaged his right arm and torso, pockmarking them with smoking holes from warhead bursts. This minor damage he attributed only partly to luck.

He heard the *hiss-pop* of an open channel. "Blast it, Cox, come out and fight me like a warrior."

He grinned to himself. Good. She was losing her composure. Her defeat was near. "I am in no rush to win this trial, Star Captain." He continued to slowly move his 'Mech around the mound. His sensors picked up a faint magnetic anomaly reading from behind another mound a few hundred meters away. It could be a trick of the ore, or it could be her fusion reactor.

"Show yourself, you *surat*," she yelled back. "This is not a child's game."

"Indeed it is not," he said, angling forward into the open. "Perhaps you would like to capitulate now and save yourself the indignity of defeat."

She paused. He knew she had picked him up on her sensors. "It will be a cold day before I lose to an unblooded warrior," she spat.

Most Clan warriors would have been infuriated by such a remark. Bloodnames, the highest honor available to Clan warriors, were won on fields of honor such as this. Star Captain Cox had only one name, the name he had been given as a child. Caitlin had won the Bauer Bloodname two years ago. *I have earned my Bloodname already; you know that. Just as I know this is not yet the time for me to assume it.*

"Bold words, Star Captain. But I do not need to hide behind a Bloodname to prove my mettle. If you were worthy of the Bauer bloodline, you would have ended this fight twenty minutes ago. You have left it to me to teach you the ways of a true Spirit Cat, and it is a task I shall finish in my own time."

Her reaction was just what he had hoped. She moved quickly, breaking into a run, determined not to let him slip away. Her *Vulture* was a birdlike 'Mech, narrow, with gangly legs that made it hop slightly when it jogged forward. Cox remained in place, concentrating on targeting her. A warning alarm beeped in his neurohelmet as she locked on with her missile tracking system. He had expected her to do that.

The missiles came like a wall of spears aimed at his head, disgorging smoke as they streaked across the space toward him. He juked his *Warhammer* hard to the right at the last moment, causing some of the shots to miss and fly past him. There was a roar in his ears as the rest of the warheads found their mark.

His secondary display flickered as it tried to track the loss of armor. Flames from one or more warheads lapped up the torso of Harbinger and blackened the lower portion of his cockpit ferroglass. His 'Mech careened under the rumbling impact of the missiles, staggering drunkenly to one side. Smoke, black and gray, wrapped around the Spirit Cat 'Mech, hugging it like a deadly snake attempting to crush the life from him.

Cox fired back with two of his large lasers, both shots hitting the *Vulture* in the legs. The emerald beams stabbed into the knee area, and he saw one plate of her ferro-fibrous armor actually pop off from the sudden heat searing a joint. The temperature in his cockpit rose slightly, but was easy to handle. His sensors painted the picture he expected to see; she was reloading her missile racks, planning to finish him off. Caitlin Bauer was probably still puzzled about why he was not rushing forward and taking away her advantage, but she also probably didn't care.

So he turned and ran.

He broke his *Warhammer* into a full run away from her, dodging around the mill tail pile to get out of her line of sight. Glancing at his tactical display, he saw that he was getting what he wanted; she was running as well. He stopped, swung hard to the right, twisted the torso of his 'Mech and fired again, this time with all four of his large lasers.

One shot missed, but the other three found their mark, biting in at the very heart of Bauer's *Vulture*. His pursuer hesitated under the assault, and from the splatter of green, he knew he had hit her coolant system. She fired again, two racks of missiles at once.

The salvo of missiles was more of a snapshot than a well-aimed volley, but it was true to the mark. This time the left side of his *Warhammer* rumbled and moaned under the impact. He felt his footing slip slightly on the gravel and his head roared as his gyro sent a nauseating wave of feedback into his neurohelmet. The neurohelmet compensated balance in the 'Mech, feeding back his own bio-impulses to the gyro control. He tasted bile rising in his mouth, but turned again and ran.

Star Captain Caitlin Bauer followed in a full run.

He moved another hundred meters around the mounds of scrap rock and ore, keeping out of her line of sight, then swung out again to the right, moving to where she could see him.

They both fired at the same time.

His large lasers reached his target faster, searing into her right arm, right torso and into the armored cockpit of the *Vulture*. The gray-and-white 'Mech reeled heavily under the cutting beams, but before he could enjoy the successful attack, he felt the thunderous impact of the missiles on his own 'Mech. Nearly every part of his *Warhammer* took a hit from at least three or four missiles. He saw one piece of armor plating peeled upward, just under the cockpit . . . a reminder of how close death could be. Cox fought the controls, leaning into the roaring blast. He sneered at the damage and fired again the moment his lasers cycled through. He heard a pop as one of the relays in the cockpit overloaded from the stress of the battle. He caught a whiff of ozone.

Three of the brilliant jade beams hit the right leg of her *Vulture,* blackening the remaining armor. From the looks of it, there was damn little left. Myomer muscle fibers, used to power the limb, were severed and flapped as power tightened and released them. The *Vulture* sagged slightly.

He saw the first indication of his success in the smoke rising from the armor joints near her right-side missile racks. Suddenly, there was an audible groan that he heard in his own cockpit, and he watched as her 'Mech rocked from an internal explosion. The entire right side of the *Vulture* burst outward in an orange ball of fire. As the flame rose into the air, he could see the right arm of the 'Mech hanging limp, held on by charred myomer and the remains of the shoulder joint. The tip of the arm touched the ground.

There was another rumble, this time from the left side of the *Vulture.* The visible results were not as dramatic this time, but he could tell that more warheads had cooked off. Cox's tactical display showed him that the fusion reactor that powered Caitlin Bauer's 'Mech was shut down and there were no readings at all from her weapons systems.

He waited for a moment before speaking, giving her the opportunity to yield before he called upon her to do so. There was some honor in that. After a long minute, he broke the silence. "This trial is over, Star Captain Bauer."

For a moment, when she still didn't respond, he wondered if she had been killed or injured. Finally he heard her voice come in loud and clear, and he knew she was broadcasting so that the other Spirit Cat warriors heard it as well. "You fight like a bandit, Star Captain Cox. You won, but your victory was not honorable."

He shook his head. "Do not blame me because you allowed your temper to override your management of your BattleMech's heat," he replied. He knew that the

Vulture required aggressive heat management. By forcing her to run and attacking her with lasers, he had methodically forced her to either not fight or to overheat. By angering her, he had practically guaranteed that she would continue attacking. Patience was a virtue that he possessed, but that most Clansmen lacked. Patience had won the battle.

"I should contest the results of this trial," she retorted angrily.

"I would not if I were you," came the voice of Galaxy Commander Rosse. "I learned a long time ago that though Star Captain Cox may not fight in a predictable fashion, he knows the ultimate honor is victory. He has won this trial fairly and within the Rede of the Clan. And with this victory, he has earned the right for his troops to travel to Wyatt and determine if it is indeed the sanctuary for our people."

4

The HPG core was large, measuring more than a dozen meters long. To the casual observer, it looked like a giant metal tank. Installed at the rear of the HPG array, it performed the hyperpulse generator's most important function: folding space to transmit data instantaneously up to fifty light years away. The core consisted of a series of circuits and specially shielded magnetic coils that rested inside a massive, metallic domed chamber nearly two stories tall.

The core was essentially the chamber end of a massive subspace cannon. The "barrel" of the HPG array extended outward to the domed ceiling, where it attached to an extension system on the exterior of the array. Outside the dome, a fifty-meter-diameter antenna could be turned and aligned to send and receive message traffic with another HPG. The entire chamber could be rotated and the extending "barrel" could be raised to 90 degrees or lowered to 30 degrees. Under the core chamber was a large fusion reactor and a series of power capacitors to help generate and store the massive amounts of power necessary for the array to operate.

The functioning of the HPG was complex. The communication system was essentially the same technology that allowed JumpShips to travel between star systems. Rather than pushing a physical object through space, however, the HPG sent data through the high-end band of hyperspace where another network would receive it. Rumors abounded that HPGs could be used as weapons, that they could be turned on BattleMechs and could destroy them—but most people considered that possibility an urban legend.

Tucker Harwell, decked out in a white lab coat and wearing specially coated nonstatic gloves, allowed himself a moment to look at the core he had brought with him from Terra. It had been installed into the array, but installation was only part of the challenge. Plugging it in and aligning it was delicate work and important, but fine-tuning the programming of the core was the real work.

When he looked at the core, he saw something beyond all of the metal, software and technology in front of him. Something beyond the raw nuclear power that would soon be pulsing through the device, something he couldn't fathom. Reaching out, he gently placed his hand on one of the closed access panels as if he were feeling the core for a heartbeat—as if it were alive. Even through the gloves the metal was cold. But it seemed hot to him, alive. This was why he had become a technician. *Patricia doesn't know what she's missing.*

"Sir," a voice said, shattering the moment. He jerked his hand away, turned and saw another tech, Adept Paula Kursk, standing behind him. "Sorry to interrupt you."

He put his hands behind his back. "No problem," he stammered. "It's just that it's so—"

She nodded. "I understand. One hell of a piece of hardware. It's the soul of this station. I felt the same way when we installed the first new core." She shook her head.

"Well, this is a *new* new core," Tucker replied. "Mounting it is one thing; calibrating it is another."

She stared at her wrist-strapped noteputer for a moment. "Mr. Harwell . . ."

"Tucker."

"Tucker," she began again. "I've got my technical team ready to begin the testing, but I need to know where you want them."

"I thought I'd first run a Tango-level diagnostic. Once that's done, I was planning on taking a look at the HPG balance readings and comparing them with the new core's balance codes and adjusting them. I figured then I'd load the Crimson diag sequence and check the load balancing and packet traffic modules." He rattled through the details as if he could do them in his sleep.

Adept Kursk said nothing for a moment, apparently studying the tips of her shoes. When she looked back at Tucker, her Asian features did not betray the tension that her voice revealed. "Tucker, you have me and my team here. I've got eight techs on this shift that have come to you and asked for assignments and were sent away empty-handed. They're sitting in the rec area playing holovid games, wondering when you're going to let them do their jobs. Bottom line: we know this station inside and out. We're here to help you. But for us to do that, *you* have to let us do what we know how to do."

"Listen, Adept," he said, his voice betraying his own tension. "I understand that your team wants to be involved. But ComStar sent me all the way from Terra to do this installation, and is holding me responsible for the results."

She flashed a fast grin. "The demi gave us the scoop on your record. You've only been in a classroom so far, right?"

He took offense at her words. "So what does that have to do with anything?"

Again the grin, this time with a soft chuckle. "Hey, no offense intended. It's just that you haven't had the chance to figure out that you can't do this alone, no matter how smart you are. You make Faulk nervous, so you must be pretty good at what you do. But spending your career in the classroom isn't the same as working on a technical team in the field. In the field you get to know each other, trust each other, work together. Nobody tries to do it all alone."

Tucker felt his face redden slightly. He knew she was right—and that made him wrong. He hated being wrong. "So what you're saying is that, in order to make this work, I'm going to have to learn to trust you and your team?"

She nodded. "Afraid so."

"I know you're right," he confessed after a moment. "It's just that it's not easy to share responsibility when everybody hangs the accountability for success on your neck. I'm sorry. I didn't mean to offend you or your team."

"No offense taken. To be honest, I'm looking forward to working with you."

"Why's that?"

This time it was her face that flushed faintly pink. "When we installed that first replacement core and it fried during the shutdown, Demi-Precentor Faulk hung me and my people out to dry—held us responsible, even though we sent it back to Terra and they couldn't figure out what went wrong. I want this installation to go right. When that happens, I'm counting on you to clear our reputations with Terra. We didn't do anything to screw up that last core, and I need someone with your level of credibility to prove that."

Tucker grinned and held out his hand. "Okay. Let's start this all over. Get your people in here and let's put together a roster of tasks."

She shook his hand. "Not my people. Not while you're here. They're *our* people."

Knight Errant Alexi Holt stared at the printout of the project plan and cast Demi-Precentor Faulk a wary eye. "So we have the new core installed, but we're still looking at several weeks' worth of tests before it can be tried?" She shifted her stance to look into the core chamber through the shielded ferroglass. In the massive chamber below, five or six technicians scurried around the newly installed HPG core.

"That is what the technical specs require," Faulk replied stiffly. "A core is a sensitive device. You can't just plug it and turn it on."

"I'm well aware of that, Demi-Precentor," she said, trying to suppress the edge she wanted to put into her voice. "I was simply stating my observation based on this revised plan."

"Yes, well," he stammered as he realized he had overreacted, "I simply wish to assure you that we are doing all that we can." He stopped talking as a tall, lanky man arrived at his side. Alexi had not noticed this ComStar tech in the HPG compound before. He was skinny, his hair was a mess, and he seemed to be averting his eyes from her. "My apologies for not getting back to you sooner, Demi-Precentor. Installation went as planned and we've begun the level-one diagnostics."

There was something in the glance she got from Faulk at that point that told her she wanted to meet this man. Turning, she extended her hand to him. "I don't believe we've met yet. I'm Alexi Holt."

The lanky man gave her a firm handshake. "Tucker. Tucker Harwell."

He had a boyish charm that made her smile. "You must be the genius that ComStar sent from Terra to help repair the HPG. I've heard quite a bit about you. Pleased to make your acquaintance."

Tucker looked at Faulk, who explained. "Ms. Holt is a Knight Errant sent by The Republic to," he hesitated, choosing his words carefully, "oversee our work in getting Wyatt reconnected to the rest of the HPG network."

Tucker bowed his head once he realized he was meeting a Knight. "I had no idea who you were, Lady Holt."

Alexi laughed. "Mr. Harwell, there's no reason to fall into court formalities here. I've simply come to ensure that ComStar has everything it needs to complete this restoration. And please don't use my title. It makes me feel old. From what I've read, we're almost the same age."

"My apologies," Tucker said awkwardly.

"Please think of me as one of your team. If there is anything you need that The Republic can provide, simply let me know."

Faulk cut in quickly. "I assure you, Knight Holt, Com-Star has this matter under its tightest control and is giving it the highest priority."

"Of course that's the case, Demi-Precentor," Alexi soothed. "I just wanted to make sure that our resident genius knows that my door is open, should he need it."

Tucker jumped on her words. "I wish you would stop referring to me as a genius. Really, I don't see myself that way."

An insincere smile crossed Faulk's face. "Don't be so humble, Tucker. Everyone knows that the success or failure of this project rests on your shoulders," he said, dropping his hand onto Tucker's shoulder and squeezing it too hard. "And don't you worry, Knight Holt, I'll make sure that this young man has everything he needs to get the job done."

Alexi nodded. "Very good," was all she said out loud. *I see how he's positioning this: Tucker Harwell will be either the hero of Wyatt, or the failure.* Either result would generate a situation that she, as a Knight Errant, would have to defend. *God, I hate politicians.*

Tucker sat at his table at The Crimson and adjusted the volume slide on his media stick, then dropped it back in his pocket. The media stick stored thousands of songs and other media and transmitted them to the earpiece he wore like an earring in his right ear. He bobbed his head slowly in rhythm with the tune he heard and poked his fork at his steak.

The Crimson was not as nice a restaurant as the one he had gone to with his sister several nights before. In fact, it was a hole in the wall, a tiny little place where the locals gathered. It was a working person's restaurant; he didn't fit in here, and the stares he gathered when he walked in emphasized that fact. Tucker wasn't intimidated by the gazes of the blue-collar locals, though. In fact, he found this to be the perfect kind of place to relax. It was far from ComStar, the ever-watchful eyes of the demi-precentor, and the hassles he had faced during a fifteen-hour day.

So he was surprised when someone flopped down on the booth bench opposite him. It was a dark-haired man sporting a day's worth of beard stubble and a wide grin. "Mind if I join you?" he asked, putting his beer down on the table. "My regular seat is taken and I prefer sitting in a booth."

Tucker shuffled together the printouts he had been studying during his meal and shook his head. "Nope."

"You're with ComStar, aren't you?"

From recent experience, Tucker considered that to be a loaded question, and he was not in the mood for an argument. "Yes. I'm an adept at the compound."

"That's cool," the unkempt man replied, taking a long pull on his beer. "It must be interesting."

"It's a job," Tucker replied.

The man smiled. "Name's Jones. Reo Jones." He extended his large hand and Tucker shook it.

"Tucker Harwell."

"You aren't from Wyatt, or at least this part of Wyatt, are you?"

"No. I'm from Terra. They sent me to help install the new HPG core."

"Well, that's something. All the way from Terra." Reo replied, finishing the last amber swallow of his beer. He signaled the waitress and held up two fingers. "Let me get you a beer. Least I can do for interrupting your dinner."

"Thanks," Tucker replied. "So, Reo, what do you do?"

Reo cocked a thick eyebrow and gave him another broad smile. "I'm something of a jack of all trades. I work for a lot of people. I secure goods and information for a fee. Though the way some people tell it, I'm something of a spy and a mercenary." He chuckled at his own words.

"And are you?" Tucker asked.

The beers arrived, allowing Reo to pause for a moment. "What I am is a MechWarrior, plain and simple."

"Is that the full truth?" Tucker said, shoving a forkful of steak into the side of his mouth like a squirrel so that he could chew and talk at the same time.

"There was a misunderstanding. An accident happened. A lot of people got killed. Damn waste. Somebody had to take the fall for it, so I did. The media, they blew it out of proportion, started pinning the blame on me for everything from the downing of the HPG network to the disappearance of Devlin Stone. I was a convenient scapegoat and The Republic doesn't keep men like that around, regardless of the truth. So I came to this isolated planet and found what work I could."

Tucker hung on every word. "Incredible. I mean, you really are innocent?"

Reo nodded solemnly. "I'm not going to defend myself, Tucker. I know the truth and I sleep like a baby every night knowing that truth. I got tired of trying to defend myself a long time ago. People form their own opinions, and rewrite history to fit their own views."

"I always wanted to be a MechWarrior," Tucker said admiringly.

"Really? Why didn't you go for it?"

He shrugged. "I never really had the chance. My family's been a ComStar family for generations. Besides, I had a knack for technical work, so that's where I got channeled for my education. Each one of my brothers and sisters went into ComStar, too."

"Here's to men who follow their destinies," Reo Jones replied in a toast. The two men tapped the necks of their bottles together and took long drinks.

Reo pointed to Tucker's earpiece. "What are you listening to?"

Tucker pulled off the earphone almost absentmindedly. "I just was listening to some chants."

"Chants?"

"Old ComStar chants. Back when the organization was a technoreligion, the adepts would chant text from technical manuals when they performed tasks related to the HPG. I find them kind of relaxing. Here." He handed the earpiece to Reo, who held it up to his own ear for a few moments.

"Weird stuff," he said, handing it back. "It's like Gregorian chants, but it's all technical terms and phrases."

Tucker shut off the media stick and put the earpiece in his shirt pocket as well. "The music is a little fringe in the organization these days. ComStar frowns on anyone trying to emulate the old days, but at the same time you can buy the chants at the company store. I've heard rumors that some techs have actually started reciting the chants during transmissions, but I have to say I find it hard to believe. For me—something about them helps me clear my head."

"Do you have that much stress, that you need that kind of relaxation?" Reo asked.

Tucker drew in a long breath and blew it out, and almost without volition he began to talk about the past few days. The pressure of Demi-Precentor Faulk's resentment. The Knight Errant poking into his work. The embarrassment of the poor start he had made at working with Adept Kursk's team. The constant reminder that many people considered him a genius. All of the frustration he had bottled up seemed to flow out as Reo listened sympathetically and asked pertinent questions. After two hours and two more beers, they suddenly realized just how much time had passed.

Tucker was embarrassed to see that the tiny restaurant had all but emptied. "Geez, Reo, I'm sorry. I didn't mean to unload on you like that. It just felt good to talk to someone who isn't part of the work I'm doing."

His new friend grinned. "I understand, Tucker. I know how it can be. Tell you what, let's meet for dinner again in a couple of nights. I'll do what I can to show you the hot spots of Wyatt. While you're here, you might as well enjoy yourself a little."

Tucker smiled. "Thanks, Reo, I'd appreciate that."

Reo grabbed the bill. "Tucker, the pleasure's all mine."

5

Alexi Holt watched Legate Singh settle back in his big, black office chair and survey the holomap display that she had projected on the desk between them. He seemed to be considering the information it provided, but there was a quality about his silence that made her suspect he was going to tell her something she didn't want to hear.

"Knight Holt," Singh began, leaning forward onto his elbows. "I appreciate that you have brought us new hardware, and that you have already enhanced our defense capabilities. But there are some realities that you must face on Wyatt."

"Such as?"

"We have a limited military budget. What we receive from The Republic of the Sphere funds a portion of our defense budget, but the rest comes from the government of Wyatt. In each of the past few years, that budget has been greatly reduced. Introducing a new series of maneuvers, while beneficial, is costly. I just don't think we can afford operations on the scale you've suggested." As if to underscore his point—and his authority—he shut off the holographic image.

Alexi wanted to yell at him to get a spine, but she knew that as legate, the world was his to command. Her position allowed her to set aside the legate and take command herself if necessary, but she preferred to find a way to work with him. "Sir, the new hardware and vehicles are different enough that we need to get your personnel up to speed with them, or they're all but worthless."

The legate offered her his best politician's smile, full of false sympathy. "I understand completely, Knight Holt," he replied. "But it's not me you have to convince. And I am confident that the government simply won't fund the maneuvers you suggest."

"And I'm confident that you could go to the governor personally and ask him to authorize more funds," she replied softly.

Singh shook his head. "I'm afraid I can't do that."

She leaned across the desk. "Try to avoid being afraid," she snapped.

"There are political consequences to asking for what you're demanding," he returned sharply. "I know the situation here well enough to know that there is no way the governor could back more funding."

She put her fists on her hips and stared at the legate for a long moment before speaking. "Your troops seem good enough, but none have worked with artillery before. That Sniper I brought isn't the newest hardware, but it's going to change their tactics in a fight. Same with the combat trikes and Guila suits. None of your troops have practiced with an armored personnel carrier on a battlefield, either, and that can alter deployment tactics from the word go. Without training, all of the defensive gear I've brought is next to worthless."

Singh leaned back in his chair again. "You talk like we are facing some sort of imminent threat. Without proof, the governor won't believe that the risks Wyatt currently faces are any different than they were a year ago."

"A year ago ComStar tried to bring up that HPG core without any fanfare. This time, many more people are aware of what we are going to attempt, and that automatically makes the risk much greater. A year ago we were not dealing with a House Liao incursion or the Jade Falcons invading. We simply can't afford to sit back and behave as if these new risks will not affect this planet."

Singh smiled indulgently. "Knight Holt, I'll go and talk to the governor myself. I'll share your concerns with him. But I honestly doubt that it will do any good."

"And in the meantime?"

"I will assign Lieutenant Johannson as your aide, and together you can see what can be done to get the troops trained under our budget constraints. Just in case the governor is not swayed by your arguments."

She narrowed her gaze slightly. "Perhaps I should speak with the governor myself."

Singh smiled back. "Why, Knight Holt, don't you trust me?"

She wanted to answer truthfully, but managed to refrain. "Of course, Legate Singh. I simply wanted to avoid burdening you with this discussion."

He broadened his smile. "I assure you, my good Knight, it's no problem at all."

Eagle's Talons Company Encampment, Bixby Plateau
McKenna, The Oriente Protectorate

Captain Ivan Casson stared at the intelligence report with a degree of contempt. He was stationed on McKenna. McKenna was not a prosperous world, not even highly populated. Its people had been battered by years of devastating fighting during the Word of Blake Jihad, and had barely begun their recovery. Most people did not expect a prosperous future, simply hoping to carve out a better life than their parents had. In other words, McKenna was a microcosm of the Oriente Protectorate.

And that sickened him.

While the united Free Worlds League before the Jihad had been a power in the Inner Sphere, its shattered remains had suffered some of the most brutal fighting and its people had remained fragmented in their thinking and beliefs. And not only the League. House mark also quickly degenerated into a civil war that left three Mariks claiming to truly represent the Great House. Captain Casson believed that the future of his tiny, fledgling state, the Oriente Protectorate, could only be seized by thinking big and bold. He knew that opinion put him in the minority. But things could change. A few strategic victories, the *right* victories, could change the fate of the Protectorate. It was all a matter of finding those opportunities. Captain-General Jessica Marik thought the same; she had shared her thoughts with him and a key handful of other officers. She had a vision, and that vision did not feature a weak and fragmented Free Worlds League.

The intelligence report in front of him, distilled from dozens of informants and friends of the Protectorate, was slightly less disappointing than others he had seen in the past few years. The collapse of the HPG network had offered a number of Inner Sphere governments a chance to exploit the weakness of The Republic. He had watched several opportunities come and go. By the time he had received permission to take his Eagle's Talons into battle, the chance had arrived and already disappeared. But that was the case no longer: now, the Captain-General had charged him with a great deal of latitude and freedom in exploiting potential opportunities.

The deal he had struck with her was a stern one. If his self-chosen operations succeeded, he would receive the full support of the Captain-General and the military forces of the Protectorate. If he failed, he would be branded a rogue and disavowed by the nation's leadership.

So all that remained was to find the right opportunity. Eyeing the report again, he found reference from several sources to another attempt to reestablish the HPG on Wyatt. He glanced at his star atlas and paused, puzzled for a moment. Then her remembered that Wyatt didn't show up on the maps without an update. He keyed in a request, stabbed at the upload button and accepted the update, Wyatt appearing as a white dot on the holographic display in front of him.

Wyatt was tempting, but it lay a significant distance from the Protectorate. If its HPG came online, it would be a prize—but would it be worth his troops' lives? The old Free Worlds League had tried to take Wyatt many times in its history, and had always failed. So there was some prestige in taking such a planet, along with the huge advantage his nation would gain by controlling a working HPG. He had to determine if the prize Wyatt represented supported the risk.

If not Wyatt, there were sure to be other choice targets in that Prefecture.

He spoke out loud. "One thing is for sure, we will win no victories sitting here on McKenna." Captain Casson rose to his feet and pressed the button on his intercom that summoned his aide de camp.

Senior Grade Lieutenant Jacobs entered and snapped a fast salute. "Captain, what can I do for you, sir?"

Casson regarded her. "How long have we been training here, Lieutenant?"

She cast him a skeptical eye. "Sir?"

"How long have we been here on McKenna?"

"Ten months, sir," she rapped out.

"Wrong," he muttered, half to himself. "We've been here too damn long. If the Oriente Protectorate is going to survive and grow, it must stand ready. That means *we* have to be ready. I want to break camp immediately. Send word to the DropShip captains to stand ready to depart. Tell space operations to inform the *Halsey* that they will receive jump orders from me in the next two days, and to be ready for immediate departure. Alert intelligence that we will need up-to-date reports forwarded to us upon our arrival."

"Sir, yes, sir," Jacobs replied. "If I may inquire sir, what is our destination?"

"The Republic of the Sphere. There is a potential target of opportunity that I plan to investigate."

Alexi surveyed the dingy tactical operations room and, for the first time, felt that she was dealing with the real command elements of the Wyatt Militia. Though she assumed some percentage of these men were loyal to the legate, she hoped to develop her own rapport with them. Her first stab at that rapport was her current dilemma, which she was in the process of laying before them as a challenge to be solved: how could they achieve the training they needed to use the materiel she brought to Wyatt?

"So that's the new hardware we've got to work with," she said flatly, having finished the list. "It changes our TO&E and gives us some serious kick. Thoughts on how to get up to speed on this equipment?"

Lieutenant Foster, the dark-skinned commander of the support lance, smoothed his fingers across his shaved head in thought. "Having real damn artillery, that's something new. We've had support mortars and such, but a Sniper is a serious crater-making machine. Well, I need the grunts in Tooley's lance to learn how to call in support and not get themselves bombed in the process." He shot a quick look at the Knight Errant.

Lieutenant Bran Tooley nodded coolly in response. A tall man with a thick paunch, he was in charge of the infantry lance of the Wyatt Militia—the Ground Pounders to the rest of the militia, The Furies to themselves. "I can convert my squads to the new hardware, the battle armor and weapons systems. Hell, they'll welcome the chance to learn something new. But I gotta agree with Foster—we need help learning the ins and outs of artillery."

Alexi frowned. "We can simulate some of what they

need to learn. But nothing beats the real experience for really grasping the essentials. Legate Singh has assured me that there is no budget for setting up full-scale exercises, and your usual combat ranges are too far away for us to mobilize just for practice. So here's the real question: what are our alternatives?"

The silence did not feel hopeful. It was the usually meek Lieutenant Johannson who spoke up. "I have an idea. Probably a bad idea. Most likely a waste of time."

"Out with it," Alexi prodded.

"Well, the old Bowie Industries works were nuked during the Jihad. It was just a satellite plant, but when the Wobbies hit it, they hit it hard. So now that area is a no-trespassing zone. Still a lot of radioactive hot spots out there, but we know exactly where those are. My guess is that we don't need a lot of terrain to get used to the new gear, just some wilderness where it's okay to try some live-fire stuff. We use the Bowie Industries area, and we just make sure we use proper wash-down procedures so that we're not dragging back fallout material."

Captain Irwin of the mobile strike lance spoke up. "You want us to practice in a nuclear hot zone? I doubt the legate will agree with that idea."

Johannson shrugged. "There's no real risk, not if we pick the right spot."

The captain turned to the Knight Errant. "Do you support this notion, Knight Holt?"

She gave him a firm gaze, the kind that only one officer could give another. "Captain. Our job is to be ready if we're attacked. We need to practice to be ready. We seem to have limited choices here, so I support the lieutenant's idea. We choose the right spot, limit the training and clean up after ourselves. And I'll help the legate see the light."

"Seems damn risky for a bunch of weekend warriors," Irwin returned, crossing his arms defiantly.

"Normally, I would agree. But the Wyatt Militia appears to be a cut above the usual militia standards. And if the option is some planning and sweat versus going home in a body bag, well, I think the minimal risk is worthwhile. I'm still open to other suggestions . . ." She glanced around the operations room and saw only slow nods of agreement.

"Very well. Johannson, draw up the duty rosters. Captain Irwin, I'd appreciate your assistance in finding us the right spot. It's time we gave the Wyatt Militia some serious teeth."

6

ComStar HPG Compound
Kinross, Wyatt
The Republic, Prefecture VIII
30 April 3135

The HPG master control board had not seen this much activity in months. Tucker sat in the control seat—"The Hot Seat," the technicians had dubbed it—and watched the readouts as the core went through the start-up sequence. He almost believed he could feel the throbbing of the fusion reactor that powered the massive machine under his feet.

He loved this room. Tucker had been in HPGs before, on Terra, but most of those were new, or just simulation rooms. Wyatt's HPG was centuries old. His love of history meant he loved this room and respected it: these walls had been standing when Kerensky served as a general in the Star League. He was thrilled to be out in the field, and now he realized that was where he belonged. *After all of those years in a lab, this—this is reality.*

"We are at seventy-five percent," Adept Paula Kursk reported from the secondary control station. "Capacitor flow steady. Power levels steady. We're getting some flux in the primary hyperspace coil."

"Variance?" Tucker asked.

"Four . . . no, six percent. Climbing." Her voice betrayed her concern.

"Adjust the beta coil plus-three megajoules." Tucker hoped that upping the power might balance out the primary coil.

"Flux has leveled off at eight percent," Kursk replied. He heard the relief in her voice.

"Okay, we're still within the pipe," he replied. The team knew what the phrase meant. They were not perfectly aligned for starting up the HPG, but were within the tolerances for the new core. "Query controllers. Go for primary HPG initiation?"

"Coil tolerances are just below the yellow line, but we are good to go," Kursk replied.

Adept Kurtis Fowler, another technician on the team, squinted at his display and reported, "I've got greens on the board here, hot seat. We're a go on power flow."

Tucker cranked his head quickly to the right. "Transmission control?"

Adept Morial nodded as she spoke. "Transmission is go. Test packets and pings loaded and coded." A technician seated behind Tucker spoke up from his controls. "Buffering clear and ready for packet receipt."

Tucker turned back to his central control panel. "All right. Begin sequence alpha one, engage."

Fingers around the room flew over panels, keyboards, point controls and even knobs. Tucker let the clicks and clacks of the HPG controls surround him. The readouts in front of him began to change as the power flow increased. He leaned forward in the black leather chair, his arms pushing against the raised padded arms. *This is it . . . .*

"Test packet release," came the voice of Adept Morial. Tucker considered it a good sign. The test transmission packet was outbound, shooting through hyperspace toward a known and properly aligned receiving HPG. When the receiving HPG indicated receipt of the packet and sent back its coordinates, they would have confirmed that Wyatt was once again on the network. This process was called "pinging." No one Tucker knew could provide the origin of the phrase.

The challenges of pinging other stations had only come into effect when the net went down. Now awkward gaps in the network that were still being discovered made confirmation a required step in the process.

Suddenly, his display showed a green indicator flash to yellow. Not a good sign, though at least it wasn't red.

"I've got yellow on the flux reading on the primary coil," Paula Kursk offered before Tucker could ask. "It's at eleven percent and holding." He heard the strain in her voice.

He leaned back for a long moment. "All right, shut down the sim," he commanded. The simulation software for the start-up ended and the test indicators came online, displaying charts and graphics of the data they had tracked during the test start-up. Tucker heard footsteps approaching behind him at a deliberate pace.

"Well, Adept Harwell," drawled Demi-Precentor Faulk. "You didn't have to shut down the simulation so quickly. The primary coil variance was only at eleven percent. We didn't blow out the core in the yellow. There's no real risk until you reach twenty percent variance."

"Sir," he replied coolly, "we shouldn't have even drifted into the yellow. This core tested perfect. We should have had no more than a two percent variation."

"Eleven percent is within the limits defined in the specs." Faulk examined his manicure.

"With all due respect, sir, we have no way of knowing what the results would have been. But the trend was toward unacceptable variance, and I chose to make the call to end the simulation on that variance. There is no new information to be gained by allowing the core to cascade again."

"But it didn't cascade. This core is within specifications. It works fine. In my opinion, you shut down the simulation prematurely." The administrator brushed imaginary lint from the lapels of his suit.

Tucker understood where the conversation was going, and decided to distract Faulk from his train of thought. "Demi-Precentor, I'd like to massage the start-up sequence before we run the next simulation. It's acting strange."

"Acting strange? Is that your technical explanation for what's happening? It seems like the original virus that took down the network is just rearing its ugly head again."

"It could be that, or something else," Tucker flushed at Faulk's sarcasm, but persisted. "I think we could compensate for the variance as it occurs using a program I could write to help rebalance the harmonics of the signal on the fly."

"You want to change a centuries-old procedure because you think we need to fine-tune the hyperpulse generator on the fly during start-up and initialization? You think quite a bit of yourself, Adept Harwell." Faulk's voice rang with contempt.

"This isn't about me," Tucker replied. "This is about the best way to get this core up and running."

Faulk chuckled, but there was no humor in the sound. "The start-up sequence was created centuries ago. Hundreds of technicians have used it successfully thousands of times, Adept. Yet you feel the need to fine-tune an operating harmonic that never changes. And you propose making this change based on what? A hunch?"

"Sir—"

Suddenly, Faulk focused intently on Tucker, pushing his face close to his subordinate. "Don't push it, Adept," he said, his voice pitched to carry to the rest of the room. "Your last two simulations have been within limits. Continue your simulations. But we don't change the operating procedures. Period." He stepped away, spun on his heel and walked out. Tucker swung his chair around to watch him leave the control room. He could feel the back of his neck burning in embarrassment. He adjusted his glasses.

He turned back to the simulation results. "We aren't going to solve this by doing it by the book. We start up this HPG his way and we'll fry this core just like the last one," he muttered. Glancing at the clock, he realized how late it was. "Okay, people. Good job," he said. "Let's go over the data tomorrow."

They sat at what had become their usual table at The Crimson, Tucker's mood solemn and bitter. Reo ate his flank steak and mashed potatoes and watched Tucker push his linguine around on his plate. The younger man stewed over the day's setback.

"So he said no," Reo said, finally ending the silence that had descended after Tucker had replayed his day. Reo shrugged as if it meant nothing.

"You sound like my sister," Tucker scowled. "It's because you don't understand."

Reo flashed a quick smile as he finished chewing a small chunk of steak. "I like you, Tucker. But you've got a lot to learn about how people work and how to get around the rules."

Tucker slapped down his fork. "You're not helping, Reo."

"Keep your temper, and I'll explain," he replied. "First off, you keep butting heads with the demi-precentor. That's a mistake."

"The man hates me," Tucker sulked, picking up his fork.

"No, he doesn't." Reo spoke like a brother offering advice to a younger sibling. "You two have a lot in common. Just like you, his career, his entire life is ComStar. The difference is that, no matter what happens with this new core here on Wyatt, you'll be packing up and going back to Terra. He has to live with the results. Therefore, he's unwilling to gamble."

Tucker pulled a sour expression. "Like I said, you sound like my sister."

Reo grinned again. "Sounds like a smart lady."

"So I should just do what he wants?"

Reo imitated Tucker's sour expression. "No way.

Look, they sent you here because you're their best chance to fix this thing. So you need to put together your solution—just don't tell Faulk what you're doing. The way you describe it, it sounds like you can have everything ready to go ahead of time. Then if you need your solution, just do what they sent you here to do. Butting heads with your boss won't get you anywhere."

"So I should lie?"

"I prefer," Reo said, "to think of it as contingency planning."

Tucker laughed. "That's actually not a bad idea."

"So how do you plan on tuning this core? From what you've told me, this kind of thing hasn't been done for so long that there aren't any rules to follow."

Reaching into his shirt pocket, Tucker pulled out his media stick. "Remember those chants I listen to? The ones created by the old ComStar religious order?" Reo nodded slowly. "Well, most of them are literally these guys performing musical intonations while quoting Jerome Blake or their technical manuals. But one chant I found is different. It references harmonics, and the singers cover a much broader musical range than in other chants." He spoke quickly, excitedly. He stopped so that his friend could gauge the impact of what he was saying.

"So?"

Tucker smiled. "It's just a hunch, but I think they are chanting the harmonics of the tuning process. If I'm right, this particular chant holds the key to fine-tuning the HPG core's operating system."

Reo whistled. "That seems to be kind of a reach."

Tucker shook his head. "No, not really. I've found that most of the chants were based on something the adepts were exposed to as part of their work, so why not the harmonics program? The real trick is to write an algorithm that adjusts the harmonics fast enough to accomplish the job before the core fries itself. I analyzed the notes used in this chant, and they produce an algorithm very similar to what I would have written if I tried to write this kind of program from scratch. Look, there's no documentation showing that adepts tuned the cores after they were up and running, but it makes sense to me that they would have needed to make tiny adjustments when they were being installed. There's hardly any piece of machinery that doesn't need fine-tuning at installation."

"You're the expert," Reo conceded.

Tucker nodded in agreement. *That's right. I am* the *expert. And Reo is right. I can put up with Faulk's attitude for as long as it takes to create my own solution.*

7

Contaminated Territory, Section A, Grid Ten
West of Kinross, Wyatt
The Republic, Prefecture VIII
2 May 3135

The rolling hills were dotted with dense clumps of trees and lush undergrowth. Rocks occasionally jutted from the tall green grass on the hills, gray and pink granite stabbing at the sky. Swampy ponds pooled in some of the valleys, with tall reeds poking up everywhere. In the distance, the slope of the hills was steeper, more menacing, forming a bowl with her units on one side, the legate's on the other. Knight Alexi Holt stared at the scene and shook her head. This battlefield had been laid waste with nuclear weapons during the Word of Blake Jihad. Faint hints of radiation still burned the soil, but it was hard to picture such a pastoral scene as a charred, blasted landscape decades before. The ground was safe, for short periods of time.

She checked her *Black Knight*'s primary display and switched to long-range sensors. They were out there, the militia troops her lance was going against in this exercise.

She picked up vehicle movement in the distance, but the hills and the bedrock underneath diminished her sensors' effectiveness.

Alexi allowed herself a smile. This was the one place in the whole universe she longed to be—the cockpit of her *Black Knight*. This was the one place where she could escape politics and the pressure of her position for awhile. Here, she was in charge, her alone. She patted the command couch armrest. *All right, old girl, let's show them what we can do.*

Alexi often spoke to her 'Mech as if it were a living entity, and in some ways she thought it was. Her *Black Knight* was named "Miss Direction," and though she had not given it that name, she appreciated the humor and had kept it. The internal chassis of the 'Mech was more than three centuries old. It had been salvaged and rebuilt under her supervision. If the records were accurate concerning the machine's serial numbers, this 'Mech had served with the Com Guards on Tukayyid against the Clans and had fought a desperate last-stand engagement against the Word of Blake during the Jihad on New Earth. She had discovered the name during the rebuild, hand-etched by a previous owner into the cockpit framing. When she decided to resurrect the name, she asked an artist friend to design a logo she felt reflected the honor of the 'Mech. On the armor plating of the right torso, she had a woman painted in knight's armor, wielding a sword over her head. Under that was painted the name of the 'Mech.

"Red Team," she signaled, "stand by to engage."

"Red One, this is Red Rain," came the voice of Lieutenant Foster, his support lance bringing up the rear. "I'm not picking up anything from our pickets yet. Are you sure they're out there?"

Alexi understood his apprehension, but she had chosen carefully the ground for their position. The slope of the hills, the surrounding high ground with tough terrain—everything would help channel the legate's Blue Team toward them. And there were other ways to get their attention and ensure the enemy moved where they wanted. "They'll be here shortly, Red Rain. I'll make sure of that. Stand by with your thunderstorm. Red One out."

She broke into a run toward the center of the battlefield. Miss Direction came up the side of one hill and at its crest, her long-range sensors suddenly lit up with a dozen or so red dots. She slowed to a walk and checked their positions. Spread out in an open semi-circle, they were slowly moving forward toward her team. *Good . . . let them come.*

The trike squad was on the right flank and accelerated the moment they picked her up on their sensors. They would drive to her rear to wreak havoc; she would have considered the same tactic. As they rose up over a hill, the trike riders lifted into the air. In her imagination, she could hear the riders howl with delight as they rushed forward.

A swift little Tamerlane strike sled, riding on a cushion of air, dove off to her right side while a more ponderous DI Morgan assault tank pulled up the rear of the legate's force. Small-arms fire from a half dozen infantry squads opened up. The snaking trails of hand-launched short-range missiles laced through the air, a pair of them slapping into Miss Direction's right leg with the distinctive thump of simulated warheads. White marking powder from the rounds rose up to indicate the hit, and her battle computer recorded the damage as if the missiles had been live. In the distance, she saw the *Panther,* piloted by the legate, attempting to push past her left flank. The regular infantry rushed toward her.

"Red Rain, drop targeting round at the following coordinates." The location she indicated on her display would put the rounds directly between her and the approaching infantry.

"Sir, there are no targets there," came a protest.

"You have your orders," she said firmly.

A round dropped out nearly fifty meters in front of the advancing infantry. A trail of bright purple smoke hung in the air. The marking round was right where she wanted it. "Red Sky, right flank punch through, just like we talked about."

"Roger that, Red One," came another voice.

"Red Wagon," she called out, walking her *Black Knight* backward up the hillside as if retreating. "Your target is on the left. Let's show the legate how this is done."

With smooth skill, she juked the joystick to bring the targeting reticle onto the DI Morgan assault tank as it attempted to go hull-down against the hillside, sod flying as it ground to a fast halt. She fired her PPCs the moment she had a target tone in her ear. They were powered to 5 percent, enough to mar the paint on the target but not do real damage. The right and left arms of *Miss Direction* whined as they discharged their blue burst of charged particles. Hits! The Morgan driver panicked, backing away down the hillside, out of line of sight.

Over the heads of the Blue Team trike squad came a Donar assault helicopter, the roar of its blades penetrating into her cockpit. She glanced ahead at the purple smoke round and signaled again. "Red Rain, fire for effect."

From the far rear, the Sniper artillery let go a vicious barrage of simulated fire. The white powder rounds went over the smoke round and to the right, smacking and exploding into the hillside grass and one of the ponds. Alexi checked her sensors and smiled. It had worked as planned. She had not targeted the approaching infantry, but had instead planned to use the artillery to halt their forward movement. The sight of the explosions in front of them suddenly had them stopping and digging in behind every little rock that poked out of the ground.

The Tamerlane hovercraft fired at her flank and its lasers showed up on her secondary display as good hits. Not enough to do any real damage against a seventy-five-ton BattleMech, but annoying. The Tamerlane was doing a good job of getting her attention, but she refused to bite. She craned her 'Mech over and fired the pair of Diverse Optics extended-range small lasers at the scout.

Her engine simulated heat by raising the temperature in her cockpit slightly as the lasers bore in on the Tamerlane, striking it on its right side. An enemy 'Mech would have barely noticed the hit, but against the light hovercraft, it was enough to force it to turn away and look for softer targets.

Unexpectedly, almost right in front of her, there came a burst of small-arms fire. Guila suits. The stealth suits that the infantry wore allowed them to infiltrate lines with a low degree of detection. Now that they had fired, she could paint them on her tactical display. *Legate Singh is better than I gave him credit for. He got those troops up pretty close.* Her damage display showed that the infantry support fire was chipping away mock damage to her lower torso and legs, enough that she opted to get out of their range. She jogged Miss Direction off to their flank. She smiled. *I have to remember to compliment Lieutenant Tooley on the efficiency of his Ground Pounders.*

Off on the left flank she watched as Red Wagon, the new J-37 ordnance transport she had brought with her from Terra, rushed toward the legate's *Panther*. The J-37 was not much to look at, but it could carry a lot—which she was hoping would be a surprise to the legate's forces. On its approach to the 'Mech, it made a sharp turn, facing its lightly armored rear towards the *Panther*. To the uninitiated, this appeared to be a foolish move that could only end in the destruction of the transport. The *Panther* hit it with what would have been lethal laser fire, damaging the transport, but not crippling it . . . not yet.

The ramp on the back of the J-37 slammed down so hard it tore up turf on the hillside. Out charged Red Wagon's surprise, a JES III missile carrier. The legate's *Panther* seemed to stop in its tracks at the sudden new threat at dangerously close range. The top-mounted missile racks roared a barrage at the towering *Panther*. She didn't bother to scan the legate's 'Mech; it was out of the fight.

The DI Morgan tank emerged from the flank of the

hillside and fired at her with its own PPCs, returning some of the damage she had inflicted, this time with simulated hits on her legs and torso. Red Rain's artillery dropped another spotting round, this time off to the left of the original position. Alexi locked onto the DI Morgan and fired. This time, she hit it with only one of her PPCs, but it was enough to show some significant damage. But this time, the Morgan was not retreating.

A modified ForestryMech emerged from a cluster of trees near the right flank and charged forward. The IndustrialMech had been converted into a deadly in-fighter, but only at point-blank range. It seemed to be trying to use support from the Tamerlane to reach Red Rain's position.

From behind it came a thunderous roar as Red Sky approached from Blue Team's rear, rushing to optimum firing range behind the ForestryMech. The MechWarrior knew he was in trouble and stopped, twisting the torso of the massive lumberjack 'Mech to face the new threat. It was too late. He had no way to engage the Donar helicopter. A blast of simulated laser fire taught that militia member an important lesson.

A signal came over the comm line on an open channel. "Blue One to Red One. Blue team capitulates. Request an end to this simulation." Legate Singh was not happy, but he was doing his best to keep his disappointment out of his voice.

Alexi grinned again. "Red One to Blue One, we accept your offer. All units, stand down. Red Team salutes Blue. Good job." She meant what she said, but her mind was already on the debriefing. Both sides had made mistakes. She needed to explain those errors, then work with the troops to incorporate the needed changes to their tactics. *They did all right, but I know the legate will try to position their performance as much stronger than it was.*

Rather than dwell on the spin the legate would give to the results of the exercise, she started walking Miss Direction to the staging area. She still had a long few weeks of training ahead of her if she was going to get the militia up to the level she knew they could reach.

She hoped they had that much time. The good news was that the commanders now knew her, knew what her training made possible. The legate was not the only one who could command their respect at this point.

Reo Jones stepped into the offices of Universal Exporters Ltd. The receptionist, ages old with wrinkles as deep as canyons, waved him past. He gave her a broad, fake, flirtatious smile. Her response was to take a long drag from her cigarette and roll her eyes as if he didn't deserve the time of day. It was the same every time he visited the dingy little office tucked away in one of the more seedy business districts of Kinross.

Universal Exporters Limited consisted of three offices, none of them too flashy. His footsteps seemed to echo as he walked down the hall on the worn, unpadded carpet. The door to the last office was open, so he stepped in. Reo always had a private chuckle at the name of the company. Universal Exporters Limited was a wholly owned subsidiary of Artemis Transport Shipping. Seventy-five percent of Artemis Transport Shipping was owned by Universal Import and Export Corporation. The majority of the stock of Universal Import and Export Corp. was held by Fidelity Financials of New Earth, which in turn had its outstanding notes owned by Brightside Shipping of Terra. Brightside was financed by Tybalt Investing, which was owned by Bannson Universal Unlimited.

In other words, it was owned by Jacob Bannson, one of the most powerful tycoons in The Republic.

The office featured a desk, a computer, a filing cabinet and a man in his thirties who greeted Reo with a sneer. He motioned for Reo to close the door and he did, then took the seat opposite the desk. The man sitting across from him did not have the look of a businessman running a trade company. A long scar ran horizontally across his forehead. His red hair was neatly cut, but his complexion was pockmarked and showed signs of age and experience beyond his years. His name was Rutger Chaffee, but he insisted Reo use his nickname, Cut-Throat. Captain was the other title he wore; Captain of Chaffee's Cut-Throats. It seemed there was something about being one of Bannson's people that required you to have a threatening nickname.

"So, Reo, I'd offer you a drink, but you can afford your own, especially with what our employer is paying you." Chaffee poured himself a drink from a bottle he kept in his desk. The air stung slightly of whiskey as he took a gulp. "I take it you have information on ComStar's timetable?"

He nodded. "Yes. They're going to try to fire up the new core in two days."

Chaffee frowned. "I take it they think it's going to work, then?"

"Yes."

"And that kid from Terra, the one you've been pumping. He's sure that the new core will work, too?"

Reo shrugged. "He says so. Tucker's smart, really smart. I think they might just pull it off this time."

"Not good," Chaffee said taking another gulp of his whiskey. "Mr. Bannson is not going to be happy with that. How about if I have the kid killed? Will that make a difference?"

Reo knew he should say yes, but didn't. "I doubt it. Why would Mr. Bannson care if the HPG is up and running or not?"

Chaffee's chair squeaked as he rolled it back enough to pull out the whiskey and pour himself another two or three shots worth, slopping it into his glass. "We're one of his little hiding holes. We've smuggled about a company's worth of hardware and mercenaries on-planet. He picked Wyatt as a rabbit hole because it had dropped off the star atlases and was isolated from the rest of The Republic. Once that HPG goes on-line, this planet is likely to draw a lot of attention. Worlds that get their HPGs working tend to attract—well, let's call 'em unwanted visitors."

Jacob Bannson was a powerhouse in The Republic. His company had vast holdings, mostly in Prefectures IV and V. The Liao incursion into The Republic seemed to have dealt a couple of solid cards into his hand, but Bannson was the type of man who hedged his bets. He had several worlds like Wyatt set up as safehouses. He kept discreet (military) forces on his payroll on each planet to help with his "aggressive business plans," and men like Reo to gather intelligence and assist him with specific missions.

"So do you think we'll have to move operations to another planet?" Reo asked.

"I don't know," Chaffee said. "It's possible. But Mr. Bannson also told me to keep my eyes open for opportunities that he can exploit. Once we have HPG communications reestablished, he may have new orders for me. I do know this much: I'm not in the mood for a change of government."

Reo grinned. "You like The Republic of the Sphere so much?"

"It's weak," Chaffee replied. "I like that. I also like the devil I know versus the devil I don't. My forces are ready for anything. I'd be willing to go so far as to cripple the local militia if it's to our advantage." He was deadly serious. What little Reo had learned of him indicated that his family boasted military leaders from as far back as the FedCom Civil War, and Cut-Throat was known to be ruthless—a potent combination.

"So," Reo pressed, "do you or the boss have any other missions for me?"

"Keep your eyes on what ComStar is up to," Chaffee said. "Look for opportunities. If there's a way to derail their start-up attempts, get in contact with me."

Reo rose to his feet. "I'll keep my eyes peeled."

"You'll do more than that," Chaffee said with a grim smile. "You'll do whatever I tell you."

Tucker walked with his sister in Kinross' small museum, one of the community's few cultural attractions. He had hoped to hook up with Reo for dinner as usual, but his friend had other commitments.

Occupying nearly the entire ceiling of the museum was a massive flying wing. Supported by metal struts that ran to the ground and heavy cables, the aerospace fighter was an impressive sight. Tucker stood under it gazing up, his mouth hanging open.

"Pretty impressive, isn't it?" Patricia said. "It's a *Chippewa*-class fighter. The only one on the planet, I think."

"I've read about them," Tucker said. "They carried enough missiles to take out a BattleMech in a single strafing run."

Patricia looked up at the flying wing with respect. "It's sad when you think of it. That fighter is probably what brought about the destruction of so much of what was Wyatt."

"Why's that?"

"The Bowie plant here on Wyatt made those fighters during the Succession Wars. Naturally, the Word of Blake took out the plant in the first attack wave of the Jihad. They used three nuclear weapons, frying the plant with the first one. Then they used the other two just for good measure. The old capital city, Hartsburg, butted up against one side of the plant compound. My research says that the city burned in a wave of radioactive fire. Close to a half million people were killed in the first hours of the Jihad—all because of that fighter."

"I take it your research is going well?" Tucker replied, looking at the kiosk that provided information on the fighter.

"Yes and no. So many records have been lost during the war, it makes my research quite tricky," she replied. "I take it from what I heard today that you're doing quite well, though."

"That depends," Tucker replied with a coy smile. "What did you hear?"

"The compound is a pretty tight little community. I heard that the new core will be ready to try in just a few days. I think congratulations are in order." She slipped one arm around him and hugged his waist.

"Don't break open the champagne just yet. Like I told Reo last evening, there's about a half-million things that can go wrong. And our beloved demi-precentor breathing down my neck doesn't make my work any easier."

The mention of Reo caused Patricia to wince slightly. "Tucker, about Reo . . ."

"Not again, Patricia," he said, waving his hand. *We've had this discussion before. I'm a big boy now.* Out loud, the words came out better. "I choose my own friends."

"I'm just looking out for you," she replied. "He has a bad history. The man's an outcast, even among the Knights who were his friends. Hanging around with him is not going to help your career."

"I appreciate your concern, but Reo's just a friend."

"You need to be careful what you say to him," she warned in a tone that reminded Tucker of their mother's voice. "He's supposedly on the payroll of Jacob Bannson."

"Bannson's on the other side of The Republic," Tucker countered. "And even if he is, which I doubt, I'm not too worried. We have a Knight Errant practically camping out in our compound. If he really was dangerous, she'd take care of him." He wasn't worried. Reo didn't have the technological background necessary to understand most of what Tucker talked about, let alone use it. Anything he told him would be of no use to anyone who was not an expert on HPG communications. In other words, it was only of use to ComStar itself.

The mention of Alexi Holt only made his sister roll her eyes. "The last thing that ComStar needs is a Knight Errant sticking her nose into our business," she said angrily. "I don't trust this new direction The Republic seems intent on pursuing . . . having Knights involved with our decisions concerning the network."

Tucker nodded. He held a neutral position on Knight Holt. She had spoken to him several times and seemed friendly, not prodding or nosey, as others at the ComStar compound had painted her. Perhaps there was another side to her that he wasn't seeing? That thought gave him pause. That was possible. Shoot, there was a side of him that even his sister didn't know. For example, he had not told her that he was writing an algorithm to fine-tune the HPG harmonics if the core initialization started to go wrong. He knew Patricia quite well. She was like the demi-precentor, and would not approve of him working outside the standard procedures. He finally said, "Knight Holt's always been nice to me."

"Of course she is," Patricia said, tucking her hand under his elbow. "She knows the same thing that I do. You're important here. Tucker, you're the future of ComStar, you and people like you. ComStar is, well, like your family . . . especially for us Harwells. I'm not just saying that because I'm your sister. If anyone is going to help get the HPG net back up, it's you."

He blushed and grinned. "So you don't like Reo Jones; you don't like Knight Holt. You know our demi is a nutcase more worried about his career than doing the job right. Is there anyone I can trust, sis?"

Patricia smiled and squeezed his arm. "You can always trust family, Tucker."

8

Tucker was sweating in the air-conditioned control room. He unbuttoned his white lab jacket and adjusted his eyeglasses on his long nose. *No pressure. Just everyone on the planet and the entire ComStar organization back on Terra counting on you . . . .* His attempt to mentally make light of the situation didn't break the tension. He gripped the armrests of the hot seat and gave the main control display another careful inspection. The indicators were all in the green, across the board.

He glanced around the room, not at the people filling it, but at the room itself. Tucker had spent a lot of time in this control room and had come to love it. Yes, it was Demi-Precentor Faulk's domain, but at the same time it was *his*. Here, he had applied all that he had learned. Within these centuries-old walls, his team had massaged the new HPG core to life. It had taken long hours and countless tests and adjustments, but they were now as ready as they would ever be. The last two days had produced only minuscule improvements to the new core.

But as he returned his gaze to the main control board, he couldn't help but worry.

The last HPG core also had tested out perfectly. It had fired up fine, then a cascade began and it had burned out in a matter of minutes. *Am I overlooking something?* It nagged him to sleep each night. *They went down this same path before and the core blew. Is the same thing going to happen to me?*

No.

Unconsciously, he patted his right lab coat pocket, feeling the tiny silver disk he had put there. It had taken all his down time, writing the program he had based loosely on the chants he had played hundreds of times. He needed to keep the autoloading program at his fingertips. It represented his fallback plan, a last-ditch tool, if he needed it. If the core began to cascade, he would have only two minutes to slot the program and use it to tune the HPG harmonics. Two minutes.

Someone moved into his peripheral vision off to his left. It was Knight Errant Holt, who had been like a shadow the past few days in the control room. She was smiling, projecting a sense of calm that he wanted to cling to. Somewhere outside the room, watching on a monitor, was his sister Patricia, and he wished that she could be with him, too.

"Good luck, Mr. Harwell. From what I've seen, you and your team have done everything you could to make this a success." Holt smiled again and stepped away. *I needed that. Though I wonder what she would say if she knew I had that program in my pocket?*

His palms were sweaty. He ran both hands through his hair, not caring that he was making his normally untidy hair look even worse. Tucker took off his glasses and pocketed them.

He heard the footsteps of the demi-precentor approaching, and the man stopped beside Tucker and put his hand on the armrest of the hot seat. Faulk's face was blank of all emotions except the stern anger that he seemed to always be bottling up. Tucker hoped he would say nothing, since he had offered the team zero support up to this point. But Faulk was not going to be quiet.

"Mr. Harwell," he began slowly. Tucker could smell the man's morning cup of coffee on his breath as he spoke. "It appears that the board is green. In your opinion, are we ready to proceed?"

Tucker glanced over at Adept Kursk, who gave him a single nod. He darted his eyes once again to the main control board, then looked at the demi-precentor. "Yes, sir, everything from the team indicates we're in the green."

"Very well." Then Faulk bent his head slightly forward and spoke just above a whisper. "Remember this, Mr. Harwell. That seat you're sitting in is mine. If this core goes active as planned, fine. If not, I'll make sure that you are hung out to dry for the failure. Do we have an understanding?"

Tucker nodded. "Yes, sir, I understand completely." His skin tightened at the threat. *I understand that you're more worried about your position here than the success of this project.* He turned away and gritted his teeth. *The last thing I needed was him trying to motivate me with a kick in the ass.*

He settled back in the chair. "All right then. We are at fifty percent power. I need a go, no-go for primary HPG initiation. Flux control?"

"Flux is go," Paula Kursk said from her position.

"Tolerance?"

"Power and flow are go," replied Adept Fowler.

"Transmission control?"

Morial hesitated for a second with a last check of her board. "Test packets and pings loaded. Hot seat, transmission is a go."

"Buffering?"

"Receiver array and storage is green. Good to go," replied another technician from behind him.

That was it. Everything showed ready to go. Tucker

glanced up at the demi-precentor at his side, but Faulk did not even look down at him. *Hung out to dry, then.* The decision was his to make, and his alone.

"Start sequence alpha one . . . engage."

There was a throbbing under his feet as the power flow from the fusion reactor pulsed through the facility. The control board in front of him seemed to come alive, bars and graphic readouts all in the green, moving and growing in front of him. It seemed to be going as planned.

"We're at seventy-five percent," said Paula Kursk.

Better than in the simulations. He found himself clenching the armrests with sticky hands. As much as he wanted to relax, he couldn't.

"Full power," Kursk said a half-minute later.

Tucker nodded. Good. He wasn't going to need the fall-back in his pocket. "Stand by for test packet release," he said.

Suddenly a green bar on his display flashed to yellow. Before he could ask, Kursk spoke, this time with concern in her voice. "Flux increase in the primary coil. Seven percent and climbing."

"Increase beta coil power levels four megajoules."

He stared at the display. The yellow bar stopped growing for a moment. He started to breathe out a sigh of relief, but then he saw it start to creep forward. Paula's voice had an even crisper tempo. "The variance in the core is growing. I've increased to ten megajoules."

"Test packet release," said Morial from her console.

Cascade. It was happening again. Just like the last core. Shutting down would take too long. It would fry the new core.

"Mr. Harwell . . ." Demi-Precentor Faulk's voice at his side actually held some concern.

Tucker rose to his feet, and in one long stride reached the control station in front of him. He pulled the program disk from his pocket and jammed it into the drive. "Paula, watch the beta coil. When you see the variance drop, manually bring down the power flow so that we don't fry it."

"On it," she replied, her voice nervous. This was not something he had walked them through.

"Harwell . . ." Faulk's tense voice rose from behind him.

His fingers danced on the keyboard with a speed and force that he didn't know he could achieve. The program loaded quickly and the dialogue window popped up in front of him. The harmonic pulse that it would run would tune the core, but part of this was him manually adjusting the pulse as the program did its work.

"What are you doing?" demanded Faulk, who was crowding his right shoulder.

"What's happening?" asked Alexi Holt, moving in on his left side. He ignored both of them. His program became his entire universe.

"Variance is about to cross the red line," Kursk called out.

"You've got to shut this core down," Faulk said, reaching for the keyboard. Tucker instinctively shifted his entire body to block his superior's reach, while his fingers continued to attack the keyboard. "Stand by," he said, loud enough for his team to hear. His own ears were pounding with the sound of his heart beating.

Then he saw it on the display in front of him. *Yes. It was so simple.* The program had narrowed the scope of the new frequency. He watched the wave line on the display and his fingers danced through the adjustments that were required. *The adepts who had written that chant were smarter than we knew.* The wave line seemed to flatten slightly as his fingers continued to fly across the keys. Then suddenly, almost as if something had gone wrong, the wave became a flat string of light. Yellow became green in the background of his program.

He turned, half pushing past the demi-precentor to look at Kursk. "Status?"

"Primary coil is at point zero seven variance," she replied with a puzzled tone.

"Bring down the power to the beta coil to standard," he said, sucking in a long gasp of air. His extremities were tingling; he didn't know whether it was lack of oxygen or excitement.

Adept Morial spoke up. "I have pings back from the network. Test packets received and processed. No degradation. I'm getting a solid signal."

"The core?" Faulk demanded.

"Stable," Adept Kursk replied. "We're receiving test data and buffering is holding."

Tucker's face wore a small smile as he ejected his program disk and slipped it back into his pocket. He stared at the main control board and saw that the green bars were all solid and unmoving. Tucker tapped the keyboard again and the control display changed to the ComStar logo, which only appeared when an HPG station was active and ready for transmission. Leaning forward, he tapped another pair of keys. The logo flickered away and was replaced with data.

Tucker read the words out loud. "We have received a confirmation code from our target station, the Thorin HPG. Standing by for secondary confirmation."

The minutes seemed to take forever to pass. The room was painfully quiet as they waited. Suddenly, almost anticlimactically, a stream of data appeared on the screen. Tucker adjusted his glasses and read it carefully.

"Well?" Faulk demanded.

Tucker turned and smiled, broadly this time. "Package received intact, and we have secondary confirmation. Demi-Precentor Hutchinson on Thorin sends the following: 'Wyatt, welcome back to the universe.' "

A cheer rose from the techs. For the first time in three years, an HPG had been restored to active status. Tucker joined in the elation. He looked around the room and saw the happy faces of the ComStar personnel. It was a turning point, he could feel it. Then he met the stern gaze of Demi-Precentor Faulk—the only person in the room who did not seem overjoyed.

"What did you do?" he demanded. The tone of his voice drew the attention of the Knight Errant, who stepped closer and gave the two men a puzzled look.

"I did what was necessary," Tucker responded. "I used

a program to fine-tune the core with a harmonics pulse, and manually adjusted the frequency."

Faulk's face flushed red. "I distinctly remember giving you a direct order not to do that."

"I apologize for going against your orders, sir, but if I hadn't," Tucker said evenly, "we would have fried this core, too."

Faulk stared at Tucker, breathing heavily.

"We will have to send your algorithms to Thorin and Terra for review," he finally said, and held out his hand for the program disk.

Tucker gave it to him. "That's only part of the solution," he replied bluntly. "Most of what I did is up here," he tapped his temple.

"Don't get cocky with me, Adept Harwell," Faulk responded.

Alexi Holt cut in. "It sounds to me like you should be congratulating Tucker, not castigating him," she said smoothly. "If what he says is true, he's responsible for saving that HPG core. Maybe he's earned the right to be a little cocky." She threw Tucker a quick smile.

No matter what that windbag throws at me now, she knows the truth. And that's got to bother him as much as I do.

"Knight Holt, you may be missing the larger picture here. This isn't just about Wyatt," Faulk replied. "First of all, what he did was reckless, even if it did work. As it turned out, the risk was worth the reward—but it as easily could have gone the other direction, and taking that level of risk is not a decision Adept Harwell is authorized to make. Second, his success has widespread implications: replacement HPG cores have died on hundreds of worlds. If Tucker has created some sort of patch for the system, there's no telling how many planets may be able to be restored to active status. A solution of that magnitude is not something that should be undertaken by the seat of our pants."

Faulk stopped talking, and Tucker realized in that moment that the stakes were much higher than his wildest imagination could have dreamed up. *What have I gotten myself into?*

* * *

Legate Singh sat back and considered her words. Once again, Alexi Holt was amazed that he kept his office so immaculate: even his desktop was completely empty of paperwork. Even from the legates on more prominent worlds, she had come to expect a certain amount of clutter. Singh was different, she reminded herself once again.

"Word will spread to other systems that we have a working HPG," he said, stating the obvious.

"The news will spread slowly, even with Thorin and Terra aware that we're active. We're not anticipating another ship in-system here for a month or so. But with each ship the word will spread," Alexi confirmed. "The risk for Wyatt increases as word spreads. With interstellar communications at a bare-bones minimum, any world with a functioning HPG is considered a prized target. It provides you with something that most worlds don't have: access to information."

"What level of risk do *you* think we're facing here?" he asked. The legate didn't seem concerned; or if he was, his voice didn't betray it.

"I don't know. The fact that we don't know the full scope of the risk was part of the reason I came and brought the hardware I did. Wyatt's been off the charts for awhile; it could be that no one will be interested in us. But we have to be prepared if someone is."

Edward Singh leaned forward in his chair and frowned. "The last thing I want to do is panic the population, Knight Holt. The governor will be furious if I mobilize the militia and get people worried over nothing."

She crossed her arms before she could stop herself. She didn't want her body language to broadcast the things she couldn't say out loud, and anyway, at the moment the legate was right—there was no immediate threat to Wyatt. But even he had to be aware of how quickly that status could change. "I understand your position, Legate. You have to deal with political implications. My only job is to protect the citizens and worlds of the Republic."

"What would you recommend?" he asked coyly.

Better preparation . . . giving the population an honest warning of what might happen. Out loud she said, "Legate Singh, if you feel declaring a full-scale alert will cause undue concern among the citizens, we should go to standby alert instead. It will be seen as precautionary by the ordinary citizen, but will allow the Wyatt Militia to effectively prepare to deal with a threat should it emerge."

He said nothing for what seemed like a long time. Finally he refocused his gaze on Alexi and leaned back. "I believe the governor will find standby-alert status acceptable. I'll contact the governor and the media. Thank you for your insight, Knight Holt."

Alexi clenched her jaw. *Stone forbid that this man be in charge of my fate if and when a fight comes to Wyatt. The planet will be overrun and the governor out of office before he makes a decision.*

"You're welcome, Legate" is all she said, and left to make her report to Paladin Sorenson.

It had been the longest day of Tucker's life, and it still was not over. The demi-precentor had interrogated Tucker and his technical staff for hours, to no avail. Tucker had not involved his team in his backup plan, so they could not explain to Faulk what had happened. And the demi-precentor refused to accept Tucker's explanation of his actions, even when he went into detail about the program he had written and his theory of the meaning of the chant that had inspired his work.

All the while, another team of technicians was busily running additional tests, and had discovered that the adjustments Tucker performed seemed to have increased the HPG's capacity to the highest level of its specifications. His program had been transmitted to ComStar on Terra, but they had yet to receive a response.

Outside of the ComStar compound, the city of Kinross seemed to have come alive. The movement of the antenna array and the throbbing of signal transmission spread the word that the HPG was operational again. His sister Patricia had found him and congratulated him, and informed Tucker that there was a line of people stretching for five city blocks outside the compound waiting to send messages.

Demi-Precentor Faulk already had assigned three administrative assistants to walk along the lines and explain how long it would be before communication resumed at anything resembling a normal level. They were also prepared to describe the procedure ComStar would use to prioritize the messages. The sabotage of the HPG network had cut off communications between families, businesses, and governments, and everyone else. Now people felt that all of that was restored.

Patricia was elated. Tucker felt trapped somewhere between numb and weary. Finally, in the late afternoon, the demi-precentor emerged from his office to find Tucker pacing the hallway. Tucker stopped short and Faulk slowly walked over to his subordinate, halting only a few inches from Tucker so that their conversation would not carry. "Mr. Harwell, you've put me in a tight position."

Tucker stared at him impassively.

Faulk continued. "Terra indicates we can begin transmitting any time. Whatever it was you did, they're satisfied that this station is now stable."

He didn't let that slip by. "You're welcome."

Faulk had the grace to look slightly embarrassed. "I deserved that, I guess." He paused. "Terra has reviewed your program and the final harmonics settings, and they agree with your claim that you performed the most critical adjustments on the fly. This poses a problem for ComStar, and I've been asked to address it."

"What do you mean?"

"The fact that you found a way to restore our HPG may mean that it is possible for ComStar to restore dozens, if not hundreds of the damaged HPGs in the Inner Sphere. Many stations have working cores but no transmission capability. If your technique can effectively recalibrate the surviving cores, it may be possible to bring back a significant portion of the HPG network."

Tucker's mouth hung open. Again, he was taken by

surprise at the scope of the bigger picture. His mind boggled at the idea that his work could solve something against which the entire ComStar organization had been struggling. The only thing he could say was "Wow."

"Wow, indeed," Faulk continued. "Precentor Buhl and the other folks on Terra have asked that, as much as you can, you document the details of what you did—every minuscule element. We will route the report through Thorin in a secured data package under my security code . . . highest priority."

Tucker nodded. "I can write down what I did, but a lot of it was sort of instinctive."

Faulk smiled at Tucker, for what seemed the first time. "I understand, and I've already warned them that that was the case. They are checking to find a JumpShip and DropShip that can be diverted here to take you back to Terra. Right now the ships are spread fairly thin with the other crises in The Republic, but ComStar is working on it."

"Is that really necessary, sir?"

Faulk glanced around to make sure they were alone. "Tucker, the solution in your head has just made you the hottest commodity in the Inner Sphere. I'm ordering a pair of our security people to shadow you from this point on. As much as I hate to, I may have to speak to our visiting Knight Errant and ask her help as well. In fact, it's important that you stay here in the compound until further notice."

"Sir?"

Faulk's breath was hot on his face. "Your work has made you a hero, Mr. Harwell, and you'll get the credit, never fear. But also know this: every faction and government out there would like to control the man who can get the HPG system working again. You've become a commodity, but you're also a risk."

"You don't really think they'd come for me, do you?" For the first time, he felt worried. The fact that the demi-precentor was willing to give him credit for what he had done was a big clue that something had changed dramatically.

"We just need to be prepared," Faulk responded. He patted Tucker on the shoulder. "I know we haven't gotten along very well so far, but I'm happy to acknowledge that you pulled this off. Congratulations."

Demi-Precentor Faulk stuck out his hand and gave Tucker a genuine, colleague-to-colleague handshake. Then his boss turned and walked away, leaving Tucker with a wave of fear suddenly rising in the pit of his stomach.

Today was a good day for ComStar, a very good day. Historically, ComStar had never been big on press conferences, so the press room in the compound was small. When Gray Monday had devastated the HPG network, the Wyatt media had camped out for weeks in this room, demanding answers that the demi-precentor could not provide. Now, three long years later, Faulk felt he had finally regained the advantage. Every media outlet on Wyatt had a representative shoe-horned into the cramped room, and as Faulk entered the room, cameras locked onto him and pulse-strobes went off like a thousand explosions. One step behind him, where he felt she belonged, was Knight Errant Alexi Holt. She had done nothing so far to help reactivate the HPG; he was happy to give her the assignment of guarding Tucker Harwell. If nothing else, it would get her out of his hair.

He strode to the podium, put his hands on either side of the wooden stand and gave the media a big grin. Tonight, all across Wyatt, his image and the ComStar logo on the front of the podium would be the most-watched broadcast in years.

"I will be reading a short statement. I will not be taking questions at this time," he began. He knew the media would ask questions regardless of his stated intentions. When the network had gone down, he had been roasted alive on holovid screens across the planet. Today, refusing to address their questions was his payback.

"This morning, at 1035 hours, a select team of ComStar technicians initiated the startup of the new hyperpulse generator core that was delivered several weeks ago from Terra. I'm pleased to report that this attempt was successful. At present, the HPG station on Wyatt is up, running and connected to the existing system." He paused and let them drink that in for a moment.

"We have begun processing transmissions from our backlog of maintenance patches and are currently sending priority Republic transmissions for the government and military. Civilian transmissions are being accepted at this time and buffered for future release. While this will create a temporary backlog, we are doing everything in our power to work through this and return to a normal operating schedule. In the meantime, I ask for your patience.

"I want to take this opportunity to thank Knight Errant Holt, who assisted us with quality assurance aspects of this project. Also, I wish to extend my thanks to my superiors in ComStar on Terra for sending in crack personnel and the right hardware to ensure that Wyatt once again is connected to the rest of the Inner Sphere.

"Finally," he said, taking another pause, "I want to thank the technical lead on this project, without whom this project would not have been successful. Tucker Harwell of ComStar Terra played a pivotal role. His solution for restoring our core may one day help restore hundreds of other HPG stations throughout the Inner Sphere. Quite literally, what happened here on Wyatt could usher in a wave of restoration of communication that could impact billions of individuals."

The questions flew at him like a tornado. Demi-Precentor Faulk smiled and nodded, and Knight Holt stood solemnly behind him. He was content for the first time in a long time. His chief problem, like a nagging headache, had suddenly been cured. He was getting a satisfactory amount of the limelight, and ComStar had scored a major public relations coup by reactivating Wyatt.

Most importantly, if there was anything else that went wrong, or if trouble came to Wyatt as a result of the HPG going live, no one would come for him. Trouble had a new target—Tucker Harwell.

Yes, today *was* a good day.

9

For Tucker, the days following the HPG restart made him feel like he'd been trapped in a hurricane. Despite his personal feelings about Demi-Precentor Faulk, he had to admit the man had media savvy. His superior hailing Tucker as the hero of Wyatt caught him off guard. Based on everything he knew about Faulk, he expected the demi-precentor to claim credit for repairing the HPG. That was before he realized the implications of Faulk's strategy.

Tucker had been hauled out like a trophy and put on display for the media. Faulk answered all the questions but constantly deflected the credit back to Tucker, keeping him in the spotlight. On the second day after the restart, he had tried to meet Reo Jones for dinner as usual but had been ambushed by holo-cameramen and reporters. Tucker had answered a few questions and tried to leave, but soon realized that he'd never make it to

The Crimson and retreated back inside the ComStar compound. Dinner was a lonely affair.

The day after that, he found himself the star attraction at a formal dinner at the governor's palace in the hills overlooking Kinross. The governor seemed a nice enough man, but within an hour Tucker's hand hurt from being gripped enthusiastically by fat men smoking cigars, who slapped his back and thanked him over and over. It gave him a headache. The only thing that made the evening bearable was Patricia's supporting presence.

So far, Patricia had been a rock for him. Instead of thanking him for his work or showering him with praise, she simply told him that she was proud of what he had done. She sent word of his accomplishment to their parents, and the response of quiet joy and shining pride in their son's contribution almost made the rest of the media circus worthwhile.

A local elementary school in the city sent him hand-drawn thank-you cards, most showing him as a stick figure next to an oversized HPG dish. They were charming and Tucker wanted to reply to each one, but he quickly realized he didn't have that kind of time. The capital city newspaper, *The Beacon,* ran an article about him and got most of the facts about his childhood and history with ComStar wrong. He wanted to ask the paper to correct the article, but Patricia assured him that it would be a mistake: a follow-up article would only generate more interest. He trusted her. She knew best about such things.

Fortunately, he got to spend some time with the technical team, Paula Kursk and her—no, their—people. They didn't treat him like a superstar; they just got down to working hard to document exactly how they had started up the new core, transmitting multiple reports to Terra. His reports on the harmonics tuning had gone through the most scrutiny and had generated the most questions from the technicians and theoreticians on Terra. He felt sure they would never be satisfied with his reports. *They want me to explain instinct. I just adjusted the settings until they* felt *right. How do you explain that?*

Four days after the restart the city threw a parade for him. He tried to get out of it, but the demi-precentor insisted. "This is a public relations coup for ComStar, Mister Harwell. Embrace it!" He found the entire event acutely embarrassing. Crowds cheering, bands playing—it was a small parade, but it seemed strange that people would be clapping and cheering for him, for Tucker Harwell. His image on the news and in print, his private life impossible to live—that was surely something he had not predicted when he slipped that tiny disk into the HPG computer and ran his program.

As he sat slumped in a chair in the compound cafeteria across from his sister, nursing a bowl of soup, he brooded over the attention.

"I should have suspected something was wrong when the demi started treating me nice," he commented dolefully, stirring his spoon around and around in the thick, white chowder.

Patricia chuckled. "I agree, that should have been a big clue." She went on, "Tuck, you've got to lighten up. The media attention will die down—eventually." She took a bite of her hero sandwich—which Tucker suspected she had ordered just to tease him—and finally got some eye contact from under his unkempt, spiky hair.

"You don't sound too reassuring there, Patricia," he muttered, finally taking a sip of his soup.

"For what it's worth, I'm happy about the attention you're getting," she replied. That made him sit up. He straightened up in the hard plastic chair and frowned at his sister.

She didn't wait for a response. "Tucker, you know the history of ComStar. For years, we were revered by the people of the Inner Sphere as the keepers of technology and the source of interstellar communications. They treated our adepts with the respect and honor normally reserved for religious men and women."

"I know our history, Patricia," he replied, trying to figure out where she was going with this train of thought. "Our family was part of ComStar back then. And they were not just respected like religious leaders; they acted like religious leaders. It was that quasi-religion that eventually led to the Jihad."

She shook her head. "I disagree. You may enjoy history, Tucker, but it's my career. What hurt us was not the religious overtones of our organization, but that fact that some of us broke with the old ways. *That's* what led to the Jihad."

She waved her hand above the table, both acknowledging and dismissing their difference of opinion on the subject. This same debate had been waged over the dinner table in their parents' house many times. Patricia Harwell continued. "But that's neither here nor there. The fact is that ComStar has been blamed for the crimes and sins of the Word of Blake for decades. When the HPG net went down, there were people in the media who said we did it on purpose, who accused us of destroying the very source of our own influence. Now, because of you, they hold parades in our honor. At least on Wyatt, ComStar is no longer a villain."

"I think you're overstating my part in this," Tucker replied, gently tipping his bowl to get the last spoonful of soup.

Patricia shook her head. "I went to the market this morning. People greeted me on the street on my way there and back. Every shop I went into, they treated me like royalty. That was what it used to be like to be part of ComStar. I have to admit Tucker, I enjoyed it."

Tucker frowned. "I'm glad at least one of us is."

Knight Errant Alexi Holt settled into the small room in the ComStar compound used for sending and receiving private messages. The room was dark, lit only by tiny recessed ceiling lights, its walls soundproofed with a dull gray-black material. It was a cramped space that felt more like a videophone booth than a communications room. It had three seats facing a flatscreen that dominated the entire wall in front of her. The ComStar logo floated in the center of the screen in front of her, the twin-star points stretched downward against a dull, royal blue background. In the lower right-hand corner of the display, a countdown ticked away the seconds until her connection was established.

Real-time communication between two or more HPGs using intermediate stations was a rare, expensive and complicated procedure. When the ComStar techs alerted her to the incoming message, it reinforced her suspicions of the level of importance The Republic gave to the events on Wyatt.

The counter ran down to 00:00:00 and the screen suddenly flickered to life. The face of her mentor and current mission commander, Paladin Kelson Sorenson, came into focus. His features were rough and weathered. Deeply furrowed wrinkles marked his forehead. The light gray eyes that she had come to know and trust stared back at her. She noticed that his hairline was freshly shaved, to give his BattleMech neurohelmet good contact with his scalp.

"Greetings, and congratulations, Knight Errant Holt," he said with a nod.

"Thank you, Paladin Sorenson. I have to say, though, my contribution to the work of getting the HPG up and running was minimal, at best."

"I read your report, Alexi. Humble as always. I grant you, you may not have been involved with the technicalities of getting the HPG up and running, but your presence there definitely had an impact with ComStar—even here on Terra." His voice hinted at the political pressures that he was putting on ComStar at the behest of the new Exarch, Jonah Levin. Wyatt was simply the first of what should be many such restorations.

"The adept ComStar sent from Terra, Tucker Harwell, was the key to the repairs here. Apparently, he exceeded his direction from the local demi-precentor in his repairs, but what he did worked."

Sorenson nodded. "Better than you may realize. I met with Precentor Malcolm Buhl in Australia just yesterday to discuss this matter. ComStar is keeping their cards pretty close to their vests, but Buhl did admit that the fix this Harwell came up with may allow ComStar to reactivate numerous HPGs."

"I've heard similar comments here."

"I've also managed to confirm they have not been able to duplicate here on Terra whatever it was Adept Harwell did when he tuned the core. Obviously, they're not sharing their data openly, but it's clear that they don't fully understand what he did, or how he did it."

"I've met Harwell several times, Kelson, and I don't think it's an overstatement to call the man a genius."

Sorensen shifted in his seat. "Then it's even more critical that you hear what I am about to say, and understand me clearly. If Tucker Harwell is the only person who can perform this tuning procedure, he is now one of the most important people in the Inner Sphere. I want you to stay close to him, Alexi. His safety is critical to the survival of The Republic. And if we've figured this out, so will everyone else."

And when they do, they'll come for Tucker in force. "I understand, sir," she replied.

"I'm arranging for a JumpShip and DropShip to come to the Wyatt system to pick up you and Harwell. I can have reinforcements in your system on 25 May at the earliest. Until then, it is your job to secure Tucker Harwell."

"That won't be easy," she replied. "He's become a minor media sensation."

"We don't send Knight Errants on easy assignments," the Paladin replied with a grim smile. "Do whatever you have to. I'm giving you wide latitude in the execution of this assignment. Until ComStar can figure out what he did, we can't afford for anything to happen to Tucker Harwell."

"Understood."

"Best of luck," Sorenson said, and broke the connection.

I hope I don't need it. "Thank you, sir," she said out loud. The image of the Paladin disappeared, and the ComStar logo returned to the screen in front of her. Alexi stared at it for a moment and tried to regain her composure. The feeling in the pit of her stomach convinced her that the nature of her mission on Wyatt had become much more complicated. She stood, moved to the door at the back of the room and opened it, her mind still focused on the new instructions from her superior. As Alexi stepped out into the hall, she bumped into someone, sending a flurry of papers to the floor.

"I'm so sorry," she said, bending down to help gather up the printouts. Adding to her embarrassment, she bumped foreheads with the person she had run into. As she straightened up to apologize again, she realized she had collided with Patricia Harwell.

"It's all right," Patricia said, quickly grabbing at the papers on the floor.

"It's entirely my fault," Alexi replied, gathering papers as she spoke. It struck her as odd that anyone would carry printouts when a data cube was so much more convenient, then chalked it up to some quirk of Patricia's historian nature. She could not help looking at the papers in her hand. They were pre-coded transmission packets; hard copies of messages scheduled to be sent. These were marked Crimson Priority, routed to Terra with a secondary routing address of "L." From what little she knew of ComStar's systems, Crimson was one of the organization's highest internal security ratings. Then she caught herself, and handed them to Patricia as she picked up the last of the handful of printouts.

"Don't worry about it—really," Patricia said, bundling the material into a stack again.

Alexi forced a smile to her face. "Your work as a researcher must keep you quite busy, Ms. Harwell." *Why would a researcher have such a high level of security clearance?*

"Patricia," she corrected. "And yes, Knight Holt, my work does keep me busy." She seemed flustered. Her nervousness, added to the high security clearance she apparently enjoyed, suddenly made Alexi very curious about Tucker Harwell's sister.

"You and your family must be very proud of your brother."

Now Patricia forced a smile. "Tuck is a smart kid. I think everyone in ComStar is proud of what he's done."

"And that's exactly why I'm planning to keep an eye on him, to make sure he stays safe."

Patricia's grin disappeared. "I'm sure that that's not necessary," she said stiffly.

"I understand your feelings. No one likes to think of their loved ones being in any danger. But there is a chance that—" Her words were cut off by a beeping from her wrist communicator. She turned slightly and activated the connection. "This is Holt," she stated.

The voice on the other end of the transmission was curt and to the point. "Knight Holt, we have a problem." She immediately recognized the voice of Legate Singh, and he sounded nervous . . . maybe even scared. It didn't take a seasoned warrior to pick up on the quaver in his voice.

Patricia nodded, acknowledging that she was not part of the discussion. She stepped into the private communications booth that Alexi had just exited and closed the door behind her. Alexi looked after her thoughtfully. "What is it, Legate Singh?"

"Satellites picked up unscheduled activity at the nadir jump point," Singh replied. Alexi understood the implications. Jump points were the gravity wells located at the poles of a star's orbit. JumpShips could fold space and arrive at these well-charted points, safely outside a planet's gravitational pull. Many planets also had less well-charted jump points, so-called pirate points where JumpShips could arrive closer to the planet, but these were secrets well-kept by those who used them. The unscheduled arrival of a ship at a jump point was always a matter for concern.

"What data do you have?" she queried.

"According to the satellite signal, the JumpShip arrived and immediately deployed a *Union*-class DropShip. The JumpShip has begun recharging operations and the DropShip is inbound."

"Merchant?"

There was a pause. "I think you should come to HQ, Knight Holt."

Alexi closed her eyes, focusing her thoughts. "I take

it you've identified the incoming ship." *Stormhammers? Possibly. Clan Jade Falcon?* She felt her stomach muscles clench at the thought.

"Both the JumpShip and DropShip bear the markings of the Spirit Cats."

The Spirit Cats? That was a wrinkle she hadn't considered. Word had it that their leader was scattering his warriors across the Inner Sphere on quests to find the Clan's destiny—a safe haven where they could ride out the storm they were convinced was coming. They were tough customers: skilled warriors, deeply spiritual, and highly motivated. When the Spirit Cats acted, they did so as if the survival of the Clan depended on their success. It galvanized them, turned them into a dangerous force.

She looked again at the door that Patricia had closed behind her and sighed. "I'm on my way," she said. She shut off the communicator.

Checking into Patricia Harwell would have to wait.

Legate Singh was nervous. It showed in his darting eyes, and how the faked smile Alexi had come to expect had been washed from his jaw. He leaned on the operations table in the Militia headquarters, his hands flat against the tabletop and his arms stiff, and stared at the holographic image displayed for his command team. The air in the room smelled ripe, a mix of nervous sweat and humidity. Singh said nothing, but let the image sink in for everyone in the room.

It was imposing. A Clan *Union*-class DropShip filled the display against a dark field of stars. The ship was painted dull gray with the growling cat-head of the Spirit Cats emblazoned on its side against a shield of blue. There was no mistaking it. The Clan was on its way to Wyatt.

Legate Singh shut off the projector. "So there you have it. The Spirit Cats are inbound on a fast-burn trajectory. We have five days maximum before they arrive." His voice rang like a bell of doom.

"So what's the plan, sir?" Captain "Fox" Irwin asked, stroking his gray goatee.

The legate's eyebrows seemed to collapse, as if they were surrendering. "Thus far, the Spirit Cats have refused to respond to our attempts at communication. We won't know where they are going to land or their targets until they get here." His answer gave his officers nothing to work with.

So Alexi jumped in. "What we need to do," she said in her firmest command tone, "is mobilize our forces. Based on their usual operating procedure, it is unlikely the Spirit Cats are coming here for a fight. But if we have to engage them, we need to be ready to do it."

Singh stared at her. "Do you really think we might be able to avoid a fight altogether?"

Alexi shrugged. There was no sense in hiding the truth. "Probably not. We don't know why they are coming here. When we learn the goal of their mission, we may be able to negotiate with them. However, they are violating the sovereignty of The Republic and of Wyatt by landing here. That alone may force us into a confrontation. If we do fight them, we need to keep the citizens out of the way."

"I believe it would be best for all involved if we could avoid a battle," the legate replied.

I'm sure everyone agrees on that. Alexi nodded rather than say what she was thinking. "We are talking a single *Union*-class ship. That's three Clan Stars' worth of troops on board, slightly more than the size of a company of our troops. Given our current numbers and the additional hardware and armaments I brought, the odds are about even—in fact, we may have an edge in numbers. But these are Clan warriors. We cannot afford to underestimate them." The officers around the table took her words very seriously. They all knew that the Clan warriors were genetically bred for combat and trained from childhood to fight and win.

Legate Singh sucked in a deep breath. "I've informed the governor of the situation. He has scheduled a broadcast to let the general population know what is happening."

Knight Holt gripped the edge of the table and squeezed hard. Making an announcement of the Spirit Cats' arrival was premature and would only cause panic. But she knew it was out of her hands. She had to work with the cards she had been dealt. "In that case, we can go to full alert. Cancel all leaves. Recall all the militia. Prep the vehicles and load them out."

Legate Singh slapped his hand on the holotable. "Don't worry, Knight Holt. We will be ready."

If we're not, we're all dead. Alexi scanned the faces of the officers in the room. She wondered if any were asking themselves why the Spirit Cats had come to Wyatt. She knew the answer: she had been sent to Wyatt because if the HPG was repaired, there was the risk that some faction might make a grab to control the planet. Of all of the possible threats, the Spirit Cats had been a distant worry. Now, that distant worry was burning in-system.

There was more to worry about than just the HPG. There was a gawky technician who was an even greater prize.

Reo Jones hated rain. He stood under the striped awning of the newsstand, leaning back to avoid a drizzle running off the edge of the flimsy canvas covering. He pretended to study the long racks of newspapers and magazines, and the owner, a bald, older man with a grungy salt-and-pepper beard, cast him a wary glance. Reo suddenly realized the rack nearest him was filled with pornography, and just for a moment wondered if the owner figured him for a pervert. He'd been called many things over the years, but that would be a new one on his record.

Rutger Chaffee ran under the awning and collapsed his umbrella. The long scar on his pockmarked face was wet, and it looked artificial. Reo knew differently. Any scars this man had acquired as a mercenary, he had earned with his own blood and the blood of others.

"So, Reo," he said, taking one of the more brazen

magazines off the rack and flipping through it as if it were a sporting publication. "You heard the news broadcast tonight?"

"I did. And ten minutes later, you called me to meet you here."

"The Spirit Cats," Chaffee said, his whole attention apparently focused on the magazine.

"Has our mutual benefactor expressed any thoughts on the situation?" The reference to Jacob Bannson was thinly veiled.

"I've got a lot of freedom to act here on Wyatt," Chaffee replied, turning the pages of the magazine more slowly. "This particular situation is one he never predicted. The only word I have from him is that if an opportunity presents itself to take control of Wyatt, I should not let it pass."

Reo smiled cheerfully. "Sounds like he's giving you enough rope to hang yourself with."

Chaffee made brief eye contact with him and chuckled. "You may be right. Here's your assignment. I want you to keep your eye on this ComStar fellow and on our Knight Errant. I want to know what's going on with the Wyatt Militia and what plans they might have for dealing with the Spirit Cats."

"Mind if I ask why?" Reo asked casually. Chaffee turned to the front of the magazine and began flipping through it again.

"Let's just say that I'm always on the lookout for opportunities to advance myself. If I can arrange it, I wouldn't be opposed to the Wyatt Militia and the Spirit Cats slugging it out with each other."

Jones understood. "And then you and your unit can pick up the pieces."

Chaffee tossed the magazine back onto the rack so that the pages bent. "It's a wonder you never became a Knight yourself," he said sarcastically. "You've got such a sharp eye for detail." His tone flattened out into something that sounded dangerous. "Just don't forget who you work for, Reo. Keep your eyes peeled and send me regular reports."

Before Reo could respond, Chaffee stepped out into the rain, popped open his umbrella and set off down the street at a quick jog. Reo watched him run down the block, and turned the collar of his coat up against a sudden cool breeze. *Cut-Throat's dangerous . . . then again, so are the Spirit Cats.* His mind racing, he picked up the magazine that Chaffee had wrinkled, smoothed out the cover and placed it carefully back on the rack. He tossed a five stone to the man running the stand as he walked out. *Rutger Chaffee was playing a deep game. The key was to work that against him. Timing was everything. . . .*

**ComStar Compound
Kinross, Wyatt
The Republic, Prefecture VIII
10 May 3135**

Up to this point, Alexi Holt had been more than courteous, on several occasions going so far as to bite her own tongue rather than say what she felt. Diplomatically prodding Demi-Precentor Faulk to action during the entire installation of the new HPG core had taken every ounce of her patience. He had been thoroughly put out by her arrival on Wyatt, and had made no secret of his feelings. All during her time in the ComStar compound, he had complained constantly about her "interfering with internal ComStar affairs," though she considered her attitude pretty hands-off. Her mission now made his complaint true, and now, the diplomatic gloves were coming off.

She had spent hours reviewing what she knew about the Spirit Cats and their quest for a sanctuary. Whenever they had appeared in The Republic before, it was a deliberate move, always motivated by an event or something specific about a location. *An event . . . like the reactivation of an HPG?* It fit the way they worked. As much as she wanted to convince herself otherwise, she kept coming to the same conclusion. It was not by chance that they had shown up in the Wyatt system when they did. The Spirit Cats had come with a purpose.

The demi-precentor sat behind his large, pristine desk, arms crossed, his expression smug. Next to her sat Tucker Harwell. He looked distracted, as if his mind were anywhere but in this hastily called meeting.

Faulk seized the initiative. "With the Spirit Cats heading toward Wyatt, I would have assumed that you would be too busy to spend more time with us, Knight Holt."

She regarded him silently for a moment. "Demi-Precentor Faulk, the Spirit Cats' imminent arrival is precisely why I am spending time with you today. Even you cannot believe it's a coincidence that they appeared in-system right after the HPG became operational."

The cocky expression seemed to melt from his face. "Do you think they want to take over the HPG?" Alexi could practically smell his fear and see beads of sweat forming on his brow.

"I don't know for sure, but I do know this: they may not have come here because the HPG became active, but they figured that out when they arrived. Regardless of the order of events, Paladin Sorenson has compelled me to take action."

Faulk gripped the desktop. "What is your plan?"

She looked at Faulk and then at Tucker Harwell. The adept seemed to have no idea where the conversation was headed. She returned her gaze to Faulk. "Beginning now and for the duration of this crisis, Tucker Harwell will be under my protective custody."

"Out of the question," Faulk protested weakly. "Adept Harwell is a highly valued member of ComStar. Until we can decipher what he did to restore our HPG, he must remain under ComStar's protection."

Alexi waved her hand dismissively. "You think your squad of security men is a match for the Spirit Cats?

This isn't the good old days of ComStar, Faulk. You don't have the elite troops and kick-ass 'Mechs of the Com Guards protecting your installation. Whatever they want—if they have to blast this compound to get it, they will, and you won't be able to stop them." She was exaggerating for effect. The Spirit Cats were Clan, true, but it wasn't their style to kill innocents or needlessly damage infrastructure. She just wanted to drive home to the demi-precentor that his attitude was placing more than just Tucker at risk . . . and that much was true.

"Your title does not give you the right to kidnap valued employees." He was stretching a point now, and they both knew it.

"That's right," she replied, wearing her best poker face. "But it is part of the Knight's creed to protect the citizens of The Republic of the Sphere. How we accomplish that is left to each Knight's—to my—discretion. Whether you like it or not, Demi-Precentor, Harwell is going with me." Her tone made it clear that if she had to, she would fight her way out of the office.

"I could call security and you wouldn't reach the outer wall."

"Yes," she replied coolly. "And if I don't leave with him now I'll come back with a BattleMech and take him out. Like I said, this isn't the good old days." She turned to Tucker. "I'll take you to gather your things."

Tucker's face was red, and he was clearly angry. Before he had the chance to say anything, however, Faulk started talking again. "You've made your point, Knight Holt. But I want you to understand that this means you are assuming full responsibility for his safety."

"Agreed."

"You'll also be taking a few of my other techs, the ones who worked most closely with him. I don't want the Spirit Cats or anyone else capturing and interrogating them for what they know."

She suspected that Faulk might actually have wanted her to take this approach, so this was an easy concession. "Agreed."

"And Tucker's sister, Patricia."

That caught her off guard. She opened her mouth to protest, but Faulk cut her off. "On this I cannot waver. My superiors would insist. His sister was sent here to be with him, and she will remain with him, no matter what the circumstances. Surely one more person will not pose a challenge, Knight Holt?" A hint of arrogance returned to his voice.

"Agreed," she said after a moment's consideration. Faulk had just revealed more than he realized. Apparently, Tucker's superiors on Terra had anticipated a problem like this and had put plans in place—including the assignment of Tucker's sister to Wyatt. She wondered again about Patricia's true status in ComStar, and decided she would deal with it.

"Good," he said, exhaling noisily. "Knight Holt, I'm agreeing to this only for his protection. Tucker is a valuable asset. If anything happens to him, I assure you that even your Paladin cannot protect you from the punishment that ComStar would demand from The Republic." It was a bold threat, but she knew he was right. It was a risk that she was willing to take.

Tucker rose from his seat, finally getting a word in edgewise. "Don't I get a say in this?" he demanded.

The demi-precentor and Alexi replied in unison. "No."

Tucker sat in the back of the room as the Wyatt Militia's command staff assembled around the holotable. They were in the tactical operations room, or so the chipped brass plaque outside said. It was buried two stories down in the bowels of the militia headquarters at the edge of Kinross. The HQ building was squat with steeply sloped ferrocrete walls that leaned in as if to deflect incoming fire. Offices filled the upper level, but the rest of the structure was a series of underground bunkers. Patricia had told him the facility was built during the Jihad. Using hidden passages and tunnels, the militia could deploy within a four-block area around the facility, and could coordinate troop movements from multiple nearby locations. Enemy forces laying siege to the command bunker would find it to be a deadly affair.

Patricia, Paula Kursk and two other techs from the ComStar compound were attempting to convert one lower chamber into adequate sleeping quarters. The space was cramped, the beds army-issue cots, and the walls nothing more than old, green woolen blankets pinned together and pegged to the ceiling. The air was not quite musty, but definitely stale, infused with the sweat of years' worth of militia use. The space allocated for his private use was tiny—and barely private—and he wasn't crazy about being there, but even Patricia admitted that the militia HQ was a much safer place right now than the ComStar facility. He had helped the others for awhile, but quickly found himself caught somewhere between boredom and frustration. Alexi Holt took pity on him and invited him to join her staff meeting. Now he was sitting in the corner of the briefing room, feeling like a kid sitting at the holiday dinner table for the first time.

She was an imposing force. For the first hour or so since her command performance at the compound, Tucker had resented Holt. She knew he was mad, but it didn't seem to bother her, and she continued to treat him the same as always. Eventually, his usual good temper resurfaced. It was hard to stay mad at her when he admitted to himself that he still found the idea of a female Knight Errant somewhat exotic. It also helped that he had half enjoyed her verbal pouncing on Demi-Precentor Faulk earlier in the day. "Look on the bright side, Adept," she had said jokingly, "at least you won't be on the evening news for a few days." That had actually made him feel better.

The Knight didn't seem inclined to give anyone much time to adjust to their new situation. It was clear that she felt a sense of urgency that she was determined to pass on to everyone else. He couldn't decide whether Holt had an agenda for him, or was just keeping her eye on him; either way, at least hanging around with her was more entertaining than hanging blankets. He was learning more about her as he watched and listened. Most of the officers deferred to her—a testimony to the respect she already had earned. Only Legate Singh, who he had

met briefly upon his arrival, seemed unwilling to acknowledge the value of her experience and knowledge.

"We need to augment our force," Knight Holt said,
slowly sweeping the command staff with her gaze.

Legate Singh spoke up. "Four squads of the city police
and a significant number of volunteers have stepped up.
We can muster them in and arm them."

"Police officers probably aren't going to give us the
edge I'm looking for," she replied. "Still, it's appreciated."

"Actually, most of these guys are militia veterans.
They may not have combat experience, but they have
training—and they're determined to protect Wyatt," offered Lieutenant Johannson.

"Well, we've got a lot of those new shoulder-launched
SRMs in the gear I brought," Alexi commented. "Har-
vester Model 10ks. A monkey can fire them, and they
can wreak a lot of havoc. We can outfit at least a squad
with them."

Johannson grinned. "I'll make it happen, sir."

"Now let's talk real hardware. We have a Forestry-
Mech," Holt continued. "Are there any other Industrial-
Mechs we can commandeer?"

The legate shrugged. Tucker was surprised. When he
saw the man on the holovid newscasts, he had seemed
so forceful. Now, without the cameras on him, he seemed
less sure of himself and less knowledgeable about his
fighting assets. "I have an inventory of all the 'Mechs on
the planet. There are ConstructionMechs in Packardston,
but that's on the southern continent, and there's no way
to move them here fast enough to use them. There are
some AgroMechs in use on this continent, but again, I
don't know if we can get them here in time."

Captain Irwin spoke up. "Too bad we can't pull some
of the old ConstructionMechs out of the ruins of the
Bowie factory. There's a lot of them left out there."

Holt's face lit up. "Why not go after them?"

Lieutenant Tooley blew a light gray cloud of smoke
into the air from his cigar. Tucker caught a whiff of the
aroma and was instantly transported back to the family

rec room and the times his grandfather would visit and
smoke. To Tucker, the grizzled face of the officer loudly
proclaimed that he was an infantryman. "They were used
to clean up the debris of the old armaments factory after
the Wobbies—uh, Word of Blake—nuked the place back
to the Stone Age. They've been abandoned out there for
decades, still hot with radioactivity."

"Were they exposed to the nuclear blast?" Knight
Holt asked.

"No," the man replied, "but what difference does that
make? They're still hot."

Tucker understood the line of questioning and Alexi
cast him a quick glance, inviting him to chime in. He
leaned forward. "Not really. I mean, they are, but it's
only because they're covered with radioactive fallout and
dirt. Radioactive particles on the surface won't turn the
equipment itself radioactive," Tucker said. The militia
officer was talking about a common misconception, but
Tucker knew that with proper cleaning, it might be possible to use the gear again.

"You mean we might be able to clean them?" Legate
Singh asked.

"It's possible. You just need some special gear and
solvents, and a place to do the cleaning. I've never actually done it, but I've taken instruction in the basics of
the process. With all of the clean-up that was done after
the Jihad, it should be easy for us to get a line on the
chemicals and equipment we need."

Lieutenant Johannson spoke up again. "Most of that
hardware has been abandoned in warehouses in the contaminated zone near the factory for a long time. I suppose we could salvage enough parts to get a few 'Mechs
in working order."

"If we could scare up some long-range armaments to
mount on them, then we'd have a real advantage," Holt
replied. One problem with using IndustrialMechs in battle was that they were best for close-up combat. Getting
them close enough to do damage and keeping them in
one piece in the process was always a trick.

Lieutenant Foster, sporting a heavy five o'clock

shadow, jumped into the conversation. "We have some replacement weapons systems we can use, but I was thinking a little more creatively. The Bowie factory used to make *Chippewa* aerospace fighters, and the museum in town has one. I worked on it as a kid during the restoration. That thing has a number of those Holly missile racks, which are modular for quick swap-out. They may be old, but the technology of a launching and targeting rack is pretty basic. With some jury-rigging, I'll bet we could get a few of them working."

Tucker found himself nodding. He had just visited that museum exhibit—what suddenly seemed like years ago.

"We'll be able to get a shot or two at range with the modifications you suggest," Knight Holt responded. Tucker understood the distinction she was making. He had studied BattleTech—battlefield technology. Missile launchers were easy; reloading systems, they tended to be complex.

Alexi smiled. "Do you have personnel who can pilot these 'Mechs if we can get them up and running?"

The legate nodded. "Militia personnel all have jobs outside of their commitment to the military, Knight Holt. Trust me, some of them are bound to have a competency in piloting IndustrialMechs. I'll have my admin go through the personnel files."

"Excellent. We'll also need to secure as much heavy transportation as possible. We have no idea where the Spirit Cats are going to land. That leaves us with two options: spread out all over the planet, or get our force as mobile as possible."

Legate Singh's eyebrows rose. "That might be tricky. We have a prime hauler, but it's more than eighty years old. If we have to go any significant distance, it's not going to be reliable. We do have an old mobile HQ down in Bay Four. I guess it would be possible to cut off the sides and top and convert it into a flatbed transport of some sort."

"You have a mobile HQ? I didn't see it on the TO& E for the unit," she replied. It took Tucker a second to remember that the acronym meant Table of Organization and Equipment.

Lieutenant Johannson answered her. "It's not an active vehicle, so we don't list it on the TO&E. The comm system died almost ten years ago. Our motor pool techs have kept the engine tuned so that it runs, but the cuts in military funding didn't leave us with enough to get the jamming and surveillance gear working. We use it mostly to haul around equipment on extended maneuvers."

She stood there for a moment, her back half turned to Tucker, deep in thought. Slowly the Knight Errant turned and faced the adept. "Mr. Harwell, you're something of a genius with HPG technology. How are you with conventional communications systems?"

Tucker rose to his feet, and felt the weight of the gazes of the military officers in the room resting on him. "I've got quite a bit of experience with the types of systems that would be used in jamming and ECM technology." He had guessed what she was thinking, and it sounded infinitely more exciting than sitting on his cot and counting the chips in the paint on the wall of the bunker.

"How would you and your techs like to take a crack at repairing the gear in that HQ? Having that vehicle operational would give us a big edge in a fight. We could tie in the command-control-communications systems and get some leverage from having a coordinating command unit."

Tucker smiled. "I can't make any promises on the results, but I'm sure they'll all agree to try. It's better than sitting around and waiting for the action to start."

Alexi gave him a somber stare. "Don't get anxious, Tucker. The action will happen soon enough."

11

Wyatt Militia Headquarters
Kinross, Wyatt
The Republic, Prefecture VIII
12 May 3135

The prime mover was a massive truck carrying heavy-duty winches and cranes and a deep bed, deep enough to carry a BattleMech. Prime movers were crucial in battlefield operations for salvaging 'Mechs and damaged vehicles and bringing them back to repair stations. This one had seen its prime at least two decades ago, if not longer. The flat, brown-and-green striped paint scheme was deeply scratched, scraped and chipped in many places, revealing other colors buried in the layers of paint. Pockmarked dents from rounds that didn't penetrate the metal marked its sides, scars of battles long past. It rumbled down the long tunnel into the bay, its transmission rattling like a baby's toy, the engine straining. Four mechanics rode on the truck bed next to the cargo that was tied down under tarps.

Alexi Holt moved alongside the old hauler as it clattered to a stop. Lieutenant Johannson hopped down from the passenger seat to stand next to her, and pointed up to the bed of the hauler. "That was a hell of a dirty job," he cursed. The logistical officer's jumpsuit was muddy, splashes of bright green coolant staining both legs. It had been torn, and black smears of grease splotched it everywhere. Alexi barely registered that he smelled as if he had been in the field longer than the two and a half days he had been gone.

"What were you able to recover?"

He shook his head and reached up to grab an armful of slick, bright yellow decontamination suits from the storage compartment, tossing them to the concrete floor of the bay. "Not as much as I'd hoped. I have parts that should allow us to rebuild two 'Mechs, a miner and a construction." As he spoke, the mechanics in the bed of the hauler removed the tarps. Alexi was surprised to see not 'Mechs, but parts. Huge industrial ICEs—internal combustion engines. A drilling arm. Nearly every part in the truck showed signs of black scarring and cutting.

"Looks like parts, all right," she said, unsuccessfully trying to keep her surprise out of her voice.

"Knight Holt," Johannson said, sounding exhausted. "There were almost a dozen IndustrialMechs out there. They've been there since the war. We decontaminated them as much as possible, but in the end we had to cut off most of the exterior metal—it was more efficient than decontaminating it. Most were in such disrepair we couldn't salvage anything. What we have is enough to build two 'Mechs, if we're lucky."

She reached up and gave his shoulder a squeeze. "You did a good job, Lieutenant," she replied. "How is your rad count?"

"We're good as long as my team stays out of the contaminated zone for a few days."

"You did a good job," she repeated. "I'm pleased with the results. Two additional 'Mechs is a big improvement. I'm not worried about the plates you had to strip off— the exterior bodywork had to be fabricated with fresh armor plating anyway, because IndustrialMechs aren't armored the way we need them to be. You think you can assemble those parts in the next few days?"

Johannson wiped his brow on his sleeve, smearing a streak of grease on his forehead in the process. "I'd like to tell you no, but something tells me that you won't accept that answer. Somehow we'll pull it off."

"I know."

"Anything pop while we were gone?"

She shrugged. "We've heard nothing from the Spirit Cats. They're three days out and still heading toward us."

"Damn."

"There is some good news. Tucker Harwell and his people have managed to restore that old Browning Mobile HQ. They've gotten the electronic countermeasures and sensor array working and they're tying in all of the IFF transponders so that it can assist in coordinating operations."

"The cowlhead pulled it off, eh? I'm impressed."

Alexi frowned at his words. "Cowlhead" was a phrase that dated back to when ComStar had been a religious organization and when adepts like Tucker had worn hoods and robes and prayed to the technology they operated. Since the Jihad, the phrase had become derogatory, usually aimed at ComStar. "Lieutenant, I'd ask that you not use that word when you talk about Tucker Harwell. I've been camped out with ComStar since I got on Wyatt, and they're a little sensitive about comments like that. He's on our side, remember?"

"Sorry," Johannson said, blushing red at the rebuff. "I meant what I said as a compliment. We wrote off that battlewagon downstairs a long time ago. The fact that they've got the comm gear working is remarkable."

"Yes, it is," she replied. "Because of their work, I'm assigning two of their people to your team for rebuilding the 'Mechs. They're not much on mechanics, but from what I've seen, these ComStar techs are pretty good with electronics and power plants."

Johannson smiled. "Great. Anyone who could fix that hunk of junk is welcome to work with my people anytime."

Alexi smiled. "Glad you feel that way." *Now my biggest problem is the Spirit Cats.*

Legate Singh stepped out of the ComStar private communications cubicle and slid the data disk back into his vest pocket. It had cost him quite a bit to send the messages he had transmitted, but the cost was well worth it. The accounts he had used had been set up years ago. At that time, no one expected to use the accounts for the kind of situation they currently faced. But with the Spirit Cats heading toward his planet, he was willing to take extraordinary risks to keep Wyatt safe.

That was his charter as legate . . . the protection of the world. If his resident Knight Errant wanted to plan for an all-out war, a war he knew they would lose, that was her prerogative. He intended to make sure that Wyatt was safe, and if that meant taking extraordinary risks—well, he was willing to do that. *History will vindicate my actions . . . and if not, my parents would.*

As he stepped into the hallway, he heard a rumble from outside the compound. For a moment, Edward Singh convinced himself it was distant thunder, but it was too short—too sharp. A heartbeat later, he knew the rumble was an explosion. Another heartbeat later, he heard shouting and the sound of gunfire.

Reaching down, he felt the comforting weight of his Settles Mark II slug-thrower. Weapons were banned inside the ComStar compound, but his position as planetary legate granted him some latitude in the rules. He was thankful for that. He unclasped the leather holster strap and rested his hand on the weapon.

The Spirit Cats . . . but how did they get here so fast? No. It couldn't be them. He tensed and moved along the interior wall, cautiously starting down the corridor. The realization that someone else was on-planet, someone unknown, settled over him like a wet blanket. *What are we up against? More important, who?*

There was another roar, this one much closer. A ceiling tile jostled loose and crashed to the floor right in front of him, and he jerked his pistol loose. Every muscle in his body tensed up, and blood roared in his ears with each beat of his heart. Whoever it was, they were getting closer.

The corridor in front of him ran straight for ten meters then turned, paralleling the outer wall on this side of the compound. Legate Singh moved forward, one cautious step at a time. From around the corner ahead, he heard the rattle of a submachine gun and the whine of ricochets off metal or concrete. Yelling—someone calling for reinforcements. He pressed his spine tight against the wall and waited.

There was a rush of wind, then a sucking sound as a blast ripped the air in front of him. Singh fell and something heavy draped over him, trapping him. His vision filled with spots, as if a camera had flashed right in front of his eyes. He felt the grip of the Settles slug-thrower still in his hand, but it was difficult to move his arm.

It took a second for him to figure out that he was covered with a length of the hall carpet. Pushing and crawling, pistol still in hand, he got free. The blast down the corridor had torn up the carpeting and tossed it right over him. Looking down the hallway, he saw that the pictures decorating the walls were gone, and a black burn mark lapped along the exterior wall from the blast. Feeling dazed, he stood in the middle of the hall.

He could see forms moving in a cloud of smoke. They were massive shapes, obviously not human but oddly human-shaped. One was walking toward him, and Singh held out his pistol with both arms in front of him, shivering slightly from the rush of fear and adrenaline. The figure moved steadily through the darkened section of corridor, the lights blasted out in the explosion.

When the legate heard the crushing, grinding noise on the exposed concrete floor in tandem with the enemy's footsteps, he knew he was facing power armor, but he still couldn't tell who it belonged to. He wanted to fire, shoot right at the face plate or the neck, but he knew that was a pointless gesture. If it was power armor, he was facing a ton of killing hardware that would shake off anything his slug-thrower might toss at it.

The lead figure stepped into the light and the legate got his first good look at what he was facing. Standing more than two meters tall, it had a domed helmet and a reflective face plate that shined like a curved mirror. A huge jump-jet tank covered the back of the armor, making the infantryman look like a hunchback. Singh knew the armor was reflective just under the paint; he could see the shiny surface where the camouflage had been scraped. Great protection from lasers, somewhat less against firearms. Still impenetrable by a handheld slug thrower. The shape of the power suit told him everything he needed to know: he was facing Raiden battlearmor.

Its left arm was humanoid looking, like a massive mailed gauntlet on a knight from a different era, though Singh knew it was more than armor. Augmented with myomer muscle fibers, microsensors and datafeeds to the CPU, it was capable of grappling a moving BattleMech and holding on for the ride. At the same time, the gauntlet was so delicate that it could be used to manipulate weapons, toss grenades and perform any function of a normal human hand.

The right arm was a barrel mounting a massive heavy machine gun—definitely not humanoid. It was not aimed at him, but he knew it could be in a millisecond. He kept his pistol aimed at the head of the battlearmor, and for a moment the two soldiers stared at each other.

His eyes dipped down past the light tan and gray urban camouflage colors of the armor to the left chest. Right above the ammo feed mechanism that led to the machine-gun arm, he saw the logo of a unit named Chaffee's Cut-Throats. He frowned. Who the hell was Chaffee?

"Who are you?" he demanded, taking a step back. The Raiden battlearmor took two steps forward, closing the distance between them.

A hiss and pop came over the shielded external speaker, followed by a deep, distorted voice that sounded as if it were broadcasting from a cave rather than the power suit standing in front of him. "You're not Tucker Harwell," it stated flatly.

"No."

"Do you know where he is?" it crackled back.

"No." He lied. It came naturally.

"Too bad," the voice responded. The Raiden suit stepped forward one more step and swept its machine-gun arm forward. For a millisecond, Singh thought he was dead. Reflexively, he fired off one shot, hitting the head of the battlearmor, but the hollow-point slug just burst and ricocheted down the hallway. Pain exploded in his temple, and Legate Singh thought he had been shot. His ears rang as he smashed into the exterior wall and dropped to the floor. Just before he blacked out, he realized that he had been thrown aside like a rag doll in the hands of an angry child.

Deep in the interior of the mobile HQ, Tucker leaned back against one of the few consoles that was not open, in pieces, or draped with fiber-optic wiring or cables. The work on the mobile HQ was progressing, but the way the officers were talking, it was already done. There was clearly a difference in the way that technicians and military personnel defined operational.

That thought flitted wildly through his mind as Tucker stared at Alexi Holt. The Knight stood at a loose parade-rest, the position she had chosen for delivering the news of the attack on the compound. Patricia had moved to Tucker's side as soon as the Knight had entered the vehicle. It was obvious Alexi Holt had experience in delivering bad news. There was no sugar-coating it. She had been blunt and to the point, dealing only with the facts.

Tucker was stunned by what he'd heard.

"How bad is it?" he finally managed, his voice barely audible.

"Three dead. Six wounded, including Legate Singh, who apparently was there on personal business. I guess we're fortunate that the legate only suffered a mild concussion. One of the attackers was killed by ComStar security—a lucky shot through the collar on the battle armor." Her voice conveyed no emotion, just the facts.

"Why?" he stammered. "Who did this?"

"ComStar and the local police are still picking up the pieces, but it appears that the units were marked with the logos of a mercenary group. As to the why," for the first time Knight Holt hesitated. "Tucker, they were looking for you."

"For me?"

"By name. No damage was done to the HPG itself or any of the operating equipment. They arrived in a converted commercial vehicle, two squads of battlearmored troops. One secured the perimeter while the other penetrated the compound searching for you."

Tucker drew a deep breath. *They were looking for me. If I had stayed in the compound . . .* "They were going to kill me."

Alexi shook her head. "Doubtful. Chances are the merc leader, or the unit's employer, realizes the same thing I did—you're a valuable prize. If he can secure you, he can control the fate of many worlds suffering from the blackout."

Patricia put her arm around his shoulders. "Tucker," she said firmly, "it's going to be all right. You're safe here."

He shook his head, his hair springing in every direction. "I thought I was safe *there.* But now people have *died* for me. Others are hurt, who knows how badly. All because of me."

Tucker's entire life had been spent studying, learning, researching, searching for knowledge. He had lived on Terra since the day he was born. It was the safe, comforting heart of humanity. Now, suddenly, everything had changed. He had come to Wyatt to help apply what he knew to help the people who lived here. Now some of those same people were dead. Total strangers had been killed because of him. His whole body sagged against the console. Patricia's arm around him was the only thing keeping him from curling up into a ball on the floor.

Alexi paused, then spoke again. "Tucker, this didn't happen because of you. This happened because people are corrupt and greedy. You've got a gift, a gift that can bring hope and a future to billions upon billions of people. It's typical that some people would want to corrupt that for their own benefit. Don't blame yourself. Blame them." Patricia caught her eye and mouthed, "Thank you." Alexi Holt spun on her heel and stepped out of the mobile HQ.

Patricia settled in beside Tucker, tipping his head to her shoulder. "Tucker, you know she's right. This isn't your fault."

"It's not right that people should die because of me."

"Most everyone feels that way," she soothed. "Do you remember when Grandpa used to tell us stories when we stayed at the cabin on Stuart Lake?" Tucker nodded. He couldn't guess her point, or what memories she hoped to conjure. At that moment, he felt that nothing could relieve the pain he felt.

"He loved to tell us stories about the old days of Com-Star, and you used to really enjoy those stories. Remember his stories about Jerome Blake? He was just like you, a technician. He was handed control of an entire interstellar communications network after a devastating war. All he ever wanted to do was to help people. Evil people rose up against him and ComStar over the years, causing wars and worse, but he never lost sight of what he was doing—helping trillions of people stay in touch."

"I'm not Jerome Blake," Tucker said sadly.

She chuckled. "I agree, Tucker. But you are special. You have a skill that no one else understands. Until we do understand what you know, we have to protect you. In that process, people are going to get hurt. Some may die."

"I don't want their blood on my hands. There's got to be another way for this to go."

"Unfortunately, you don't get to make a choice anymore; this is bigger than you. Events will become violent no matter what we decide." She paused. "Our family has been a part of ComStar for generations. Mom, Dad, even Grandpa would want you to hold true to your commitment to ComStar. You've made all of us proud. Don't give up now, Tucker."

He gave his sister a hug. "You're right, Patricia. You always are."

She sighed. "Don't worry, Tuck. ComStar takes care of its own."

JumpShip **Halsey**
Nadir Jump Point
Irian
The Republic, Prefecture VII

Captain Ivan Casson hovered above the floor of the bridge while the comm officer watched the data retrieval status scroll past on the screen. Casson would have preferred to pace, but in the zero-G of the bridge, he had little choice. Even worse, he was waiting. He hated waiting. Fighting, that was something he understood. Waiting, that was something for junior officers to contend with.

The *Halsey* had used false transponder codes to pose as a commercial JumpShip and was now sitting at the jump point, waiting for an update of information to be relayed to the tiny satellite that SAFE, the intelligence arm of the now-dissolved Free Worlds League, had placed in the system. No one seemed to care much about the provenance of the JumpShip and its attached DropShips, as long as they were willing to relay news from the Oriente Protectorate and everywhere else they had traveled to or from. Even the Dragon's Fury, which had seized the 'Mech production facility on Irian, did not seem to care about the Oriente ship—as long as it did not attempt to land any DropShips on-planet. News and data was a commodity that everyone respected.

It was a sign of the times. The Republic was weak. The Dragon's Fury knew it, the Capellan Chancellor knew it, and his own leader, Jessica Marik, knew it. Ripe for the taking . . . that's what the Republic was. But taking and holding, those were two different things. •

He didn't know the origin of the information he was downloading from the SAFE spy satellite—most likely beamed from the planet, or possibly a JumpShip passing through the system. He didn't care.

"Data dump complete, Captain," the comm officer announced.

He grabbed a handhold and levered himself around to face his dedicated workstation. Grasping the armrests of his chair, he seated himself firmly, allowing the material of his uniform and the surface of the chair to establish the connection that would keep him in place. "Transfer to my station," he commanded. Smoothing his left hand across his salt-and-pepper hair, cut in a maintenance-free flattop, he surveyed the information. Reports from numerous sources, some confirmed, many not. SAFE's information-gathering was impaired by the HPG network failure, just like everyone else's. The available intelligence, however, was delivered to operatives such as Casson using their own network of spy satellites to secretly transmit data.

Most of the material was boring. Updates on the Liao incursion into The Republic . . . old news. Reports on the Jade Falcon presence on Skye. The usual rumblings of discontent on Terra. His eyes skittered across the screen impatiently until the data on Wyatt finally came up. Poor little Wyatt. Now that they had a working HPG, it seemed inevitable that other splinter groups and governments would make a play to control the planet. Not him. Taking an isolated planet, even one with a working HPG, wasn't worth the risks.

One line toward the end of the report caught his attention. According to SAFE's source, a long-term operative—some might say a turncoat—planted on Wyatt over a decade ago, a single ComStar adept was credited with restoring the HPG. The operative suggested that this man, Tucker Harwell, might possess the knowledge and skills to restore other HPGs, perhaps hundreds of them. His personnel profile, complete with holoimages, was attached.

Captain Casson leaned back in his seat and stared at the screen. A single man who could control the fate of entire worlds—now that was a prize to be captured, taken back to the Protectorate. His little fragment of the once-mighty Free Worlds League would suddenly be a power in the Inner Sphere again.

The details were sketchy; still, he was inclined to believe an onworld, deep-cover operative, even if the data was unfiltered, unverified and unconfirmed. That level of risk, he was willing to accept. A lopsided smile curved one side of his mouth. Too many times in his career confirmed intel had failed him, and he had developed a sense for the information he could trust.

"Captain Hassin," he called to the dark-skinned JumpShip captain. "Are we in range of the Wyatt system?"

The man checked his command-seat display in the center of the JumpShip bridge. "We are two jumps away," he replied, his deep voice rich with an accent Casson never had been able to identify. "But with the lithium-fusion battery, we can double-jump and get there quickly."

"What are the available jump points?"

"I assume you mean pirate points?" Hassin asked in return, his bland tone somehow managing to convey his opinion of risking the safety of his ship by jumping to a point in space where a temporary gravity well, commonly called a pirate point, could be leveraged.

"Yes. Do we have any pirate points on file?" Pirate jump points were tricky to calculate, and there were risks in using them. But successful use of a pirate point brought a JumpShip into a system undetected, and much closer to the planet than the traditional jump points.

The captain of the *Halsey* manipulated the small key-pad on his command seat armrest. "The Free Worlds League attacked the Wyatt system several times during the Third Succession War. On two occasions, they used pirate points. We have them on file, but there is no record of their use in more than a hundred years."

"Pick one that will get us close to Wyatt prime."

"Yessir," the captain replied. "This will take some time," he added. He didn't bother to disguise the concern in his voice as he continued, "I assume I don't need to remind you of the risks associated with this kind of jump."

Ivan gave him a broad grin. "I'm well aware of the risks. Begin your calculations and prep the ship for departure." He pushed off from the seat toward the pressure door at the rear of the bridge.

"Where can I reach you?" asked Hassin.

"I'll be on the *Deathclaw*," he replied, "meeting with my staff. We have an operation to plan. I have an appointment with someone named Tucker Harwell." As he moved through the door, he missed the puzzled looks of the bridge crew.

Book Two

Blake's Blood

New Earth
One Jump from Terra
The Secaucus Plains
The Jihad

Demi-Precentor Seagrams Harwell angled his LNC-25-01 *Lancelot* toward the grass of the rolling plains. Seagrams ran a long-range scan of the fields and saw a mass of the magnetic signatures of fusion reactors at several kilometers. Dark purple clouds rolled in over the fields and the occasional flash of lightning flickered down as the winds whipped the tall grass. Eerie shadows seemed to spring to life out on the plains with each burst of electrical energy. The use of numerous nuclear weapons had devastated the weather patterns of New Earth and countless other worlds. It was as if the planets themselves were screaming in agony, an agony that Harwell and the others often believed they could feel.

Seagrams had seen too much fighting the last few years. Thanks to young Devlin Stone, they had taken back several worlds, but at a horrific cost. His Com Guards unit was a fragment of its former self. It had once flown the Star League banner above its own. Now there was no more Star League. It had melted away into history, just like the original commanding officer of his division, who had been ambushed and slaughtered six months earlier. The unit itself was fading into history right in front of him. Thanks to the Word of Blake, many of the personnel who had reported to him were dead, wounded, or had deserted to join their former brethren. His personal losses were far too many to count. Fortunately, his two sons were safe . . . for now.

"Form up on my position," he signaled to the remains of his company. "We'll lay down a pattern of suppression fire, rolling forward. Infantry will hold the right flank with the Demons. Sweep Lance will form on the center and charge the Word of Blake's lead units as the artillery barrage passes to their rear—while they're still dazed." Elsewhere on the plains, other elements of Stone's forces were already starting to move forward, slamming into the Blake forces, probing, prodding—killing.

"Artillery standing by. Marker rounds ready to fire," came the call from the Long Tom that was the heart of his support lance.

His headset crackled with an incoming transmission. The popping told him it was on an open channel, so it was coming from the Blake forces. *What is this, a taunt?*

"Your transponders are familiar," a female voice said. Though the tones were distorted, they wrapped around his heart and squeezed. "Does this Division still follow Demi Harwell?"

"Kari," he responded on the same channel. "You know I'm here."

"My husband," she said, and he closed his eyes in gut-wrenching agony. She had turned against ComStar, against her own family, her own children, to follow a madman determined to destroy the Inner Sphere. "Surrender now, my love. I will make sure you are spared."

He reined in his emotions. "You are not my wife," he replied coldly, realizing that he was on an open channel, that all of his troops could hear their exchange. "My wife died years ago."

A sigh sounded in his ear. "You never understood the true calling of our people. May you drink the Blood of Blake."

A tear ran down his cheek as Seagrams switched to a

direct line to the Long Tom artillery. "Fire marker rounds, validate your targets, fire for effect." *Kill them all.*

He heard hesitation in the voice of Adept Konrad, his artillery officer. "Sir?"

They had been listening. The story of his wife's betrayal and her defection to the Word of Blake was not unique. Everyone in the Com Guards and ComStar knew someone who had changed sides when the holocaust of the Jihad had begun. His wife was an officer. Her betrayal had been to release a nerve agent in the Bachelor Officers Quarters. Forty-six men and women had died in their sleep. She had given him children. She was a war criminal.

She was no longer his wife.

"Adept Konrad, I want that area saturated with fire. Take out the 'Mechs first. Everyone of them that you kill is one that can't kill us."

Adept Konrad acknowledged the order. "Artillery going downrange. And sir, my apologies."

He stared out into the distance and identified the *Kintaro* that his wife piloted. She would be one of the first to fall. "Blake's Blood be damned. . . ."

Behind him, the roar of the Long Tom artillery shook his *Lancelot*. Lightning flickered as the spotting rounds, belching purple smoke, dropped almost directly on top of the Word of Blake line. The rain began to pour at almost the same instant. Seagrams charged up his Krupp large lasers, focusing his mind on the whine of the capacitor coils charging.

The only things that would change by the end of the day were that his long-dead wife would finally have a grave, and a part of his soul would be lost in the fight.

Choking back his raw emotions, he signaled his people. "Guards—charge!"

12

Scout Position Beta Five, East of the Bowie
Factory Ruins
Kinross, Wyatt
The Republic, Prefecture VIII
14 May 3135

Lieutenant Tooley crawled up the slope to where his team had settled in. It was a little pocket on the steep hillside, a perfect place to hide. A lone tree hugged the hill, gnarled and twisting upward. At its base, a small boulder jutted outward, and around that grew a clump of ground brush, one of the few bushes growing on the grassy hills. The nook in the hillside gave a commanding view of the surrounding hills and deep, flat-bottomed valleys.

Tooley opened the enhanced camouflaged Guila suit covering that draped over his head and body and a fine yellow-green powder, pollen, blew away in the breeze. Under the wrap he wore light body armor consisting of a chest plate and coverings for his thighs plus a heavily padded helmet with built-in comm and enhanced range-detection gear. The wrap was designed to reduce his in-frared signature and improve his ability to blend in with his environment. The nanosensors in the cloak sensed the background and light levels and adjusted the preprinted camouflage pattern in the wrap to match. It was not a perfect system; troops wearing Guila suits still were visi-ble, but they were able to sneak forward with a better chance of avoiding detection.

Corporal Pusaltari, already in position, gave him a quick nod in lieu of a salute. This wasn't the place for formalities. Tooley nodded back and elbow-crawled his way to where the corporal lay in the brush, scanning the horizon using Falcon-Is Model B enhanced sighting gear. These electronic binoculars gave him a commanding view of the area.

"What do you have, Corporal?"

"Cats and a nasty head cold, sir," he replied, handing over the Falcon-Is. Tooley took off his helmet and put it on the ground next to him, then leaned forward into the brush, staring out through the low growth.

Pusaltari wasn't kidding. The Spirit Cats were on the ground and deployed. He saw their DropShip, a massive, spherical *Union-C* class. "Range, one-point seven-eight kilometers. *Union*-class ship is typical Clan combat trans-port," he commented softly. This one was a dull gray color, with white streaks on the four support-strut legs that held it up. Its bays and drop-ramps were open and extended, and the Spirit Cats were deploying their equip-ment. As soon as they had pinpointed the Cats' landing zone, the legate, prodded by Knight Holt, had deployed pickets and monitors.

The Cats didn't seem to be in a hurry to go anywhere. There was no evidence of the rapid, focused deployment Tooley would have expected. He was a seasoned combat veteran, having served in the Hastati Sentinels and "re-tired" to the Wyatt Militia in order to serve his home planet. He'd been in enough battles in his life to know that most deployments were accomplished quickly and with the goal of being highly mobile. This one was not. The Spirit Cats were on the ground, moving slowly, practically milling around the base of the DropShip.

Kinross was to the east of him, behind him. No units were heading in that direction. Instead, they were fanning out to the west. There was nothing for them there but the contaminated zone, and that area had been abandoned for decades. The zone wasn't particularly dangerous, but the government had ordered long ago that the area of radioactive contamination left by the Jihad was best avoided.

Tooley felt in one of his hip packs under the armor plating and pulled out a small tube. "Pollen getting to you, too?"

"Always does at this time of the year," Pusaltari replied, wiping his nose on the sleeve of his Guila suit.

"Been there and done that. Squirt a dab of this in each nostril," the lieutenant said, handing him the tiny tube.

"Decongestant?"

"Jalapeno pepper juice," Tooley replied with a toothy grin.

"You trying to kill me, sir?" Pusaltari asked jokingly.

"It'll get your nose to run. I used to use it under my eyes when I was on fourth-watch sentry duty. Anything to help you stay awake."

The corporal nodded and squirted a painful glob of the clear gel into each nostril, tears springing to his eyes as the juice did its work. "What are they up to, sir?" Pusaltari asked.

Tooley reached for the small welded pocket positioned right over his heart on his armored chest plate. Inside it was a small brown stub, the remains of a cigar that had been with him for a long time. He stuck it in the corner of his mouth, but didn't light it. This particular stub had nothing to do with smoking, and everything to do with tradition and superstition. "Beats the shit out of me," he cursed, shifting the cigar to the right side of his mouth as he talked. "Did you get their numbers?"

"Some. The gear they deployed on the far side of the DropShip was next to impossible to scan."

"Let's see what they've got," Tooley said, taking the noteputer from the corporal and thumb-scrolling through the list. "A *Warhammer IIC*, a *Black Hawk*, and a Behemoth? You might get the idea that they plan on staying a while, wouldn't you?"

The corporal smiled. "I'm pretty sure I also picked up Elemental armor and at least one IndustrialMech."

"How's the radiation level here?"

Pusaltari waved his hand side-to-side in a cutting motion. "Minimal background radiation on this end of the zone. We could stay here for weeks—and so could the Cats."

"That's all we need. You send this back to the base yet?" he queried.

"No, sir."

Tooley handed back the noteputer. "You'd better do it. Tell the legate and Knight Holt that the Cats don't seem interested in us right now. The heading that they are on will take them to the ruins of the old Bowie factory." He rolled to his back on the hillside and held up his hand to block out the light of the sun. "If the Spirit Cats want to go and play in that radioactive waste pile, then I say let them."

Knight Holt sat at the holotable, which was projecting a miniature layout of the terrain where the Spirit Cat DropShip had landed. The detail was fine enough to show a five-kilometer area surrounding the DropShip, complete with points of light where her pickets had been posted.

As soon as she had been able to pinpoint the vicinity of the Spirit Cat landing zone, she had ordered the Wyatt Militia infantry to deploy. Their goal was simple: try to learn what the Spirit Cats had brought with them, and their target. Everything they had gotten so far was confusing.

Legate Singh slumped slightly in his chair, his eyes looking a little glazed from the painkillers he was still taking. A bandage the same color as his skin decorated the right side of his brow, mute testament to the result of his losing battle with the Raiden battlearmor. He watched the blinking green light that indicated the position of Scout Beta Five on the hillside above the Spirit Cat DropShip; then he glanced over at Alexi Holt.

"Knight Holt, you know more about the Spirit Cats than the rest of us. Can you explain their behavior?"

She stared at the display, hoping some sort of insight would jump out at her, but that didn't happen. "The most likely explanation for their arrival is that the Spirit Cats are following a spiritual vision or quest. As for their interest in the factory ruins—I don't know. It doesn't give them any sort of tactical advantage."

"Given the radiation levels near those ruins, they won't be there long," Singh replied.

"Well, their 'Mechs could remain there a long time without suffering any ill effect," she replied. "But I think you're right, they won't stay." She paused, then continued thoughtfully. "I have seen intelligence documents reporting that the Spirit Cats have visited ruins created by the Jihad on other planets. Given their general level of mysticism and spirituality, my guess would be that they're paying their respects to the victims."

The legate shifted in his seat. "That's very interesting, Knight Holt. But I spoke with the governor a short time ago and his official position is that they are violating the sovereignty of Wyatt and The Republic of the Sphere. He asked me to pose this question; 'What is our Knight Errant going to do about this violation?' I must admit I'm curious about your strategy now that they are here." The legate was still challenging her, but at the moment he seemed genuinely interested in her answer.

The governor made it sound so simple: come up with a strategy for dealing with a Clan force that had decided to drop onto their planet. Unfortunately, the situation was a little more complex than just the Clan threat. The mercenary group that had attacked the ComStar compound had yet to be tracked down and apprehended, which meant they were still a threat to Kinross. Which meant she couldn't leave the capital unprotected in order to deal with the Spirit Cats.

Deal with the Clan force, but make sure that Kinross is protected in case the mercs make another move. Damned if I do, damned if I don't.

She'd been considering alternatives for hours, but the list of options kept getting shorter. So far, the Spirit Cats had ignored all their attempts at communication. In order to force the issue, she would have to confront and attack them. Quite frankly, most of the planetary militias that chose this option had not been pleased with the results. As with all Clans, the Cats were formidable fighters. Against mostly untested militia, they were more than a match.

She rose to her feet. She needed to play the role for which she had trained. "I'm not too enthusiastic about the proposal I'm about to make, but I don't see an alternative."

"Go ahead," Legate Singh prodded.

"I'll go out and attempt to parlay with the Spirit Cats."

"Negotiate with them?" Singh asked, his voice rising an octave.

"I've dealt with Clansmen before. One of the few things they respect about the people of the Inner Sphere is those who make a sincere attempt to honor their traditions. I will meet their commander and issue a batchall, an invitation to a combat trial. Their presence on Wyatt will be the prize. If they win, they stay and do what they feel they need to do. If they lose, they leave." She stared at the legate, who seemed stunned by her words. His mouth hung open, as if the right words to respond to her statement simply didn't exist.

Alexi didn't wait for him to find his voice again. "Right now we don't know why they're here. If we manage the combat trial properly, we'll learn the reason they're here, and maybe even their objectives. This option also leaves the militia protecting Kinross in case the mercs raise their ugly heads again."

"You are going to risk yourself by going alone?"

She nodded. *That's what separates you and I, Legate Singh.* "It's in my job description. 'A Knight of the Sphere protects the citizenry, if necessary with his life.'

But don't worry. I'm not sacrificing myself. A single trial combat just represents the best, most logical choice—the least amount of risk for the largest number of people."

The warehouse of Universal Exporters Ltd. squatted in one of the seediest sections of the oldest part of Kinross proper. It was a run-down structure that appeared to the casual observer to be nothing more than a storage facility way past its prime. Vines wound their way up to small windows on the upper floor that shed minimal light to the interior. No one on the street would remember the last time they saw a vehicle enter the building, though there had been people going in and out for months.

Reo stood at the personnel entrance door, casually rocking back and forth on the balls of his feet as the security camera hidden in the brickwork scanned and validated his identity. A buzzing sound unlocked the apparently unsophisticated entry system, and Reo walked into the warehouse.

The outside of the building was unremarkable, but the interior had the look of every military post that Reo had ever seen. Overhead cranes draped myomer hoisting cables alongside gantries where the 'Mechs and vehicles were berthed. The 'Mechs grabbed his attention, three-story-high machines that could raze a city block in minutes. Reo had never seen all the elements of Cut-Throat Chaffee's military assets assembled together in one place, and it was impressive.

Rutger Chaffee had been busy over the last three years building this little operation for Jacob Bannson. Reo had helped coordinate the transport of the 'Mechs, which had been the trickiest part; most had been sent in separate shipments labeled AGRICULTURAL EQUIPMENT. The rest of the gear had come from Chaffee's other sources. Not counting infantry, there looked like nearly a company's worth of armor and 'Mech assets. A fair match for the entire Wyatt Militia, if it came down to a slugging match.

Chaffee, wearing a military jumpsuit with the rank of captain on his shoulder, swaggered over to Jones, looking like anything but a regulation military leader. "Nice of you to make it, Jones," he said with a thin smile. "I've gotta tell you, I'm a little pissed off at you right now."

"*You're* pissed off at *me*?" Reo responded. "That's funny as hell."

"Your report said that the last time you saw Tucker Harwell, he was in the ComStar compound," Chaffee said belligerently. "He wasn't there."

"What were you thinking, Chaffee, striking at ComStar that way? You could have damaged the HPG. In case you missed the news, Sorenson has a Knight Errant on planet. Do you really want her breathing down our collective necks? I thought you were going to wait until the Spirit Cats duked it out with the militia. You jumped the gun." Reo kept his voice low, but the intensity of his words carried. Even the technicians moving crates on the far side of the room seemed to pause for a moment. Few people talked to Rutger Chaffee the way Reo did.

"You of all people know that plans change. I was following orders, just like you. I received a coded message from the boss himself, and you don't question Jacob Bannson. He says jump, you say, 'How high?' Mr. Bannson wanted us to grab Harwell, so that's what we were trying to do, no thanks to you. And the HPG was never at risk."

Reo was tired and frustrated. Since the attack on the compound, someone in authority had made a guess at a connection between the mercenary attackers, Reo, and Jacob Bannson. As a result, he was spending too much of his time evading capture by the police, and it was starting to wear on him. "You should have told me that you were planning the operation. I could have confirmed Tucker's position before you went in. Hell, I eat with the kid from time to time. I could have arranged for a simple kidnapping."

Chaffee stiffened and his face darkened in anger. "I don't clear my ops with you or anyone else, Jones. Get that straight."

Reo took a half step backward and forced a conciliatory note into his voice. He wondered if Chaffee was even working for Bannson anymore, or if he was just pursuing his own agenda. Reo's information-gathering worked both ways, and the intel he'd been receiving about Bannson lately was very interesting. If the rumors were true, Jacob Bannson was currently on Sian cementing his relationship with House Liao by marrying into that crazy family. In Reo's opinion, Bannson was going to be way less available to his minions for awhile. But this was not the time or the place for a confrontation with Chaffee. "I was just trying to say that I could have helped if I had known the plan."

"Instead, you let us down," Chaffee snapped. "Now try to make it up to me. Where do you think they've taken Harwell?"

Reo already knew. He just hadn't had the chance to file a report today. "I've confirmed that Tucker Harwell is in the protective custody of Legate Singh and our visiting Knight Errant. From what I've gathered, he's in the militia HQ."

"Singh's not a problem," Rutger chuckled. "He almost wet himself when our squad entered the building. According to the media, he emptied his weapon at our forces at point-blank range attempting to defend the building. But I saw the battlerom from the Raiden suit that knocked him out. He was shaking like a leaf. One badly aimed shot, and then a whack upside the head."

Reo already knew the media had exaggerated the legate's performance under fire; his public image had always been his strongest suit. "I agree that the legate is just a paper tiger. But Alexi Holt can't be dismissed so easily. She's got the skills and experience to cause us some real trouble."

"I'm less worried about her since the Spirit Cats made planet fall," Chaffee replied, watching a pair of techs paint a Fox hover scout with a dull gray-and-black urban-combat camouflage pattern. "Our Knight has more than enough to keep her pretty head busy."

Use that tone with Alexi, and she'd snap you like a dry twig. "So you're thinking of striking at the militia headquarters?"

Chaffee's expression turned sour. "I don't think so. Not that we couldn't pull it off if we wanted to. My troops are seasoned mercenaries, not weekend warriors like the militia. But I don't like the odds of going up against a heavily fortified and well-protected bunker."

"What about your orders from Bannson?"

Chaffee shrugged. "He's not here, so that gives me room to maneuver. I just have to get this kid. I was hoping to do a snatch-and-grab from ComStar. That didn't work, but that doesn't mean that another chance won't present itself. For now, we lay low and exercise some patience."

"What do you need from me?" Reo asked.

"I want you out on the streets. Find out what you can about how the militia is planning on handling the Spirit Cats, now that they're on the ground."

Corporal Pusaltari adjusted the Falcon-Is rangefinders and squinted, trying to get the best possible view. The Spirit Cats were sticking to their camp, close perimeter patrols of their landing zone constituting the bulk of their activity. They had launched a Crow scout that had buzzed nearby twice, and he was convinced that they had spotted him on the second pass. Pusaltari had grabbed his assault weapon and prepared to face a strafing run, but it had never come. Pusaltari was just about to open fire first when Lieutenant Tooley reached over and toggled his safety. He figured that's what separated him and the lieutenant—experience.

The action he was focused on at the moment was a BattleMech slowly making its way across the valley toward the DropShip. He knew the 'Mech, even if he couldn't see the heraldic banner on its torso that identified it as belonging to a Knight of the Sphere. It was the only *Black Knight* class 'Mech he had ever seen up close. Its humanoid form moved fluidly, almost gracefully, a testament to the piloting skills of the person in the cockpit. As it walked, it left deep footprints in the sod, a trail stretching back toward Kinross.

"Lieutenant, you'd better take a look at this." Tooley

rolled over from his position on the other side of the tree and re-focused the corporal's binoculars for himself. "Creeping crudstunk," was all he said.

"Any idea what she's doing, sir?"

"Since Paladin Ezekiel Crow betrayed The Republic by abandoning the Highlanders on Northwind and then fighting against them on Terra, I'm suspicious—anything could be possible. But I assume she's going in to parlay with them."

"Parlay?"

"Negotiate," he said, handing back the rangefinders. "Signal HQ and let them know what we've seen, just in case."

"Yessir," Pusaltari replied, wiping his nose on his sleeve again. "You don't think she's going to negotiate our surrender do you, sir?"

Lieutenant Tooley gave him a grim smile. "I haven't spent much time with the Knight Errant. She's a little above my station. But I've seen her on maneuvers, and so have you—so you know she's a fighter. I know this, too: they offered to put her up in the Royale when she came on planet, and she opted to stay in the BOQ. Alexi Holt is regular people, and regular people don't sell each other out."

"I hope you're right," the corporal replied, keying in the wrist-comm system codes for access to the militia transmission frequency.

"Me, too," Tooley said.

13

Spirit Cat Landing Zone
East of the Bowie Factory Ruins
The Republic, Prefecture VIII
14 May 3135

The shadow of the DropShip crept across Miss Direction, and still Alexi Holt stood facing the ship. She had powered down her BattleMech, dismounted and waited for the Spirit Cats to acknowledge that she casually had walked up to their LZ. The warriors and technicians performing their various tasks around the DropShip ramps eyed her, but they showed no other reaction to her arrival.

As the shadow fell over her, the chill in the air caused goose bumps to rise on her arms and legs. MechWarriors always dressed sparingly because 'Mechs generated such intense heat in the cockpit. She had left her neurohelmet in the cockpit along with her cooling vest. That left her in shorts, short boots, and a T-shirt. She usually carried a pistol in a holster on her hip, but that would have been contrary to the message she wanted to send here. She had come to speak with the Spirit Cats, not fight them. Given the raw firepower of the DropShip looming over her, it seemed a good choice.

By now Alexi was tempted to accost one of the warriors and demand to meet with their commanding officer. She had been waiting for more than two hours already, but she managed to keep her patience. She had dealt with the Clans before, so she knew that the Clans had their own way of dealing with negotiations, and ceremony was integral to their culture. She wondered if the test of patience was something they had picked up from their association with the Draconis Combine.

Finally, a solitary man approached her from the camp. He wore a dull, green-gray jumpsuit that did not hide his muscular build, and his reddish-brown hair was cut short all over. On his belt he wore what appeared to be a hunting knife on one hip, and a small leather bag on the other. His face appeared to be chiseled out of stone, offering her no emotion whatsoever. She maintained parade rest as he approached to within a meter of her and stopped. He surveyed her BattleMech for a long moment, then locked his light blue eyes with hers.

"A *Black Knight* is a BattleMech worthy of much honor. It is said that many served during the first Star League. Yours is particularly interesting."

"Why is that?"

The man offered her nothing but his words. "It bears the markings of a Knight Errant of The Republic of the Sphere. That makes you either a thief or a potentially worthy adversary."

"I am no thief," she replied flatly.

"And you have walked into our camp alone," he nodded once. "That must make you a Knight. How did you know that I would not order my forces to attack you as you approached within range?"

Faith . . . and hope. She didn't dare say those words out loud. When she replied, she was careful to avoid contractions, knowing that the Clans considered that they weakened the language. "I have dealt with the Clans before, and am somewhat familiar with their traditions.

I knew that no Clan warrior would attack a lone BattleMech approaching on low power. No honor would be
gained in such a victory, *quiaff?*" She added the "query-
affirmative" of the Clans' language, to underscore her
experience with their culture.

"*Aff*, Knight Errant. Well spoken. I am Star Captain
Cox of the Spirit Cats. I bid you welcome."

"I am Knight Errant Alexi Holt of The Republic.
Thank you for your welcome." She bowed her head
slightly as a gesture of respect.

"I have a fire on the other side of the landing zone.
Join me, Knight Alexi, and we can discuss what would
prompt a Knight of the Sphere to come to this place."
Like most trueborn Clan warriors, he did not acknowledge her last name. For the Clans, a last name, what
they designated as a Bloodname, was a prize to be won
in a combat trial, not something provided simply by birth.
He turned back toward his fire, and she joined him, walking a half step behind him and to his side.

The fire was small, surrounded by stones that some
member of the lower caste had dug up and positioned
in a circle. A few feet from the fire lay two dull-green
blankets, opened on the grass. No chairs, as she had expected. Star Captain Cox sat cross-legged on one blanket.
Alexi sat on the other blanket, only three feet away and
on the same side of the fire.

For a moment she said nothing. She had many questions to ask, but Cox was not likely to reveal his purpose
on Wyatt just because she asked. She would learn more
if she kept quiet and let him talk. He unhooked his canteen from his hip and held it out to her. She took it,
drank the warm water and handed it back. She found
the silence uncomfortable. Her eyes drifted down to the
leather pouch that hung from the Star captain's belt, and
it gave her an idea for opening the conversation.

"I work for a Paladin named Kelson Sorenson. You
have heard of him, *quiaff?*"

Cox nodded once. "*Aff*, I have heard of him. We give
Knights greater regard than others, and so seek to learn
about the Knights and Paladins of The Republic."

She wanted to smile. "We also seek knowledge of those whom we respect. The Spirit Cats are said to be kindred to Clan Nova Cat. Do your Clans share traditions?"

"Our customs and traditions are the same as and yet different from the Nova Cats," he said, revealing nothing. "Those who confuse us with our kindred would be making a mistake. In the end, we are our own people."

"Do you keep the Clan tradition of collecting vineers?"

Cox glanced down to the pouch at his belt. *"Aff."*

"As I understand it, these are the relics of your greatest fights. If I may inquire, what is your most treasured vineer?" Though vineer was an ancient derivative of the word "souvenir," she avoided using that word because most Clansmen reacted violently to any suggestion that their traditions or language were a debased version of a Terran concept.

The Star captain unfastened the pouch from his belt and opened it. She could tell that the pouch held several objects, things that he would consider important in his life. After digging in the small pouch with his large fingers, he finally pulled out a small red button and handed it to her.

Alexi examined it. *A firing stud of some sort?* "It is a firing stud from a joystick, *quiaff?*"

"Aff," he replied. "I took it from the 'Mech of a warrior named Jackel in a combat trial. During the fight, one of my shots, a gauss rifle round, slammed into his cockpit. He was killed instantly." Alexi handed the button back to him, and he stared at the red piece of plastic broodingly. Then, carefully, he replaced it in his vineer pouch.

"You won the trial?" she asked.

"Aff. I won. But I killed someone that I cared for a great deal. Jackel and I were raised together as sibkin. We had fought many times at each other's side. He had saved my life. As a child, I had saved his. Our paths were woven together like the strong strands that make up a rope." There was a longing in his eyes, as if he

were hoping that speaking of his former friend would somehow summon him to the fire.

A darkness hooded his expression. "My eagerness to fight took his life. We fought a Bloodname trial that day." He glared at her for a moment. "I had intended my shot to disable the arm of his *Summoner*, but it did not. He moved at the last possible moment and spoiled my aim. I was a good fighter, but not good enough that day to adjust my shot, not so quickly. The Galaxy commander awarded the Bloodname to me, but I refused to accept it." His voice became deep, rumbling like the threat of thunder.

"I have never heard of a Clan warrior refusing a Bloodname," Alexi said with wonder in her voice.

"As I said, our customs and traditions are different. Few have refused a Bloodname, but it is allowed. Galaxy Commander Kev Rosse told me the Clan would reserve the Bloodname for me. To possess such a name is a great honor, and it is often won at a high price. I will know when I have performed a deed that redeems my blemish sufficiently to allow me to claim the Bloodname. Our leader believes that there will be a time when I find redemption in my heart for what had happened. For now I remain Cox—nothing more, nothing less." He returned his gaze to the fire and the silence returned.

Alexi could tell there was more to this Spirit Cat than met the eye, and she was determined to tread carefully with him. "The fire is nice," she said, shifting her position slightly. As the sun set, a cool breeze seemed to rustle through the valley. "Relaxing."

"Our fire helps us to honor those who died here in the Jihad," Cox replied. He picked up a stick resting on the edge of the stone circle and tossed it toward the center of the fire, sending two or three glowing embers upward into the early evening air.

"I was not aware that any members of your Clan fought on this world."

Cox looked at her solemnly. "They did not. That does not mean we should not honor those who did die here at the hands of a common foe. Spirit Cats often come to these places, the burial grounds of the innocents, the battlefields of the honored dead. We believe such places give us unique insight into the matters of the here-and-now. For example, you are wondering why we have come to Wyatt, *quiaff?*" Clansmen were fond of rhetorical questions.

"*Aff,*" she replied.

"What would you say, Knight Alexi, if I told you that I did not know for sure myself?" The Star captain gave her a coy grin.

"Star Captain, I know a little about the Spirit Cats. They do not travel to a place for no reason at all."

Cox surprised her by laughing. "That is one thing about my people," he agreed. "We do not do anything in life without a purpose, without a reason."

"Then I will ask," she said carefully, "why have the Spirit Cats come to Wyatt?"

The Star captain turned from her to watch the flickering flames of the fire and said nothing for a moment. "We always have regarded the Knights of the Sphere as honorable warriors, a trait we share with you. Today, you have supported that belief by showing respect for our traditions. Even so, I cannot simply tell you why we have traveled to this planet."

"Because I am not of your people."

He nodded, still staring into the flames. "You are not Spirit Cat. You would have no context for my words."

"Star Captain Cox," she replied courteously. "You must know that by landing on Wyatt, you have created a problem that we must share. Your Clan is violating the sovereignty of this world, and I and others like me have sworn to protect The Republic from such actions. I have no desire to fight you without first understanding why I must fight you. I hope you can understand this."

"Knight Alexi, the reactivation of the Wyatt hyperpulse generator reached beyond ComStar's network. It has stirred our leader, Kev Rosse. I myself was awakened on the fifth of May with a vision of a star burning bright in the hands of a Lightbringer."

Visions were an important aspect of the life of every

Spirit Cat warrior. Alexi didn't place any weight on them, but these warriors considered visions a pivotal part of their lives. "And you realized when you arrived in-system that the fifth was when the HPG was activated. I might tell you that it was coincidence that you had a dream that woke you at the same time the HPG went active."

"You could speak the words, but I would not hear them," Cox replied, turning away from the fire and locking his gaze on hers again.

She understood. Alexi didn't agree, but that was irrelevant. "Why come here first? If your interest is the HPG, why not land nearer the compound?"

Cox smiled wryly. "Imagine what would have been the result of us landing at the local spaceport—a Spirit Cat DropShip debarking personnel and equipment. What would have been the response of the local militia? You and I both know they would have been forced to attack, in an urban environment where the count of pointless deaths and waste of resources would have been high."

Alexi smiled back. "You are right, of course." The images painted by his words were impossible to dismiss. "And I seek to avoid that same outcome should you go to Kinross."

The Star captain waved his hand toward the hills that surrounded them, now darkening as the sun dropped lower. "We came here first to honor the spirits of those who died at the hands of the Word of Blake. We hoped those spirits might shed light on the visions of myself and our Galaxy commander. So far, they have not. That means that the answers we seek may be in Kinross."

"If you go to the city," she said in a low tone, "we will be forced to fight you."

Cox responded immediately. "If that is what happens, I assure you it will be a glorious fight, one worthy of a line in The Remembrance of the Clans."

"Perhaps," she said, "there is another way."

For the first time since she had arrived, she had obviously caught him off guard. Before he could ask for more detail, she explained. "Clan warriors fight combat trials.

Rather than us both risking waste of our troops and forces, we could fight a Trial of Possession for safe passage in Kinross."

Cox pondered her words for a long moment. "Single combat?"

"Yes—*aff*," she corrected herself.

"Only a Knight Errant would be considered honorable enough to fight such a challenge. Far too many times have the Clans faced individuals who corrupted our traditions to their own advantage. I would only accept a challenge to fight *you* in combat."

"Agreed."

"And the terms of this trial?"

"If you win, you gain access to Kinross in order to pursue your vision. We would not cede ownership of the city, merely allow access to it. Should we—er—I win, the Spirit Cats leave Wyatt altogether."

Cox shook his head. "*Neg*, Knight Alexi. If you win, the Spirit Cats will not attempt to enter Kinross. However, we will depart Wyatt at our own discretion and timing. Those terms are fair."

"I accept these terms, Star Captain."

"Our venue will be out here, in these hills," he spread his arms apart.

She looked around. The choice of venue was Cox's, and she wished she had thought through this part of her plan more thoroughly. She might have been able to suggest terrain that gave her some sort of advantage. Instead, she replied, "This land has been scarred by the Jihad. Is it good to injure it again?"

Cox cocked his left eyebrow at her words. "You surprise me, Knight Alexi. You speak as if you have Spirit Cat blood in your veins, if these hills so speak to you. However, I think a single-combat trial will not stir the dead here."

"Who will fight for your Spirit Cats?" *As if I have to ask.*

Star Captain Cox said solemnly, "One does not lead from the rear."

"I must discuss this plan with the civilian government.

I believe I can convince them that this is the best way to proceed, as it poses the least amount of risk to the city and infrastructure."

"I suggest we fight in two days' time," he said. "And during that time, I ask that in the spirit of honor, you withdraw those troops you have watching us in the hills. With a combat trial pending between us, there is no need for spying. I assure you that I will fight with honor, and we prefer privacy in which to perform our rituals of preparation."

"Agreed," she said, casting a glance over her shoulder. Out there somewhere were Lieutenant Tooley's pickets, probably watching her right now.

"Well bargained and done," he said, extending his hand to her. She took it and they exchanged a firm handshake.

She had much to think about on her journey back to the city.

=== 14 ===

Wyatt Militia Headquarters
Kinross, Wyatt
The Republic, Prefecture VIII
14 May 3135

Tucker watched Alexi climb down the rungs of the ladder hanging down her 'Mech's right side. The noisy chaos of the 'Mech bay did not seem to reach her—the hissing, pounding, metallic clanking and muffled shouts that merged into white noise. Her lithe frame always conveyed barely contained energy, and he caught some of that energy as she dropped down the last two steps next to the massive pad-foot of the BattleMech.

There was a lot to this Knight Errant that appealed to him. Part of it was the way she carried herself. While he was caught up in the events surrounding his bringing Wyatt back in contact with the rest of The Republic, those events seemed to control him. It wasn't that way with her. She seemed to create circumstances rather than react to them.

He wished he had that ability. The last few days had

been a blur. He wasn't sleeping well. Some of it was due to the snoring of one of the other technicians bunked with him—he'd already given up his sort of private space—but most of it was because he couldn't stop thinking about the attack against the compound that had cost ComStar the lives of good people. Patricia had done as much as she could to ease his conscience, but what seemed to help the most was just keeping busy, and working on the mobile HQ accomplished that in spades.

The vehicle itself was amazing; not just because it was a working antique, but also because its impressive capabilities had been ignored for so long. The onboard battle computer and communication systems were still considered top of the line, even by current standards. With these systems, an officer or operator could pull in data feeds from any friendly vehicle or 'Mech on the field and develop a tactical and strategic view of the battlefield and the enemy strength. Fire missions and other orders could be centrally coordinated. The comm system could be used to jam enemy transmissions and communications. If the comms were properly adjusted, Tucker felt that he could even jam enemy targeting and tracking systems, if the 'Mechs or vehicles were close enough to the old war wagon. Its ECM suite would make the HQ vehicle difficult to lock onto for indirect fire, as well. The old girl offered the militia some wonderful advantages. Trying his best to seem casual about the Knight's return, Tucker leaned against the exterior of the HQ, belatedly remembering that a crew of techs had given the HQ a fresh coat of paint just that morning, and it was probably still a little tacky. Fortunately, the arrival of Alexi Holt had everyone's attention.

She had taken only two steps away from the *Black Knight* before Legate Singh appeared beside her. Tucker had learned a little bit more about the legate during the days spent working on the mobile HQ. The militia maintenance team working with him had given the ComStar personnel the cold shoulder at first, but as they saw system after system come online in the old battlewagon, they warmed up to him and his team.

According to the two members of the motor pool who were helping replace the power transfer relays, Singh's family had come to Wyatt as refugees from some other part of the Inner Sphere and had risen quickly through society based on the success of its specialized line of work—hauling toxic wastes. A shrewd man, the legate's father had secured numerous government contracts and made his fortune: a fortune that he invested in the promotion of his son Edward.

A mechanic named Darrell who helped him re-run the fiber optics to the extended long-range sensor array was happy to speculate on how Edward Singh became legate. Darrell was also quite willing to expand on the changing perception of the legate based on the comparison between Singh and Knight Holt. Among the militia members, most considered Singh to be a nice guy, friendly and cordial if not a dynamic leader. Until Alexi Holt arrived on Wyatt, the militia thought they had a pretty fair military commander. Now that they had witnessed her leadership skills and experienced the effectiveness of her decision making—they understood how bad they had had it.

From where he stood, he could see that the discussion between the legate and the Knight Errant was picking up in intensity. Another officer, Lieutenant Johannson, stopped at the periphery of the debate and was listening in. As Tucker watched, a number of other people— militia soldiers and officers, even ComStar techs, moved closer to hear what was happening. Tucker immediately decided to join the gathering crowd.

"The governor will not like this plan and will not back it," Tucker heard the legate complain.

Alexi did not seem moved. "With all due respect, Legate, perhaps the governor would like to face them—alone."

"You should have ordered them off Wyatt," he persisted.

The Knight Errant flashed a contemptuous grin. *Order the Spirit Cats?* "I would never presume to give orders to Clan warriors. You knew my plan."

"I knew the plan you chose to discuss with me," Singh

seethed. "I had no idea what terms you were going to present to them. The risks are too great. I don't feel bound to honor what you've negotiated."

Alexi laughed, which somehow reassured Tucker. "Hell of a time for you to change your mind, Legate Singh. What would you have us do, attack the Spirit Cats?"

"I'm not afraid of them," he returned, false bravado ringing in his voice. Even Tucker flinched at his words. *Are you insane?*

"You should be," the Knight of the Sphere replied seriously. "This isn't like facing a bunch of armed mercenaries. These are *Clan warriors.* For generations they have been bred for war, and are trained from birth to fight and win."

She paused, drew a deep breath and exhaled as she straightened to her full height. "If you betray the terms and conditions I have negotiated," she stated formally, "I would be forced to stand against the militia."

Tucker was caught off guard by her words. He thought he understood why she spoke so passionately, but for a Knight to threaten to stand against a legate—that seemed extreme. Singh wiped perspiration from his face in a nervous gesture before he responded. "You would fight against us?"

"If you betray my word to the Spirit Cats, you'll be unleashing them on Kinross or anywhere else on Wyatt they choose to attack. Clansmen are oath-bound to fight by a clearly defined set of rules. You violate that honor, and it's like setting loose a pack of wild hounds on the civilian population and anyone who opposes them. Your militia would be wiped out. Would I fight you? Yes, I'd fight you to prevent you from bringing total war on your people and having them die at the hands of a Clan." She spoke with unmistakable conviction.

"They wouldn't dare," Singh said weakly.

She nodded once, decisively. "They would."

Tucker believed her. He knew the history of the Clans, how they were the descendants of the Star League Army led into exile by the great General Aleksandr Kerensky.

The founders of the Clans had tried to ensure that they were an honorable people, but when crossed, they could be savage. Tucker remembered reading an account of an incident involving the city of Edo on the planet Turtle Bay during the Clans' initial invasion of the Inner Sphere decades ago. The local population had risen up against one Clan, the Smoke Jaguars. In response to that show of defiance, the Clan had used their WarShips to blast the city into slag. Even the river running through the city boiled to steam under the bombardment. He knew that history had recorded other examples of Clan excesses; these were not a people to be trifled with.

"What if you lose?" Singh asked.

"We honor the terms I've negotiated, to the letter. The militia will abandon Kinross and let the Spirit Cats enter and depart it as they see fit."

The legate turned until he could pick out Tucker's face in the crowd. He pointed at him as if wielding a dagger. "And what about Mr. Harwell, whom you insisted on bringing here? What happens to him?"

"He goes with us," Alexi said, casting Tucker a reassuring glance. "The terms I've negotiated are for the militia to leave. As of yesterday, Tucker Harwell is temporarily attached to the Wyatt Militia."

I am? Tucker didn't remember agreeing to anything of the sort. He opened his mouth to protest, then he thought about what she was saying. If being part of the Wyatt Militia kept him alive, he was happy to have been signed up.

"You are gambling with our planet," the legate added. "All for the life of a man who doesn't even belong to this world."

She shook her head. "This isn't about Adept Harwell. The Spirit Cats didn't even ask about him. They are here for something else. If the option is taking an untested planetary militia up against them or letting them pass through, I say let them pass. Besides, there is one thing you have overlooked, Legate."

"And what is that?"

She grinned a white smile. "I have no intention of losing."

The gathering in the 'Mech bay broke up almost as quickly as it gathered. Tucker, Patricia, and Paula Kursk left the rest of their team working on the mobile HQ and offered Lieutenant Johannson their assistance on reconstructing the IndustrialMechs. He accepted their offer so quickly and graciously that Tucker was immediately suspicious of what he was getting into. When he saw the challenge facing him, he understood Johannson's reaction.

IndustrialMechs operated on the same principles as BattleMechs, but were not built for battle. These two creations were being converted to war machines, but to say they were BattleMechs was akin to commandeering a bulldozer and declaring that it was now to be referred to as a tank. Equipped with internal combustion engines, these civilian-use vehicles generated comparatively low levels of electricity to power their myomer muscles for movement. They were strong, but very slow, and ungainly when they moved. These two machines had been stripped of their irradiated exteriors and new sheet metal, worrisomely thin, was being spot-welded to the frames.

The modified ConstructionMech didn't look much different at first glance. Its cockpit was low and exposed. The standard-equipment roll bars had been covered with metal plates, but the pilot's compartment was so close to the ground that small-arms fire could easily kill the driver. The 'Mech's arms were huge, nearly the size of traditional excavators. One was a scoop bucket, which had been modified with spikes that would allow it to rip and gouge at anything that got close to it. The other featured a massive set of clamps used for lifting. If these hydraulic monstrosities locked onto an opposing 'Mech or vehicle, they were bound to inflict some damage—if the pilot could last long enough to accomplish it.

The MiningMech seemed to show the most promise;

it at least looked like a military vehicle. One arm had been removed to make room for armor plating to be welded in around the cockpit. The burrowing right arm was in the process of being replaced with what appeared to be an autocannon salvaged from some other vehicle. The dump-trucklike back of the gray-green beast was filled with long tubes, wiring and maintenance people.

"The MiningMech is our priority right now," Johannson said. "Those missile tubes are a one-shot affair, but wiring them to usable cockpit controls is beyond my people's skills. Anything you can do to lend a hand is appreciated." Tucker began to walk toward the massive 'Mech, his mind already puzzling over the challenge, when a beep at his wrist caught his attention. Glancing at his personal communicator, he saw the face on the tiny digital display and immediately felt his jaw tighten.

"Tucker," the voice said.

"Reo," he replied tersely. He had ignored his sister's warning about Reo; now the police were looking for his friend, and he appeared to have links to Bannson's Raiders. The merc attack on the ComStar compound, apparently ordered by Jacob Bannson, still was a very raw nerve for Tucker, and all those things together made him suspicious of his friend—and that made him feel even worse. "I thought the police were looking for you."

"They are," came the casual reply.

Patricia noticed his agitation and headed his way. He shook his head and took a step away from her, letting her know he wanted some privacy. "I just want to know one thing, Reo: were you involved in what happened at the compound?"

Jones shook his head on the tiny wrist display. "No. The people running the show for Bannson kept me out of the loop. Apparently, they don't trust me, either." Tucker thought he heard a note of bitterness in Reo's voice.

"People got killed." He almost added, "because of me," but didn't. Maybe, just maybe, he was past that feeling. Now wasn't the time to explore it.

"I saw that on the news," Reo replied. "I'd tell you I'm sorry, but I won't apologize for something I wasn't involved in."

"How do I know I can believe you?"

Reo frowned heavily at the words. "Listen up, Tucker. If I wanted to kidnap you, I had plenty of chances to do it without causing any collateral damage. The guy running the show for Bannson on this rock is playing his own game right now."

"But you admit to being on Bannson's payroll."

Reo nodded once. "I've never denied it. The fact is, however, I work more for myself than for Bannson. I have a lot of contacts and usually know what's going on, but that doesn't mean that everything I know gets passed on to Bannson. For example, I know about the salvage work the Militia pulled off on that fighter in the city museum two nights ago, but my report with Bannson doesn't. Nice job, by the way. I assume those missile racks they pulled from that *Chippewa* aerospace fighter will go to good use."

Was he fishing for more information or a confirmation? Tucker shook his head impatiently and ran his hand through his hair so that it all stood on end. Everyone was quick to tell him what and how to think when it came to Reo Jones, but he could form his own opinions. It was one of the few things he could control in his current situation. "What's Bannson's interest in this world, anyway?"

"Apparently, Jacob Bannson originally intended to use Wyatt as a safe house, one of a few locations he set up as places to fall back to if his plans ever totally collapsed. A fairly minor operation: smuggle in some mercenaries and gear, stockpile some money and equipment . . . your basic backup plan. But something in his strategy has changed now that you've fixed the HPG. And that's why I contacted you."

"Go on," Tucker said, carefully weighing his friend's words.

"Tucker, Bannson has ordered his forces to go after

you personally. I don't have details; like I said, they don't trust me. But I consider you a friend, and I don't want anything to happen to you."

The words hit him hard, because Reo was confirming the speculations of everyone around him. *Damn.* Tucker suddenly felt like he had a target painted on his back. "So what can I do?"

"Stick close to the Knight Errant. Unlike Legate Singh, she inspires a healthy fear in the people I'm associated with."

"I'm already doing that," Tucker replied grimly. "Anything else?"

"Even though everyone's focusing on the threat of the Spirit Cats, I don't think they represent anything close to the problems that Bannson's people could cause. Just be ready for anything. I'll warn you if I can find out their plan."

"Reo, you're putting your life at risk by going against these high-priced killers. Why not just turn yourself into the police?"

Jones laughed. "First, I have a reputation to maintain. The last thing I want to do is let it be known that a small-potatoes police force like the Kinross PD could capture me. Secondly, I'm willing to bet that you're the only person on this planet who would believe I'm telling the truth. Third, if I turn myself in, I can't keep my eyes on these guys."

Tucker heard a snort and looked around. His sister had moved up behind him and stood listening to the conversation, her arms crossed and a scowl on her face. He frowned back at her and said, "Reo, I have to go."

"Watch your backside, kid."

"You, too." Tucker shut off the communicator. Patricia opened her mouth, but he beat her to the punch. "We need to go talk to Knight Holt."

"I was just going to say that," she replied, jogging to keep up with him as he headed for the upper levels of the headquarters building. It took them ten minutes to find the Knight Errant, and Tucker said nothing to his sister the entire time. He wanted to talk, but he didn't want a debate with his sister.

They found Alexi Holt walking down one of the corridors. She had changed into a dull green jumpsuit and had tucked her hair under a cap that bore the insignia of The Republic of the Sphere. She looked more like a mechanic than a Knight Errant. The moment she saw Tucker, she stopped.

"Is something the matter, Adept Harwell?"

"You keep doing that," he replied cordially. "Call me Tucker. And to answer your question, I don't know."

Patricia butted in. "My brother just received a call from Reo Jones."

Alexi cocked her eyebrow. "I see. Well, Tucker, what did Mr. Jones have to say?"

Tucker shook his head. "Not much of use. He admits to working for Jacob Bannson, and confirmed that the mercs attacked ComStar on Bannson's behalf. And he told me Bannson's people were changing their strategy. Like you and everyone else suspected, I'm the target."

"Can he help us?" the Knight asked.

"Doubtful. I don't think he's working against us, though. I think that counts for something. Oh, and he did tell me to stick close to you."

She smiled. "Maybe Jones is smarter than I thought. At least we agree on that point."

Patricia cut in, anger coloring her voice. "That's it? You don't seem surprised or concerned that a known criminal is in contact with my brother in the middle of a crisis."

Alexi's smile abruptly disappeared. "I was just coming from the communications center," she gazed steadily at Tucker. "I anticipated that Jones might try to reach Tucker. I took the liberty of having his wrist communicator monitored. We heard the conversation live, and tried to run a trace. I'll say this for Jones. He's savvy enough to have cut off his signal before we could pinpoint him."

Tucker felt his face redden. "You bugged me?"

"Tucker. A lot of people are counting on you. Until we get you off Wyatt and to a safe place, my job is to protect you. It might seem contrary to the spirit of The Republic, but if I have to violate your privacy to accomplish that directive, I'm prepared to do it. The day after tomorrow I will face the leader of the Spirit Cats on Wyatt in single combat; not just to protect the people of Kinross; not just to minimize losses to the militia; but to make sure that you are safe. In the hopes of finding Jones, I ordered you 'bugged,' as you put it. To be honest, I also wanted to be sure you didn't do anything through lack of experience that the rest of us would regret."

There was a moment of silence that he used to think. He trusted Alexi Holt. Reo trusted her. Even his sister had grudgingly admitted that Holt was right more than once. He didn't like what the Knight had done; he particularly didn't like what she was implying about his judgment. His brain ticked through his options, and he arrived at his decision.

"I'm going with you when you face the Spirit Cats," he announced.

"Tucker," his sister began.

He interrupted her. "Patricia, this is my decision." He threw back his shoulders and faced Alexi Holt. "I'm not sure anymore who else I can trust, but I know I can trust you. If I'm a target, I'm going to be a moving target. If there's a chance that anyone else is going to get hurt or die because of me, I'm going to be there doing everything I can to prevent it. From now on, I will have a say in my own destiny."

Alexi Holt surprised him. "Frankly, Tucker, I wouldn't have it any other way. Welcome to the team."

15

Circle of Equals
East of the Bowie Factory Ruins
The Republic, Prefecture VIII
16 May 3135

The Circle of Equals that Star Captain Cox had declared for their fight was four kilometers in diameter, much larger than she expected. Alexi's first instinct was to challenge the size of the circle, but she couldn't think of a reason for doing so that she felt she could successfully defend.

Her second surprise was that the Spirit Cats had marked the perimeter of the circle with LZ buoys. These small metallic cylinders were usually dropped from low orbit or positioned by ground forces to mark a landing zone. She had to admit that their electronic pulses showed up clearly on short-range sensors, with one placed every hundred meters.

Alexi stopped Miss Direction on the steep grade of a grass-covered hill and ran through her systems check. Targeting and tracking, long- and short-range sensors, weapons cycles and preheats on her PPCs, coolant systems; everything appeared to be working perfectly, just as it should be. Using her joysticks, she performed a final calibration of her 'Mech's arm movements, fine-tuning the alignment of the shoulder and elbow actuators.

She checked the connection between her coolant vest and the command couch one last time. In battle, the temperature in a 'Mech cockpit ranged from sauna to oven. On her first mission as a cadet, her coolant hose came loose and she nearly had died from the unalleviated heat. Since that time, she always checked the coolant hose connection just before she entered any battle. Finally, she checked to make sure her neurohelmet was perfectly seated on her head and tested the gyro that controlled the balance of the massive war machine. *The field of combat does not matter,* she told herself, *I intend to win.*

Her strategy for fighting Cox was based on what she knew about Clan warriors: known for their aggressive nature, they almost always rushed in for a quick kill. This wasn't to say that they were sloppy fighters; a man did not rise to the rank of Star captain in the Clans by being careless. She expected Cox to exploit his two pairs of arm-mounted heavy large lasers. He would hold his *Warhammer IIC* at the far end of its long-range weapons and whittle away at her. When he felt he had softened her up, he'd close to point-blank range, making it impossible for her to use her particle projector cannons. Then he'd attack with short-range missiles to try to finish the job.

Considering the 'Mechs, the terrain and the expected fighting style of her foe, Alexi Holt could almost see in her mind's eye how the battle would unfold from her enemy's perspective. If she understood her enemy, she could beat him. Her plan was to keep him at long range, firing as often as possible to allow her PPCs to wreak maximum havoc.

Looking down from her cockpit, she saw a Fox hovercraft and a hovertruck from the militia. Legate Singh and several of the officers had come to the trial. She appreciated the show of support, though naturally, Singh had positioned it as observational training on Clan fighting styles. On a field this size she doubted they would see much, but she appreciated the thought of friendly faces nearby.

Tucker Harwell was also in the hovercraft. As she watched, the upper hatch opened to reveal his lanky form. She couldn't see his features, but the untidy mass of black hair was a dead giveaway. He waved up at her, a half-salute of sorts. Alexi smiled and waved back, though it would be impossible for him to see her gesture through the laser-deflecting tinting of the blast-resistant cockpit glass.

All right. It's time for me to do my job.

The steep hills limited some of her long-range scanning, but there were very few trees or other terrain features. Star Captain Cox was Clan; in a real battle, he might use the hills to hide his movement, but not in a combat trial. The Clans approached combat trials very efficiently, and the most efficient tactic would be to come straight at her.

A comm channel hissed open in her ears. The communications console in her cockpit showed it was an open channel, keyed for anyone in the area to hear. "Knight Alexi of The Republic of the Sphere, you have come to face a Spirit Cat warrior in honorable battle. By the rede of our people and your own honor, I compel you—enter this Circle of Equals and meet your fate." Star Captain Cox's words rang with ritual and pride.

"Seyla," she answered, the ritual Clan response that translated roughly as "let it be so." She throttled up the Vlar 300 XL fusion reactor under her cockpit and stepped into the circle. She could feel the barely discernible throbbing of the reactor that powered the 'Mech. Her long-range sensors were sending out signals to the hillside, feeding her information and painting her own position on her heads-up display.

She walked Miss Direction along the slope of the hill, which gave her a wide view of the open grass-covered valley in the center of the Circle of Equals. He was out there somewhere, though her sensors showed nothing

yet. Perched near the top of the hill, she had a commanding view. Alexi stopped her *Black Knight* and stared at
the long-range sweeps on the secondary display.

A minute passed, and there was no sign of the Clan
warrior. Both their 'Mechs could stride at 43 kph, and
moved even faster at a full run. Any minute, she knew
he'd come, cresting the hilltop, most likely right across
from her position. Then she'd have him.

Another minute, still nothing. She switched to magnetic anomaly scans, but the mag scans showed no movement. She stared at her display, and glanced from time
to time at the hill across from her.

Nothing.

She bit her lip in thought, a nervous habit she'd developed as a child. She considered her options, and made
her choice. By moving to the top of the hill, she'd present
a bigger target and his instruments would pick her up
easier as well. Time to play the role of bait. She angled
Miss Direction up the hill and climbed steadily to the
top. Once she reached the top, she turned again, half-
expecting to see him on the top of the facing hill across
the grassy valley.

Another minute passed, then another. Not even a hint
of Star Captain Cox presented itself. Alexi shook her
head. It didn't make sense. She'd dealt with Clansmen
before, and this wasn't their style. She had to admit to
herself that she had misread Cox, and for a moment, she
wished she could kick herself in the butt. He wasn't going
to come for her. Obviously, Star Captain Cox was waiting
for her, attempting to lure her to his chosen terrain. Now,
the extra-large Circle of Equals made sense. Suddenly,
the usually comfortable cockpit seemed small, cramped
and dangerous. Her nerves were on overdrive, and it
wasn't because she couldn't see her opponent; it was that
she had been wrong.

I hate being wrong.

Tweaking her long-range sensors to display the maximum area, she studied the Circle of Equals with a new
eye. If her enemy was making her come to him, she
would have to change her tactics. Alexi looked down

into the valley below her and at the hill across that vast opening. If she went into the valley, it would limit fire coming at her, cutting both her own and Cox's line of sight. Then, she could cut back to the east, just along the edge of the circle, skirting the base of the hill and giving herself a chance of coming up behind him. She moved the throttle control forward to a walking gait and swung Miss Direction down into the valley.

She reached the bottom of the hill with no sign of the Spirit Cat Star captain. She began moving to the east, then suddenly a red dot lit up on her tactical display— an enemy IFF transponder. She planted one foot and turned to face up the steep green slope.

As she pivoted the 'Mech's torso, four laser beams, brilliant green in color from their modified optics, stabbed into her 'Mech. One shot burrowed deep, Miss Direction's right shoulder absorbing the energy blast with a sizzle and pop. The other three beams gouged at the armor plating on the BattleMech's torso. One carved a long, blackened scar across her chest. The other two cut smaller lacerations deep into the lower torso of the *Black Knight*, right above the hip actuators. The 'Mech swayed slightly from the attack, but Alexi leaned into it in order to gain a good angle for firing back up the hill. A slight ripple of heat rose in her cockpit from the hit, but she barely noticed the increase in temperature.

Then he was gone. The signal disappeared from her sensors and she lost him from her sights. She jammed the throttle forward for a full run and continued around the base of the hill, trying to catch him on the back side. She switched to short-range sensors and prepared for the assault.

She wasn't disappointed. Star Captain Cox's *Warhammer IIC* was standing and waiting on the hillside. Again he fired first. This time, two of his large lasers missed their mark completely, searing the green grass into blackened trenches just past her.

Two found their mark in her right arm and torso. One shot bore into Miss Direction's forearm with such fury that a piece of the Durabond armor melted away with a splatter that rained down on her legs. The other shot cut loose one armor plate, damaging some of the myomer muscle fibers underneath. Her damage display showed that the armor was still holding.

Alexi swept her two extended-range PPCs upward and locked her targeting reticle onto the towering *Warhammer*. She activated her primary target interlock, which tied together the firing of the two weapons. She heard the familiar whine of the particle projector cannons unleashing their brilliant blasts. Blue lightening bolts stabbed up the hillside at Star Captain Cox. One found its mark square in his upper torso, just under the cockpit, while the other one stabbed into the sky. The *Warhammer* rocked backward, then turned and ran back the way it had come, over the top of the hill and out of her line of sight.

Not this time. Alexi was not going to cover the same ground twice. She moved the throttle forward again, all the way. She charged up the steep slope in pursuit. After the first hundred meters, she began to feel the heat from the myomer muscles straining under the full-speed uphill run. Beads of sweat formed on her brow and she tasted salt in the corners of her mouth. Her vest flexed as the coolant pumped across her chest, chilling her slightly as it attempted to compensate for the spike in heat.

She picked up his mag reading at the top of the hill before she could see him. Miss Direction's PPCs were recharged, but she knew this was a job for her close-range weapons. Her medium and small lasers were ready to fire.

The *Warhammer*'s humanoid shape came into view. At the very moment she saw a flash of missiles launching, she instinctively dropped her crosshairs on the upper torso and head of the 'Mech and squeezed off a shot before she lost target lock with the missile impacts. With all her lasers tied to a single trigger, they discharged simultaneously in a burst of brilliant death.

The tom-tom thumping of the short-range missiles mangled the armor on her 'Mech's upper torso and left arm, pushing Miss Direction's torso and Alexi both to the left. Her tactical display showed that three of her four small lasers had found their mark. The lancing beams of light cut long surface scars on the gray-white armor of Star Captain Cox's *Warhammer*. Unfortunately, none of the shots cut deep. Cox seemed to contort his 'Mech at the last moment and started down the far side of the hilltop.

Alexi was determined to not let her foe get away, but she was already running hot. Pushing her 'Mech harder and faster would only add to her heat, but it couldn't be avoided. She rocked her foot pedals side-to-side and Miss Direction seemed to lumber drunkenly up the hill. She reached the top and saw Cox's *Warhammer IIC* nearing the bottom of the slope in the valley where she had been only a few minutes before. She followed cautiously along the slope and moved her targeting reticle onto her foe. *I never thought I'd see the day that a Clan warrior would run from a fight.*

Cox stopped his trot down the hill. As his 'Mech's torso twisted all of the way around, she realized that he wasn't fleeing, he was setting up for another blast. She fired first, sending two azure blasts of charged particles ripping down at the Spirit Cat. One hit and one missed, but the one that hit slammed into the right thigh of the *Warhammer* with such energy that she saw a secondary arc of blue electricity dance up the torso. The white smoke from the hit rose like a puff from an old man's pipe, leaving a deep black hole where the armor had been breeched. She tried to wet her lips, only then realizing just how hot her cockpit had become.

Star Captain Cox did not react instantly. He waited a moment, then fired. His own four emerald laser beams knifed up the hill at Miss Direction. Two missed, but two hit her already mangled and blackened chest armor. These shots were well aimed and burrowed deep into her weakened armor plating. A deep grinding sound told her that at least one of the shots had severed myomer muscles under the armor, sending them snapping like deadly whips. Miss Direction listed backwards for a moment, long enough for Cox to start up the next hill and break her target lock.

She wanted to run after him, but her heat indicator was at the top of the yellow zone. One more attack or running-speed movement, and her 'Mech would begin the countdown to automatic shutdown. Miss Direction was a fantastic 'Mech in most aspects, but it was not so good at venting heat. Grinding her teeth in frustration, Alexi walked steadily forward as her PPCs recharged for another volley.

When she reached the bottom of the hill, she leveled her 'Mech and attempted to lock onto Cox's 'Mech, already halfway up the next hill. It was tricky given that he was moving uphill. It got trickier when he suddenly turned and fired one of his large lasers at her.

The shot punched into Miss Direction's hip, blowing her target lock for a moment as the seventy-five-ton BattleMech sloughed off the burning damage. She swung back toward the *Warhammer* and saw a fearsome sight— a 'Mech charging in a full run down a hill straight at her.

Her thumb jerked toward the firing stud, and a target lock warning blared in her ears. She brought her small lasers online and started a hot charge to their capacitors, but a second later she saw the open missile hatches on the right and left torso of the *Warhammer* suddenly blossom with orange and red flames.

Eight short-range missiles twisted and spun in as Star Captain Cox continued to run down the hill straight at her. She attempted to juke out of the way, but his target lock was solid. Six of the missiles found their mark in the chest of her damaged BattleMech.

Instantly a wave of nausea hit her. The quality of the heat in the cockpit of her *Black Knight* suddenly changed and she felt as if she were fighting a fever rather than sitting in a sauna. Bile rose into her mouth, and she felt like she was going to throw up. Alexi fought to keep her balance as a wave of dizziness pulsed through her body. The missiles must have hit a neurolink or the gyro itself, sending a wave of feedback into her brain. Her left eyelid fluttered and she strained to stay in control of the situation. Miss Direction seemed to moan as metal strained. Something was wrong, but she couldn't focus long enough to figure out what it was. It was taking everything she had at the moment just to keep from being sick.

Alexi felt her BattleMech fall—rather, she felt it hit the ground. Her head bounced off the padded rests of her command couch, and the noise of the impact was deafening. Red lights blinked frantically on her damage display, but she couldn't focus her vision to read them. A soft light illuminated a green expanse outside the viewscreen. When she realized it was sunlight on the grass, she knew for sure that Miss Direction was on the ground. When she tried to move, she figured out that her 'Mech was on its left side, since that's where the safety straps were digging into her shoulder. Her chest ached. She had bruised or broken a rib in the fall, guaranteed.

The heat was unbearable. Alexi tried to take a deep breath, but couldn't seem to get air. She hit the button to pop open the front of her neurohelmet and the plexvisor swung up. Hyperventilating, her ears ringing, she spit to get the bile out of her mouth, then threw up. Her vomit fell sideways, confirming which way was up. Coughing and gagging, she closed her eyes. The smell of her stomach contents was as sickening as the taste in her mouth. Alexi spit again to try to get the taste out of her mouth.

She looked sideways at her damage display. The armor shielding her right arm was damaged. Her chest and torso had armor plating left, but what was there had been savaged in the assaults. There was a damaged heat vent on the side of her fusion reactor, probably a coolant leak. The holed torso armor had allowed some damage to penetrate to her gyro housing, which was what had created the feedback. Her left arm, pinned under the weight of the entire BattleMech, showed the worst damage. The PPC and medium lasers there were offline, which meant she was down to about half her firepower.

She had been vaguely registering a grinding noise and the ground shaking for the past few seconds, and so she turned her attention to the tactical display. It showed the red dot of the Star captain's *Warhammer* right on top of her position! To make it worse, the rocking motion of her 'Mech was reinforcing her nausea.

She snapped her plexvisor back down and managed to toggle the comm switch. "Star Captain Cox," she called. "I know you're out there."

The reply came immediately. "Knight Alexi. I have my right foot on your 'Mech. You cannot stand. I have a weapons lock on your cockpit. My remaining firepower is more than enough to destroy you. However, I do not wish to destroy you, because you are a worthy opponent and you pilot a valuable machine."

The words formed in her head slowly and painfully. *He beat me.* "Let me stand so that we can finish this," she challenged him.

His words were dispassionate. "It is already finished. You are defeated. Any further combat would risk your life. You fought with great skill. If we had faced each other outside this trial, I would claim you as my bondsman. Knight Alexi, this battle is over." The words rang in her ears.

"Until now, I have never lost a fight," she cursed, to herself more than to the Spirit Cat. "But I have lost this one. I submit, Star Captain Cox."

"You fought with honor," he replied. If Clan members were capable of the feeling, she would swear he was gloating. "You will honor the terms of this trial, *quiaff*?"

"*Aff*," she replied, licking her lips. The salt from her sweat at least was better than the bile of her stomach.

"We have both learned something today," said Cox. "You have learned what defeat feels like. I have learned the mettle a Knight of the Sphere brings to a battle."

There was a grating sound as he lifted the *Warhammer*'s foot off her *Black Knight*. The 'Mech could be repaired. It was her pride that had taken the heaviest damage. "It is a lesson I only intend to learn once," she returned. "I salute you and your Spirit Cats. But this will be your only victory here." With those words she cut off her comm channel and closed her eyes.

* * *

The warehouse for Universal Exporters Limited was abuzz with activity when the security system admitted Reo Jones. Something was happening. The holovid newscast was playing and people were pointing to the talking head on the screen, apparently intent on the story. Reo hated hearing the news; he preferred to be the one controlling the flow of information.

Rutger Chaffee stomped over to him and pointed at the screen. "Did you hear the news yet?" Jones shook his head.

"That idiot Knight Errant lost the duel. That stupid bitch has handed over Kinross to the damn Spirit Cats."

Jones cocked his eyebrow, but simply said, "If Knight Errant Holt lost her trial against the Spirit Cat commander, then he must be a heavyweight 'Mech jockey."

"Bah," Chaffee said, dismissing Reo's words. "The government will spin the story six ways to Sunday. But no matter how you twist it, the results are the same. The militia is leaving the city and the Spirit Cats can come and go as they please."

"Does this change your plans?" Reo asked.

"Of course it changes my freaking plans," spat Chaffee. "This puts that buddy of yours on the road. Instead of holing up in the city HQ, he'll be somewhere out in the wilderness. Any world is a big place if you want to hide. Even worse, it leaves a Clan force sitting in the middle of my town. I can intimidate and manipulate the local government officials and even the militia. I think that Clan commanders are unlikely to tolerate behavior like our little raid on ComStar."

Reo was surprised that Chaffee had such a firm grasp of the situation. The Spirit Cats were, in some respects, dangerous animals. If cornered or pushed too hard, they would strike back, and do so with force. "So how do you plan to deal with the new situation?"

Chaffee smiled the kind of smile that Reo hated seeing on his face, because it always meant something bad was going to happen. Cut-Throat glanced at a Fox-class hovercraft near an interior wall of the warehouse, then looked back at Reo with a chilling expression. Three personnel were spray painting the tan vehicle to match the urban combat patterns used by the Wyatt Militia, right down to the Wyatt Militia insignia—the image of the planet with a large Roman letter "M" in the middle.

"What are you planning?"

"Don't you worry, Jones. You'll find out the details soon enough. Let's just say that I don't intend to let those kitty cats interfere with my operation here." Reo noted with some alarm that Chaffee was no longer referring to it as Jacob Bannson's operation.

His boss' lethal grin grew slightly wider. "If that bitch-Knight can't do the job, I'll just have to finish it for her."

16

"**I** would ask you what went wrong, but my knowing won't change anything," Legate Singh sneered, seated safely behind his desk. Opposite him, still wearing her sweat-soaked gear, stood Alexi Holt. Her arms were crossed over her breasts. Her slick, matted hair almost matched the mess that Tucker Harwell usually sported.

It had been a long time since she had been dressed down by anyone. In fact, she couldn't remember the last time someone had addressed her in the tone that Edward Singh was using. She wanted to lash out at the man. At least she had taken decisive action to protect Wyatt. His only concerns had been political, perhaps even personal. But talking back to someone like Singh was a waste of time. He had already painted her as the scapegoat for whatever happened next.

"One of Star Captain Cox's missiles apparently hit the

neurocontrol circuits on the outside shield of the gyro housing. It sent a pulse of biofeedback into my neuro network and that pulse incapacitated me." The technical explanation of her defeat was analytical and boring. The truth of the matter was that she had been outfought, and a lucky shot had taken her down.

"You're a Knight Errant. This sort of thing isn't supposed to happen to a MechWarrior of your skill. Because of your failure, we now have to allow the Clan free reign in Kinross." If it was possible, his tone became even more scathing.

"I'm feeling fine," she said contemptuously.

Her words caught the legate off guard. "What?"

"I am fine now," she repeated. "Keeping in mind that I was engaged in a live-fire combat trial with a Clan warrior who could have killed me, and that I suffered a level of electronic feedback that could have inflicted permanent brain damage—I wanted you to know that I am *just fine*." She was still trying to control the full force of her anger, and not just at the legate. *He wouldn't have the stones to go toe-to-toe with a Clan warrior, but he sure is quick to criticize my failure.*

Singh suddenly grasped what she was implying. "Ah— I assumed you were feeling better since you were able to report so quickly," he said in a much more controlled tone.

"Legate," she began, trying to match his level tone, "let me get to the point of our conversation. I accept full responsibility for my failure to end the situation with the Spirit Cats in the Circle of Equals. I will accept whatever punishment the governor, or the prefect, or Paladin Sorenson considers appropriate. However, right now we need to deal with the facts, and the facts are as follows: I lost the combat trial. Therefore, we need to evacuate our facility here and exit Kinross. If the Spirit Cats wish to enter Kinross, we need to let them."

"The governor was unhappy about this arrangement when he believed you were going to win," Singh pressed. "I can't guarantee that he's going to let us leave the city defenseless."

"We *will* leave," she repeated. "I gave my word as a Knight of the Republic. So far, the Spirit Cats have behaved honorably, and we must do the same. If we betray their trust, we will be forced to fight them."

"Obviously, I'd rather not," Singh replied. "But we do have superior numbers."

Alexi leaned forward over his desk, slapping her sweaty palms on the sleek wooden surface. "If you choose to slug it out with the Spirit Cats, superior numbers will not save you," she said fiercely. "They will smash the militia, fast and furious. Study history, Legate!"

"So we give up?" he said, recoiling from her intensity —*and perhaps my body odor,* she thought with grim humor.

"We honor the terms of the batchall," she corrected.

He considered her for a moment. "Where do you suggest we go?"

She had thought about it for two days; while she had been confident of winning the trial, a true leader plans for all contingencies. So she had studied the maps and calculated what was required to move the militia. It was not just a matter of the gear and the personnel; there was fuel, expendables, provisions, spare parts and more. It was a significant amount of war materiel to move, and Alexi also wanted to keep her force mobile and her options open—especially because she still considered Bannson's merc force a viable threat of unknown size and composition. "My inclination is to take Highway Seven, north of Kinross. The map shows it as essentially a long stretch of road running parallel to the Kalamazoo River into the mountains, so we can move quickly. The highway cuts through several hills and the sides are heavily forested, which could potentially give our enemies cover, but we can compensate for that with light scouts. The road ends in a wilderness camp near the Crater Lakes. Camping season doesn't start until later, so we can use the empty buildings up there for shelter."

The legate appeared to hear her words, but he began talking as soon as she stopped. "I was thinking of moving us to the city of Madison. It's a small city approximately four hunded kilometers from here, but it offers facilities we can use to set up a temporary base."

She frowned. "Legate, Madison is so far away that we would be unable to respond to Kinross if there was trouble. My plan takes us only 180 kilometers from the city. Also, Madison is an urban setting, and since we are still protecting Tucker, we will continue to draw the attention of Bannson's people. We do not want to fight them in an urban environment."

"It's easier for us to establish our base in a city," Singh returned. "We'll have better access to resources."

We'll be hemmed in and trapped. "Sir, this is a military unit. It can set up anywhere. We aren't doing these troops any favors bunking them down in a hotel in the middle of a city. The sooner they realize that this could be a shooting war, the sooner we treat them like the soldiers they are, the sooner they'll start to believe it themselves and act accordingly."

"The fight is over," Singh said. "You lost it for us."

She didn't react. "Legate, I assure you, this fight is just beginning. My recommendation that we head north stands."

He stared at her for a few moments, perhaps thinking that the silence would intimidate her. It didn't. "Very well, Knight Holt. But should anything else go wrong, I will hold you accountable."

Alexi wanted to laugh. Plenty had already gone wrong. "I assure you, whatever happens, I will take responsibility."

Tucker walked to the massive mobile HQ and leaned in the driver's-side hatch. It was like a bank-vault door, heavy, thick, mounted above the half-track drive train. He saw his sister heading for the opening and moved out of the way. She swung through the hatch by holding on to the bar above the interior of the door, shooting her legs out first. Patricia dropped to the floor and dusted off the working jumpsuit she had borrowed from Wyatt Militia supplies.

Tucker had been working with Patricia on the MiningMech that was being modified for combat when the
techs assigned to continue work on the mobile HQ had
encountered a problem with the tracking systems that
they couldn't solve. Like most ComStar personnel, Patricia was trained in basic electronics and communications
systems maintenance and repair, so his sister had gone
to help troubleshoot it. That had been three hours ago.

"Get it fixed?" he asked.

"A while ago. I was just working with one of the other
techs on fine-tuning the satellite relay system," she replied. "Guess what I found? That vehicle was ComStar
at one time."

He glanced back at the huge, armored cab-and-truck
assembly, its new paint job concealing any sign of the
age of the beast. "Really? Wow. It's been a long time
since ComStar fielded any military vehicles." The Jihad
had destroyed the Com Guards, ComStar's military wing,
first in battle, then through attrition as the Guards
hunted down and eliminated the remains of the Word of
Blake out of guilt and anger. Because the Word of Blake
considered the Com Guards traitors to the true vision
of Blake, the attacks against the ComStar military were
particularly vicious, most involving suicide bombs or
weapons of mass destruction. Tucker shivered involun-
tarily at the thought of such wanton destruction. The
Com Guards were nothing more than a memory.

"How do you know?"

She smiled. "I'm a researcher. Behind one of the access panels was an old ComStar insignia. It was hard to
see, but of course it caught my eye immediately."

Tucker listened intently. "But how do you know the
vehicle wasn't used by the Word of Blake?"

"I don't," Patricia said, as if surprised that he thought
it made a difference. "It doesn't matter."

Tucker seemed shocked. "It *does* matter. The Word
of Blake killed billions upon billions of people. They
almost destroyed ComStar. They conducted a jihad, for
heaven's sake. Hell, you know the stories better than I
do, Patricia."

She glared at him. "I do know them better than you, and it still doesn't matter to me, Tucker. ComStar is an organization to be proud of. Throughout our history, we have guided mankind to a better future. What the Word of Blake did does not reflect on ComStar, and I'm tired of being forced to apologize for a war that happened before we were born. The Jihad is in the past. We—you—are making the future."

He had struck a nerve without meaning to. Remembering his treatment by the customs official at the airport when he arrived, he had to concede that there was some justification for her outburst. But he also had to believe that so much death would somehow count against ComStar until that blood debt was paid. As he struggled to collect his thoughts into a convincing argument, someone walked up and stepped between them. At first he didn't recognize the man. He wore his left arm in a sling and had a bandage over his left ear. Tucker did a double-take when he realized he was looking at Demi-Precentor Faulk. Gone was the immaculate suit, gone was the arrogance that had seemed permanently etched on his face.

"Ms. Harwell, I have been asked to deliver this message to you," he said, handing her a data disk. He either didn't see Tucker or chose to ignore him.

"Demi-Precentor," Tucker said in recognition. Faulk turned to face him. His face showed multiple small cuts, with one or two larger ones bandaged. His eyes were dark and sunken, with bags under them. He had the look of a man who has seen war as he met Tucker's gaze.

"Adept Harwell," he replied.

"What happened?" Tucker stammered.

He hefted the arm in the sling. "When those raiders came looking for you, I thought they were coming to seize the HPG or worse, destroy it. I tried to fight them."

Patricia cut in. "They were in battlearmor."

Faulk gave a wry smile. "I am aware of that." For the first time since he'd met him, Tucker felt sorry for the demi-precentor. Worse, Tucker felt a pang of guilt. *It's because of me that he's hurt.*

"What are you doing so far from the compound?" Tucker asked.

"I'm just following orders," he said. "I received a coded message for your sister along with orders to deliver it, by hand, in person."

Tucker was confused. "I've never heard of any message that had to be delivered in person by a demi-precentor."

"I have, but it's rare," Faulk said. "My orders came from Precentor Buhl. As you know, it's not good to question Precentor Buhl. My duty is to serve." Faulk's spine stiffened as he spoke, like he was coming to attention, but Tucker would swear that there was a hint of humor in the man's eyes.

"Thank you, Demi-Precentor," Patricia said.

"I'll take my leave of the two of you," Faulk replied. "And Mr. Harwell?"

"Yes?"

"Be careful." And with those words, Faulk walked away. Looking puzzled, Tucker turned to Patricia. "Do you have any idea what that was all about?"

She shrugged, tucking the disk in her shirt pocket and snapping the flap shut. "I asked for some data from Terra a few days ago. I'm sure that's what it is."

"But delivered by person?"

Patricia's smile seemed forced. "Tucker, just chalk it up to the vagaries of my profession and leave it alone." Before he could ask anything else, Patricia had started back through the hatch into the mobile HQ.

Alexi stepped off the gantry platform onto the back of the MiningMech. The dump-truck back of the 'Mech had been converted into a missile bay, now filled with eight meter-long missile tubes. Tucker stood down at the loading end of the missile rack, attempting to sort through the colorful, tangled mess of wiring harnesses. Knight Holt walked carefully down the length of the missile rack until she was standing over him.

Tucker didn't notice her, he was buried in his work.

He pulled gently on one harness, tracing it to where it wired into the missile tube, and clipped the feed back on. He held up his wrist communicator. "I just reseated number ten. Run a systems check." Tucker stretched his back and suddenly saw the Knight Errant standing over him. He managed to fumble to his feet without getting caught in the harnesses.

"How's it going, Tucker?" she said, for once using his first name.

He seemed tongue-tied for a moment, probably wondering how long she had been watching him. "Uh, fine. Just some last-minute wiring issues for the TICs."

"Will she run?" Alexi asked.

"Oh, yeah," Tucker replied enthusiastically. "We've got most of the replacement armor welded into place. The autocannon weapons system that Lieutenant Johannson salvaged from storage turned out to be a good addition. She's not a BattleMech, but this old miner has a few surprises that I think will catch anyone going against us off guard."

"Excellent," she said, putting her hands on her waist in a relaxed stance. "From what I understand, you've been a big help to the teams here. I wanted to thank you, and to let you know we're moving out soon."

"Where are we heading?"

"North. First thing in the morning."

"That's not much time," Tucker frowned. "We haven't had a chance to really test out the IndustrialMechs at all."

"We'll have to test them on the road," she replied. "I struck a bargain with the Spirit Cats, and I intend to honor it."

"Were you hurt in the trial?"

Her expression didn't change. "I was injured, but I'll recover."

Tucker stared at her for a moment. They were both silent. She kept thinking of Tucker as a kid, but he was fully grown. He had restored Wyatt to the HPG network and had the potential to perform the same miracle on hundreds of other worlds. Saving this one man might just save The Republic from the chaos that it had been struggling against since the HPG blackout.

"I wish none of this had happened," Tucker finally said.

"I understand the way you feel. At the same time, I'm glad you came here and did what you did."

Tucker knew he looked confused. Alexi continued. "Tucker, we'll get through this . . . I'll make sure of that. And when it's all over, you are going to help restore The Republic and the rest of the Inner Sphere. The universe fell apart when communications broke down. You are the only person right now that has the aptitude to fix this."

"It's not easy," he said wearily.

"Great things rarely are," Alexi replied. She reached out and squeezed his shoulder.

17

Adam Steiner Memorial Park
Kinross, Wyatt
The Republic, Prefecture VIII
16 May 3135

Star Captain Cox stood at the feet of his *Warhammer*
in the center of the city park and surveyed the surrounding area. Kinross enfolded the ten-acre park at its
exact center, its buildings creating a perfect set of walls
from where he stood. It was an old city, its architecture
dated, but somehow it seemed *quaint*. As the sun set in
the distance, fresh understanding rushed through him of
what it meant to be a Clan warrior . . . master of all he
surveyed, his dominion won in combat. *Things could not
be better,* quiaff?

Cox stared up at Harbinger and saw the replacement
armor, primed a dull black-gray, not yet painted to match
the rest of the 'Mech. His memory of the battle with
Knight Alexi was still fresh, as fresh as the repairs. He
had won because he had suppressed his instincts as a
Clansman. While his training dictated that he rush in for

a fast victory, he knew that his foe would expect that. Instead, he had lived up to the insignia on the torso of his 'Mech, a leaping black cat—a Pouncer.

Victory belonged to him and to the Spirit Cats. Victory opened the city of Kinross to his Clan. He was pleased with what he had achieved, but not arrogant in the defeat of the Knight Errant. Defeating her had been a matter of calculation and skill. If he fought her again, he was not sure the end result would be the same. Alexi had demonstrated great skill in fighting. The damage to his *Warhammer* had been sufficient to validate the prowess of his opponent. He had lost a heat sink in the trial, and another hit to the torso would likely have damaged his fusion-reactor housing.

His forces deployed in the park, posting a light perimeter guard around the clump of trees and fountain that marked the center of the green fields. The fountain was centered on a statue of some figure from the history of the world, and from the look of it, a military man. He wore a uniform and a stern expression. Star Captain Cox frowned. Only the Inner Sphere sought to pay such tributes. In the Clans it was much easier. Honored leaders did not seek stone effigies; instead, they considered their honor complete if their genetic heritage was passed on to future generations.

Star Commander Monique stepped away from the footpad of her *Black Hawk* and stood next to him, attempting to see the park through his eyes. "Are you sure that this is where you wish us to set up our encampment, Star Captain? There are plenty of structures that we can commandeer, including the militia headquarters."

"We will camp here," he replied. "I believe that sleeping here under the stars will help us in our search."

"As you wish," she responded, as a Condor hovertank came to rest on its armored skirt nearby. "Though I expect that wherever we set up our base, we will disturb the locals. Did you see the lower castes stare at us as we entered the city? They are afraid of us."

"*Neg*, Star Commander," he replied coldly. "They hate us. It is a somewhat more dangerous emotion than fear."

She seemed unimpressed, and that worried him. He was well-versed in Clan history, as every warrior should be. When the Clans first returned to the Inner Sphere decades ago, on the Great Crusade to liberate the citizens of the Inner Sphere from war, their experiences taught them much worth remembering. While the populations of some worlds submitted peacefully to Clan rule, others rose up against the Clans, taking up arms and successfully using guerrilla tactics against the warrior caste. But the Crusade ended without any Clan claiming the prize of Terra, and the younger warriors had begun to display some of the overconfidence that had cost the Clans so dearly early on. "Post pickets," Star Captain Cox replied. "I want our Elementals positioned for rapid response should trouble arise."

"Do you feel that it is necessary, Star Captain?"

He nodded firmly. "See to it personally, Star Commander. We will enjoy the fruits of my victory here, but we will not place ourselves at unnecessary risk."

"Where will you be, sir?"

"I am going to meet the ComStar administrator for Wyatt. The reactivation of this HPG may be the root of the visions that Galaxy Commander Rosse and I have experienced. Understanding what has happened here may help me interpret my visions."

Reo Jones sat comfortably on top of the Fisher Building, an old office building near the edge of the park. From his perch, some twenty stories up, he had full view of Adam Steiner Memorial Park in the twilight. Using his e-binocs, he was able to identify every detail of the Spirit Cat deployment and camp. He sighed as he looked at the 'Mechs and tallied the number of armored infantry that he saw—for the tenth or twelfth time. It was something to do and it made him feel useful.

You faced a lot of problems when you were labeled as incompetent or a traitor, chief of which is that no matter what, you are never fully trusted. The Republic, formally, had turned its back on him. Jacob Bannson kept his leash fairly tight, and Reo didn't blame him.

Rutger Chaffee trusted him as far as he could throw him, and the feeling was mutual. Lack of trust didn't consume Reo's thoughts, it was simply something that came with his job—his life.

Today, lack of trust was making Reo's job more difficult than usual. Reo knew that Chaffee was planning something. There was something in that yellow-toothed grin that told Reo plain as day that the mercenary commander was holding something back. He refused to share his plans, so Reo went to plan B. Spying on Cut-Throat's force would only cause problems. Spying on the Spirit Cats, however, would eventually reveal what Chaffee was up to. If Chaffee was going to make a move, it would be here.

Only a Clan warrior would camp in the open in the middle of a hostile city. And then he had the gall to make his next move a meeting with the planetary leader of ComStar. Reo had seen the news broadcast of Cox meeting with the bandaged form of Demi-Precentor Faulk an hour ago on his portable holovid viewer. He leaned back in the folding chair, pulled out a drink and popped the top, taking a sip. Even though the conversation between the two wasn't broadcast, he was sure that the Star captain didn't learn anything useful from Faulk. The real brains behind the restoration of the HPG was Tucker, and he was unavailable for comment. Which made him wonder just how much the Spirit Cat commander had learned about Tucker Harwell, and if the Clans now considered him as much of a prize as did Chaffee and Bannson.

At the edge of his field of vision he saw something moving toward the park. The early evening twilight made it hard to identify without visual aids. He grabbed his e-binocs and brought the image into focus. The digital enhancement system built into the binoculars corrected for the lack of light. It was a Fox-class hovercraft. This one was not the gray, white, and black of the Spirit Cats. This one was painted in an urban camouflage pattern of greens and browns. Flickers of firing lasers flashed in the early evening darkness and he saw at least a few Elemen-

tals light their jump jets and rise into the air on plumes
of orange flame, casting odd shadows.

Reo had seen this vehicle before, in Chaffee's warehouse. *This is very, very bad.* He drew in a long breath.
"What in the hell are you up to, Cut-Throat?"

Machine gun and laser fire erupted on the north edge
of the park, catching the attention of Star Captain Cox.
He stepped out of his duraplex dome tent, wearing a
T-shirt and shorts. He emerged ready for a fight, even
though he carried only a combat knife for a weapon. He
stared off in the direction of the weapons fire and heard
the whining roar of a hovercraft getting closer.

There it was! A Fox hovercraft. He saw the insignia
of the Wyatt Militia on the front of the craft as it swung
wide along the edge of the camp. His pickets, Elementals
of the Striker Star, swept in after the Fox, firing at it
from the rear and sides. Ricochets tossed up sparks on
the armored hull as the craft danced to the side, sliding
toward where the 'Mechs were parked.

Personnel ran across the camp to pick up their weapons or man their vehicles. The hovercraft was not firing,
but instead seemed determined to taunt the warriors by
invading their camp and breaking their perimeter defenses. *This is not honorable behavior.* He lifted his left
wrist and activated his communicator. "Pouncer One to
all commands. Alert One. Air support get up. Neutralize
that vehicle." The words didn't sound threatening, but
they were. It was difficult to neutralize or cripple a vehicle. What he was really saying was to destroy the
hovercraft.

Star Captain Cox heard the engines engage at higher
revs and the Fox seemed to roar almost twice as loud.
An Elemental sentry landed near it at the apex of its
floating turn and blazed away at it with an arm-mounted
laser. A burst of emerald energy sliced up the side of
the hovercraft, cutting right through the logo of the
Wyatt Militia. It wasn't enough to stop it.

The hovercraft slewed toward the area where he stood.
Cox reached down to his hip and pulled out his knife.

His mind raced, reviewing what he knew of the approaching craft. If he could time a jump just right, he might be able to get on top and get to the access hatch there. If he could get inside, he could kill or incapacitate the driver. The Star captain stepped forward to meet his foe.

The Fox juked to the right, away from him and toward the 'Mechs. He heard the thunder of a diesel engine starting up and knew it was the ConstructionMech Mark II behind him. He expected to hear the *Locust* and *Black Hawk* firing up their fusion reactors as well.

The Militia Fox roared past him, kicking up dust as it raced away. He jogged behind it for several steps, but it widened the distance between them too quickly. The hovercraft was bearing right for his own *Warhammer,* shut down for the evening. The tech caste members were trying to get out of the way. Star Captain Cox watched as three Elementals jumped past him in pursuit. He watched as the ConstructionMech stepped forward. The *Locust,* some fifty meters away from his *Warhammer,* came to life and started to move, lining up a flank shot on the Fox.

At first, he thought that the Fox was building up speed to ram into his 'Mech. It was a pointless move. The vehicle would inflict damage, especially if the ramming attack toppled his 'Mech. But the pilot of the Fox could not hope to get away. He was in the heart of the Spirit Cat camp, and the Clan warriors were on the move. The hovercraft was trapped.

When it got within a dozen meters of the *Warhammer*, right between it and the ConstructionMech, the Fox exploded.

The blast was incredible. A bright white flash, followed by an orange-yellow ball of fire that seemed to have no end. One of the hovercraft's rear propeller blades came out of the blast like a deadly spinning knife, flying into a clump of trees and burying itself deep in the largest trunk.

One of the Elementals was knocked back and down, and Cox flew ten meters, landing on his back. There was a deep ringing in his ears and he coughed, struggling to breathe. His sight narrowed to tunnel vision for a few beats of his heart, and he worried that he was going to black out, but slowly his sight returned to normal.

There was nothing left that resembled the Fox; only a shallow black circle marked where it had been. The *Warhammer* had been toppled by the blast; through the flames from the burning supplies and repair gear he could see the bottoms of the footpads of the BattleMech. The ConstructionMech was still standing, but was blackened from the blast; its left shoulder-guard armor plate had been mangled and twisted into scrap by flying debris. Fires seemed to burn everywhere.

The force of the blast clearly had a higher yield than just the armaments of the Fox cooking off. It was safe to assume that the militia had stripped some of the armor plating off and loaded on at least several tons of military-grade explosives—making perfect shrapnel of the remaining armor. There was no question that this was deliberate.

His ears heard nothing but a dull roar, like the rush of water, as he watched his personnel spring into action, putting out fires, recovering the scattered gear, tending to the injured. He felt nothing but cold fury. The Wyatt Militia fielded a Fox hovercraft. It had been turned against him as a moving bomb.

Knight Alexi had efficiently destroyed the bond of honor between his forces and hers. Now, he would take the fight to her. The Wyatt Militia would pay for what they had done. The Republic of the Sphere would learn what it meant to test the Spirit Cats.

Tucker sat in one of the communications console seats in the cramped interior of the mobile HQ, feeling claustrophobic with everyone looking over his shoulder. The Wyatt Militia had left Kinross at almost the same moment that the Spirit Cats had entered it. The convoy moving up into the highlands along Highway Seven had been slow and ponderous, a situation made worse when

the ConstructionMech that had been pieced together suffered a hydraulic failure that dropped its excavator arm
onto the pavement and brought the entire convoy lumbering to a complete stop. It had taken the motor pool
mechanics nearly two hours to repair it, during which
time the rest of the unit had formed up around it. Legate
Singh did not want to spread out the troops too far. By
the time repairs were done, it had been time to set up
camp for the night.

"Are you sure it was a military-band transmission?"
Legate Singh pressed.

Tucker nodded. "It only lasted a few moments. I have
a copy in the buffer," he flipped a switch and the speaker
system repeated its tinny message. "To the Wyatt Militia.
Your violation of the terms of our trial has left us no
alternative. We will come after you and teach you the
price of treachery." The message came to an abrupt end.
Tucker turned to the legate and saw the color drain from
his face.

"What is he talking about?" Singh stammered.

Alexi Holt stood with crossed arms, defiant, refusing
to react to the message. "Something has happened. See
what you can pick up on the civilian channels."

Tucker switched frequencies. "Current broadcast from
Kinross coming in on that monitor," he pointed to one
of several flatscreens that lined the control panel. It
flickered on and the image showed the city at night.
Flames danced several blocks behind the reporter, a
young woman, who gestured to indicate the scene of the
event. ". . . and the Spirit Cats have not made a formal
statement, but sources indicate that some sort of terrorist
attack took place at their base an hour ago. Witnesses
interviewed by Channel Four news have confirmed that
an attack by the Wyatt Militia, apparently a suicide attack, has occurred at Adam Steiner Memorial Park."
Alexi indicated that Tucker should cut the feed.

Tucker watched her in the silence of the confined
space. The legate was nervous, but she was calm, almost
relaxed. "Get the Donar in the air. Recon the highway

to make sure the Spirit Cats are not sneaking up on us. Order our troops to full alert and get ready to break camp in two hours."

"It's a mistake," Legate Singh said. "We should open a channel to them, explain to Star Captain Cox that it wasn't us."

The Knight Errant shook her head. "It doesn't matter now. Most Clans have no tolerance for political intrigue or subterfuge. They won't believe us without evidence, and to get evidence we'd have to go back to the city— and that's not going to happen."

"It had to be Bannson's mercs," Tucker blurted out. She gave him a nod. "Most likely."

"We've been set up," Singh added.

"Definitely," she replied. "I'd hoped to avoid this kind of battle, but it looks like someone is serving it up for us. Fine. If the Spirit Cats want a fight, we'll give it to them."

18

"I need a layout of the terrain here," Alexi Holt said firmly. Tucker's fingers attacked the keyboard, and he brought up the surrounding kilometer on the viewing screen. The owners of eight or nine sets of eyes instantly leaned over his shoulders, shoving him further forward in his seat in the mobile HQ.

"Back it out to show five kilometers," she said. Tucker slid the control and the image backed up to a higher altitude. The image showed green and gray, with two lines representing the roads crossing in the middle of the display. Everyone leaned back a bit, taking some of the pressure off Tucker, who gave a general scowl to the officers and troopers huddled around him.

The image was clear. Highway Seven was a wide ribbon of gray running straight north and south. The east-west road was Viewtown Road. He tapped the keyboard and brought up more icons on the screen, now showing that that intersection was labeled Ben Venue Corners.

North of the intersection was a gray mass representing a mountain or rocky terrain. Highway Seven cut nearly through the middle, and that was the section Alexi chose next. "Overlay the topographical elevation lines on that section." The road ran up the long slope of the mountain and down the other side. The majority of it seemed to cut significantly into the hill, creating an embankment on either side of the road that was so steep it would be difficult for anything other than jump-capable equipment to climb. Past the peak of the mountain, the road ran down the hill at a long angle to the flatlands further north. Light, second-generation forests dotted the road once it came free of the mountains.

Knight Holt studied the map and Tucker studied her. Her eyes darted back and forth, and she rested her hand under her chin, flicking her fingers upward as she pondered courses of action. "It looks like that roadway cut through the mountain is going to be our best bet."

Legate Singh nodded. "You are planning to drive the Spirit Cats up the highway that direction. The highway is wide, but not too wide. Their maneuverability will be greatly reduced."

"That's what I was thinking," she returned. "Except that I wasn't planning to drive them there. Star Captain Cox would expect that."

"How do you know what he would expect?" Singh retorted.

"I fought him. Now I know him."

"You *lost* to him."

The Knight parried the verbal barb with a grin. "Which makes me the best candidate to understand how he thinks. Not to mention the person most motivated to not let it happen again." Either she was as good as she implied, or was so overconfident that they were doomed. Tucker chose the first option.

"He's bound to see that the terrain will bottle him up

there," Patricia inserted. "He'll be expecting us to attack at that exact point."

Alexi nodded. "Yes, but going around will cost him too much time. He's going to spread his forces out, put his heavy-hitting 'Mechs in the lead of the column so they can punch through. He won't want his people bunched up."

"How do we take advantage of that?" Singh queried.

"Step one is to make him think he has outthought us," the Knight replied. "That makes him believe he has the initiative. Then we hit him where he doesn't expect it," she stabbed her finger at the map near the crossroads, south of the mountain pass.

Patricia leaned forward over Tucker's workstation, intent on the map. "You'd have to divide our forces in front of a superior enemy. You'll need enough force on the north end of the mountain cut to make him think he has you where he expects you. At the same time, you'll need enough firepower left behind to hit the rear flank hard enough to cripple them."

Alexi stared at her with a puzzled look, and Tucker wore the same expression. Her analysis of the operation did not sound like the opinion of a ComStar researcher. It sounded much more like someone experienced in combat operations, and that just wasn't possible. ComStar no longer had the Com Guards. And anyway, Tucker had never once known his sister to demonstrate even the slightest interest in military tactics.

Patricia felt their eyes on her and shrugged. "What? You can't research old battles for as many years as I have without picking up some of the strategies and tactics. Did I get it right?"

Alexi chuckled. "A pretty accurate assessment, Ms. Harwell," she returned. "The trick is that the Spirit Cats have air support. If they spot us, Star Captain Cox will be able to turn on our own plan against us."

Tucker chimed in. He had spent the evening helping monitor the Militia's Donar assault helicopter covering the rear. Every time it got close to the Spirit Cats' force on the highway south of them, it had taken fire from a Balac Strike VTOL and a pesky little Crow scout. "We have to find a way to take care of their helicopters. Every time we get close to them, they swamp our lone air support."

Alexi smiled grimly. "I think that's doable as well. We have a lot to accomplish before tomorrow," she said, looking at Tucker. "And thanks to you, we have the mobile HQ to serve as a communications coordination point. Mr. Harwell, I'll need you to help me orchestrate this battle. Are you up to it?"

Tucker's mouth opened, but nothing came out for a moment. Finally, he managed to stammer, "I'll do my best."

Alexi responded, "That's all I want from everyone."

DropShip Deathclaw
Northeast of Kinross, Wyatt
The Republic, Prefecture VIII

The *Deathclaw*'s fusion engines still glowed muted red, and white streaks marked the condensation of the slowly cooling surface. The ground underneath the DropShip was baked. Captain Casson moved out his *Sun Cobra* as the rest of the Eagle's Talons Company deployed along the edge of the woods where he had ordered their drop. The narrow, boxy shoulders of his 'Mech were marked with regal purple, one of the traditional colors of the Free Worlds League, and now of the Protectorate. On the armor plating just in front of his cockpit ferroglass was painted a swooping eagle with an open claw—the symbol of his Eagle's Talons.

They had arrived several days earlier at a pirate jump point in the Wyatt system. No one had detected their arrival. Since their arrival, they had spent their time monitoring commercial and military communications, studying events unfolding on the world. The most important thing he had learned was that his target, Tucker Harwell, was still somewhere on the planet. Harwell was with the militia, he had pieced that much together. And the militia was on the move.

Wyatt was a mess. The Knight Errant gave the capital city to the Spirit Cats by losing a combat trial. Then the militia had attacked the Spirit Cats. Now the militia was to the west of Casson's LZ, apparently fleeing from the pursuing Spirit Cats force. In the middle of all of this, Bannson's Raiders, who had no business even being on this world, had attacked the ComStar compound—looking for his target.

Tucker Harwell.

For a few moments, Casson had actually considered conducting a full-scale, highly visible military assault on Wyatt. It appealed to him on only one level: to impress on everyone that the Oriente Protectorate was not to be trifled with . . . that they were a major power in the Inner Sphere. It had been a tempting thought, one that appealed to his nationalistic pride. At the same time, the last thing he needed was to give everyone on Wyatt a common enemy. No, the solution he had chosen was best. Achieve orbital insertion in the least populated area of the planet, skim to a landing zone in the wilderness, and hope like hell that everyone was too occupied with current events to notice.

His officers wanted immediate action, but he was confident enough to wait for the right moment to strike. Casson expected that the Spirit Cats and the militia would tangle with each other and wear each other down. That was logically when Bannson's people would strike, for Bannson ran his mercenaries like his business: attack when your enemies are weakest, and you will have fewest losses and greatest profits. The profits, in this case, were the man who could rebuild the HPG network: Tucker Harwell.

So Ivan Casson deployed and stood ready to move. Once Bannson's people showed themselves, then he would mop up whatever forces were left on this world. Tucker Harwell would be his prisoner, to be taken back to the Oriente Protectorate in his custody.

And Captain Ivan Casson held a trump card. There

was his deep-cover operative on Wyatt, the source of his information about Harwell. He could now tap this same agent for intel on the militia if needed.

Let them slug it out. In the end, we'll prevail. "All right, Talons, establish a perimeter and establish passive communications jamming. Sit tight and wait. We'll strike soon enough . . ."

"You son of a bitch!" Reo swore at Captain Chaffee. Jones tossed his kit bag to the floor of the warehouse and stood toe-to-toe with the mercenary commander. Chaffee seemed unshaken by his words. "You've started a war."

"Not at all. I'm just taking advantage of the existing situation," Chaffee replied. "And you may want to watch your mouth, Jones. We work together, remember? Technically, I'm your boss."

Reo was in no mood to listen to Chaffee's insinuations. "You framed the militia with that attack. Now the Spirit Cats are mobilized and moving out after them. Did it ever occur to you that Tucker Harwell might end up getting killed in the fighting? If he dies, Bannson will have both our asses in a sling."

"You worry too much," Chaffee scoffed, taking a swig of coffee from his mug and putting the empty cup down on a barrel of coolant. Behind him, technicians were calibrating the arms of a BattleMech looming along the back wall of the warehouse. Reo's trained eyes noticed that a few of the vehicles and one of the 'Mechs he had seen on his last visit were missing from the warehouse. Reo didn't have to ask where the assets had gone; the mercenary force was on the move. "Besides, Bannson will love the press we're going to get out of this. We'll be the ones who got the Spirit Cats out of Kinross."

Reo knew he wouldn't win this argument, so he switched gears. "Was that hovercraft piloted by remote control? How did you get it so close to their 'Mechs?" He figured if he gave Chaffee the chance to brag, he'd learn more about the mercenary's operation and plans.

There was too much he didn't know, and he had to take every opportunity to learn what he could.

"Don't be stupid," Chaffee replied. "I had a local kid driving it. I promised him 10K stones if he helped me with a practical joke. All he had to do is drive our hovercraft up to the Spirit Cat 'Mechs, then bug out of there. It cost me 5K up front, but I got him right where I wanted him. Then, one quick laser signal from a nearby building, and poof!" He gestured with his hands simulating an explosion. "Instant war. The Spirit Cats never bothered to go through the debris. They got their gear repaired and set off after Legate Singh and his pet Knight."

Reo felt the color drain from his face. He had always known that Rutger Chaffee was a tough, heartless man. It made him sick to think of the kid's family. "You blew up a kid?"

"You have to break some eggs to make an omelet," Chaffee chuckled. "Besides, if they did check the debris, there had to be some organic remains there or they'd suspect something." He eyed Reo skeptically. "Don't act so shocked. You've done worse in your life. You allowed an enemy force to kill hundreds of people, including your own family. So don't try to come over all high-and-mighty on me."

Reo heard his words but said nothing in his defense. "Now what?"

Chaffee smiled. "We move out tonight. My men in the field tell me that the Spirit Cats should be on top of the militia tomorrow. That should be a hell of a battle. Nothing gets Clanners up for a fight more than a slight against their honor. Even so, it seems like the odds are pretty close. Some of the men are running a pool if you want in on the action. We let them hammer each other, then we pick up the pieces."

"Where do you want me?" Reo asked tiredly, feeling drained by Chaffee's callous attitude.

"You scout the action for us," Chaffee said. "Get out there and monitor the fighting. Let me know when the time is right to come in and finish this job."

Reo nodded. Chaffee slapped him on the back. "Quit worrying about the dead, Jones," he said. "In a few days time, we're both going to be richer than we ever dreamed. Trust me on this; Jacob Bannson takes care of those who show initiative."

Reo said nothing. There was nothing he could say. The entire Inner Sphere knew he was a betrayer. Fighting that image was pointless, because he couldn't reveal the truth. He only hoped that Tucker didn't find his shell cracked at the end of the day.

Star Captain Cox sat in the cockpit of his *Warhammer IIC* and glared at the communications console. The message was being sent in a loop on an open channel: both the legate and the Knight Errant claimed that the Wyatt Militia had not been responsible for the attack on his people. It bothered him that they thought he was so ignorant.

He had trusted Knight Alexi, and the militia had violated that trust and wasted lives in the suicide attack. Now, they must pay, on the same terms they had dictated to him—no formality of honor, no quarter asked or given.

He gazed out at the Spirit Cats force assembled before him and let his pride in them burn away his anger. His eyes lingered on the Purifiers tattoos many in his command carried on their faces and bodies. He himself did not have visible tattoos, but he admired the stunning colors of the marks of determination, purity and honor.

He would leave Kinross and take the fight to his enemies, wherever they were. But there was one whom he would spare. His Watch officer, a Clan intelligence specialist, had determined that there was one man responsible for restoring the HPG on Wyatt, a man named Tucker, an adept of ComStar. This member of the technician caste was currently with the Wyatt Militia.

Perhaps this man is the Lightbringer of the vision I share with Galaxy Commander Rosse. If he is, then this may be indeed the new home of the Spirit Cats. "Remember," he said on the Star command channel, "we offer no quarter to the militia. We honor the great Kerenskys by our retribution against them. Further, we must find this Tucker of ComStar to explore his role in our destiny. I so command."

A series of "*Affs*" echoed in his ears. Star Captain Cox smiled. "Pouncers, we strike now!"

19

Highway Seven, Ben Venue Corners
North of Kinross, Wyatt
The Republic, Prefecture VIII
18 May 3135

Tucker studied the screen intently, unconsciously adjusting the headset and mike as he absorbed the data. "Stay sharp. You should be right on top of them in two minutes, Air One," he signaled. South of their position, their lone Donar assault helicopter was closing in on the Spirit Cats. They had played this hand several times already, and each time evoked the same response. The Cats would scramble their air assets, two helicopters, to pursue. The Donar would turn, run for the safety of the militia lines—and at the last minute, the Spirit Cats would break off and head back.

This time was going to be different.

"Holy freaking crap," came the voice of the pilot, Lieutenant Aulf Michelson, in Tucker's earpiece. "Here they come."

Patricia Harwell cut in on the channel. "Just as

planned, Air One. Let them get close, then go to nape of earth and bring them in low and fast to the coordinates." Her soothing voice reminded Tucker of their mother's.

"Roger that, Command," came back the pilot's voice, interrupted by a roaring sound—probably a short range missile going off. "Needless to say, I have their attention."

Tucker watched the transponder track the course of Michelson's Donar heading back to the intersection where Highway Seven crossed Viewtown Road. The transponder signals also clearly painted the Spirit Cats following suit. The last time they gave chase, they went almost a kilometer past the intersection. This time they would get a little surprise there.

He toggled the comm channel. "Miss Behavior," he began, but was immediately cut off by the voice of Alexi Holt.

"Tucker, that's Miss Direction," she said. He glanced at his sister, who gave him a big grin.

"Uh, sorry," he said. "You'll have company in twenty."

"No problem, Command. We're ready."

The Donar was flying up Highway Seven a short ten meters above the roadway. Lieutenant Michelson was weaving and dodging as the Crow scout and Balac Strike VTOL dropped to the same level in a coordinated dive. They were attempting to get weapons lock, that much was obvious from their aggressive movements.

The intersection was just a crossroads atop a tiny hill, barely high enough to qualify as a rise. The Spirit Cats were intently focused on their prey, determined that this time they would overtake the Donar before it reached the safety of the rest of the Wyatt Militia. Michelson banked hard and pushed lower to the ground, heading right for the top of the paved rise. The Crow anticipated his move and fired its nose-mounted laser, hitting the back end of the Donar. If the militia craft had a tail rotor, it would have been lost, but this was an airstream-controlled craft. The Donar danced slightly from the laser's impact and passed over the intersection . . .

. . . just as the Partisan anti-aircraft vehicle pulled up and locked on its weapons.

The Defiance Shredder LB 5-X autocannons littered the air with depleted uranium slugs. The Crow scout slammed right into the fire. It attempted to pull up and away, to turn and run. The shells stitched a line up the bottom of the copter, splaying away armored plates. The Crow quaked under the impacts. Suddenly, fire erupted from two other sources, Legate Singh's *Panther* and Knight Holt's *Black Knight*. Both had been hull down behind the rise waiting for their chance.

The *Panther* unleashed a blast from its PPC, a flash of raw, blue-white energy that tore off part of the Crow's rotor. The Spirit Cat craft's attempt to rise above the fight was cut short. It spun out of control, finally diving straight down toward the ground. The Spirit Cat pilot never had a chance. A ball of orange fire plumed into the air, marking the pilot's grave.

The Balac pilot bore in on the legate and fired a barrage of armor-piercing rounds, hitting the *Panther* in the legs and nearly knocking the BattleMech back. The return fire from the *Black Knight* was an incredible light show of death and carnage. Flashes of the extended-range PPCs both hit the Balac, seeming to stop it dead in the air, its forward momentum shattered. The pilot immediately began to turn to face the greater perceived threat, but Alexi Holt was not intimidated.

The turn was cut short when Lieutenant Michelson's Donar joined back in the fight. While most of his shots missed, one emerald laser beam cut a scar along the lower edge of the cockpit, just under the ferroglass armor that kept the pilot alive. The Balac began to belch smoke, whipped by the rotors, and it spun to limp back toward the Spirit Cat lines. A parting shot from the Partisan AAV autocannon fell short of their mark, but ensured that the copter would not continue to be an issue.

Alexi toggled back to her comm channel. "Command, dust one Crow and count the Balac out of the fight."

She was impressed by how quickly Tucker had adjusted to helping her and Legate Singh coordinate the defense from the mobile HQ.

"Good work. Our sensors are picking up movement your way," Tucker's voice came back. "I can't tell for sure, Miss Direction, but it looks like we may have pissed off the Spirit Cats."

"Roger that."

They retreated from the intersection at a full run, heading to the wooded areas sheltering Viewtown Road to the west. Her sensors, and the data feeds she was getting from the mobile HQ, told Alexi what she wanted to know. The Clan warriors had swarmed over the small knoll where the fighting had been, ready for a quick fight. But there was no one there, only the fresh tire marks from the Partisan, 'Mech footprints in the sod, and the burning remains of what had been a Crow scout.

Alexi watched the display. "Come on, Star Captain. You're pretty sure we're up north. You know it'll be hard fighting, but that's where you've got to go to find us. . . ." It was a lie. They had split their force. The more mobile elements, sans the ConstructionMechs, were down Viewtown Road. The infantry had dug into reinforced positions high on the embankments over the roadway, while the rest of the troops held the bottom of the mountain cut to the north, right where the Spirit Cats would expect them to be.

The icons on her display showed that the Cats had stopped, as if the Star captain was thinking about what to do next. *The last thing I need is for him to get a vision of some kind as to where I* really *am.*

She switched to the channel used by Lieutenant Tooley's Furies—the Ground Pounder forces. "Lieutenant Tooley, have Rainmaker fire a volley at maximum range at the intersection."

Tooley's voice came back. "Any specific targets, sir?"

"Just the road."

A long ways off, at the bottom of the mountain cut, the Sniper artillery unleashed a wild volley. Even from her *Black Knight* cockpit she heard the thunderous roar of the artillery's awesome destructive force. The shells from the mobile artillery landed all over the area, drifting toward the rear of the Spirit Cats' location. Elemental infantry scattered for cover, and only the 'Mechs seemed unimpressed by the attack.

The Spirit Cats took the bait.

They formed up into ranks and spread out along Highway Seven heading north, just as she hoped. They moved quickly toward the cut. She was tempted to rush in quickly on their flank, but Alexi had learned long ago to resist such impulses.

"This is the Command wagon," came Tucker's voice. "They are heading north as planned. Furies, you're about to have some company."

Lieutenant Tooley's voice came in loud and clear. "We're as ready as we can be." Alexi heard a crackle of weapons fire. The battle was joined.

The leading edge of the Spirit Cats force raced past him and his squad as if they weren't there. It helped that they hadn't done anything yet to attract attention. Hidden in the rocks high over the highway, Corporal Pusaltari watched as the *Black Hawk,* a *Locust* and a more distant *Warhammer IIC* raced up the roadway followed closely by a lance—no, a Star of armored support.

"Hold your fire," came the calm whisper of his commanding officer.

"Sir, I'd be nuts to fire down at all that crap," he replied in a low whisper.

The *Locust* fired at the DI Morgan assault tank as it ran in reverse, attempting to keep its distance from the advancing 'Mechs. The lightweight *Locust*'s medium laser slashed at the tank, cutting into its armor over the right side. The Morgan paused for a moment right at the peak of the roadway cut and unleashed a volley from its triple PPCs. One shot went wide, doing nothing more than casting a spark at the *Black Hawk* as it passed, burning the paint. The other two shots, bright white, hit the squat *Black Hawk* hard and low, just to one side of the cockpit. An armor plate splattered under the melting blast, showering the *Warhammer* behind it with glowing, red-yellow globules of melted armor plating.

The *Black Hawk* then locked on with its weapons and fired everything at once. Four streak missiles followed the powerful jade bursts from the large lasers, stabbing out in a massive volley of death and destruction. Pusaltari had never seen an alpha strike before, but he knew what one was. By firing everything at once, the *Black Hawk* would overheat, but if it hit its target, the target was dead. He looked up the road and saw something where the tank had been. It was a black mass, burning in a shallow crater that had been the road a moment before. The turret was gone, or so badly cut and burned that it simply was not identifiable. A secondary explosion from the twisted remains of the DI Morgan tank confirmed that it had taken the brunt of the assault. The *Black Hawk* was so hot that steam rose as fresh paint burned. It was dead in its tracks.

Suddenly, the ground erupted as the militia artillery started to rain down. The *Warhammer* juked to the other side of the road, but the *Locust* moved almost directly under his Guila squad. The artillery rounds tore up the roadway in a series of ripple-blasts that threatened to shake him from his perch in the rocks. Pusaltari held on to the ground and his assault rifle and watched as several of the blasts paid back the *Black Hawk*, knocking it down as they engulfed it.

Then down the hill, back from where the Spirit Cats had come, there came the staccato of gun and laser fire. That would be the Knight and the legate, springing the trap. He watched with satisfaction as the *Warhammer IIC* and the *Locust* turned to face their rear. In that one moment, the young corporal knew the Spirit Cats had lost the initiative. And more importantly, he knew *they* knew it, too.

He looked over at Lieutenant Tooley, who gave him the nod. "Third Squad, concentrate on that *Locust*!" He rose up from his perch and fired down right at the ferro-glass cockpit of the 'Mech below him. Pusaltari yelled as he ran, yelled at the top of his lungs. There were no words, only a guttural sound that came from deep within him. Small-arms fire popped off everywhere around him as a squad of Elementals attempted to cover the *Locust*. He didn't care. His head pounded with the red flow of battle.

"Uh-oh," Tucker said unconsciously as he stared at the tactical display in the depths of the HQ vehicle.

"You'd better be a little more specific," Patricia said, spinning her seat to face his screen. She looked at the display as well. "Uh-oh."

Patricia saw the same problem he had spotted. The *Locust* BattleMech had slugged it out with several squads of infantry, but now had broken free. It was heading to the rear of the Wyatt Militia. There wasn't much there, two squads of SRM-armed infantry and the precious Sniper artillery piece. The Clan *Locust* wasn't alone. A battered squad of Elementals and a unit of Purifier armored infantry were punching through as well. If they made it, they could get under the firing umbrella of the Sniper and rip it apart.

Everything he had ever read or studied about Clan warriors was being confirmed by the action on the screen in front of him. They were being hit from two directions at once. If it were him, he'd surrender. Not these warriors. They were not just fighting, but breaking through to the rear of the enemy that had trapped them.

Tucker stared at the display, the dots of light representing each of the units, friendly and enemy. "Two choices. Break off the Behemoth, or pull the artillery and us back and out of the fight."

Patricia nodded as she toggled on the command circuit and adjusted her headset. "Legate, we have problems. The Spirit Cats are heading to the rear."

"Cover our assets," came the battle-strained voice of the legate.

Knight Holt's voice broke in. "You've got the best information, Mr. Harwell. Make the call."

Patricia looked at her brother, locking his gaze for a

millisecond. "Either way should work, Tuck. But you've got to do it now."

Tucker gulped and activated a channel to the units on the field. "Armor Two," he signaled to the Behemoth. "Break off your attack, turn 180 and go after that *Locust* and infantry heading to the rear."

A distant voice crackled in his ears. "I've got infantry on top of my turret trying to cut their way in, damn it."

"Turn around now," Tucker repeated.

"Damn!" the voice swore. "Who the hell is this? Confirm that order."

"Command One," Tucker responded, with a tone of authority he never expected to hear from his own throat. "Get moving now, or good men are going to die."

"Roger that, Command One," the tanker replied. Tucker watched the dot of light representing the IFF transponder for the tank. It blinked once, indicating firing. The *Locust* took the shot from the rear and stopped. It was either down, or stopping its rush to the artillery to turn and fight the new foe.

"You did the right thing, Tucker," Patricia said.

He looked at her. He knew that he was either sending men to their deaths, or sending them to kill others. It may have been the right thing, but it wasn't easy.

The Spirit Cats' charge to attempt to shatter the militia's rear force was not a surprise to Alexi. The warning of their sudden turn had come from numerous sources, including Tucker's semipanicked voice from the mobile HQ. Their subsequent retreat also was not a surprise, but their pattern of fighting did catch her a little off guard. Her opponents did not seem as interested in engaging in battle as they did simply in getting out of the trap she had set. The Star captain's *Warhammer* slowed only long enough to level a blast at the legate's *Panther*. The shots from the *Warhammer*'s quartet of heavy lasers sheared off the left leg of the *Panther*, dropping it like a hamstrung warrior in a medieval battle. She returned fire to the Star captain with her PPCs, turning the *Warhammer*'s left arm into a torn, burned and mangled mess that hung limply from the elbow joint. Even then the Star captain did not stay and fight her.

A ConstructionMech Mark II B tore into the Militia ForestryMech, but only for a moment. It hosed down the smaller ForestryMech with its arm-mounted flamer and scared the Militia pilot into breaking off his assault and fleeing. The Spirit Cat pilot must have been pleased with himself—the Militia's Fox armored car rammed the ConstructionMech at full speed. The impact was a grinding moan of metal and armor, and the right leg of the ConstructionMech wobbled for a moment, fighting for balance, then the 'Mech toppled down, right on top of the Fox. White and gray smoke rose from the carnage. Alexi was glad to see it drop; she had watched it nearly fry her own MiningMech a minute before.

A Condor hovertank came down the road to the intersection, bleeding black smoke, dragging part of its armored skirt on the pavement and showering sparks in its wake. As the Spirit Cat vehicle limped away, it was followed by one other 'Mech, a *Black Hawk*. True to its name, it had been hit so many times by fire it was blackened, its gray and white paint long gone. It limped slowly along, dragging its left leg with each step. She lined up a shot on it, but its course took it to the far side of the legate's fallen *Panther*.

The militia Donar swept in, strafing the Condor, but banked off when a Clan Demon tank came into view and began firing. The Demon crew held their ground, refusing to fall back until the last possible moment, sending several well-placed shots into the Fox as it struggled to get free of the 'Mech on top of it. Then, as quickly as it had jumped into the fight, the Demon broke off and fell back.

Alexi wanted to pursue, wanted to order a full assault, but she knew better. She had been lucky so far. "Tucker, get on the horn. Signal everyone to hold and secure their positions."

"Yes, sir," he replied. "Did we win?"

"For now," she replied. "For now."

*   *   *

From the small clump of brush above the highway, Reo watched the Spirit Cats turn to face a pursuit that just wasn't coming. He took stock of what was missing: a *Locust* that he had seen in Kinross was not there, and also a modified ConstructionMech. From the look of the Star captain's *Warhammer IIC* and the limping *Black Hawk*, Reo Jones had to say this round went to Knight Holt.

But as he watched the repair vehicle extend its mobile gantry and the teams of techs pour out to repair and refit the damaged force, he knew that a battle won did not mean the war was over. Also, he was very curious about this Clan commander, having now seen him in action; he had never heard of a Clan force breaking off a battle.

Reo set aside his binoculars and uncapped his canteen. He'd report what he'd seen to Captain Chaffee . . . in his own sweet time.

20

Tucker stood on the battlefield after the fighting had ended. The smell made an overwhelming first impression: a mix of the aroma of diesel and burning rubber and armor. As he walked through the debris littering the pitted, cratered highway, he caught the sharp smell of feces. He turned reluctantly to find the source, and recoiled in horror at what he saw. Lying on the road only five meters away was a blackened pile of what looked like clothes. It was a trooper—actually, half a trooper. He, or she, was burnt black from whatever had blasted him apart. The smell came from the intestines tangled on the blacktop. The legs were simply gone. Tucker pressed his hands against his mouth, fighting the urge to throw up. Looking away, he saw what he thought was a log on the road surface, then realized it was the severed armored arm and hand of an Elemental warrior.

The Spirit Cat *Locust* loomed ahead, what was left of it. The legs were stripped of armor; snapped and burned myomer muscles hung limp where they had been severed. A sickly green liquid, 'Mech coolant, oozed from one of the holes in the armor of the podlike body, forming a puddle under her legs. *Her.* There was something about 'Mechs that seemed inherently feminine, at least in his mind. Two technicians were standing on the ladder rungs on the legs, one half inside of the cockpit.

Through a light haze of smoke, he spotted the Behemoth II on the rising slope of the road, back toward where the Knight Errant had led the assault against the rear of the Spirit Cats force. The Behemoth was operational, its hull pitted with laser gashes and cratered bursts in the armor plate. Tucker allowed himself a brief, satisfied smile. He had worried that he had sent those men to their death. They had survived—or at least the tank had.

Tucker looked around. He saw wounded, bandaged infantry all around. Their uniforms and body armor were stained the brown of dried blood. They all seemed dirty enough to have been in the wilderness for weeks, rather than two days. When he looked into their eyes, they seemed harder than before the battle.

"You shouldn't be here," said a voice at his side. He turned and saw Legate Singh standing next to him. The commanding officer was wearing only the T-shirt and shorts of an ordinary MechWarrior, with no rank or insignia to identify his position.

"My sister is handling the HQ," Tucker replied in a flat tone.

"This is still a combat zone," the legate replied.

"I had to see for myself," Tucker said, looking around at the carnage.

"I knew these men and women," Singh returned, following Tucker's glance. "It is now my responsibility to contact their families and tell them that their children, their brothers or sisters aren't coming home."

Tucker wiped his eyes and ran his hands through the mess of his hair. "Devlin Stone brought us peace. Maybe that was a mistake."

"I beg your pardon?" came another voice, this one belonging to Alexi Holt, who had moved up on his other side. She looked more tired than he had ever seen her. Her eyes looked bruised.

"Many planets have been so insulated from war in The Republic that we've forgotten what it's like. Maybe if we had seen war from time to time, we wouldn't be in such a hurry to start a new one."

He looked into her eyes and saw that she understood. In the next moment, she closed her eyes and turned away, but he knew that his words had struck home. "The legate is right, Tucker, you shouldn't be in the open like this. The Spirit Cats might regroup any time and strike back."

He resented that both leaders were so concerned for his safety. "Knight Holt, Legate Singh," he said bitterly, "I sent some of those troops into battle. They're all here because of me in some way. I'm not going to hide in the mobile HQ while good men and women die to protect me. I want everyone to see I'm willing to fight, too."

Singh cut him off. "I know how you feel, Mr. Harwell, and your support from Command One was appreciated. But you are too great a prize to risk being killed by a random shot."

"You don't know the first thing about how I feel. I'm not some prize," he gritted out between clenched teeth. "I'm a man, just like you, just like them," he gestured to the armored infantry. "I won't hide."

The legate didn't acknowledge his words, but he saw compassion on Alexi's face. "Tucker, I don't know what you're feeling, but I think I understand what you're saying. You're not qualified to pilot a 'Mech or fire an assault rifle. But you're still qualified to help us. Our equipment is damaged. We've captured enemy gear that might be repairable. Your skill is with technical things. Use your skills to help, so that when the Spirit Cats come back, the rest of us can do our jobs."

That wasn't the answer he wanted. He wanted to fight. He wanted a gun, or a shoulder-mounted missile launcher. But she was right, and he knew it. "Thank you, Knight Holt," he said. "Where do I start?"

She turned and pointed to the Behemoth. "That tank packs a hell of a wallop. See what you can do to make sure she's operational."

Tucker nodded and jogged away.

"Are you mad?" Legate Singh asked as Tucker took off at a trot to catch up with the repair team heading for the tank. "If he gets killed, all of this was for nothing."

Alexi gave the legate her best stern gaze. "You heard him on the comm channel, Legate. He ordered that crew into the fight just like a trained soldier. He needs to deal with his guilt over any losses they suffered, and this is the best way. Anyway, he could be killed in the mobile HQ just as easily as in the open."

"This is reckless. Their remaining helicopter has already skirted us twice, taking potshots."

"We are taking a risk," Alexi corrected him. "But we'll hedge our bets," she said, signaling one of the men wearing Guila suits to join them. "We'll assign a trooper to protect him—from a distance, of course."

Tucker and one of the tank crewmen, Private Ugus, held the temporary armor-plate patch in place while a tech welded it. Glancing over his shoulder, he saw an infantryman standing only ten meters away, with his massive assault rifle at the ready. As the white-hot metal tossed sparks from the welding torch, Harwell averted his eyes and considered the trooper.

"Hey," he called.

The corporal cocked an eyebrow. "You callin' me?"

"Yeah," Tucker said, casting a quick glance at the armor plate on the hull of the tank to see if the welding was finished. It wasn't.

The corporal walked forward a few steps. "What?"

"Are you watching me?"

"Something like that," he replied. He was now close

enough for Tucker to make out the infantryman's name on his uniform. Pusaltari.

"The legate put you up to this?" Tucker asked.

"Nope. Knight Holt ordered me to protect you."

Tucker cursed silently. *Damn it.* He didn't want this kind of help, and he knew he didn't need it. "You can go. I'm fine."

"No offense," the corporal said calmly, "but I don't take orders from you. She told me to watch you, and that's what I'm going to do." As he stopped speaking, both men heard a low, thumping sound in the distance, getting louder. Tucker wasn't sure what it was at first, but then the noise became clear. Rotors. A helicopter. He checked the tech working with him and noticed that he was welding much faster, much sloppier.

"Is that ours?" Tucker called out to Corporal Pusaltari.

They both saw it as it came over the edge of the cut in the highway. It was a beast, a predator. It was the Spirit Cat Balac again. The copter paused for a moment at the apex of the hill, then turned toward the Behemoth where they were working.

It fired.

Tucker half fell, half dove off the hull of the tank the moment he saw the puff of smoke from the Balac. He hit the road hard and rolled to get away. The Behemoth crew leapt into action as well. The tank roared to life and began to back up, turning its turret to fire. Private Ugus disappeared down a hatch and buttoned up.

An explosion rocked the ground near where the tank had been. Tucker instinctively, uselessly threw his arms over his head for protection as coin-sized chunks of concrete rained down on his body. Next to him, the corporal raised his assault rifle and poured a barrage of fire upward. Other infantry troops joined in. Laser shots stabbed upward at the Balac. Tucker looked in front of him and saw something he had missed before—a pistol.

The gun wasn't much. Against the helicopter, it was a toy. But these men and women were fighting, and he felt the need to be doing the same. Picking up the heavy weapon, he rolled onto his back, leveled it at the Balac and pulled the trigger. The gun jumped in his hands as he emptied the clip. He was convinced that every shot missed, but it felt good. He was trying to kill that craft— kill or be killed. The infantry fire rocked the Spirit Cat craft, and it broke off.

Corporal Pusaltari looked at Tucker down on the ground. "You okay?"

"I guess so," he stammered. It wasn't the truth. Physically, he was fine. He dropped the pistol to the road. Mentally, he now understood what it was to be in combat. All of his boyhood daydreams were shattered. This was not the heroics he envisioned. This was dirty and deadly.

As he rose, he dusted off the most obvious chunks of roadway debris. He looked over at the Behemoth II, where repair work had already begun again. "Where are you going?" the corporal asked.

Tucker turned to look at him, resolve gleaming in his eyes. "I have work to do."

Pusaltari paused for a moment. "Right," he said slowly. He followed his charge by a few meters, rifle at the ready.

For Alexi, the hours passed quickly into the evening as the battered force of the Wyatt Militia regrouped. Overall, their personnel losses had been light, but the damage to equipment was heavy. The good news was that they had managed, with help from the ComStar techs, to repair the former Spirit Cat *Locust* to fighting condition, though it was made mostly of spare parts. Most of their vehicles sported patchwork armor, and some had makeshift replacement weapons, a few of those salvaged from the equipment the Spirit Cats left behind.

The amount of equipment the Cats had left behind showed that they had taken a hit as well. Her trap had worked as well as could be expected; they were hurt, but as dangerous as an injured animal. The Spirit Cats had sent several recon sorties to test their perimeter defense, but each time they got close Patricia jammed their comm systems from the mobile HQ. It was enough to keep the suspicious Spirit Cats from pressing too far forward, fearing they might stumble into yet another trap. *Good,* Alexi thought. *In just six days a DropShip will arrive in-system, and I can get Tucker Harwell out of here and to safety. I just have to hold off until then.*

As she walked across the encampment, a whistling noise caused her to duck instinctively. There was a thump and hiss some fifty meters ahead, near the militia's Sniper artillery. Shouts rang out from the infantry and she saw people running—with good reason. A wisp of phosphorescent smoke rose into the air, glowing yellow-green in the twilight.

A spotting round.

A whooshing roar followed a moment later with a blast that knocked her off balance. Artillery! She kept her feet under her but was staggering like a drunk as she headed toward Miss Direction. This was the first she knew of the Spirit Cats boasting artillery among their assets. "Fan out! Move that artillery piece out of here!" she shouted.

All around the Sniper artillery rounds exploded, eating the ground as the slow-moving piece tried to get clear. A chunk of its side armor twisted away in one bright-orange blast. Damn! Alexi rocked back from another concussion in the evening air, this time losing her footing.

Then, as suddenly as it began, the rain of artillery stopped. Personnel shouted status reports, sounding oddly quiet compared to the blasts. People still were running in every direction. Her right ear was ringing from the last burst, and Alexi barely heard her wrist communicator beeping.

"This is Knight One," she said.

She heard Tucker's voice. "We're getting a message for you."

A message? "Send it."

The wrist communicator crackled and a booming, arrogant voice drowned out the ringing in her ear. "Knight Holt, this is Captain Chaffee of Chaffee's Cut-Throats. You've just experienced a taste of the firepower at my disposal. I know you've been fighting the Spirit Cats and are in no condition to face fresh troops.

"Turn over Tucker Harwell to me and the Wyatt Militia will be spared. If you refuse, I'll just kill you all and take him anyway. You have fifteen minutes."

21

The Knight Errant stood in the road for a moment, just thinking. This was what she had trained for her whole life, to lead men and women in battle. She always won her fights—with the exception of her trial against Star Captain Cox. No, now was not the time to think about losing or surrender. This was the time for action. Through the haze of the artillery barrage, the jogging figure of Legate Singh emerged, his face spotted with black dots from blast-smoke. Alexi saw him coming and spoke into her wrist communicator.

"Tucker, have Lieutenant Johannson scramble our air defenses and fan our ground forces up into the hills. Chaffee has to have some forward fire controllers up there for that artillery to be so accurate."

"I heard the message," Legate Singh said, huffing

slightly from the run. "You intend to fight Bannson's people?"

She shook her head. "No, I intend to beat them."

"But the Spirit Cats . . ."

In her mind the entire topography of the area came into focus. "He must have used a secondary road and come cross-country to our east. That's the only way he could have gotten a force from Kinross close enough to hit us. Chaffee thinks we've been bloodied pretty badly by the Spirit Cats—"

"He's right."

"We're not as battered as he thinks we are, Legate," she returned. "We'll leave behind our modified MiningMech—what's left of it, in case the Spirit Cats push us at the same time. That covers our rear enough to give us warning." Overhead, the Donar rose into the air and headed for the high ground over the roadway, looking for the Cut-Throats spotters. "The rest of the force will move a half kilometer north, then go off-road to the east. If we clear out his observers, we should be able to turn his flank and come down on him from the north."

"Knight Holt," Legate Singh pleaded. "That terrain up there is rough. Our people are tired."

"We roll," she said. "Better tired than dead."

"Knight Holt," he persisted. "You must be objective. We are still talking about just one man, here. Is keeping hold of Tucker Harwell really worth all this risk? I'm asking you to at least entertain negotiations with Bannson's folks, or even the Spirit Cats. So much loss of life for one man's safety makes no sense."

Fear. She could almost smell it on the legate's breath. "Tucker Harwell is a citizen of The Republic and deserves the same protection we would extend to anyone else. More important, he's the best shot the Inner Sphere has at restoring the HPG network—maybe bringing an end to all of the fighting everywhere. For the last time, Legate, this is not up for debate."

"I am in charge of these forces," Singh countered.

"Ah. As a point of order, as Knight Errant, my authority supercedes yours. Up until now, I have been as diplomatic as possible to accommodate your existing infrastructure and your feelings. But I no longer feel obligated to do so. I am under orders from my Paladin to take whatever measures are necessary to secure Wyatt and protect Tucker Harwell. If that means relieving you of command, Legate," she said in a tone pitched only for his ears, "then I'll do it. Otherwise, deploy your forces as I have ordered. Have I made myself clear?"

He was stung by her words, and he looked as if he were sucking something sour. "Yes, Knight Holt. I understand completely."

Captain Rutger Chaffee saw his trike squad roar over the hill at full speed, heading straight toward him. He had lost their signal a few minutes ago, when they claimed that the militia Donar was harassing their position. Now they were running back. He swore he would chew them out good for leaving their post as forward fire observers.

"Sweep Two," he said, from the head-shaped cockpit of his *Blade*. "You mind telling me why you're here?"

"We were being fired on and jammed," replied the squad leader's voice. "Sir, I think the militia is moving out to the north."

"Trying to flee, most likely," Rutger guessed. "They fought hard with the Spirit Cats. That had to cost them dearly. Nobody tangles with the Cats and walks away without some serious scratches. They know they're not a match for us."

"Sir, they looked mostly operational," the voice of Sweep Two contradicted. "I even saw some captured Spirit Cat gear."

Chaffee chuckled. "Trust me. They tangled with a Star of Clan warriors. These weekend fighters are no match for that kind of skill. We've got them on the run." In a way, he was glad the militia was running. The rush to get up into the hills had spread his own company out over several kilometers, with the slower supply vehicles pulling up the rear. This meant the Cut-Throats were not at their peak in terms of strength, but in his mind they still were more than a match for the battered militia. "Stand by on my orders to head west to the highway. Upon intersect, we'll start whittling away at their rear guard until they give in."

He had taken a single step forward in the *Blade* when a voice burst in his earpiece. It was clouded in static, hard to hear, but he knew it was one of his pickets. ". . .'Mechs on the outer marker . . ." it crackled.

He boosted the gain on his comm gear to try to get a better signal. "Say again, unit reporting. Your message is breaking up."

There was a roar all around his *Blade*, manmade thunder that shook him wildly. His portly body slammed into the restraining straps and he felt them dig into his flesh. Orange and red fireballs and explosions rose up with rings of black everywhere he looked. He throttled the 'Mech into reverse, taking a step back, almost losing his balance. *Artillery? Here? How?* For a moment he felt a chill. Maybe the Spirit Cats had learned of his deception. That thought scared him more than any other. Or maybe the Clansmen had mistaken him for the militia. Over his comm system he heard multiple voices overlapping a wave of static that seemed to drown out everything audible.

"Sit rep!" he barked. "Where in the hell is that artillery coming from?"

Suddenly a voice came in loud and clear. "They're on our flank! We've been turned!"

He turned in time to see vehicles of the Wyatt Militia plow into his strung-out force.

"Crudstunk!" he muttered, turning his *Blade* to face the battle line.

Alexi Holt was surprised at the small size of the mercenary force Chaffee had brought to engage her. Then she thought about it and realized how far his unit must be spread out, given the speed and distance they had been forced to cover to pursue the militia. The mercenaries thought the militia had been much more badly mauled than they were now learning—a mistake for which they would pay. She raised Miss Direction's left arm with its deadly PPC and medium lasers and switched all those weapons to the same target interlock circuit. As she ran down the hill she locked onto the first 'Mech she saw, a *Blade* standing in the middle of a cratered piece of turf, compliments of her artillery barrage. With smooth precision she moved the targeting reticle onto the center of the *Blade* as it lifted its foot to move forward.

As she fired, she felt a wave of heat rise in her cockpit and the hairs on her bare arms lift slightly as the particle projector cannon discharged its manmade lightning. The green laser beams seemed to coax the charged particle blast right into the lower torso of the *Blade*. The mercenary 'Mech rocked back as if it had been punched. Her lasers cut swaths, black and glowing red from the heat, along the crotch of the *Blade* while her PPC left a craterlike mark in the gut, sparks flying about wildly in the center of the blackened hole.

Off to her right flank, she could see a squad of Cut-Throat minigun cycles rushing her ConstructionMech. These were nothing more than dirt bikes armed with a pair of side-mounted armor-piercing missiles. They roared up to almost point-blank range of the lumbering beast and fired. The missiles ripped into the under-armored sides and front of the 'Mech. It wobbled and attempted to turn. Sweeping out its excavator arm as it fought to stay upright, it struck one biker, sending him and his vehicle flying. A series of crimson laser bursts splattered up the side of the IndustrialMech, mauling the left claw arm and severing the hydraulics, spraying a cloud of white mist into the air. The ConstructionMech listed to the side and went down hard, grinding into the sod. Alexi noticed with some satisfaction that at least one of the minigun cycles had been too close when it fell and had been crushed under its weight.

She turned to see where the shot had come from. A fifty-ton *Ghost* BattleMech, painted light green and bearing the insignia of Bannson's Raiders on the torso, seemed to come out of nowhere, looming up near a Padilla artillery vehicle and blazing away with its large pulse lasers. The red bursts of energy were like fireworks all around her, some ripping into her right-arm replacement armor, splattering globs of the unpainted plates around as if they were mercury.

Legate Singh's still unsteady *Panther* stopped for a moment near her and fired at the *Ghost*. His shot was true, hitting one of the legs of the *Ghost* at the knee with a PPC shot that sent raw energy arcing around the waist of the merc. She turned her attention back to the *Blade*, which seemed to be targeting the militia's J-37 ordnance transport. No, that vehicle was too damn precious. Not only could it ferry troops into battle, it was a repair vehicle. "Furies, concentrate on that *Blade*, now!" she barked as she lined up her own shot.

The tiny dune buggy–like Shandra scout reacted first. It raced right at the *Blade*, apparently unafraid of its towering foe. The twin guns on the rear swung forward and fired. The shots hit, though the armor of the *Blade* seemed to mock them, sending more sparks up from ricochets than any real damage. But the Shandra didn't slow down. It bore down and slammed into the left leg of the BattleMech, its rear rising slowly into the air, then dropping down with a thud as its bumper became tangled with the *Blade*'s shin.

Alexi didn't wait. She fired her left-arm PPC at the *Blade*, striking again near her first hit. The shot dug in deep and cut a jagged, blackened rip in the armor. The *Blade* rocked back and toppled over, just in time for a squad of militia to swarm over it. She saw the arms flaying in the air, but there was no hope. They would be in the cockpit in a few heartbeats.

The mercenary *Ghost* let go with a salvo of short-range missiles at the militia's Tamerlane strike sled. The missiles crossed in the air with a larger salvo from the militia's JES missile carrier, aimed at a hoverbike squad that disappeared in a cloud of smoke, shrapnel and death. The Tamerlane, struck by the *Ghost*, rocked sideways under the impact, scooting a full fifty meters into a clump of trees. The *Ghost* MechWarrior was good. He rushed in to draw fire from the already damaged Padilla artillery piece, giving the vehicle a chance to make a break for it. Legate Singh fired at the *Ghost* and missed, but the *Ghost* returned the salvo, this time with a full barrage from its pulse lasers. The legate's 'Mech was pitted with black spots where the armor had been burned and melted from the onslaught. Wisps of smoke rose from the tiny holes as Singh throttled to a run, juking right, away from the fighting.

The two minigun cycle squads swung around for a parting shot at the Shandra as it wrenched itself free from the leg of the defeated *Blade* with a metallic moan. They hit it from behind and the tiny scout bloomed with yellow flames and black, rolling smoke. The gunner and driver never had a chance. Alexi did not mourn them yet; instead, she turned her attention back to the *Ghost* in hopes of another shot.

Another Bannson vehicle, a low-riding Mars assault tank, came up on Alexi's tactical display. It appeared at the top of a nearby hill long enough to unleash a hellish barrage of missiles. The wave of death and destruction rose up over the battlefield in a long arc, then dropped down on the *Locust*, which was blasting away at a squad of nearby infantry. The light 'Mech, more parts than original equipment, was engulfed in a series of tiny yellow explosions. The Knight could only make out the raised, podlike missile laser racks on the sides. As the smoke cleared, the remains of the Locust came into view. This time there would be no repair. It listed slightly, then collapsed. The Mars vehicle broke into a flat-out flight before anyone could lock onto it.

Across the battlefield, the Cut-Throats *Ghost* was a fading image, retreating over the crest of the green hill before she could acquire a weapons lock. Surveying the battlefield, she saw parts of the Padilla artillery vehicle marking a trail to where it had finally ground to a halt. A JES III missile carrier lay on its side, belching gray smoke from what had been its cockpit. A roaring fire rose from what was left of the Militia's Construction-

Mech. They had taken down the lightweight *Blade*, but the *Ghost* had gotten away. The *Ghost* had to be Chaffee—merc commanders almost always piloted the heavier BattleMechs.

The mobile HQ appeared over the ridge behind her. Then, and only then, did she know that they had won the battle. *But are we in any condition to win the war?*

Captain Casson swung his *Sun Cobra* to a stop at the edge of the wooded area and checked his long-range sensors. His scouts were out ahead, tasked with creating a picture for him of what they were facing. They had been on planet for a few days now, and the situation was shaping up to be intriguing, to say the least.

The satellite report from his deep-cover operative had told him that the militia was on Highway Seven outside Kinross, heading north. And there were two other military forces on Wyatt. The Spirit Cats had tangled with the Wyatt Militia and had been lured into an ambush by the Knight Errant. *What was her name? Ah yes, Alexi Holt.*

In addition, Jacob Bannson had a little-known mercenary unit, Chaffee's Cut-Throats, on Wyatt. They had rushed in to catch the militia out in the open following the militia's battle with the Spirit Cats, apparently assuming that the planetary defenders would simply succumb to them. Far from rolling over, the militia had slammed into the leading edge of the spread-out mercenary force and had driven them back, at least for the moment.

Casson figured Knight Holt was going to be a problem. His source said that she was taking Harwell's safety as her personal responsibility and keeping him buttoned up in the mobile HQ. That being the case, acquiring the ComStar adept would be tricky. Harwell was only of use if he was alive, and mobile HQs were slow vehicles, lightly armed and armored—easy to destroy, but hard to capture.

Ivan Casson planned to leverage the strategy that Bannson's people had tried. Each fight that the Wyatt Militia engaged in weakened them; one more battle

should soften up everyone involved enough so that his
Talons could ride in and sweep the battlefield. Not that
Captain Casson was not afraid of a tough battle. He had
fought and been badly injured in the fighting for Oh-
rensen, so he knew how to survive a stand-up fight. But
on this mission, his goal was simply to secure Tucker
Harwell and get off-world with minimal losses.

His scouts reported that the Spirit Cats were nearly
ready to resume the fight. The Cut-Throats were re-
grouping for a counterassault. Let them both hit the militia at least one more time.

This is far too easy. . . . He throttled his *Sun Cobra*
into a faster stride. Behind him, the rest of his company
pulled into formation and followed. With any luck, this
fighting would be over in a day or two, and when the
dust settled, the Oriente Protectorate, the last true fragment of the once-great Free Worlds League, would control the fate of The Republic of the Sphere. *Once more,
we will assume our rightful place in the seats of
power. . . .*

He keyed in the encryption codes and transmitted a
coded message to the DropShip at the LZ, then activated
the relay coding to bounce and boost the signal up to the
satellite in orbit. He needed more intelligence in order to
proceed, something that his operative would be able to
provide him. His fingers rapped on the keyboard, coding
the message for the deep-cover agent. All that remained
was to designate a code signal for when to strike.

Book Three

The Peace of Focht Be with You

"We were in the Allegheny Operations Theatre, Roanoke Valley. It might have been 3078—no, maybe 3077. Wait, that's right, it was in the Midwest, outside of Cleveland. All right, it was Terra—I'm sure of that much. You'll have to forgive my memory—like a lot of us, it's fading (crowd laughs).

"We were rooting out the last desperate little fragment of the Word of Blake. That's when I first met him. I reported to his mobile HQ with my new orders and he came out just as I got there. I saluted him. Just stood there like a jackass, facing one of the greatest military leaders in the history of mankind.

"Anastasius Focht looked a lot older than I expected. His role in the Jihad had been more political than in the field, so why he was there, I don't know. I just know this, it was a real treat to see him. My father and my grandfather both knew the man. He returned my salute and took a glance at my noteputer with my orders on it. He asked me if I was related to Demi-Precentor Seagrams Harwell. I told him I was his son. He told me that he knew my father and thought highly of him.

"He was just handing back my orders when an artillery round came down on the far side of that mobile HQ. It went off like a thunderclap. I was tossed around and landed on top of Focht. I remember spitting the dirt out of my mouth and checking him, rolling him over, to make sure he was all right. He was a little dazed, so was I.

"I asked him if he was okay and he said he was. I let

out a sigh and said, 'Peace of Focht be with us.' That lit
him up. He got to his feet and told me to never say that
again. The old man told me that so many crimes had
been committed by the Word of Blake as their warriors
screamed, 'Peace of Blake be with you,' that he hated
that we had changed it to reflect him. I apologized like
hell; I admit it—I was embarrassed.

"You know what he did? He smiled at me and said
that we shouldn't be ashamed of our past. ComStar was,
and is a great organization, he said, but no single man,
him and Blake included, deserved to have their name be
used as a prayer, and he didn't want to hear Com Guards
members say that sort of thing. 'I'm just a man doing a
man's work,' he said.

"There aren't many of us left. Most of our comrades
were purged, and Focht is gone. I marched in the ceremony to honor him and served as part of the honor
guard. And I never forgot what he said to me that day."

—*Com Guards Veterans Association,*
Terra Chapter 4 Gathering
8 November 3129
Presentation by Demi-Precentor (Retired) Drake Harwell

22

"**S**o there you have it," Legate Singh said wearily, leaning against one of the consoles in the cramped space inside the mobile HQ as he surveyed his officers. "We've suffered nearly fifty-five percent casualties since we left Kinross."

Alexi didn't flinch at the numbers. She had expected worse losses for a planetary militia unit going up against a Clan and a trained mercenary unit. The choice was to see the glass half empty or half full. "Legate, your assessment is correct. We lost our ConstructionMech and the *Locust* we repaired. We recovered the *Blade*, several of those missile-armed motorcycles and a hoverbike or two. The *Blade* can probably be repaired. And we captured several prisoners."

"That doesn't change the fact that we're way below our operational combat strength. These kinds of casualties—

well, we need to consider another option." His gaze drifted over to the corner where Tucker stood. Displaced by the impromptu meeting, he and his sister Patricia stood in the farthest corner of the HQ vehicle. Tucker felt the stares of everyone in the tight quarters, but crossed his arms and said nothing.

Holt ignored the opening for another discussion about giving up Tucker Harwell. "Operational strength is not an issue, in my opinion. Your troops have proved themselves against two different forces, both with superior experience. We need to recover whatever ammo and gear we can gather, execute repairs with priority to the BattleMechs, and get moving as quickly as possible."

Lieutenant Tooley rubbed his face. "The men are tired, but if we keep them moving they won't have time to bitch about it. Where do you suggest we go, ma'am?"

"My original plan was for us to move north to the lakes. We can use the camp there," she replied, pointing to the topographical map on the wall display unit of the console next to the legate. "We've hit both the Spirit Cats and the Cut-Throats hard, but it's only a matter of time before one or both of them regroup and come after us." Alexi's bet was on the Spirit Cats; they had been far too quiet since the battle of Ben Venue.

"We'll have tough going," Captain Irwin added. "The terrain up there is difficult for the wheeled and tracked vehicles."

She nodded. "Understood. The sooner we take off, the better," she replied, glancing over at the legate. Singh shook his head in reluctant agreement.

"We have another problem," Lieutenant Johannson, his head bandaged from injuries suffered in the last attack, spoke up. "We lost three of our techs in the fight with the mercs. We're going to need some help."

"We've got to get that *Blade* operational or abandon it," she returned. Her eyes found Tucker. "We've asked a lot from you already, Adept Harwell, but we still need you and your ComStar team."

He gave her a thin smile. "We'd be glad to help."

"Good," she said. "We have half an hour. After that, we go mobile."

Star Captain Cox stood on the roadway looking at the pile of wreckage that had been combat vehicles earlier that day. His nostrils stung from the smell of burned ferrofibrous armor and insulation that still hung in the air. He laid his hand on the metallic surface of the mangled hovercraft lying under the wreckage of the ConstructionMech Mark IIB. The metal was still warm, and he rubbed the soot-smeared green paint with his thumb, as if touching it would tell him something.

The Wyatt Militia was long gone. His scouts had ranged two kilometers up the highway but had found only indications of their movement, no sign of troops or vehicles. As he leaned on the savaged wrecks, the Star captain considered what had happened.

He had taken the bait Knight Alexi had laid out for him, and she had closed the trap. His force had pushed in both directions at once and gotten free, but they had lost equipment and personnel. Even with repairs, he was at 60 percent combat capability.

The losses were replaceable. What bothered him was the defeat itself. He had taken out the Knight Errant in single combat—now she had returned the favor. The loss stung in his mouth like bile.

All that remained was his honor.

Another warrior walked over to him, noteputer in hand, and saluted. Cox stood up, taking his hand off the hovercraft, and returned the gesture. "Tell me, Point Commander Barton. You are my Watch, the unit's eyes and ears. Intelligence is your responsibility. What is your analysis?" He waved his hand at the wreckage.

Barton was a tall man, commander of a Point of Elemental warriors, genetically engineered infantry that fought in power armor. His face bore swirling, red-and-green tattoos and his right eyebrow was pierced with tiny rivets taken from the seat of the first 'Mech Barton had destroyed in battle. Even out of his battle armor he was an imposing and dangerous figure. Barton silently stared at the carnage for a moment. "I see betrayal, Star Captain."

Cox's eyebrows rose at his short answer, "Explain."

"This is a Wyatt Militia Fox-class hovercraft."

"Aff."

"The Wyatt Militia has only one Fox hovercraft in its TO&E. A Fox-class vehicle painted with the insignia of the Wyatt Militia was loaded with explosives and detonated in our encampment in Kinross." His voice betrayed no emotion.

Cox had arrived at the same conclusion when he had seen the wrecked hovercraft. That was why he had stopped his Spirit Cats on the ruins of the battlefield. "What does this mean to you?"

"One of two things. First, the militia may have had more than one Fox in their arsenal. Second, the Fox used in the terrorist attack against us did not belong to the Militia, but was owned by another faction on the planet."

The Star captain understood the implications of the second option. "It is possible that someone deceived us into fighting the militia, *quiaff*?"

"*Aff*, Star Captain," Barton replied.

"Prepare to move out," he said. *We have directed our retribution at the wrong target. We will correct this mistake.*

Tucker walked over to the three prisoners. Patricia pointed to one of the men and said, "That one." She had chosen an older man wearing a faded jumpsuit and a rough look. Tucker reminded himself to ask her later how she decided that he was the MechWarrior. The man was handcuffed with his wrists behind his back and restrained by a plastic tie between his ankles, loose enough for a hobbled walk if he needed to relieve himself. His jumpsuit was missing his rank insignia; even his name patch had been torn off.

"You," Tucker said to the man. "What's your name?"

"Lieutenant Rod Blakely," he replied gruffly.

"You were the MechWarrior piloting the *Blade*, right?"

"Yes," he said bitterly.

"All right," Tucker said. "I need your access codes."

The man calling himself Blakely laughed out loud. "You're kidding me, right?"

Tucker frowned. "No, I'm quite serious. I need your codes."

"Why should I give them to you?"

Tucker paused, unsure of what to say. His sister, however, did not hesitate. Stepping forward, she planted her right foot carefully into the mercenary's crotch. The portly man flinched, but, there wasn't a lot he could do to protect himself. She flexed her knee, pushing hard enough to get his attention. Tucker stared at Patricia, more stunned by her action than was the mercenary she was torturing.

"Hey," Blakely squeaked, twisting slightly on the ground but unable to get away.

"My brother asked you for the access codes. You asked why you should give them to him. How about this for a reason? If you don't give him the codes, I crush your crotch flatter than a snake on a busy highway?" To emphasize her point, she leaned forward, grinding her heel slightly as she did so.

The man's face reddened. "This is against the damn rules of war. Soldiers can't torture fellow soldiers. Ares Conventions, damn it."

Patricia smiled. "Those rules don't apply to us. We're not soldiers. We're ComStar."

The mercenary glared at her, his eyes filling with tears of pain. "My override code is Alpha-two-two-one-Victor-five."

Tucker jerked his gaze away from his sister and scribbled down the code. Patricia lifted her foot. "Thank you for your cooperation. Peace of Focht be with you."

Tucker stared at Patricia again. This was not the sister he knew. There was an edge to her, an anger he had never seen before. Then, as quickly as she had turned it on, it disappeared. *It must be the stress.*

As they turned and walked away, the MechWarrior cursed softly. "Screw you. I'll show you peace when I get out of this." Captain Rutger Chaffee leaned back against the tree and wondered how his unit was faring and how long he'd be able to keep up the act of being a flunky officer.

The Protectorate *Sun Cobra* slowed slightly as the message came to Captain Casson. "Recon Three reporting, sir" came the signal, crisp and clear.

"This is Eagle One, go Recon Three," he said, punching up the long-range sensors. The scouts were fanned out far and wide in the countryside, attempting to locate the Wyatt Militia and the prized ComStar adept. Recon Three was a good ten kilometers ahead, piloting a Scimitar Mk II hovercraft. They were the northwest point of the search pattern. "Right where I thought the militia'd be," he said to himself with a grin.

"We're picking up chatter on the comm channels, sir; military in origin. I'd estimate their range at twenty-five to thirty klicks on a northwest bearing."

Captain Casson stared at the display. The sun was setting. Night operations carried inherent risks. The last thing he wanted was to accidentally kill Adept Harwell. "Can you ID the forces you're picking up?"

"We believe it to be the mercenaries under Bannson's banner," came back the voice of Recon Three. "Confidence is sixty percent; six-oh."

"Roger that," Casson replied. He pondered for a moment. This wasn't the target he was looking for, but it was the next best thing. The mercenaries would follow the militia. "Recon Three, maintain your station. Monitor transmissions and activity." He switched to the broadband channel to send a message to the rest of his unit. "Talons, this is where we camp tonight. I want a tight perimeter and three watches."

Casson toggled the comm system to send a message to his DropShip, to relay to the satellite. He keyed in his map coordinates, date and time. His operative was out there somewhere, and he was counting on him to help bring home victory.

*   *   *

It was early evening when Star Captain Cox arrived at the battlefield his scouts had located. He saw the mangled wreckage of a Wyatt Militia ConstructionMech, its few remaining spots of paint and half the image of Wyatt on its torso the only indication that it was indeed a militia machine. There were craters, torn sod, scorched soil—all the telltale marks of a fierce battle. These remains were fresh, fresher than the field he had come from earlier in the afternoon. The smell of the fight was still in the air.

Point Commander Barton emerged from the fallen 'Mech and jogged over to his commanding officer. He held a torn scrap of cloth, part of a uniform, that he had obviously pulled from under the 'Mech. It was crusted with blood.

"Who were they fighting?" Cox asked.

"The mercenaries," replied Barton, handing over a pair of shoulder patches. One showed the battle-ax insignia of Bannson's Raiders, one blade forming a distorted B and the other an R. The other patch was a scull and cross-bones design, with the bones replaced by two bloody daggers with the words CUT-THROATS at the top of the logo.

"Bannson's Raiders," Cox said aloud.

"*Aff*, Star Captain," Barton replied. "Infrared scans show that the tracks from the militia are hours old, heading north. The tracks of the mercenaries following in pursuit are newer."

Cox crumpled the patches into a ball in his fist. "These mercenaries are interfering with the honor of our Clan," he said coldly. "This will not stand."

23

Crater Lakes
North of Kinross, Wyatt
The Republic, Prefecture VIII
21 May 3135

Under normal circumstances, Crater Lakes must have been a restful campsite. The dense, second-generation forest surrounding the lakes came up almost to the edge of the water. The rustic log and stone cabins were hidden among the trees. Further north were the logging camps, but here, where Highway Seven terminated in a dirt road, Crater Lakes was a resort.

For now.

Alexi Holt surveyed the area with a sigh of relief. They had been moving north for a day and a half when the highway turned east for two kilometers and abruptly came to an end. Here, she hoped they could recoup, repair and hole up. Paladin Sorenson had said that reinforcements would come sometime after 25 May. If the Wyatt Militia could hold out long enough, the forces chasing her might suddenly face a more equal fight.

The dense forests would limit the mobility of any attackers, which was good. Open meadows had been cleared for the tourists near the shore of the largest body of water, Higgins Lake, and they provided a discreet area where combat could take advantage of direct line of sight. They could build breastworks at the far end of the fields, making them deadly places to fight. The water of the lake would help cool their 'Mechs, allowing her troops to push themselves with less risk of overheating. And the cool mountain waters supplementing the work of the heat sinks would be a blessing for a MechWarrior in the heat of battle. But Alexi knew even all these factors were not enough to tip the tide of battle in her favor.

There has to be another way. Her pursuers would come and come hard. The planetary militia was already under strength. Legate Singh was right; his troops were on the edge. With 55 percent casualties, the men and women were holding on by sheer force of will. Most units would have fallen apart with losses so high. They should have fallen apart a while ago, but she did not allow that to happen. *I didn't have a choice.*

She had done her part, leading from the front, talking to nearly every member of the command personally during the trek up. She prodded, slapped backs, yelled, complimented and did everything else she could think of to motivate them to keep going. Now a handful of them were taking a much-deserved swim and bath in the lake. Alexi closed her eyes in weary restraint. She wanted to yell at them, tell them to work on defenses. A gentle mountain breeze ruffled her hair, and she caught her own scent; earthy, sweaty, the stench of battle.

How to turn the tide? The dense forest seemed to offer the most possibilities. Burn it? Much of it was green wood, and the rains in the last few weeks made a successful fire improbable. She looked along the cleared area of the lakeshore and the formidable wall of trees. Down along Higgins Lake, nearly three kilometers back, she knew that Highway Seven ran parallel to the lakeshore—separated by the forest. Any attacking force would have to come up the highway.

Continuing her survey, she turned and saw a technician stringing a diesel refueling hose to the Militia's Forestry-Mech. The small IndustrialMech was burned almost top to bottom from its battle with the Spirit Cats. The militia troops had begun to call it "Hot Dog," in reference to its blackened paint. It carried a heavy claw for a left arm and a massive chainsaw tipped with industrial-diamond cutting teeth for a right arm. Even massive, first-generation-growth trees would fall easily to a fast swipe with those dangerous cutting blades. Alexi had seen what the blade could do to 'Mechs and vehicles, and the results were not pretty.

Thoughts of Hot Dog and the woods suddenly clicked. There was only one road up here, one way in or out. *What if we make our own road?* Using the ForestryMech and perhaps the modified MiningMech, they could move along Higgins Lake and make their own shortcut back through the forest to Highway Seven. If they made their cut far enough back from the road, they could remain hidden and punch through the last few meters as an enemy approached the camp, hitting them either in the flank or the rear. With a small force left at the camp, she would set nearly the same trap she had used successfully on the Spirit Cats.

For the first time in several days, Alexi Holt felt a ripple of hope. She would be able to rotate the troops between rest, repairs and cutting the road. *Now we just need to identify the forces on our tail.*

Tucker stared at the communications console inside the mobile HQ, his eyes running down long columns of numbers. His sister came in, her hair still wet. Since their arrival at Crater Lakes a few hours earlier, the one luxury that everyone, including Tucker, had enjoyed, was a long overdue bath.

"So," she said, combing her hair with her fingers to help dry it, "you're the armchair general in the family. What do you think of the defense the Knight is planning?"

Tucker snorted. It struck him as funny that she considered him the armchair general since, from what he had seen, she seemed to have a solid grasp of military operations herself. "Seems good. I ran some long- and short-range topographical scans and found the optimal path for the new road, given the range of the weapons, the curve of the highway, the position of the camp and the cutting rate of the ForestryMech." He rattled off the parameters as easily as if they were the guidelines for a systems check he had performed a hundred times. *Hard to believe that just a few weeks ago, I thought my work on the HPG core was a big problem. Now I'm practically a veteran.*

She chuckled, and that annoyed him. "What's so funny?"

"You. Grandpa would be proud. Not only have you redeemed ComStar's reputation, but you've become quite the military man."

"Me? It seems like you're the one with unexplained military knowledge," he retorted.

Patricia ignored his comment, instead pointing to his display and asking, "What are you looking at?"

Tucker shrugged. "This? This is a riddle. I picked up a relay signal from the transmission system. It was pretty well buried, but the security routine I wrote picked it up."

"Where was it sent?" she asked, taking the seat next to him to get a better view of the numbers.

"Up."

"Satellite uplink?"

"That's right. From what I know, there are no planetary-defense satellites in-system. If there were, we'd be getting signals from them. That means it's a commercial satellite. Well, I checked all of the known commercial satellites, and found nothing in the flight path of this bird. But laser signals confirm that it's up there."

As he spoke, Patricia's face slowly became rigid, as if every muscle on her face had tightened. "Have you been able to replay the message?"

"It's encrypted," he said.

"You're the genius," she replied.

He smiled. "Needless to say, I'm working on it. While the battle computer runs the algorithms, I've been trying to figure out why anyone would send a covert message to a satellite."

She shook her head in response. "It's not good news, that much is for sure."

"What makes you say that?"

"If it was a legitimate transmission, the officer sending it simply would have come in here and used the equipment. This was bounced from a vehicle or 'Mech comm unit to us, and relayed up." As if to emphasize her words, she tapped the screen over the numbers indicating the routing of the message.

"A spy?"

Patricia nodded. "You'd better tell the Knight about this."

"What about the legate?"

Her eyes narrowed, just a tad. "Who do you trust, Tuck? Unlike the Knight Errant, Legate Singh has expressed an interest in surrendering you to anyone and anything that threatens the Militia. I don't necessarily like Alexi, but I trust her."

"Let me break the encryption first," Tucker replied. "Then we bring in Alexi."

Captain "Fox" Irwin swung the arm of the Forestry-Mech like a knight wielding a sword. The spinning chain-saw blade slammed into the base of the trunk of two trees at once and both were felled in a millisecond, toppling with a whooshing noise. The blade roared like a jet engine as it revved for another sweeping pass. Alexi watched in fascination and admiration. Progress was slower than she had projected, but they were definitely making headway on the new road. Captain Irwin used the massive claw hand of the 'Mech to grab the felled trees and toss them off to the side of his path as if they were merely matchsticks.

Surveillance said the closest pursuit force was the Cut-Throats Company of Bannson's Raiders. The Donar had spotted them several hours away, apparently setting up camp for the evening. From where they sat, they believed the Wyatt Militia was trapped, bottled up at Crater Lakes. Captain Chaffee, the mercenary commander, had to be chuckling at the fact that the militia had run out of road. *I will wipe the smirk off his face, and make him pay for what he did at the ComStar compound.*

Surveillance reported no signs of the Spirit Cats, but she had no doubt that Star Captain Cox was still out there. This was a matter of honor to the Clan warrior. She had bested him in battle, and he was not going to leave Wyatt with a loss against her on the books. That was something she liked about Clansmen—they had some predictable elements in their personality.

Alexi turned to walk back to camp and discovered two people wearing dull-green jumpsuits standing only a few meters away. The Harwells. Brother and sister stood with their arms crossed and serious expressions on their faces. *This can't be good news.*

She acknowledged them with a wave and closed the distance between them until they were all standing face to face. "What brings you out here?" she yelled over the churn of the ForestryMech's blade.

Tucker yelled back, "We have a problem."

"Go ahead."

"I picked up a message last night. It was relayed from one of our vehicles and bounced to a commercial satellite using the systems in the mobile HQ. It was encrypted, so I set up an algorithm that would allow me to—" His sister cut off his long technical explanation by yelling, "Knight Holt, there's a traitor in the militia. He's apparently working with another faction on-planet."

"On Wyatt?"

"Well, someone accessed the messages he sent, and they used a military prefix code," Tucker replied.

Alexi held up her hand to stop Tucker from talking so she could focus on what Patricia had just said. "Another faction. Who?"

"The Oriente Protectorate," Patricia yelled.

"Are you sure?"

"Yes. The traitor blocked certain IFF transponder codes

in the HQ. If we were attacked by these troops, we wouldn't be able to see them on long-range sensors," Tucker added.

Alexi didn't feel her hands ball into tight fists. She didn't feel the blood rush to her face in anger. *After all we've been through, and there's been a traitor undermining us all along? And working with the Oriente Protectorate?* "Who is it?" she demanded.

Tucker looked at Patricia, and she nodded. He looked at the Knight. "I was able to break his encryption and pull down at least part of his last set of orders. I have confirmed it. Legate Singh has sold us out."

Tucker drew a deep breath and sighed heavily. "His orders are to allow the militia to be wiped out. The Protectorate forces will sweep in and rescue him and capture me. Apparently, I'm the reason they're here."

24

Crater Lakes
North of Kinross, Wyatt
The Republic, Prefecture VIII
21 May 3135

Alexi watched as he scanned the eyes of the men and women of his command, people he had betrayed. Legate Edward Singh was bound by the wrists and feet and seated against a log next to the bonfire they had lit to keep warm. She had thought about giving him some measure of privacy, perhaps interrogating him alone, in the mobile HQ, but had thought better of it. Weariness of days of fighting and fleeing had left the Knight Errant bitter and angry. Worse, there was a part of her worried that if she was alone with him, she might do something she would regret.

Singh had tried to rally some of the officers to his aid, to convince them that the evidence was false. He had even invoked the Black Paladin's name in hopes that his deeds might tarnish Alexi. It didn't work. She had been with them for weeks, helped train them, fought with them, kept them together as a cohesive unit. She was their leader now, in reality as well as in name. When the legate realized that he had lost his hold over his own command, she saw the energy drain from his face.

"How long have you been working for the Oriente Protectorate?" she demanded, standing over him with crossed arms. The semicircle of personnel closed in a half-step closer with her words.

"You can't prove anything," he replied confidently.

"Actually, I can," Tucker said from the ring of people. "I broke your code. I even downloaded your last set of orders. You were going to let this unit get wiped out just so that the Protectorate could get their hands on me."

For a moment Singh said nothing. He drew a deep breath. "My family was from the Free Worlds League. We were part of the refugee movement into The Republic. We are intelligence operatives. I am a loyal son," he answered with a hint of desperate pride.

"What Protectorate forces are on Wyatt?"

He laughed in response. "You're vastly outnumbered. Bannson's mercenaries will hit us in the morning. Even if you take them out, there's the Spirit Cats. And even if you survive them, the Protectorate forces are fresh and ready for action." He pleaded his case to everyone within earshot. "You'd be better off turning over the adept and letting them leave. Save yourselves."

Alexi stepped closer and watched him squirm. This time she spoke louder, firmer. "What Protectorate forces are on the planet?"

The legate still clung to his veil of assurance. "You don't really think I'll answer that, do you?"

Alexi knew what she wanted to do, and it took every bit of restraint she possessed to refrain. The legate had betrayed The Republic that he had sworn to defend. He was placing countless lives at risk, including hers. She wanted to beat him, hit him until she was covered in his blood. She wanted to hear him scream in agony in her grip. Alexi uncrossed her arms and reached for him. Then she caught herself. *No, I'm a Knight of the Sphere. I'm better than this.*

She reached down and grabbed him by his uniform collar, instead. In a swift move, she lifted him to his feet and stared him in the eyes, her face inches from his. "No, I guess I don't expect you to answer me. So I'm putting you in the mobile HQ. If we are attacked, your own people may kill you. When we get through this, you will stand trial for treason. Being a traitor is still one of the few crimes that carries the death penalty." She shoved him to the ground near the bonfire and stepped away. She was satisfied when she saw fear in his eyes. For now, that was the best she could hope for.

"Take this scum to the HQ and secure him there. If he causes a problem, do what is necessary to silence him."

Adept Kursk, seated at the long-range sensor station in the mobile HQ, spotted the vehicle first. "I have a contact at maximum range," she said. Tucker and Patricia moved in behind her to check the display. There was a lone target moving at the extreme edge of Higgins Lake, coming out of the dense forest. As the ComStar staff stared at the display, Tucker noticed that former Legate Edward Singh, secured on the floor in the back of the HQ with a plastic tie, was squirming around to try to get a better view of the screen as well.

Patricia activated a secondary display window in the lower right corner of the sensor screen. "Punching up the war book now for ID," she said calmly. The war book was a battle computer technical readout of every known vehicle and 'Mech made in the last three hundred years. It took the computer only a second to identify the vehicle and show its schematic. "Maxim Mark II class, hover armored personnel carrier."

Tucker transmitted the information to Alexi Holt. "Command One to Miss Direction," he spoke into his headset mike. "We have a contact on the southern end of Higgins Lake. One Maxim Mark II transport." He checked the long-range sensors. "It looks like it's heading right across the surface of the lake right at us, moving slow, though."

Knight Holt's voice replied a moment later. "Sound

the alert. Everyone hold your fire until we get target ID confirmation."

"You'll see," Singh sneered. "This is just the start. Surrender now, Harwell, and spare the lives of your sister and the others. I can help you make contact with the Protectorate."

In perfect unison, Tucker and Patricia turned and barked, "Shut up!" then turned back to the screen.

A voice came over the broadband channel into the mobile HQ speakers. "This is Reo Jones in the Maxim approaching the Wyatt Militia. Hold your fire. I'm bringing in supplies."

Tucker smiled for the first time in days. "Reo, is that really you?"

Jones voice boomed. "Sure is, kid. You didn't think I'd miss a party like this, did you?"

The Maxim was resting on the grassy shores as the members of the militia surrounded it. Reo was leaning against the deflated hoverskirt of the craft, casually smoking a cigarette, despite the fact that numerous weapons were trained on him. Tucker was amazed that he remained so relaxed after taking the risk of driving into an armed camp in an enemy vehicle. But then again, he had come to know and appreciate that laissez-faire attitude in his friend.

The Knight Errant approached him first with Tucker and his sister a few paces behind. Reo glanced at her, then returned his attention to savoring his smoke. "Jones, you mind telling me what you're doing here?"

"I thought it was obvious, Knight Holt," he said, tossing the butt of the cigarette to the ground and grinding it with the heel of his boot. "I'm here to help you." Tucker was glad that Reo had showed up, but so far he seemed to be the only one.

"Why should I trust you?" she asked. "We've had our share of betrayal here already."

Reo smiled his trademark casual, confident grin. "Well, to start with, I snuck into the Cut-Throats' camp and stole this from their supply train," he patted the

Maxim with his hand. "It's loaded with ammo, repair armor and parts."

"How do we know that the stuff isn't sabotaged, booby-trapped, or that this isn't a bomb?" Alexi pressed. Her last words caused the ring of troopers to take a half-step backward, making Tucker smile—like a half step would make any difference if it was a bomb.

"You have a lot of reasons not to trust me," Reo said. "The Cut-Throats set you up with the Spirit Cats, but I didn't know they were going to do that. I admit that I'll do what is necessary to get by, but I don't start wars and I don't kill children. Chaffee may condone that stuff, but I don't. When you captured Chaffee, you threw the Cut-Throats into confusion, so I took advantage of the chaos to borrow the Maxim. They're panicking now, because they need to succeed in their mission. People who stick it to Jacob Bannson and fail him don't usually find work anywhere else."

"What do you mean?" Tucker cut in. "We didn't capture Chaffee."

Reo frowned slightly. "You took out a *Blade*, right?"

Alexi nodded.

"Chaffee piloted that *Blade*," Reo said. "If you have the pilot, you have Chaffee."

Alexi called for two of the infantry. Tucker heard her give them an order and they took off at a jog, rifles at the ready.

Tucker felt vindicated by the arrival of his friend. Everyone had told him to avoid Reo. Now, when they most needed reinforcements, he showed up on their side. "How did you get that hovercraft through the forest?" Tucker asked.

Reo looked back across the calm waters of Higgins Lake to the dense forest beyond. "It wasn't easy, but I've had a lot of experience piloting vehicles through worse terrain. Needless to say, it needs some body work and a paint job now."

There was a commotion behind Tucker and he turned to see the two infantry returning, the older, overweight prisoner struggling between them. As the crowd parted, he saw Reo. Tucker almost burst out laughing when he saw the smile that came across his friend's face.

"You traitor!" Captain Chaffee howled.

Reo leaned back against the Maxim's hull and crossed his arms. "They took you down first. . . . That's funny, you old fart."

"Bannson will see you hang," Chaffee cursed.

"You might be right," Reo said. "That assumes that you'll be alive to tell him what I've done. Right now, your precious unit is being commanded by a junior officer. I'm willing to bet that these folks can take them out. Cut-Throat, you'd be smart to signal them to stand down. It's not worth getting everyone killed."

Captain Chaffee swore again. "I'll be damned if I'm going to take suggestions from a traitor. I won't call them off. I won't tell them to stand down. They're going to hit you, hit you all," he turned and yelled at the troops surrounding him. "When they do, they'll take that Com-Star wimp and leave the rest of you dead."

"That's not very honorable," Reo pressed.

"It's that or face Bannson's wrath. Do you know what happens to mercenary units that break their contracts with him?"

"Why don't you tell us?" answered Alexi.

Chaffee grinned nastily. "You never hear from them again. They disappear. Killed to the last man. Hunted down like animals. My people will come because that's what they face if they don't do their job."

Reo stepped away from the Maxim and walked over to Alexi. "It sounds like we're in the same boat, Knight Holt."

"What are you suggesting?"

Reo smiled. "Well, Chaffee's not going to be needing that *Blade* for a while. I'm a MechWarrior. Tucker here is the only person I've met lately that hasn't branded me one thing or another. How can I let him down?"

Star Captain Cox came to a bend in the highway and slowed his *Warhammer IIC* to a walk. His long-range sensors had greater distance than their Inner Sphere counterparts, so he already knew the exact location of the mercenaries he had been pursuing. The maps of Wyatt in his battle computer told him that the highway ended up ahead in a mass of lakes and dense forests. If the militia was still ahead of the mercenaries he was following, they were bottled up there.

There was more. His rear guard had picked up some military comm traffic. It was faint, but it suggested that there was at least one unit *behind* his command. Whoever that force belonged to, they were smart enough to stay out of his sensor range. *It was beginning to seem like everyone in The Republic and beyond had an interest in Wyatt.*

No. That was not correct. They had an interest in the man who had restored the HPG on Wyatt—this Adept Tucker of ComStar. Even he was on Wyatt for Tucker, to find out if this man was the Lightbringer from his vision. The difference between his goal in finding Tucker, and the goals of the other forces seeking the man was not lost on Cox. *I have come to save people, to keep my Clan alive. These other factions seek him to gain profit or power. My path has honor, theirs does not.*

He slid the throttle to a full stop and the rest of his command followed suit. Point Commander Barton was a good intelligence warrior. He worked only with facts, leaving the extrapolation to his commanding officer. It was likely that Bannson's mercenaries had triggered the conflict between the Spirit Cats and the militia for their own benefit. It was also possible that they were somehow working together. The unknown force to their rear could be tied to one of them, or an entirely new threat to be dealt with.

The Star captain popped open the visor on his neurohelmet and rubbed his tired eyes. He pushed hard, and in the darkness he saw the twinkle of lights, like multicolored stars. Cox paused and drew a long breath, holding the pressure against his eyes. Help me find the right path. Let the right choices come to me at the right time.

Removing his hand, he closed the neurohelmet. "Pouncer

Trinary, prepare to move out. Shut down your active sensor sweeps and kill all nonessential chatter. We need to move like our name, the predator that stalks its prey and strikes with fury. Pouncers, follow me and I will give you victory and honor."

Tucker blatantly listened in on the conversation, as did all of the techs in the HQ. Lieutenant Tooley was one of the most outspoken members of the militia. His Furies, the infantry and vehicle support, had been battered but had held their own so far—mostly due to his expertise and experience. When he approached the Knight Errant, he spoke with authority.

"Do you really trust this SOB?" he asked, chomping on his cigar.

"Jones?" she verified. "No, not entirely."

"But you're going to put him in a 'Mech. Do you really think that's wise, sir?" Tooley was trying to keep the conversation private, but his normally booming voice carried even at a whisper.

"Lieutenant," Alexi began, "I understand your reservations. I share them. But let's face facts. We've got the Legate's *Panther*, operational even with a bad leg, and the *Blade*. We need them in the fight, but we don't have MechWarriors with the experience to pilot them. Personally, I have little use for Reo Jones, but he is a skilled MechWarrior. I'm making the call. We put him in the *Blade*."

"He's a known traitor, ma'am," Tooley added. "Hell, he's just turned on the freaking mercs he was supposed to be working for."

"Point taken," she replied. "But trust me. Jones won't turn against us."

"Why?"

"Because," she ground out through gritted teeth, "if he does, I will kill him with my bare hands."

Tooley said nothing for a moment, only shifting the cigar to the other side of his mouth. "Well then, sir, as long as you have a plan, I'm comfortable with it." He turned with perfect military precision and made his way to the forward hatch. Alexi Holt turned and saw Tucker watching her. They said nothing, but it was clear Tucker had heard every word she'd said. It was also clear that she meant them.

25

Crater Lakes
North of Kinross, Wyatt
The Republic, Prefecture VIII
22 May 3135

Only a thin screen of trees concealed the newly cut road from Highway Seven. The militia forces that were dug in a quarter of a kilometer distant from the end of the cut kept low and powered down, watching as the last of the Cut-Throats passed. Each squad or vehicle that passed was tagged with an ID number and fed to the mobile HQ. Alexi Holt watched them from the powered-down cockpit of her *Black Knight* and nodded to herself.

"All right," she said into her mike in a low whisper. "Fox, on my mark, cut down the last trees and rush through. Your target is the Mars assault tank. Infantry, go for that Padilla. Capture or destroy. I'll take out the MiningMech and the *Ghost*." Alexi switched off the comm channel and her eyes swept the cockpit. The confines of Miss Direction had become her home—no, more than that, her universe. "One more time, old girl," she muttered to herself, patting the targeting console.

A voice rang over the command channel. "Contact!" called out Lieutenant Foster. "Anchor force has contact."

This was it. "Captain Irwin, mark." She gripped the controls and throttled up Miss Direction's reactor. "Command One, send to all units. Fire at will."

The mobile HQ was positioned near the center point between the two militia forces. Anchor force under Lieutenants Foster and Tooley was at the end of Highway Seven. Their job was to blunt the mercenary assault. Tucker hadn't seen the *Blade* in the last two hours, but he knew that Reo was out there, somewhere, too. Most of the prisoners had been taken to a hovertruck, but the legate was still in the back of the HQ. He sat there sulking.

Outside, the roar of the Sniper artillery shook the entire mobile HQ. The jarring rock of the blast was enough to get his attention. Standing next to Adept Kursk, he looked at the long-range sensors and saw the mercenary force along the road suddenly disburse, fanning into the forest on either side of the road seeking cover. Their point force drove right into the dots of green light that represented the Anchor force. From where he sat, it didn't look like Knight Holt's forces were moving at all.

Tucker was suddenly nervous. His palms began to sweat. The Sniper artillery fired again, rocking the vehicle. He heard a distant roll of thunder from the impact. He switched his attention to the sensor screen his sister was monitoring and immediately saw a problem. The enemy was punching through at the head of the highway. "What's the situation, Patricia?"

"Our Knight needs to get moving or we're toast," his sister replied bluntly.

He flipped to the command channel. "Knight Holt, the enemy is punching through up here. You need to get moving."

There was no response for a few seconds. Then a frustrated, angry voice came through. "The forest was a little thicker than we thought, Command One. Help is on its way now."

Knight Holt stepped out of the forest and saw the rear line of Bannson's Cut-Throats. Somehow, miraculously, they had not noticed the signatures of her force powering up. A MechWarrior could not hope for a better angle— a rear shot at an unsuspecting enemy. She toggled her PPCs to the same trigger and carefully centered her targeting reticle on the back of the MiningMech. The mercenary 'Mech was hugging the edge of the forest, attempting to avoid the incoming artillery fire blasting up the ferrocrete roadway. She zoomed in the angle and targeted the bulky industrial diesel engine that powered the 'Mech. It was a perfect shot. She squeezed the trigger firmly, and brilliant blue energy beams ripped the space between her and her target.

They hit with such force on the thinly armored rear of the 'Mech that it seemed to leap forward to land on its face, plowing into the sod and knocking down several saplings. Brown smoke rose from wicked-looking gashes. Her *Black Knight* had been modified to accommodate the extra PPC by sacrificing some of her armor, and today she saw that as a good trade-off.

One of Chaffee's Cut-Throats turned, a JES missile carrier. "They know we're here," she said out loud. She watched as the Mars assault tank, a low-riding missile launching platform, spun in place to face them as Captain Irwin charged it. The roaring blades of his ForestryMech came down like a scythe, slamming into the rear corner of the Mars tank and shredding armor plating. It was a good hit, but not good enough to take out the tank. A Demon skated up to cover its comrade, firing its lasers into the underarmored sides of the ForestryMech. Irwin struggled to stay upright against the force of the attack, and in that moment of distraction the Mars broke free and put distance between them.

She caught the movement of an SM1 tank destroyer sweeping into the mix. Alexi raised her arms and heard the whine of the charging PPCs. In a second, she could ravage the SM1. But it didn't need a second. Its turret cut loose with a stream of autocannon rounds. Two missed to her right, but the rest slammed into the chest of Miss Direction. The recoil dug her restraining straps into her shoulders, and she grunted in pain.

The Anchor force seemed to melt away under the on-slaught of the Cut-Throats. The patchwork Behemoth II came into range of the mobile HQ's armored viewports. Tucker could see that the militia tank was running in full reverse, firing wildly as it fell back. Then he saw the salvo of missiles come snaking after it. Two hit, some missed. The Behemoth paused long enough to cut loose with a blast from its gauss rifle. The silvery nickel slug hit a Galleon tank, tearing a long nasty gash up the side of the vehicle and rocking it heavily to one side, but the shot didn't punch through the armor.

Behind it, the legate's *Panther* attempted to fall back to the edge of Lake Higgins. It began a running arc to the shore as a mercenary Regulator hovertank locked onto it. Tucker stared in horror as the Regulator disgorged a gauss rifle slug at the *Panther*. The shot was a whitish blur as it slapped into the right leg of the militia BattleMech. The *Panther* reeled under the kinetic force of the impact, twisting violently at the hip and knee. Chunks of armor splashed into the lake behind it and the *Panther* fought to stay upright.

The Galleon joined in, its lasers stabbing into the *Panther* as the MechWarrior wrestled for control of his machine. The mercenary Regulator spun slightly and its turret turned toward the mobile HQ. For one, terrifying moment, Tucker felt as if he were looking right down the barrel. Someone yelled, "Blast shields," and the armored doors over the cockpit of the HQ dropped into place. A millisecond later the entire vehicle was pushed violently backward. Tucker lost his footing and went down on the floor between Adept Kursk and his sister. The lights inside the HQ flickered. He tasted something salty in his mouth and realized it was his blood.

Dizzily, he rose to his hands and knees and smelled a tang of ozone in the air from damaged circuits. *Damn, we've been hit.* He felt hands on his arms, helping him up. His brain slowly prodded him to wonder how bad was the damage. Then the lights came back on full strength, and he saw for himself.

From the edge of her vision, Alexi watched Captain Irwin use the massive mechanical claw of the left arm of the ForestryMech to grapple with the Mars assault tank's torn armored surface, punching downward like a pile driver. It seemed like she could actually hear the grinding of the mechanical fingers gouging in deep, tearing up internal systems, digging deeper into the guts of the tank. The Cut-Throats' vehicle attempted to pull back but Irwin held on. There was a rumble from inside the Mars, secondary explosion, probably one of the missile racks.

The SM1 was no longer locked onto her, but was targeting Irwin's machine. Alexi swept her lasers into play. Even at long range, the green beams of laser light were deadly, playing up the side of the tank, sending hot splatters of melted armor into the air like silvery sparks.

It was too little, too late.

The SM1 fired. Its autocannon rounds hit not just the ForestryMech, but also the Mars tank it was supposed to protect. There was an eruption of black smoke and orange fire as the rounds cooked off in quick succession. The IndustrialMech was never designed to survive this kind of punishment. Its claw arm, still digging deep in the Mars tank, broke off at the elbow joint, spilling hydraulic fluid all over the enemy vehicle. The ForestryMech collapsed to the ground, furrowing into the ferrocrete highway with a scraping thud. The cockpit hatch popped, and a dazed Fox Irwin crawled out.

In the distance, the MiningMech she had hit was slowly rising to its feet, which were actually tanklike treads. Her PPC hits had left an oily black spray over the back of the 'Mech, and a charred hole just above the engine. One of the exhaust vents had been blown, and the 'Mech was generating an unintentional smokescreen as it moved forward. It was unbelievable that the IndustrialMech could take such damage and still function.

Alexi's HUD showed an image at extreme range, near the Padilla artillery tank that was still slugging it out with her infantry. It was the *Ghost*. Fifty tons of firepower centering the opposing formation. *Great—at least I have a choice of targets.* Using instruments only, unable to see the 'Mech clearly through the smoky haze of the fighting, she acquired target lock at maximum range and fired.

The cockpit heat soared as the pair of PPCs fired. The bright blue bolts crackled downrange. One hit the *Ghost* in the torso, but the other went wide into the forest, sending up white smoke. The *Ghost* sagged from the hit, turned and started away, back up the road.

She was about to break into a run after it when her comm unit signaled. "Command One has been hit!"

Oh no . . . "Command One," she called. "Tucker, are you there?"

Tucker wiped the blood from his lip as his sister scrambled to regain her seat. "Patricia, what's the sitch?" As if in answer to his question, the mobile HQ rocked from another impact. Sparks flew from the console behind him and the power to that system went down. The reek of ozone filled his nostrils and something was burning that coated his throat with a coppery taste.

She stared at her display, which now flickered every few seconds. "We've got to get out of here," she said, jumping to her feet. Tucker saw in her face that there was no argument. "Another hit or two and this vehicle is a goner."

Patricia reached over to the long-range communications system and fed in a small data disk. Tucker saw a transmission confirmation signal and asked, "What was that?"

"No time to explain," she said. "Everyone out of here!" The remaining techs started up from their seats and quickly moved to the back of the mobile HQ. The first tech swung out the egress hatch. Tucker took two more steps and another explosion rocked the HQ, spinning Tucker into the side of the vehicle. He looked up and saw smoke and flames break out in the front, and hoped the men in the cockpit had managed to escape.

His sister pulled on him, shouting, "Come on, Tuck, time to go." He started for the hatch again, then saw Legate Singh, immobilized and with his bonds tied to a hook in the floor. He was crying with fear, calling for help. "Harwell, you have to save me!" he gabbled.

Paula Kursk grabbed the egress bar over the hatch and kicked back, swinging her legs through and letting go. Tucker could hear the Sniper fire again and the staccato of small arms fire erupting everywhere. He started toward the legate, but Patricia pulled at his arm again.

"Tucker, don't leave me here to die," the legate pleaded.

A hand grabbed Tucker from outside the hatch. Tucker resisted. He hated the legate for betraying his men, but no one deserved to die like this. Patricia pushed and a strong set of hands pulled him out of the mobile HQ. His sister jumped out right behind him, pushing him forward. Tucker turned and saw Corporal Pusaltari standing over him, obviously the one who had pulled him out of the burning vehicle. "You?"

The corporal smiled. "The Knight never countermanded my orders. Your safety is still my responsibility."

"We have to save Singh."

He took a few unsteady steps back toward the mobile HQ. Flames roared out of the cockpit. Smoke poured from the rear hatch. Suddenly, the entire vehicle was engulfed in crimson and orange flames. Tucker thought he heard a scream, almost not human, over the roar of battle.

With a sick feeling in his stomach, he pulled his eyes away from the burning vehicle, blinking to ease the afterimage of the fire. His line of sight was interrupted by the mercenary's Regulator turning to engage the militia's Sniper. Past that fight, the water of the lake stirred slightly, then seemed to erupt. From the cool waters, a figure rose, almost three stories tall. It was the *Blade*, the huge Mydron Excel LB-10X autocannon in its right arm trained on the Regulator's light rear armor. The Cut-Throats' hovertank never suspected that the 'Mech was waiting in the lake.

It fired a barrage of armor-piercing rounds. The Regulator dipped down under the weight of the impacts as the rounds dug into the armor, hammering the rear exhaust fans and armor. One shot penetrated the top of the turret, sending up a plume of pressurized gas.

The Regulator broke off its attack, turning to face its new foe. Then another 'Mech appeared at the end of the highway, a massive beast, a *Ghost*. The *Ghost* cut the air with its shoulder-mounted pulse lasers. Crimson dots of light bored into the *Blade*, the shots that missed hitting the surface of the lake and sending up clouds of steam where they struck.

"Let's move," shouted Corporal Pusaltari, holding his assault rifle up and ready as he pulled Tucker with him. Half running, half stumbling, Tucker headed for the forest just beyond the Sniper artillery tank. The Regulator completed its turn just in time to face the *Blade*'s lasers. The wider medium beam hit the tank right at the turret, while the narrower small laser dug into the front cowling of the hovercraft skirt. The Regulator dipped down nose-first into the shore, furrowing a long trench as it ground into the sod. Its engines whined loudly as the rear of the tank lifted into the air; then there was a grinding sound, metal against metal, then the Regulator dropped to a complete stop.

Tucker glanced back. All that was left were the *Ghost* and the *Blade*. The *Blade* simply stood in the water, cycling through its weapons systems without pausing. The *Ghost* moved, then fired, groping for some sort of advantage.

"We have to take cover," Patricia yelled.

"We have to help them," Tucker yelled back, struggling against Pusaltari's grip.

"Adept," shouted the corporal. "If you don't take cover,

I'll knock you out and drag you there." As if to emphasize his words, a mortar round went off nearby. It was
targeting the Sniper, but it was enough to shake Tucker
back to his senses.

"Right," he said, and ran.

"Are you sure?" Star Captain Cox asked.

"Affirmative," came the voice of Point Commander
Barton. "The battle is two kilometers ahead, sir."

"Very well," the Spirit Cat replied. "Pouncer Trinary,
full assault. Now is the time for redemption!" He
jammed the throttle full forward on his *Warhammer IIC*
and broke into a run. "Find Adept Tucker and secure
him!"

26

Crater Lakes
North of Kinross, Wyatt
The Republic, Prefecture VIII
22 May 3135

Alexi Holt's short-range sensors suddenly came alive with lights, red ones, heading for her. Her tired brain had trouble making sense of what she was seeing. As her PPCs recharged, she glared at the display. The IFF transponders finally identified the incoming threat as the Spirit Cats. They were moving up Highway Seven at full speed, and her console was already chiming the tone signals of enemy weapons lock.

Damn, damn, damn!

"Militia units," she called. "Break off. Fall back to the lake. We have Spirit Cats closing at Grid Coordinate 185, flank speed."

She turned Miss Direction up the highway and broke into a run. The enemy SM1 must have thought that she was charging at him. Likewise the Padilla artillery vehicle, which dove for cover off the side of the road as well.

The hovercraft rose high on its skirts as its engines revved and it rushed past her, probably to get a shot from the rear as she passed. *Go ahead—in just a minute you'll know why I'm heading this way.* The SM1 banked around, then must have checked its sensors and seen the wave of Spirit Cats heading toward them. It turned to face the onslaught.

"Jones, you out there?" she signaled on the channel she had designated for Reo Jones in the *Blade.*

There was a hissing sound, but no return signal. "Jones, damn it, the Spirit Cats are heading this way. I'm closing on your position." She reached the end of Highway Seven and saw the Militia MiningMech standing like a sentry on the last bit of paved roady. The IndustrialMech was badly disfigured, pockmarked everywhere from missile and autocannon hits. Its left leg was a gnarled, twisted mess, which explained why it was stationary. Under its machine guns lay a pile of empty shell casings. "You have incoming 'Mechs," she told the pilot. "Hold them here."

"Roger, sir," came a weary voice.

As she rounded the edge of the forest, the carnage she saw was appalling. Several vehicles lay burning, including the mobile HQ, which was a hollow tube of roaring fire. The solid tires in the front had melted to the ground. There was no hope that anyone inside could still be alive. For a moment, her entire body slumped deeper into the command couch.

She saw Reo Jones' blackened *Blade* standing in the water of Lake Higgins. Steam rose from both of his legs as his heat sinks vented the extra heat. Her infrared sensors painted the 'Mech as searingly hot. By standing in the water, Jones had been able to push the *Blade* way beyond its specifications. The BattleMech was horribly scarred, pockmarked by multiple pulse-laser barrages. Her systems showed the 'Mech as operational, but badly damaged. It wouldn't last more than a couple of shots in a fight.

The culprit of the damage was nearby. Limping, the

mercenary *Ghost* was almost as disfigured and damaged as the *Blade*. Its right arm was gone, lying nearly a hundred meters from its current location, near the lake's sandy shore. Thin strands of myomer hung down from the shoulder, some still sparking in a phantom connection. To the left of the *Ghost* was the still-living remains of the legate's *Panther*. The small 'Mech showed no signs of the militia's repairs. The savagery of the fighting had left it mangled and blackened. Green coolant oozed like blood from an open wound at its hip. Like the *Ghost* it was fighting, it was in a slow dance of death.

She cycled her PPCs and put one each on a different trigger as the *Ghost* cut loose with another salvo of short-range missiles at the *Panther*. Half of the flight missed, riddling the woods and topping a large pine tree behind the *Panther*. The others hit the hips and legs of the 'Mech, burrowing deep into the internal hardware and frame. It quaked violently, but somehow held up.

Alexi fired her right-hand PPC at the *Ghost* from behind at the same time the *Blade* fired another barrage of autocannon fire at the *Ghost*'s front. All of the shots hit. The *Ghost* twisted halfway around under the furious assault. The MechWarrior tried to use the momentum to turn and run away, but lost his balance. The machine dropped with a thud on the ground.

"Took your time getting to the party," Reo's voice came over the comm channel.

"Any sign of Tucker?"

"He's in the woods down shore," Reo replied.

Alexi dropped her head and sighed out a deep breath. "Good." Then, "We've got company coming."

"So I hear," he said. Alexi heard a rumble behind her. Twisting Miss Direction's torso, she saw the MiningMech suddenly bathed in a barrage of laser and PPC fire. The ad hoc fighting machine burst into flames. She watched in horror as one of the lasers burned through the cockpit, killing the MechWarrior instantly. There was no hope of ejection, no system for it in an IndustrialMech. It seemed to sag at the waist joints, then toppled forward.

Reo's *Blade* moved toward shore, stirring up more steam. "One thing about this planet, it seems to be popular as all hell."

The mercenaries' Mars assault tank, complete with the ForestryMech's arm stabbing upward from the rear like a strange standard, fired a wave of missiles. At the closest range possible for the tank, the missiles had little chance of missing the Spirit Cat *Black Hawk.* They engulfed the squat 'Mech. The *Black Hawk* emerged from the billowing smoke, a bit worse for the wear. Smoke still streamed from the impact holes as the 'Mech pressed forward. A trio of minigun cycles leapt to the attack, discharging their short-range missiles as the *Black Hawk* lumbered forward, but their missiles caused more irritation than damage.

Star Captain Cox swung his four large lasers to target the Padilla artillery tank and brought the vehicle into target lock. The Padilla seemed to be ignoring him, instead unleashing a volley over the trees—probably at the militia near the lake. He heard the lock tone and fired. A blast of heat rose in his cockpit, but he watched with satisfaction as three of the four emerald beams found their mark. The Padilla's armored right side bore the brunt of the assault. It rocked from a secondary explosion, and a second later another one went off, tossing the split remains of the artillery piece into the air on a rising column of black smoke. Molten red globs of hot armor rained down like hail.

The SM1 tank destroyer skirted past him and fired at his Condor hovertank. At first, most of the autocannon rounds went past the front of the Condor, but as the gunner corrected his aim the munitions devoured the front glacial armor. Fire broke out, and the Condor came to a drop-stop on the pavement with a sickening, grinding sound. Two troopers made it out of the vehicle before the missile ammunition on board cooked off, blowing out the back of the tank.

The *Black Hawk* suddenly stopped and twisted its torso, bringing the Mars assault tank into its scope. In a heartbeat, it fired a pulse barrage from its laser array. The brilliant red burst molested the side and rear of the Mars until the vehicle came to a sudden stop. White smoke rose from every missile tube and from the rapidly opening hatches.

Star Captain Cox smiled. *My debt of honor is repaid, money-warriors.*

Tucker and Patricia huddled behind a thick log near the freshly cut roadway. Over the low ridge and through the forests, they could hear the roar of battle still raging. From within the mobile HQ, the fight had been frightening. Outside, in the open, Tucker realized his insignificance against the machines of war. They crouched behind the log and did what they could to avoid drawing attention.

A shrieking sound filled the air as incoming artillery rounds landed around them. The rounds hit near the Sniper artillery piece, tossing up huge rocks and pieces of sod as they exploded. The Sniper's return-fire rounds had a different, deeper sound. The shells ripped the air over them.

"This seriously sucks," Tucker muttered, looking at his sister. Unlike him, she didn't flinch with each blast. Either she wasn't afraid, or knew something he didn't.

"We can't stay here," she said, looking around. "We should make a break for the south end of the lake." Corporal Pusaltari leaned in so that he didn't have to shout. "We should move. Sitting in one spot is a bad idea."

Tucker poked his head up over the log and saw a fearsome sight. From the roadway that the militia had cut from the forest, a Bannson's Demon wheeled tank roared in. Running in full reverse, facing the roadway, it blazed away with its side-turret-mounted medium lasers stabbing back at whatever was pursuing it. It rocked over a tree stump and almost rolled over as it came down the shoreline of Higgins Lake, pulling a forty-five-ton, high-speed jackrabbit turn to come about. One thing was for sure, the mercenaries piloting the craft were very good.

Out of the same ad hoc roadway emerged a Clan BattleMech. Tucker recognized it after a few seconds as the 'Mech piloted by the Clan Star captain. It had taken some damage in the battle, but seemed intent on finishing off the fleeing Demon. Its large lasers flared as they fired, sending a streaming beam of emerald energy at the Demon as it fled. Two missed, but two found their mark on the thin rear armor. As the Demon turned, one of the lasers sliced into one of the rear tires, cutting it neatly from the hub and sending parts flying into the air.

Tucker wasn't sure if he was supposed to cheer or not. Turning back to the 'Mech, he was stunned to see armored infantry, Elemental troops, fanning out across the roadway. Several lit off their jump jets and rose into the air, heading right for where they were hiding. Corporal Pusaltari saw them as well and shouldered his assault rifle, leveling off a shot. Patricia pulled at Tucker to run for it, but he was mesmerized by the incoming infantry.

The Elementals landed only twenty meters away. They seemed like giants. Standing more than 2.5 meters tall in their huge power-armor suits, complete with short-range missile racks over their shoulders, they were the epitome of close-quarters combat soldiers. One hand was replaced by a mechanical grappling-ripping device, while the other was replaced by a laser—which was now leveled at the techs behind the tree.

"Drop your weapons," a voice boomed, the warrior's voice amplified by an external speaker system.

Pusaltari hesitated, but Patricia grabbed his rifle and tossed it to the side. The corporal glared at her, but knew there was little his assault rifle could have done against Clan Elemental armor.

"You have chosen wisely, trooper. You are all prisoners of the Pouncers Trinary of the Spirit Cats Purifiers," the augmented voice intoned. "One of you is Adept Tucker, *quiaff*?"

Tucker thought fast. *Perhaps I should lie?* He thought back to Captain Chaffee. No. Eventually the truth would come out. Tucker rose to his feet. He thought he heard

his sister whisper, "No, Tuck," but he couldn't be sure.
"I'm Tucker Harwell."

"Very well. You must meet with Star Captain Cox,"
the Elemental said, motioning with his laser arm toward
the Clan 'Mech.

The Spirit Cat *Black Hawk* rounded the edge of the
tree line and found itself facing two BattleMechs—a
Blade and a *Black Knight*. The *Blade* reacted first, sending a barrage of autocannon rounds into its right side,
eating away at the arm and leg of the *Hawk* as it slowed
its pace to get a better firing stance. The armor on that
side of the 'Mech was gone, and it moved sluggishly, so
that the 'Mech looked more like a drunken sailor than
a deadly war machine.

It swung its deadly battery of lasers to bear on the
Blade only because it was the closest target, and let go
with everything it had. The air seemed to come alive
with scarlet bursts of laser energy which bathed the
upper portion of the militia BattleMech in coherent light.
Five or six of the bursts melted the ferroglass armored
cockpit, almost burning through where they hit. The rest
tore into the little remaining armor on the upper torso,
some digging in deeper into the internal workings of
the 'Mech.

The militia 'Mech bent slightly forward at the waist as
the MechWarrior fought to keep it upright. Then, without any preamble, it toppled face first into the three-
meter-deep water. A flash-cloud of hissing white steam
rose into the air from the overheated 'Mech.

The *Black Knight* pivoted at the waist and unleashed
a torrent of particle projector cannon fire down on the
stout little *Black Hawk*. One shot hit the right shoulder
actuator, fusing it into a solid part, locking the aim of
the arm down at the ground a few meters in front of the
'Mech. The other shot hit the cockpit glass. Unlike the
pulse-laser burst on the *Blade*, the PPC shot gouged
the ferroglass like a blowtorch on a thin sheet of ice.
There was a brilliant burst inside the cockpit as the blue

energy beam seared inward and destroyed the interior of the 'Mech.

The *Black Hawk* teetered and then, perhaps as a malfunction, the ejection seat charges fired. The mangled remains of the cockpit hatch were fused in place from the PPC hit, so what was left of the cockpit simply exploded as the 'Mech fell to its side.

The battered Behemoth II, the J-37 transport, the Maxim, the Sniper, a handful of infantry and her own *Black Knight* were all that was left of the Wyatt Militia when Alexi received an incoming message. She had watched Reo Jones fall into the shallow water and hoped that he had survived, but she was honestly more worried about the loss of the *Blade*. Likewise, she hoped that Tucker and his team had managed to get clear from the HQ. The incoming signal was sent in the clear from nearby.

"Knight Alexi, this is Star Captain Cox. I urge you to stand down your troops. I have Adept Tucker under my protection. My fight is no longer with you, but we will return fire if fired upon. Let a truce be called between us."

She sat for a moment. The militia had fought and fought hard. Now it seemed like the war was over. Tucker was their reason to fight, and if Star Captain Cox said he had Tucker, he did.

"Very well," she replied on the same channel. "Wyatt Militia, this is Miss Direction. Stand down. Hold your fire. I say again, hold your fire. We are under a truce." The words tasted bitter, but she knew she was doing the right thing. *Twice this Clansman has beaten me.*

She opened a private channel to the Star captain. "Star Captain Cox, I have complied. What is it that you propose?"

"Come meet with me, Knight Alexi. I need to see this adept for myself."

"Confirmed," reported Captain Casson's forward scouts. "Multiple elements on the road ahead, weapons signatures from PPC and laser fire. There is a battle ahead, sir, where the highway ends."

Ivan Casson stared ahead. *The end of the road, indeed.* "Any indication of how long the fighting has been going on?"

"Comm traffic would indicate the better part of an hour," his intelligence officer replied.

The Wyatt Militia, already weakened. Bannson's mercenaries, ambushed once and routed. And the Spirit Cats, trapped once by Knight Holt. Yes, an hour's fighting would leave very little opposition. He switched to the broadband channel. "Eagle's Talons, form up in a Pattern V as in Victor formation. Prepare to move out at flank speed. Remember our objective—find the ComStar adept and capture him alive." He pushed the throttle forward on his *Sun Cobra* and aimed for the center of the formation. "In battle, timing is everything." He had learned that a long time ago as a cadet. "Talons, forward—'arch!'"

The small group stood at the feet of the *Warhammer IIC* as Star Captain Cox climbed down. He and Alexi were dressed in the shorts, coolant vest, T-shirt, and sweat common to every MechWarrior emerging from his or her machine. The Clan warrior stood tall as he walked over to where Tucker and Patricia waited. Tucker was nervous, but refused to show it. *What do they want? Am I now a prisoner of the Clans?* He had read about bondsmen and wondered if he was now going to be absorbed into the Spirit Cats. The Knight moved to stand next to him, wiping the sweat from her face onto her sleeve as she strode quickly through the broken sod. Having Alexi nearby gave him strength to face whatever would happen.

What was left of Chaffee's Cut-Throats had broken and run. There wasn't much left of them anyway, after having been hammered by both the militia and the Spirit Cats. Most had abandoned their equipment and fled into the forests. Some had surrendered, but only to the Militia. They seemed to have a healthy and reasonable fear of surrender to the Spirit Cats.

Star Captain Cox walked over to where Tucker stood and looked at him silently for a long moment. Reaching out with his right hand, he cradled the left side of Tucker's face, turning the adept's head slightly as he did so. Tucker forced himself to do nothing, concentrating on not flinching away from the warm, sweaty hand on the side of his face. Cox closed his eyes, in thought or meditation, Alexi was not sure which, then he let go of Tucker's head.

"This is Adept Tucker, restorer of the HPG on this world, *quiaff*?" he asked Alexi.

She nodded. "It is."

Cox turned his gaze back to Tucker. "You are not the man of my dreams."

Tucker almost laughed with the relief of the tension, and the meaning of the sentence out of context. "I'm not sure how to take that. I guess it's a good thing."

The Star captain was not amused. "I shared a vision with my Galaxy commander that led me here to Wyatt. We saw a star flickering to life, and a man holding the universe in his hands. I thought that you might be that man, and the star Wyatt. I see now that neither is correct."

"What will happen now?" Knight Holt asked.

Cox turned to her, resting his fists on his waist. "I see now that we were misled into attacking you. These mercenaries of Jacob Bannson, these Cut-Throats, tricked us into believing you had betrayed your rede with us. They have paid the price for their treachery. You, Knight Alexi, have my apologies."

Tucker was stunned. All of this fighting, all of the destruction—the loss of lives. It was over with an apology? "So that's it? It's over?" he asked. Alexi gripped his arm in warning.

Star Captain Cox turned back to Tucker. "*Neg*, Adept. It is not over. My pickets have detected another force heading for these coordinates. While you are not my people's salvation, you are still a prize in the eyes of others.

My honor has been injured by these mercenaries. It is time to cleanse the wound. We shall join your Knight in defending you."

Tucker's mouth hung open. Cox allowed himself a broad smile. "Do not be surprised, pup. We are Clan. Honor is our blood. If your Knight will allow it, we will join you."

Alexi nodded, her mind obviously already racing to calculate how best to meet this fresh attack. "Yes . . . we would be honored."

"Well bargained and done," he said, and turning, jogged back to the foot of his *Warhammer*, then climbed the ladder to the cockpit.

27

**Crater Lakes
North of Kinross, Wyatt
The Republic, Prefecture VIII
22 May 3135**

"Incoming targets," Alexi called out on the channel that she now shared with the Spirit Cats. "Sniper, mark targets at maximum range and roll it up to minimum. Prep for fire-for-effect."

"Roger, Miss Direction. HEAP loaded, ready for rolling thunder max to min, at your order."

"Turn that highway into slag. Sniper—fire!" she barked. The artillery piece at the rear responded with a deep roar, sending its shells downrange at the advancing force. Alexi watched on her short-range sensors as the Oriente Protectorate forces suddenly felt the brute force of the artillery barrage. They didn't hesitate or break formation. Instead, they moved faster, to stay ahead of the fire, attempting to punch under the umbrella of shrapnel and explosives.

She bit her lip. These were seasoned soldiers. That was

good to know. "Star Captain, they are almost on top of you," she said on the command channel. "I'm moving up to cover you."

"Do not worry, Knight Alexi," responded the cool, confident voice of Star Captain Cox. "There are plenty of them for all of us."

Alexi charged her PPCs. *That was the least of my concerns.*

The Oriente forces came on like a wave hitting a shoreline. Alexi targeted a charging *Hatchetman* with her particle projector cannons. Both shots hit, once again baking the interior of her cockpit. The cobalt energy beams slammed into the legs of the Oriente BattleMech at thigh level, literally melting away all of the front armor. Smoldering black holes from the hits spewed smoke as the 'Mech continued to run up to a Spirit Cats Scimitar Mk II hovercraft. Her last image of the hovercraft was the massive ax of the *Hatchetman* slicing through the thin top armor and burying itself in the cockpit. Flames bellowed up from the wound as if they came from a blast furnace.

She caught a glimpse of Star Captain Cox's *Warhammer IIC* blasting a modified AgroMech with its short-range missiles while it cut into a rushing *Sun Cobra* with its large lasers. Half of the lasers missed, but the Agro-Mech came out of the encounter looking more like a wadded-up foil ball with legs than a war machine.

A boxy Zahn armored personnel carrier raced toward her Sniper artillery piece. The Zahn skidded to a halt and popped open its rear hatch. Combat engineers and Purifier battle armor troops jumped out and tossed satchel charges on top of the Sniper as it attempted to back away and gain distance from the close-range threat. It was too late. White-flash explosions went off, punching through the top armor. The Sniper stopped dead in its tracks and its barrel drooped down.

A salvo of missiles slapped into Miss Direction from a fast-passing Pegasus hovercraft, rocking her hard to one side. She fired her pair of medium lasers into the hovercraft more out of spite than need. The beams hit the flank of the gun platform, cutting two black furrows from the front to the rear of the vehicle.

Her damage display was flickering red from the holes in her armor. Glancing out the side of her viewscreen, she watched the *Sun Cobra* riddle Star Captain Cox's *Warhammer* with autocannon rounds. Cox's 'Mech contorted and Alexi could see the massive holes in the armor, the shredded fibers of myomer hanging limp around the waist. His reactor was shifting to low-power mode. The Clan warrior was out of the fight.

A bright flash filled her cockpit as a PPC shot cut into her 'Mech's right shoulder. *Miss Direction* listed heavily to one side under the impact. She heard a metallic tearing sound, then her damage indicators flashed red and went out on her right side. *Miss Direction's* right arm had been blasted off.

Gritting her teeth, Alexi knew that they were in way over their heads.

Tucker, Patricia, and Corporal Pusaltari rushed forward to the remains of the Tamerlane hover sled that Chaffee's Cut-Throats had taken out of the fight. Hunched down, they watched the carnage of the one-sided fight take its toll on what was left of the militia and the Spirit Cats.

The images, sights, sounds and emotions of the battle almost overwhelmed Tucker. The fighting was close-in, at point-blank range. The Oriente Protectorate was literally swarming through the thin lines and overwhelming the defenders. For Tucker especially, the prospect of defeat was chilling. It was beginning to look like he would be a prisoner of these invaders. It was as irrational as it was tempting to break and run, but he knew he would not get far. *Where would I go . . . into the woods?* Outdoor survival was not his forté. Still, all his instincts were urging him to do something to survive the battle.

Oddly, his sister seemed confident and unworried. She was fidgeting with her wrist communicator, but seemed to be paying little attention to the fighting. Tucker watched in horror as Star Captain Cox's *Warhammer IIC* staggered away from an Oriente *Sun Cobra*, its front armor reduced to twisted, jagged fragments hanging from the internal structure. The *Black Knight* that Alexi piloted was missing its right arm; all that remained was a mangled, blackened stump under the shoulder joint.

Tucker practically leaped to his feet when someone slapped him on the back. He turned and was surprised and delighted to see a wet, winded Reo Jones. A smear of blood ran from his hairline down to his jaw. He gave Tucker a grin. "Remind me never to let Knight Holt plan any of my parties," he joked.

Tucker slapped his friend on the shoulder as a voice emerged over his sister's wrist communicator. "This is Captain Ivan Casson of the Oriente Protectorate. All forces hold your fire. Enemy forces, you are overmatched. Prepare to stand down for parley." An uneasy lull broke out over the weary battlefield. The only sounds were the popping snaps of burning vehicles and the charging whir of lasers and PPCs.

Tucker wasn't sure what to do. He didn't want to surrender, but he was tired of watching people be injured and killed because of him. *We are outnumbered, outgunned, surrounded.* Standing up, he stared at the *Sun Cobra* in the distance. He willed his feet to move, but they seemed stuck to the ground. He was frozen with fear.

Patricia stood up next to him and grasped his forearm. She was trying to protect him, just as she had his entire life. But this was a journey that he was going to have to make alone.

Suddenly, another voice sounded from Patricia's wrist comm, this time keyed to the militia command channel. "Now hear this. All ground forces, stand down and prepare to surrender all ComStar personnel. Say again, stand down or be destroyed." He heard a deep, bone-shaking roar that seemed to alter his heartbeat. Looking up, he saw a spheroid DropShip on a low, sweeping approach. At first, its paint scheme, flat white with thick, black jagged stripes that seemed to distort its configuration and shape at a distance, made him think it was the

Spirit Cats' vessel. The ship arrived over the forest on a trajectory toward the south end of the lake. Tucker could make out the round bumps of turrets as it approached the battlefield.

The wash of the engines kicked up dirt into a swirling storm. As the DropShip passed overhead, a cargo bay door opened and three 'Mechs dropped into the middle of the camp. Tucker shielded his eyes with his hand like a visor over his glasses and leaned into the hot blast to avoid being knocked over.

It's over. Tucker slumped, as if the wind had been knocked out of him. The ship slowed its approach to a low hover and landed on Lake Higgins' south shore. Tucker knew enough to recognize two of the BattleMechs as an *Atlas* and a *Mad Cat.* The other was a configuration and shape that he didn't recognize. All three 'Mechs were painted stark white and were pristine—and obviously deadly.

Then he stared at the ship, in shock. On the side of the DropShip was painted a familiar symbol, a star with the two bottom points stretching downward set against a blue field. The symbol of ComStar. *But that was impossible!* ComStar didn't have a military force, not since the end of the Jihad. Next to the ComStar logo was a stylized insignia, the words "Sword of Focht" emblazoned in red paint set under a flaming sword. He felt relief and confusion at the same time.

Patricia walked toward the 'Mechs, pulling him with her.

"How is this possible?" he asked his sister.

"I contacted our superiors right after the HPG came up," she said. "We took matters into our own hands to ensure your safety."

He followed numbly behind his sister. Suddenly, he saw Alexi Holt jogging toward them. It was obvious that she was as shocked as he was. "What is the meaning of this?" she asked Patricia.

"We protect our own," Patricia replied flatly. "ComStar will evacuate Tucker and me."

"Are you serious?" Alexi exclaimed.

Patricia looked grimly amused at Knight's response. "Saving Tucker is what all this has been about. Be thankful that a rescue team has arrived, even if it's not the one you expected. What's important is that he not fall into the hands of the Protectorate."

"I'll come with you," Alexi replied firmly.

"No," Patricia Harwell said. "You will not."

Captain Casson stared at the DropShip, stunned that the message to stand down had been transmitted on his command channel. His fists were clenched so tight that the tendons were cracking. *ComStar. Who were they to interfere like this?* His jaw clenched as he stared at the deploying 'Mechs. Where did ComStar get BattleMechs? And a DropShip? The Com Guards had been wiped out in the Jihad; ComStar had no military arm! This should not be possible.

Two people were moving toward the 'Mechs. Casson watched as the Knight Errant rushed to join them. One of them had to be Tucker Harwell. *He had been so close.* Casson stared at the DropShip, its cannons aimed at his 'Mech and his troops.

He rapidly sifted through his options, then signaled his forces to retreat. He had failed to secure his target, but the intel he had gained on ComStar was a prize worth presenting to his leader.

Patricia made hard eye contact with the Knight Errant. "Captain Casson is showing good judgment. I hope you also will show good sense."

Alexi Holt refused to be intimidated. "Where are you taking him?"

"Home," was all that Patricia offered in reply. She spoke into her wrist communicator. "All remaining ComStar personnel, report to my location immediately."

"Republic forces will be in system in just a few days," Alexi pressed. "If your forces remain, we can ensure Tucker's safety together."

Patricia laughed out loud. "Look around you, Knight Errant. Look at the devastation here. Think of how many people have died. The Republic can't protect Tucker. ComStar will take care of him. It is our way. More important, it's our choice."

Alexi looked at Tucker, her expression both frustrated and sad—at least that's how she looked to him. "My orders are to ensure your protection."

He couldn't think of anything to say. His mind was reeling, trying to make sense of the situation.

"I'll miss you, Tucker," Alexi said. "But at least you'll be safe." She leaned forward and gave him a hug. He held her stiffly, too surprised and uncomfortable to hug her back. He felt her slip something into his pocket as she leaned back and stepped away. She gave him a solemn nod in parting.

Tucker turned to Reo Jones. His friend smiled, winked and gave him a firm handshake. "See you around sometime, partner."

As Paula Kursk and Kurtis Fowler joined them, Tucker turned to face his sister. "Where are we going?"

She looked at him expressionlessly. "We're going someplace safe, where even The Republic can't reach you." She led him past the 'Mechs, and the huge machines turned to follow them like an honor guard. Tucker glanced over his shoulder and caught a final glimpse of Alexi Holt and Reo Jones.

"What about my work?"

"You serve ComStar," Patricia replied, "as our family has for decades. You will do what you are told, as have we all."

What was she saying? "Patricia, I don't understand. . . ."

She smiled at him. Raising her hand in a gesture he had seen only in historical accounts of the Word of Blake and the Jihad, she spoke words that chilled him to the bone. "Peace of Blake be with you, Tucker."

He let himself be led aboard the ship.

Epilogue

Republic Internal Affairs, Office 2-B
Geneva
Prefecture X, Terra
23 August 3135

Alexi Holt stood at attention at the conference table as Paladin Kelson Sorenson entered the room. She admired her superior officer. Paladin Sorenson was a veteran of the Jihad who had fought alongside Devlin Stone. His critics sometimes referred to him as the Paladin of Lost Causes and, to his credit, he embraced that reputation. It was just one of the things she liked about him.

"Please sit," Sorenson said, waving her to a chair and taking one himself. "I meant to meet with you sooner, but I wanted to make sure that I had all of my intel in order first."

She understood. Her official report from Wyatt and the copy of her battlerom from Miss Direction must have been unnerving to officials of The Republic. Men like Sorenson did not enjoy these kinds of surprises. "Alexi, your recent performance was admirable. You performed exceptionally under difficult circumstances. I know at times it must have seemed overwhelming."

"Thank you, sir," she replied. Alexi knew that from her Paladin, this was no faint praise. She dove right into the subject foremost on her mind. "What has ComStar said about Tucker Harwell?"

The older MechWarrior frowned heavily. "I met with Precentor Buhl weeks ago to ask about Mr. Harwell, and he assured me that the adept was safe under the protection of ComStar. When I confronted him with the evidence of ComStar fielding BattleMechs and DropShips, he would only say that, like every large Inner Sphere corporation, ComStar has always maintained security forces for its own protection."

"You've got to be kidding."

The Paladin shook his head. "It gets better. I met with Primus Mori, and she denied that ComStar possessed 'Mech forces, even reminding me that the Com Guards had disbanded after the Jihad. I showed her the sensor data you gathered, and she claimed that it had to be another faction attempting to frame ComStar. When I asked her about Harwell's status, she referred me back to Buhl. And now Buhl's gone on some tour of the Inner Sphere."

"Convenient," she said. "And a little unsettling. Is it possible the primus doesn't know that someone in ComStar has outfitted a small army?"

He waved his hand in the air. "In the end, what she knows or will admit to is irrelevant. What we know is this: ComStar has a secret military arm that includes DropShips and 'Mechs unique to their ranks. Based on those unique designs, we have to assume they have their own military production capability. They have Tucker Harwell, a man capable of restoring HPG service on countless worlds, and they clearly have no intention of turning him over to The Republic or even giving us access to him."

"So a military threat exists that we had not anticipated. That's not good."

"We're in the dark—not where I like to be."

"And the production capability to create new 'Mech designs?"

"The design you saw is not in any of the war books. And that DropShip represents an even bigger mystery; its profile doesn't match any known design or prototype. Apparently, ComStar has some incredible assets at their disposal. But all I got from Buhl and Primus Mori was that it was none of our business."

The implications stunned her. "I—I don't know what to say. We have to find Tucker and help him. They're obviously holding him hostage."

"I tried to argue the hostage angle myself, but Buhl came back with a perfectly reasonable answer: how can someone be a hostage if they have not asked for release or been reported as taken?"

"ComStar has secreted him away. We have to help him," she repeated.

"I agree with your goal," he replied. "Though maybe not your motivation. It's pretty clear you've developed a fondness for the man."

Alexi felt her face redden. "He's a friend. More importantly, he's a citizen of The Republic. I swore to protect him . . . and I failed."

"You didn't fail," the Paladin corrected. "Your report and the corroborating report from the Ghost Knight on Wyatt both painted a very accurate picture of events there. You performed with the highest possible degree of integrity."

"Ghost Knight?"

Sorenson leaned back and grinned at her. "You didn't think you were the only asset in play, did you? We've had an operative on Wyatt for two years now, monitoring Jacob Bannson's activities."

She frowned for a moment in thought, then said, "Not Reo Jones?"

"Yes," he replied. "We created his cover years ago. Mr. Jones is a loyal servant of The Republic who has shown a remarkable amount of creativity in fulfilling his mission. Your bringing back Rutger Chaffee for interrogation has proven to be a bonus for us. He's already helped us ferret out several other of Bannson's covert hiding holes in The Republic, and we're finding ways to

legitimately seize his assets on those worlds. His involve-
ment with Liao is making that pretty easy."

She closed her eyes. The days after the fighting on
Wyatt had been chaotic. The arrival of Republic reinforcements, ushering the Oriente forces off-world, rebuilding the militia, even the interviews with Chaffee
were more a blur than a memory. Reo had stuck by her
side through it all. Even as he proved himself to her time
and again, she had continued to see him as a reckless
traitor who was trying to do good. Now she knew the
truth. A Ghost Knight—one of the secret protectors of
the realm. It made sense.

"The last agenda item of this meeting," Paladin Sorenson said, "is to determine the direction of your next mission, Alexi."

She faced her mentor and sponsor with a determined
look in her eye. "I need to finish this mission, first. I
need to find Tucker Harwell."

The Paladin smiled. "Oddly enough, not only was I
thinking the same thing, but so was Knight Jones. I suggest that you rest up and get ready to tackle your next
assignment. My mission is to restore the communications
network. I need Tucker Harwell to do that. That makes
your job a little more complicated. First, you need to
disappear, which I think Jones can help you with."

"I need to disappear? Why?"

"You, Alexi Holt, are going to infiltrate ComStar."

Outside McPherson
Marcus
The Republic, Prefecture VIII

Star Captain Cox arrived at the hard-shell field tent and
stood at attention outside. He said nothing, nor did he
knock. Galaxy Commander Kev Rosse had called for
him, and he knew that his commander would know that
he was there. He had that level of gift about him, an
ability to see the unseen. Just as he assured himself of

that, the door panel opened and the leader of the Spirit Cats stood before him.

"Star Captain," he said. "Enter."

"*Aff,*" he said, stepping in. The tiny flexplastic tent was Spartan, showing no signs that the slender man who lived there controlled such a powerful faction.

"It pleases me that you and your Trinary have returned," the Galaxy commander began, taking a seat cross-legged on a rug and motioning for Cox to join him. Along the edges of the rug was a running list of the names of Inner Sphere worlds on which the Spirit Cats had fought great battles. Cox saw new stitching had been added to include Wyatt on the list. The implications were not lost on the Star captain.

"You honor my troops, Galaxy Commander," he said solemnly.

"You honor the Spirit Cats," Rosse replied. "I am disappointed to learn that Wyatt was not the sanctuary we seek. But you found other things there of importance to our people."

"Sir?"

"Intelligence. You have proven that ComStar is more than it seems. That the darkness that engulfs the stars may or may not have been caused by them, but they seem uninterested in helping to banish that darkness. They have a military force. That makes them dangerous. I have foreseen that the intelligence you gathered is important for our future."

Cox bowed his head. "I am glad that you are pleased."

"There is more I would discuss with you," the leader of the Spirit Cats added. "You fought bravely against and with a Knight Errant of the Sphere. You have won in battle both enlightenment and honor. You made difficult choices, and chose your alliances carefully while in the heat of battle. Star Captain, you must now accept what you deny yourself."

"I do not understand, sir."

"You will take the Bloodname you have already earned. It is time. From this point forward, you are Cox

Devalis, Star Captain of the Spirit Cats. Your Bloodname has been earned in test and trial."

Star Captain Cox Devalis bowed his head again. "I do not know what to say."

"No words are required," Rosse replied. "You have won this honor. Any taint you placed against yourself has long since been purged. You will do this for our people."

"It shall be done, then." The Star captain found himself grinning, not from pride, but for the honor he now held. A Bloodnamed warrior of the Spirit Cats.

DropShip **Deathclaw**
Orbital Approach
Amur, The Oriente Protectorate

His fingers hovered over the keypad as he considered how to cast the facts of his defeat on Wyatt. Captain Casson now preferred to think of his mission as a successful fact-finding sortie, and that's how he planned to present his results to Jessica Marik. The information about the HPG, Tucker Harwell and the status of Wyatt was enough to keep him in her good graces. The intelligence he had gathered on ComStar, especially the images captured on his battlerom, could vault his career to a whole new level.

ComStar Secret Research Facility Omega One
Luyten 68-25
Exact Coordinates Unknown
Prefecture X

As Precentor Kerr stepped off the DropShip gangway onto the obviously old ferrocrete runway, she at first thought the planet was a desolate wasteland. They had landed in a crater, she could tell that much, surrounded on all sides by what looked like an endless ring of steep, jagged hills. The air was thin, forcing her to breathe deeper to avoid feeling lightheaded. In every direction she could see ragged clumps of lush foliage, occasionally interrupted by twisted, rusted pieces of steel stabbing the sky, but mostly the bottom of the crater was blasted rock and debris. She didn't recognize any of the scrubby trees and brush fighting to grow on this world.

Precentor Malcolm Buhl stepped out from a small, bunkerlike structure that was covered with thick vines, and greeted her with a strong handshake. He was accompanied by a woman wearing a grayish-white military coverall that bore the symbol of ComStar on the left chest. "Welcome to Luyten 68-25, Svetlana. Or, as we call this place, Omega."

She looked around. A technical crew was already draping her DropShip with a holotarp to help camouflage it. "What is this place, Malcolm?"

The older man smiled and invited her to the doorway, pausing to complete a retina scan for entry. "A relic from the Jihad. ComStar terraformed parts of this world ages ago. Our Explorer Corps ships brought back the plant life you see here, what's left of it. The world is more desert than anything. But here, a little life blooms."

"Does The Republic know of this place?"

Buhl cocked an eyebrow. "Yes and no. The Word of Blake took over the facility from ComStar and used it as a base of operations, then the Com Guards routed them out near the end of the war. At one time, the shipyards in orbit were quite extensive, used for building WarShips. Now that capacity has—changed—somewhat.

"For years, The Republic patrolled this world, ensuring that no one came back to set up operations. But after a decade or two, they became lax. Eventually, they wrote this off as a dead world—their mistake. We smuggled engineers here to begin refitting the underground facilities that had survived the fighting, then we waited; but The Republic never bothered to check up on the planet. So we set up base. Thanks to some well-placed viruses, we were able to delete the majority of references to the world in the star charts."

"And we use it for?" she pressed.

"Let's just say it's home to many secrets of ComStar." The door hissed open and Buhl gestured for her to enter. She entered a well-lit corridor, the logo of the Com Guards emblazoned on the wall at nearly the size of an average human. The corridor sloped down and opened up to a series of rooms. People moved busily through the hallways. She could guess that the underground facility was vast in scope and size.

"I assume you have reconstituted the Com Guards?"

Buhl smiled but didn't immediately answer. Instead, he took her elbow and steered her down the hall. "I needed a place, someplace beyond prying eyes, where the real work of ComStar could be conducted. This world suited my needs. The Com Guards are simply one of many projects here."

"Should I ask where this world is located?"

Buhl smiled again. "You don't want to know. Suffice it to say, the best place to hide something from The Republic is right under their noses." Svetlana wondered, not for the first time, why Precentor Buhl was sharing this secret with her. She wondered who else shared Buhl's confidence. Did the primus know of this facility and the projects it contained? How big was the group— *dare she even think the term cabal?*—that supported this particular effort? Were there other facilities like this hidden in plain sight?

She wasn't sure just where she stood on the concept of factions within ComStar, though the existence of Buhl's secret project proved they were alive and well. Any good historian would point out that factionalism is what brought down the organization once before. She did know this: she would have to watch her step. For all that her superior had presented this trip as an opportunity to observe Tucker Harwell's progress, she now understood that there was much more at stake in her relationship with Precentor Buhl.

They walked down several corridors, descending short flights of stairs between each new hallway, all lit in such a way that seemed to leave darkness rather than cast light. Passing through a set of heavy doors, they arrived at a window draped in blue curtains. Providing no explanation, Precentor Buhl pulled back the drapes.

The window was revealed to be a one-way mirror look-ing in on a well-lit lab. Technicians in long, white lab smocks moved about on the other side of the glass. One sat at a table, a tall man with spiky black hair. The others moved in and around him, seeming to defer to him. Svet-lana Kerr leaned toward the one-way glass. "Harwell, I presume?"

Buhl shot a quick glance at his aide. "Yes. I have relocated the DeBurke Institute here. The facilities on Terra are really just a blind to keep The Republic's Knights in the dark about our operations. Tucker is help-ing us train a new breed of technicians who will find a way to lift this communications blackout. We're very close to quantifying what he did on Wyatt. But the most exciting element is that we may be able to use his knowl-edge to find a new way for ComStar to communicate between worlds. Something, perhaps, beyond the HPGs we know today."

She looked at the man through the glass, and some-thing about him gave her the impression that he was more than just a technician. There was a gritty quality about him, as if he might be tougher than expected. "How does Mr. Harwell feel about all of this?"

"He serves ComStar—as our family has done for years," the woman at Buhl's side replied. "He does what he is ordered to do." Her voice held no inflection.

Kerr looked at the woman, then at Buhl. The precen-tor feigned politeness. "Svetlana Kerr, this is Demi-Precentor Patricia Harwell of the Com Guards, First Division, The Avenging Angels." Patricia clicked her heels and bowed her head in Kerr's direction, then turned back to look at Tucker.

"You're his sister," Kerr added.

"Yes."

"How has he held up after his success on Wyatt?"

Patricia looked at her, devotion and duty clearly writ-ten on her face. Then she looked away again. "The af-fairs on Wyatt changed Tucker. I have expressed to Precentor Buhl that all this may be a mistake."

"A mistake?"

Buhl cut in. "Patricia feels that the events Tucker experienced on Wyatt changed him, perhaps encouraging him to identify with The Republic."

"He is not the same man we sent to Wyatt," Patricia continued. "Tucker has seen too much of the real world, experienced too much of the harsh realities of life and war. I know my brother. He has changed."

"How?" Kerr pressed.

Patricia shook her head. "In many ways. He is less open, more cunning. His attitude is less optimistic, and certainly less naive. When we talk, he tells me what he thinks I want to hear, and that makes me suspicious. I'd say he no longer trusts me, and if he doesn't trust me, he doesn't trust ComStar."

"None of that matters long as he does what we want," Buhl said impatiently.

Patricia cast Buhl an icy look. "His loyalty is an important factor in his performance—sir. It may merit strong methods of interrogation to discover what my brother is up to." Her voice was cold as a winter breeze. This was not just a military officer, this was someone willing to strike out at her own flesh and blood.

Buhl waved away her words. "What is important is not how Tucker feels, but that he does what he's told. Besides, he's been given every resource imaginable, access to research on interstellar communications that dates back centuries, and the personnel to help build whatever he wants to create. For a man of his technical background, this is heaven."

"Heaven with airtight security," Precentor Kerr commented.

"As I have told Mr. Harwell himself several times, all of this security is to *protect* him. With his help, ComStar will usher in a new era in The Republic . . . in all the Inner Sphere." As they watched Tucker, he looked at the two-way mirror and appeared to smile at the people standing behind it. Patricia averted her eyes, but Buhl smiled back. Kerr wondered at that moment who was really pulling the strings.

*   *   *

Tucker handed the noteputer back to Adept Sorrenteno after updating it with his new set of calculations. The formulas weren't complete. He never told his keepers everything, reasonably sure of his fate the moment they understood the sum of his knowledge. *As soon as I'm of no use to them, I will become a liability they can't afford.* He reminded himself of that every day.

"Sir, you adjusted the harmonics rate on my algorithm," the adept said questioningly.

"Yes," he replied. "You're really close to grasping what I did on Wyatt, but your calculations are still slightly off. Study those modifications, and I think you'll see where you need to go next."

"Thank you, sir," the adept replied. He stood there for a moment, then added, "Sir, that mirror. Does it bother you knowing that someone is watching us, even if it is for our own protection?"

Tucker bit back on his impulse to explain in the most scathing terms possible how many kinds of a fool Adept Sorrenteno represented. The problem was that, only a few months ago, he had been just like Sorrenteno. *It's amazing what a few months in the real world can do for your outlook on life.* Tucker knew that the security was there to keep him in, not to keep unwanted visitors out. They were all prisoners, including Adept Kursk, who was working in another wing of the complex on a prototype HPG for which he had created the specifications.

Tucker knew he was in control of his own destiny. The crucible of war had taught him how to take responsibility for his own actions, and for the lives of those who depended on his judgment to survive. He was taking advantage of the opportunities Omega provided him, and working his people hard to help them reach their full potential. When the time was right, his team would usher in a new era for ComStar.

He thought about the Knight Errant rank pip he fastened under his collar every morning when he dressed, and knew he had a friend waiting on the outside for his signal.

He smiled at Sorrenteno. "No, Adept. It doesn't bother me at all."

About the Author

Blaine Lee Pardoe lives in Amissville, Virginia with his wife Cynthia, his son Alexander and his daughter Victoria. During the daytime hours, he works at Ernst & Young LLP as an Associate Director. An armchair historian, he is completing his first military history book on Count Felix Von Luckner. Blaine has written eight other books in the *BattleTech* and *MechWarrior* series. This book is his first in the *MechWarrior: Dark Age* era.